GEEKTASTIC

GEEKTASTIC

Stories from the Nerd Herd

edited by Holly Black and Cecil Castellucci

LITTLE, BROWN AND COMPANY
New York   Boston

Little, Brown and Company

Hachette Book Group
237 Park Avenue, New York, NY 10017
Visit our Web site at www.lb-teens.com.

Little, Brown and Company is a division of Hachette Book Group, Inc.
The Little, Brown name and logo are trademarks of Hachette Book Group, Inc.

First Edition: August 2009

The characters and events portrayed in this book are fictitious. Any similarity to real persons, living or dead, is coincidental and not intended by the author.

ISBN 978-0-316-00809-9

10 9 8 7 6 5 4 3 2 1

RRD-C

Printed in the United States of America

"The Song of the Stars" quotation in "The Stars at the Finish Line" on pages 352–353, *Stars of the First People: Native American Star Myths and Constellations* by Dorcas S. Miller, published in 1997 by Pruett Publishing Company, PO Box 2140, Boulder, Colorado, 80306, p. 43, reprinted from *The Algonquin Legends of New England; or, Myths and Folk Lore of the Micmac, Passamaquoddy, and Penobscot Tribes* by Charles Godfrey Leland, p. 379.

Contents

All text for comic interstitials by Holly Black and Cecil Castellucci. Comics marked by  illustrated by Bryan Lee O'Malley, comics marked by 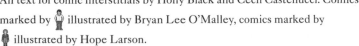 illustrated by Hope Larson.

EDITORS' NOTE

It didn't matter which one of us had married a rival Dungeon Master (that would be Holly) or lived for six weeks in the line for *Star Wars* (that would be Cecil), the moment that we met one another, we knew instantly that we were of the same tribe.

And so, while hanging out at Comic-Con in 2007, or as Cecil likes to call it, "the nerd prom," waiting in line for what we were promised was "the best burrito in San Diego," we spoke giddily of the amazing costumes we'd seen, books we'd read, comics we picked up.

Cecil told Holly about breakfast, where while eating eggs, she noticed that the table next to her was filled with a bunch of Jedi in full Jedi outfits. We remarked how we had noticed a lot of Jedi. And we had noticed a lot of Klingons. Personally, we'd been looking for Slave Leias, because we'd been told there would be a bunch, but actually there weren't that many. There were just a lot of Jedi and Klingons.

Holly mentioned that she had noticed that there was a panel on how to live your day-to-day life as a Klingon. We kind of wanted to go to that. We thought it sounded kind of cool. We wondered what kind of domestic clues we could get from learning to live Klingon.

So there we were, in line for this burrito. The line was really long. We stood there swapping Comic-Con stories while we waited, because probably we'd been waiting for a table for about an hour already. And we both kind of said at the same time, "What would happen if you were a Jedi and you woke up with a Klingon in your bed?" "Would it be like Romeo and Juliet?" "Could you even tell your friends?"

We decided then and there that we needed to write that story. The story of a Jedi and a Klingon and true love. We thought we could write it and sell it and it would be awesome.

Only then we realized that no one would publish that story.

Later, while Cecil was walking the floor looking for Gama-go T-shirts, standing between Wonder Woman and Phoenix and getting a crush on Scott Pilgrim, Holly called and left this message:

"Cecil! No one will publish our story! That is why we need to create an anthology that is geektastic so that we can have a home for our story."

"Oh! And we have the geekiest friends!" Cecil said.

"Yes! An anthology about the geek and the geek observed," Holly said.

And thus an idea was born.

We hope that you enjoy the stories within.

They sing to our geek heart.

AMHERST, June 4, 2008

ONCE YOU'RE A JEDI, YOU'RE A JEDI ALL THE WAY

by holly black and
cecil castellucci

I. KLINGON

I awake tangled up in scratchy sheets with my head pounding and the taste of cheap alcohol and Tabasco still in my mouth. The spirit gum I used to attach my nose ridge and eyebrows sticks to the sheets as I roll over. Immediately, a wave of nausea makes me regret moving and I try to lie as still as I can until it passes.

The thing about advancing in the Klingon ranks is that you have to be badass. So when Kadi and D'ghor decided last night that we had to make blood wine with Everclear instead of tequila, and twice as much Tabasco as the recipe called for, I had to drink it or be a wimp.

I open my eyes and reason with myself that if I can crawl into the hotel bathroom, I can get some ibuprofen from my bag and stop my head from hurting quite so much. Also, water. Water would definitely help.

Pushing off the sheets, I realize that I'm still wearing my uniform and that my bra is still on. My pants and boots are missing.

"Arizhel?" someone says from the other side of the bed as I stagger toward a door I hope isn't a closet. The voice has an accent that might be Irish. I don't know anyone Irish.

I also don't know this room. It must be in the same hotel, but none of my stuff is here and there is only one single big bed instead of the two doubles that Kadi, D'ghor, and Noggra were sharing with me. The only thing that's familiar is my *bat'leH* leaning against the wall, the curved blade gleaming in the little bit of sun sneaking through the drawn shades. The glare hurts my eyes.

In the bathroom, I turn the lock and go over the night before. I think back on how we sang rousing battle songs in our hotel room, accompanied by swigs of that horrible blood wine. Then we rode the escalator, raising our weapons in the air with a single shout, to the party that was happening on the main floor. A party seething with costumed people for us to growl at: Peacekeepers, Cobra Command, Stormtroopers, Browncoats.

I splash water on my face and chew up a couple of aspirins. Whoever is in the bedroom is really tidy; his toiletries are still in a little bag. There's even aftershave. I don't see any pots of makeup or prosthetics, so I figure he's not a Klingon.

Maybe he's a member of Starfleet. There were a couple of cute guys with really proper costumes and phasers that glowed a little bit when they were fired. I remember arm-wrestling a cadet, but I can't believe I would have gone back to his room. For one thing, I won way too easily. For another, he had a Vulcan girlfriend who was watching us both like she wanted to have some kind of pon-farr excuse to kick my ass.

I remember hoping she was going to try.

Maybe it was that guy. I groan and rub my face.

I pull off the braided wig that's twisted around anyway, peel off my ridge and bald cap, and wash off as much of the makeup and adhesive as I can without cold cream or Bond-Off. Blinking at my own face in the mirror, I realize how different I look. Tame. Like I used to be.

"Are you okay?" comes a voice from beyond the door. He definitely has an accent.

"Yeah," I yell.

"I ordered coffees and some food," he says. "Grease will fix us right up."

I've never ordered room service. Only rich people order room service.

"Uh, thanks." I fill a water glass from the sink and guzzle it. I feel better, like the aspirin is kicking in, and I take a deep breath.

I wish I had my pants, but I pull down my pleather tunic as low as it can go and walk out of the bathroom.

There, sitting on the bed, is a thin guy with blond hair and a cute, lopsided smile. He's still wearing his uniform, too. His *Jedi uniform.*

I know I look completely stupid, but I just stand there in the doorway. The buzzer on the door rings, but I'm still staring. Tall riding boots, outer tunic, tabard, obi. *Jedi.*

No. I couldn't have. Not with an Ewok-cuddling, Force-feeling, Padawan-braid-wearing, lightsaber-rammed-up-his-ass Jedi.

He gets up and I fumble around in the covers until I discover my pants. Pulling them up and shoving my feet into my boots, I turn around as he opens the door. He signs something and comes back with the tray of dishes in metal domes.

"I feel totally thrashed," he says as though we haven't committed a terrible crime. As though we haven't totally betrayed the stupid uniforms we're standing around in. Everyone knows that trekkers and whatever starwarsians call themselves aren't supposed to have anything to do with one another.

He pours coffee into two cups and asks me how I take it.

"Black," I say.

He smirks. "I should have guessed that, shouldn't I?"

"And you take your *raktajino* with milk and sugar."

"Ouch," he says, but he's laughing. Maybe at what I said,

maybe at the Klingon word. I want to know how we met, but I don't want him to know that I don't remember. I don't even know his name.

It turns out he does take his coffee with milk and sugar. "Makes it more like tea," he says.

I eat some toast with raspberry jelly and a sausage. After that and three cups of coffee, I start to feel a lot better. I feel good enough to realize that the room service receipt has his name on it. Leaning over, I take a quick glance. There it is. Thomas.

He sees me looking. "Thomas," I say.

"I told you it was my real name. Unlike *Arizhel*."

At least he didn't seem to realize that I don't remember him at all.

"So," I say, "are you here at the con with a lot of other...," I hesitate on the word, "...Jedi?"

"Yeah, yeah," he says, holding up his hands in a gesture of surrender. "I already know what you think about *Star Wars*."

"Oh, you mean that it's lame that *Star Wars* worships monarchical, secretive, and monastic systems and tries to tell you that anger is evil?"

"It's pretty funny that a tough, angry girl like you is all about a goody-goody idealistic show like *Star Trek*."

"It's pretty funny that you find that kind of girl attractive." I can't help smiling. I take another sausage.

"Oh, come on!" he says. "Like your attraction to me is any less screwed up?"

"I'm a Klingon," I say. "Of course I'm attracted to my enemy."

II. JEDI

A Jedi is never supposed to give over to his passions; he is always supposed to be in control. But last night, at some point between

4

Coke Pluses, Master Sven must have spiked mine with a little bit of rum. My being such a lightweight might be a contributing factor in the mess I find myself in this morning.

I know that most of my Order don't go for anything outside of the *Star Wars* universe. It's all *Star Wars* all the time with them. Which is cool. I get it.

There is something about the Jedi in *Star Wars* that feels more right to me than any other made-up alien life code. It's the Force, really. I have this thing inside of me that is light and wants to do good, but I struggle with my own dark side. I try to keep it in balance, but it's hard. I like the idea of there being something larger than yourself that guides you. The Jedi code.

I am not adverse to liking a bit of this and that from other universes, though. Heck, I like *Star Trek*. I even own all the original series on DVD. And this Klingon girl, Arizhel, whose real name I still don't know, isn't like any girl I've met before.

"Careful there, you might break something," I say.

I'm watching her wolf down some breakfast and I'm trying to act all cool and all that in front of her, because she's witty.

"You are in more danger of being broken," she says. "I am a Klingon. I could break you with a roar."

And funny. God, she's funny. That's what I liked about her at the party last night, the way she made me laugh when she came over to my Master and me.

"So you're a Jedi Knight," she said, brandishing her scary sword. I lifted my lightsaber and parried with her.

"Apprentice," I said. "An honorable start, for a human," she said.

"I've mastered many levels since I've started my training," I said.

"Have you done battle?" she asked.

"Well, we do fight exhibitions," I said.

"So you are a dancer," she said. "No wonder you wear a skirt."

"It's a tunic," I said.

And then I blushed and felt embarrassed. I was worried that she wouldn't think much of a Jedi Apprentice.

Master Sven just handed me another Coke Plus with rum and left me alone with her. He told me he'd find another place to crash, and I took that as encouragement that I was doing well.

"Every dog has his day," Master Sven said.

I make sure my clip-on braid is in place while she pushes the button to call the elevator. I am wearing my Jedi uniform and she is wearing her Klingon costume, but not her ridges or wig piece, nor her makeup. She's very different from what I remember about last night.

I'm watching her out of the corner of my eye as we enter the hotel elevator.

First off, she's Asian. And not dark and orange. She's tried washing off most of her makeup but it's still a little streaky. Still, she's pretty. She also looks soft, almost shy for someone who seems so commanding. She's got a great body. Really curvy and she's an inch or two smaller than me, but I notice that she walks with a swagger that makes her seem taller. Her walk makes me want to get a little attitude in my step.

It makes the idea of turning to the dark side a little bit sexier.

I can't believe I just thought that. Annakin went to the dark side for love and look what happened to him. I don't care how cool this girl is. I'm not about to let that happen to me.

I'm a Jedi.

To become a Jedi requires a serious mind and a deep commitment, and here I am, feeling kind of giddy standing next to a Klingon.

She turns to face me.

"I didn't hurt you or anything, right?" she asks. "Klingon mating rituals can be violent. It's not unknown for there to be bruises, or broken bones."

"Oh, no!" I say. "We Jedi are tough. I just used the Force."

"Oh, yeah," she says. "Good."

"Yep."

"So, you know, I hope you don't take this the wrong way, but when we get downstairs, I'm going to pretend that we don't know each other," she says.

"Right," I say. "Of course."

But secretly I'm crushed because I thought maybe I could ask her to meet me for lunch between the Lightsaber Demonstration I'm attending and the Darth Maul signing I'm going to later.

"Good," she says. " 'Cause you know…"

"Yeah," I say. "I mean, we were. Whew!"

I make a little hand gesture that is supposed to mean "drunk" but probably looks more like "I'm a loser."

"And no matter what you've heard about Klingons," she says, "it doesn't mean anything. We don't have to mate for life."

"Good to know," I say, and now I am just embarrassed. I don't know how to tell her that we didn't even mate at all. I wanted to. Oh, God, I wanted to. She is so hot. And we'd been talking at the con mixer all night and we had everything in common. Well, except for the whole Jedi / Klingon thing. And then I invited her back to my room, and I have never done something like that before! It was like the best night of my whole life! And Master Sven even gave me the thumbs-up. And then there was a hot girl in my room! And she wanted me. I could tell—she sniffed me! I was all set to lose my virginity. I even had a condom ready. But sleeping with drunk Klingon girls, even if they're ravishing you, seems wrong.

So does defying the Jedi code.

Jedi are monastic. Celibate.

We're quiet for a few seconds and I think our awkward conversation is over. And I'm glad, because I feel a little sad. So far, this was the best time I've ever had at a convention. And I think I liked talking to her last night way more than I did to my own Jedi Council.

So, I'm kind of looking down at my feet 'cause I don't want her to see that it kind of meant something to me. Not mate-for-life something. But maybe get-her-real-name something.

And that's when she does it again. Just like she did last night. She sniffs my arm, and pushes me into the corner of the elevator and growls. And then she kisses me and I feel weak in the knees. I give in to the dark side. I grab her. I kiss her right back.

She pushes me away right before the elevator door opens and she walks out of the elevator and away from me.

I still don't know her name.

And I only have twenty minutes to get to the convention center for the Jedi Lightsaber Demonstration.

"Hey! Thomas!" Master Sven waves me over to where he's sitting onstage before the demonstration. He's cleaning his lightsaber and he's smiling big, like he thinks he knows how it all went down.

"Thanks, Master Sven, for finding a place to crash last night," I say.

I don't want to tell him that I didn't score, so I just let him keep smiling.

"No sweat, my little Padawan," he says. "Besides, I had no idea the Battlestar people could party so hard! I ended up crashing with five Boomers last night!"

"We're about to start," one of the other Jedi, Padawan Pete, snaps. "Could you guys focus?"

"Careful, Master Sven," I say. "Don't defy the Council again."

"I will do what I must," he says.

The music begins and we start our choreographed lightsaber routine. Master Sven is the star of the show. That's why no matter how much of a rebel and sort of code-breaking Jedi he is, our Council won't ever kick him out.

I'm just learning my lightsaber technique, so I just have one little fight. But I do well enough that people clap.

When we're done, it's always the same. The people swarm us and want to take our pictures.

While we're posing, Padawan Pete starts laying into me.

"I heard you guys were mixing a little too hard last night," he says. He's got a green lightsaber that won't stay on, so he keeps shaking it. "We have an image to maintain and it's a Jedi image."

"Leave me alone, Pete," I say. He is really bugging me.

"Figures with a Master like Sven that you would get funny ideas," Master Doug says.

"Give me a break, Doug," Master Sven says. "All Thomas did was meet a girl."

"She was a Klingon," Padawan Pete says.

"When was the last time you hooked up with a girl, Pete?" Master Sven asks.

"That's not the point," Padawan Pete says.

But my anger is rising and I can't take it anymore.

"Okay," I say. "That's it. I challenge you."

"What?" Padawan Pete says. "You can't challenge me."

"Right here, right now. Lightsaber fight."

"You are totally going dark side," Padawan Pete says.

"Trust your feelings, Thomas," Master Sven says.

"What kind of Master are you for encouraging your Padawan like that, Sven?" Master Doug asks.

"Better than you," I say, which is exactly what gets Padawan Pete to whip his cape up and pull out his lightsaber to fight me.

A ring of people form around us and I start to use my lightsaber technique to wipe that smugness off Padawan Pete's face.

And just as I am getting into my rhythm, I see a bunch of Klingons walk by. Including Arizhel, in full makeup again. She stops. She looks at me. I smile at her, wanting to say hello, and I get sliced right in the stomach.

"Gotcha!" Padawan Pete says just as she's stopped for a second and is watching me fight.

9

I've been killed. There is nothing I can do.

By the rules of the lightsaber fight, I have to fall.

III. KLINGON

My plan is to go back to the room and sleep for pretty much the rest of the day, but when I get there, Kadi, D'ghor, and Noggra are dressed up and waiting around for me. Noggra smooshes my cheek against her leather breastplate in a bruising hug.

"Oh, honey," she says. "I feel so guilty for losing track of you." She gives Kadi and D'ghor a frown, more severe because she's got her ridges on. "And those two should never have let you drink so much."

"I'm fine," I say, even though I know I look like a hot mess.

"You're underage."

I hate when Noggra gets like this. She's D'ghor's mother, but she's been a Klingon for her entire adult life. She basically raised him Klingon. Most of the time she just acts like our *totlh*, but sometimes she forgets and acts like a mom.

"Where were you last night?" Kadi asks. "We called your cell, but it turned out that you'd left it here."

"I need a shower," I say.

"Was it that cadet guy?" D'ghor asks. "I'm going to kick his ass."

"My honor is mine to defend," I say, and growl to show how serious I am. "I'm a warrior and I can take care of myself."

"Let her be," Noggra says, and I nearly flop down on the bed with relief because there's no way I can explain where I actually was. I'm the youngest Klingon in our group, so I'm always struggling to be tough enough. I figure that if I match the others swig for swig, blow for blow, they'll forget how young I am.

Unless I do something really dumb, like, say, spend the night with a Jedi.

Under the hot spray, though, I can't help thinking about Thomas. About his soft and lilting voice and the fierce way he kissed. When we were in the elevator, he kissed me so hard he bit my lip. Of course, hot girls in *Star Wars* are always princesses and queens with elaborate looping hair, so maybe he figured he didn't have to be so careful with a girl like me.

I used to be a good girl. Everyone expected me to be quiet and studious and I was good at fulfilling expectations. Chung Ae, perfect lab partner. Princess.

But inside, I knew I was a Klingon. I could feel the growl in the back of my throat when I spoke, itching for me to give it a voice. Honoring my parents and grandparents was a big deal in my house, but Klingons allowed for a different kind of honor. One that didn't make you small and quiet. One that venerated you for belching the loudest, louder even than your brothers. When I met D'ghor in debate club, it was only a matter of time before I was attending a dipping party and having a life cast made so I could sculpt my first ridge.

It doesn't take me that long to get cleaned up and ready. Kadi comes in and helps me blend my base and disguise the edges of the latex. Then we're back on the floor, stomping in our big black boots, frowning and growling and prowling.

"Hey, look." D'ghor smirks and gestures with his beard.

I turn and there he is. Thomas is holding a lightsaber and he's swinging it in an elegant arc. He might be a Jedi, but he's beautiful. A warrior.

Our eyes meet and at that moment, a plastic saber slams into his chest. He turns his head toward the blow and, stunned and furious, he looks at me again right before he falls on his knees.

"Ha!" D'ghor says, lifting up his *bat'leH*. "You call that fighting? Those are oversized cocktail picks you're swinging."

I groan. I know he's just looking for an excuse to do some chest pounding, but the Jedi are staring at me like they're waiting for something. All I do is get really hot in the face and hope no one can see me blushing under a ton of orange base.

Kadi rests one of her hands on her metal-studded hip. "Cocktail picks being swung around by a bunch of toothpicks."

"Let's go," I say, and Noggra gives me a weird look because normally I would have been egging them on.

One of the older Jedi pulls Thomas to his feet. He's younger than Noggra, but not really young, with the top part of his hair pulled back into a ponytail. After Thomas gets up, the Jedi puts both his hands on his shoulders and gives him a shove in my direction. I scowl at them both.

"That's your girlfriend?" says another Jedi, the one that beat Thomas. "Talk about beer goggles."

For a moment, everything stops. D'ghor's laugh dies and I feel cold all over. Frozen. Then Noggra gives a horrible roar and grabs that skinny Jedi Apprentice by the throat. She might be in her forties, but she pushes him against the wall of the escalator and bares her teeth against his throat.

IV. JEDI

As the Klingons and the Jedi rush toward each other, the spectators start clapping. They must think it's part of our show. But as the hits begin to actually land and people begin to get hurt, they kind of look confused and start getting out of the way of danger. They make a kaleidoscope of colors as they run. Brown shirts and people of all sizes wearing flowing capes, alien masks, and spandex.

"Go! Go! Go!" Jedi yell all around me as they let out their battle cry and we rush forward to meet the enemy.

What I really want to do is find Arizhel.

The Klingons seem to have multiplied, but really it's that other

Star Trek people have joined in. Non-Jedi *Star Wars* people have joined our side as well. I fly past a Queen Amidala, her dress ripped, her makeup smudged, grappling with an Original Series Chekov. Even Emperor Palpatine is kicking some Vulcan ass. It is now a full-on *Star Trek* vs. *Star Wars* battle. It is as though we have been moving toward this moment for years and now it is finally on.

No one looks scared. Everyone looks happy.

"Watch your back!" Master Sven says as he pushes a Jean-Luc Picard away from me. Master Sven then starts parrying blows from a Jadazia Dax. I can tell he is fighting and flirting at the same time. I hear him try to get her cell phone number.

In the distance, over by the elevators, and near the coffee cart, I see Arizhel. I make a beeline for her, dodging swings and weaving in and out of the crowded arena. On my left, I see Padawan Pete.

"This is your fault," he cries.

He comes after me again.

"Brother!" I say, trying to fight the dark feelings that are rising inside of me. Or maybe more like my Irish temper. "Let us not fight each other when we are at battle."

But he keeps coming at me. He's got a mean look in his eye. He's already killed me once today and this time he is going down.

I use a three-move combination of my own design, one that I haven't even shown the Council yet, and when I finish, Padawan Pete is on the floor, his nose bloodied. I can't say that I am sorry.

"I'm reporting you to the Jedi Council and getting your ass kicked out."

I hear his voice trailing me, but I've moved on. I am doing my best to fend off attacks from every imaginable kind of character from the *Star Trek* universe. At this point, his threats don't slow me down.

I have an anger inside of me. I have turned to the dark side. And I don't mind at all.

To my right, Master Doug is putting on a show. He is trying out his best lightsaber moves, trying to outdo anything he's ever seen Master Sven do by ending each basic stance with a flourish. It doesn't look effective, but it looks good.

Someone grabs my tunic and spins me around.

I put my lightsaber up, ready to hit my mark.

It is Arizhel.

"Thomas," she says. Her makeup is running a little bit from being sweaty from the fight. She looks like she wants to say more, but she leans over and puts her hands on her thighs to steady herself.

When she looks up, she smiles.

Then she punches me in the face.

"Ow!" I say. "Why'd you do that?"

"It is my way," she says.

I see stars. My face really hurts. I bet I get a black eye. "I feel.... This whole thing is silly."

"This is not the time to talk of our feelings," she says. "This is the time to fight."

She scrambles out of my reach and shoves me up against a pillar. I hear the roar of Klingons near me.

"Fight me," she growls.

And then I get it. I think maybe what she is really saying is *please help me save face in front of my friends; they're watching.*

She does like me.

I shove her, hard, but not too hard. I shove her to show her that I like her.

I want to tell her how I feel, but I know she likes action and not words, and besides, I see something out of the corner of my eye, but I ignore it. I'm too into fighting her. It's as though we are really in the moment, as if we are really together. Every time a blow connects, I feel a thrill.

But after a few minutes I can't ignore what I'm seeing. I stop fighting.

14

"What are you doing?" she asks. "The battle is not over."

"Stormtroopers," I say.

The 501st Legion of Stormtroopers arrives and within minutes they have all of us, the Jedi and the Klingons, surrounded, separated, and under control.

"Surrender your weapons," the stormtrooper who has us says. His voice sounds just like in the movies. He must have a microphone under his helmet.

"There is no glory in surrender," Arizhel says.

"Yeah, besides, some of those Jedi deserve to get kicked out of the con just for being dicks," I say.

"You guys can choose. If you don't settle down, I'm going to have to escort you out of the convention area," the stormtrooper says.

"Lead on," I say.

Arizhel takes my hand.

The stormtrooper talks into his little walkie-talkies and ejects us from the building. Others are already outside, among them Master Sven, Master Doug, Padawan Pete, and Arizhel's friends. They are all too busy yelling and trying to blame each other for not being able to get back into the convention to notice that we are there and that we're still holding hands.

"Battle always makes me hungry," I say. "Want to go get something to eat?"

"With you?"

I nod.

We head away from our arguing friends and leave the convention center and head toward a coffee shop.

I realize as we sit down at an empty table with our cheeseburger special and bowl of chili that I still don't know her real name.

"I have something to tell you," I say.

A little kid walks by our table and Arizhel growls at her because she's staring. The kid starts crying and her mom whisks her away, muttering "freaks" under her breath.

"About last night," I say.

"Look, I have something to say, too."

She looks so good to me. Like a moonset on Naboo. Like the colors on an X-wing fighter. Like a costume that Queen Amidala would wear.

"Nothing happened between us last night," I say.

"I don't remember anything about last night," Arizhel says.

"Really?" we both say at the same time.

Tell me your name, I think.

"So, just so you know," she says. "My name is Chung Ae. It's nice to meet you, Thomas."

Damn!

That Jedi Mind Trick does work.

Holly Black is the bestselling author of several contemporary fantasy novels for younger and older readers, including *Tithe*, *Valiant*, *Ironside*, *The Spiderwick Chronicles*, and the graphic novel series, The Good Neighbors. She is an unrepentant geek, having met her husband when they were rival Dungeon Masters and currently living in a house with a secret library hidden behind a bookshelf.

Cecil Castellucci is the author of three young adult novels—*Boy Proof*, *The Queen of Cool*, and *Beige*—and the Plain Janes graphic novel series. Her books have received starred reviews and been on the American Library Association's Best Books for Young Adults (BBYA), Quick Pick for Reluctant Readers, Great Graphic Novels for Teens, and the Amelia Bloomer lists. Cecil waves her geek flag high. She waited on the *Star Wars* Episode One line on Hollywood Boulevard for six weeks, she invited Batman to her fourth birthday party, and she has a collection of broken action figures.

TOP FIVE
Words or Phrases You Need to Know in
KLINGON

Text by Holly Black and Cecil Castellucci. Illustrations by Bryan Lee O'Malley.

Dochvam vISop net pIH'a'?

Am I supposed to eat this?

nuqDaq 'oH puchpa''e'

Where's the bathroom?

bI'IHqu'. Ha' maroSchuq.

You're hot. Want to make out?

Hab SoSlI' Quch!

This is just about the worst insult in Klingon— use only in extreme circumstances.

Duck!

Jun!

*Klingon translation by Dr. Lawrence M. Schoen

ONE OF US
by tracy lynn

THE SETUP

Montgomery K. Bushnell, captain of the varsity cheerleading squad, could almost *hear* her entrance being narrated in the freakish minds of those she approached. Something involving "damsel in distress" and her blond hair being like a "sack of gold coins" or something. In her own head it would have sounded more like the voice-over in an old detective film—the only kind of movie she and Ryan could both watch without fighting.

She slapped a wad of bills down on the desk in front of Ezra. Three pairs of eyes in the room went to the money. And then to her shapely legs. And then back to the money.

"I want to hire your services," she said, biting back each word with a little disgust. She didn't want to be there. And it was no surprise.

Sprawled around the media room like it was their personal cave were the four most prominent members of SPRInGfield High's Genre and Nonsense club (SPRIGGAN). Ezra, David, Mica, and Ellen (she was the only member whose eyes stayed on the money the whole time).

They looked at her with a wide range of emotion: from almost anthropological surprise that someone like her even knew where the media room was (David, Mica), to wondering with lustful disbelief if all of their wishes were about to be granted (Ezra), to hatred so intense it bordered on audible snarling (Ellen).

"You, um, what?" Ezra said, hypnotically caught between Montgomery's blue-sky eyes and her money.

"I want you to teach me about your…stuff…." She waved her hand impatiently around the room, at the *Star Wars* posters, the action figures glued to the ceiling, the cans of Mountain Dew and bags of cheese puffs. She retracted her hand a little at the last. "I have a hundred bucks here. I need you to tell me everything about, you know, video games and science fiction shows and movies."

"Thank you…dear Lord…," Ezra whispered.

"Why?" Mica asked, not looking up from the handheld game he was furiously stabbing at with his thumbs. His tongue came out once in a while, as if hoping it could help. It curled and wavered in the air a little before he finally sucked it back into his mouth.

Montgomery tried not to gag at the sight. "My boyfriend's all into that stuff. You know — Ryan?"

"Yeah, we all know who Ryan is," Ellen snapped. " 'Quarterback.' Dating 'the cheerleader.' "

Montgomery ignored her. "He's really into it and I don't get it at all. Any of it. We fight about it all the time. I thought maybe if I actually learned something about…this…we would communicate better."

Ezra blinked at her. She could see into his head: a muscled and manly football player was tackling his dreams to the ground. Assuming he knew it was football where tackling was done, and not basketball.

"You're paying us a hundred bucks so we can teach you to speak geek so you can communicate with your boyfriend better?" Mica asked, making sure he understood properly.

"Yes," Montgomery said, trying to sound sure of herself. Trying to convince herself that this wasn't the absolute worst idea she'd ever had.

22

"Works for me," Mica said, going back to his game.

"Awww, the little cheerleader is looking for some personal growth," Ellen cooed.

"Okay, not helpful," Ezra said, shaking his finger at her. Then he composed himself and turned to Montgomery with what he obviously hoped was a professional smile. "Now. What…um…areas of our expertise did you have in mind?"

"Well, Ryan likes *Star Trek*…."

"Really?" Ezra said in disbelief before he could stop himself.

"Quarterback's a Trekker!" David laughed.

"How old-school," Mica snorted.

"Which series?" Ellen asked.

Montgomery looked confusedly from one to the other as they fired off their remarks. She tried to respond calmly, and in order.

"Um, yes; I thought it was *Trekkie*. What do you mean *old-school*? He watches…the one with the Klingon. And the other one with the doggie. Plus he likes the really, *really* old one."

"True Trek?" Ellen asked gleefully.

"There are two with a Klingon as a main character," Ezra pointed out.

"'Doggie,'" Mica snorted. "Well, actually, it was a nice doggie. Beagle, right?"

Then: "HA, TAKE THAT, YOU BRICK WALL!" Probably to his video game.

The cheerleader took a deep breath and decided to just continue, hoping that if she braved it out, maybe it would all make sense eventually.

"And-he-also-likes-playing-on-his-Xbox-and-all-of-those-big-dorky-movies-like-*Star-Wars*-and-the-one-with-the-little-guys—"

"Xbox or Xbox 360?" Mica asked, suddenly sitting up and paying attention.

"'Dorky?'" Ezra demanded, a little insulted.

"'Little guys,'" David snorted. "Hobbits suck...."

"You know, it was a book, too," Ellen said snottily.

"Oh my gosh, this was a terrible idea," Montgomery realized forlornly.

"No, wait, we can do this," Ezra said, leaping up, ready to physically stop her from leaving the media room if he had to. "We'll be organized. So he likes *Star Trek*, and all of the...*great* major motion pictures, and video games. We have experts on all three right here. Mica is a total vidiot. He knows everything about every computer and video game ever made. His name's on half of the machines down at the arcade. Plus he's a real fantasy freak. If it's got dragons, he's read it. My specialty is science fiction, genre and cult films. I'll handle that."

He gave her what was obviously supposed to be a smooth smile. Even David rolled his eyes.

"And Ellen is," Ezra added as delicately as he could, "our book and sci-fi TV expert."

Ellen might have actually hissed.

"Ryan doesn't read...a lot of books...," the cheerleader said slowly, realizing just how awful that sounded.

"Quelle surprise," Mica muttered.

"Well...what about books with *pictures*? We'll throw in comic books for free."

"Thanks," David said, waving his hand without looking up from the latest *Captain America*.

"We'll come up with a syllabus and a class schedule," Ezra continued, growing excited. "Also, we'll give you reading assignments. And we'll put it all on Google Calendar so we can arrange class time with, um, minimum interaction."

"That's perfect. The part where the interacting is all minimum-y," Montgomery said eagerly.

"That was almost a Buffyism," Mica pointed out to Ellen.

"Almost," Ellen admitted grudgingly.

"And for a final, we could take her to Locacon," Mica suggested, smirking.

"What's that?" the cheerleader asked. She liked the idea of a final and assignments. She was good at standardized education. "It sounds familiar. I think Ryan talked about it...."

"It's Springfield's answer to World Con," Ezra said proudly.

"It's a sci-ence fiction and fan-ta-sy con-ven-tion," Mica explained, slowly and carefully.

"It's incredible," Ellen said.

"It's got a great dealer's room," David pointed out. "I got the Jimmy Olsen 'giant' Number Ninety-Five—from the sixties, yeah?—for like twenty-five bucks."

"Huh," Montgomery said, nodding. "My final exam. That's a great idea. So by the end of this little course I'll be able to fit in and talk with everyone and completely impress Ryan? And maybe not be completely bored?"

The four geeks looked at each other uncomfortably.

"Ah, I think, that might be, uh, blue-skying it," Ezra said carefully, coughing a little. "Er, really ambitious. We're looking at just getting you through the day without losing your patience. Or saying anything too insulting."

"Yes, that's probably a more workable end goal," the cheerleader agreed, thinking about it.

"Sports metaphors," Ellen said, rolling her eyes. "How *typical*."

TREK 101

"All right, let's start with the basics," Ellen said, marching back and forth in front of the blackboard. She clasped a yardstick behind her back like a nun or a commandant, just waiting for a chance to strike.

Montgomery sat in Mrs. Tiegwold's English classroom, all alone in the front row. The clock ticked sadly past two thirty: school was out for everyone else who didn't need special help in the area of high geekery. She really was trying: she had her little bobbly feather-topped pen poised over her favorite pink notebook, legs crossed studiously.

Unfortunately, she wasn't able to do much about removing the look of boredom and disdain fixed on her face.

Why they were doing this at school was a mystery. Montgomery could understand Ellen's embarrassment at maybe taking a field trip to a coffee shop (the poor girl often had dribbles of something—milk, juice, coffee—on her shirt collars), but why not at least at her own house? She probably had tons of backup material. Dolls, action figures, fun props…

"We need to get you to the point where you can at least tell the difference between the Star Treks," Ellen continued. "We'll start with a good mnemonic device. THE FIVE RULES OF GIRLS."

She suddenly lashed out with the yardstick and thwacked a pull-down Shakespeare character chart. The chart rolled up violently, revealing the five carefully chalked-in rules. Ellen smiled smugly at her trick. Not that she had obviously practiced a bunch of times the day before.

"Rule one."

THWACK! She hit the board.

"Kirk always gets the girl."

"Kirk, he's the captain of the old one," Montgomery said, remembering. "With the short skirts and stuff and the funky music."

"True Trek," Ellen corrected. "But you should probably just refer to it as the Original Series. Good for you for recognizing it, though."

(Mica may have taken her aside earlier and pointed out the value of positive feedback; a grumpy cheerleader wasn't likely to fork over more money if instructed by a constantly insulting Trekspert.)

The smile on Ellen's face was forced, just like the cheerleader's interest, but Montgomery took the compliment anyway and grinned, drawing a little congratulatory smiley face for herself.

Then she realized something.

"Hey, Ellen—you know, that shirt looks good on you. You should really wear light colors more often. With, um, better shoes."

The yardstick almost broke in Ellen's hands.

Almost.

STAR WARS AND THE WORLD OF LUCAS (NOT INCLUDING A VERY WOOKIEE CHRISTMAS OR WILLOW)

"Ah, welcome to Château Ezra."

He was wearing what he probably thought was a nice shirt, a colorful Hawaiian number whose coconut buttons weren't too badly chipped. It looked freshly pressed.

In fact, Montgomery was pretty sure she could detect a whiff of starch and burnt cotton in the air. There was even…product in his hair, something that made it shiny, spiky, and not very twenty-first century.

Someday he would make a perfect mid-level manager at some sort of computer company: he already had the nondescript build, a slight tub at the tummy, and a sneeringly curved nose made shiny by the wrong use of cleansing products.

She rolled her eyes.

"Your parents are home, right?" she demanded, not coming through the invitingly open door.

"*Mais non*," he answered with a bow. No doubt he had made darn sure of that.

"Let's get this over with," the cheerleader muttered, stomping in. Ezra went to take her coat, then realized it was spring and she wasn't wearing one. Without pausing she followed what looked like the most likely route to the living room. "All right, I—whoa, that's a big TV," she said, struck despite herself.

It was the largest, flattest, high-def-ist one she had ever seen. And it almost distracted her from the low lighting, stinky candles, artfully arranged bowl of popcorn, and what looked a lot like a fake fur throw.

"Can I get you anything to drink? A diet soda, maybe?" he offered.

"'Diet soda, maybe?' What are you, a waiter in training? Get me a Coke if you've got one," she said brusquely, settling down into the incredibly comfortable, overstuffed leather couch. Too bad this wasn't the house of *any other person in the universe*. Even Ellen's. Movie night would have almost been fun.

She didn't hear Ezra leave or come back. He proffered her a can of Coke and a glass of ice—on a tray—then sat down. Right next to her. Almost on top of her.

"Um," she said, using her best glare.

Ezra happily ignored her, picking up an incredibly sleek and shiny black remote. A veritable stealth plane of a remote. "What you are about to see is what some may consider the absolute pinnacle of human artistic achievement, the peak of cinematic experiences."

"I've seen *Star Wars*," she snapped, sliding over and putting her purse in between them.

"Yes, but have you really *watched* it?" Ezra asked dramatically.

A couple of clicks on the remote lowered the lights even more and turned the great glowing box on. There was a pause as the DVD booted up, and the darkness was complete.

A muffled creaking of leather indicated movement on the couch.

"Touch me and I'll kick your ass," Montgomery warned. "And then I'll have Ryan kick your ass, and then everyone else on the football team kick your ass, and then Eddie the towel boy kick your ass."

(Eddie was an enthusiastic nine-year-old with autism who always wore a Steelers football helmet that the cheerleaders had pitched in to get him—he even wore it to sleep.)

But then the movie music came on, and everything changed.

He completely ignored her!

The cheerleader watched Ezra curiously. His eyes grew extra wide, drinking in every second of screen action. His breathing slowed (easy to tell; his mouth was open most of the time). His lips moved a little when people spoke. At mysteriously critical moments he would choose to pause the action and explain to her—eyes still on the screen—why this line was important, or what this meant in terms of character development, or how this was inspired directly from basic human archetypes à la Campbell's *Hero of a Thousand Faces.*

Most of the time, he didn't even look at her.

It was kind of weird.

There they were, in a dark room, sitting on a couch together, all alone . . . but when the screen was on, she might as well not have been there at all.

Of course, during the inevitable pee or phone break, everything changed. He accidentally rubbed up against her when sitting down or getting up, and reached directly across her chest for the popcorn—until she wordlessly dumped the entire bucket into his lap.

"Um. So this might be easy for you to start with. *Ranma 1/2*. It's a classic," David said, handing her a bootleg DVD.

They were sitting on a bench outside the local comic shop. He had just taken her on a tour of the store, which she genuinely appreciated. It was almost like a shopping spree. She walked out with *Batman: The Killing Joke*; *Sandman: Dream Country*; *X-Men Visionaries: Chris Claremont*; and an action figure she thought was "kind of cute" and "might look good on my dashboard." David hadn't laughed at her; he had merely smiled.

Too bad he was so overweight. With his shy little smile—and maybe a slightly cleaner red T-shirt—he would have been almost cute.

A haircut wouldn't have hurt, either.

"And, um, this is *Negima*. It's a good intro to manga. Very popular. Um, there's a little weirdness, with girls—it's called 'fan service,' but it's pretty light compared to other ones. We'll start reading it together—I know that totally sounds retarded, but Japanese comics read a lot different from American ones. Like, you start on this side of the book." He turned it to show her how it opened from the back.

"I'm sorry if this is totally rude," the cheerleader said as politely as she could, "but are you interested in this because of your background?"

"Um, my grandparents are from Singapore. Not, uh, Japan. I just like it…'cause, you know, it's *like* comics. But they can be about anything. Mythology or history or regular life—but with art, you know? It's not words with pictures. It's art. It's a whole different way of…experiencing a book."

"Hmm," Montgomery said, swinging her legs on the bench, thinking about it.

Susan walked by with a couple of football players. With her

long black hair and dark eyes, she was the perfect cheerleadery complement to Montgomery. Of course they had been friends forever.

The three waved and gave her a questioning look, pointing at David behind his back. Montgomery shrugged. Susan said something and the two other boys laughed. Meanly.

David turned to look.

"Oh, friends of yours," he said, more of a statement than a question. "You want to take off?"

"No," she said, a little sadly. The answer was yes; they were probably meeting Ryan at Café Not-Tea, to gossip and talk and have general fun. Not read comic books.

But Locacon was coming up.

She steeled her shoulders.

"Okay. So it reads backwards. What else?"

LOTR, PART I

"But *Rings* is an epic movie; it falls under *my* jurisdiction!" Ezra whined.

Mica shrugged. "I would argue that movies *not* based on a book fall under your jurisdiction. High fantasy literature is clearly mine. Besides, according to the schedule, you've sort of…um…monopolized most of the classes this week," he pointed out, tapping at the Montgomery Calendar they had taped to the door of the media center.

"He's got a point," David said, nose buried in *Johnny the Homicidal Maniac*. Just a refresher; he was going to talk the cheerleader through it next week.

The student in question walked in as the two boys began to shout at each other. Ellen frowned into her book, trying to shut everyone out.

"What's up with them?" Montgomery asked. She didn't think members of Team Geek ever had anything to fight about.

Ellen made a face. "They're arguing about who gets to watch *The Fellowship of the Ring*. With you," she added a little spitefully.

"I am not spending another evening with Ezra," the other girl insisted. "Not alone."

Ellen's look changed, becoming something like understanding. "I don't blame you," she agreed.

LOTR, PART II

Hanging out with Mica in his bedroom fell somewhere between David-on-a-bench and Ezra-in-his-gigantoid-living-room. While it was weird to be by herself with this boy, it didn't necessarily reek of danger. In fact, she was impressed that it didn't really reek much of anything, except for maybe the slight musty scent of hundreds of paperbacks that lined the walls. A small TV sat on a wooden crate in a corner; the home-theater experience was completed by a neatly folded Mexican blanket on the floor and a child's stool (it said 'Mica' in big bright hand-painted letters).

Tall, short, and occasionally pretty people droned nonsense on the tiny screen. Montgomery found herself losing interest almost immediately.

"Hang on, this is an important bit," Mica said, with the tiniest bit of an affected British accent. But he did it without thinking, so it was almost excusable.

"What? They going to get on miniature ponies and ride off into the sunset?" the cheerleader asked, pulling out a book and blowing dust off it.

"No, they're—come on, this is serious." He didn't turn his

head from the TV, his lips slightly parted around his surprisingly cute, slightly bucky front teeth. His dirty blond hair was tousled into his eyes—but unlike she'd assumed, it wasn't actually dirty. It might even have had some gel or something in it.

"This is no mere ranger. He is Aragorn, son of Arathorn. You owe him your allegiance...."

The serious one, blondie with the ears, the *elf*, was getting all self-important. She remembered that from the first time her boyfriend made her watch it. It would continue like this for the next two movies.

"Ugh, would you *listen* to them?" Montgomery sighed, rolling her eyes and shoving the book back onto the shelf. It had looked intriguing at first, but none of the characters mentioned on the back had any vowels in their names; only a lot of *w*s and *y*s and far too many double *l*s. "It's ridiculous the way they talk!"

"It's supposed to be epic and therefore archaic," Mica explained patiently. But there was an edge to his voice. "Like...well, you take French. Think of the formality of their speech like *vouvoiement* versus *tutoiement*."

"I didn't know you took French," Montgomery said, impressed. "Wait, you're not in my or Shaniqa's class...."

"I take French Five with the seniors," the boy said dismissively. Not bragging. Like he wanted to get over it and back to the subject at hand. He pressed *play*. "Anyway, think of it as trying to sound like an English version of romantic, archaic French."

"It *sounds* retarded," she said tartly.

"Montgomery." Mica was the very picture of barely controlled exasperation. "Not only are you paying us to show things like this to you and explain them to you, but this—*this* movie, is one of my Favorite. Things. In. The. World. If you don't like it, could you at least keep the comments to yourself? How would you like it if I made fun of..."

He paused. He could have suggested any one of a thousand

nasty things, from nighttime soaps to the worst sort of trashy romances.

But he didn't.

"...whatever it is *you* like?"

They locked eyes for a moment. She bit her lip.

Whenever it was her turn to watch something *she* liked, Ryan wouldn't stop making awful comments. Like the reality show where young designers had to sew things quickly. She didn't even bother trying to watch it with him anymore. Hence the noir after noir after noir...

"Sorry," she finally said. Grudgingly. She flopped down on his bed.

"Why are you doing this, anyway? I don't really get it," Mica admitted, crossing his legs and relaxing a little.

"Ryan likes all of this sort of...stuff," she said as she waved her hand around. "I mean, a little. Not like you guys like it. And I don't get it at all. I thought maybe if I did, I would get him more. I really like him, you know."

"That's..." Mica thought carefully. "Kind of generous."

"Um, yeah," Montgomery said, picking at his *Star Wars* quilt.

The obvious question was finally spoken.

"Is he doing the same thing for you?" Mica finally asked.

"What is this, Geek 101 or the *Dr. Phil* show?" the cheerleader snapped. "When I want relationship advice, trust me, I won't be paying the dysfunctional club."

He made a face. *"Touché."*

"What about you?" she relented. "Like...you and Ellen seem perfect for each other. How come you never dated?"

"Who said we didn't?" Mica said quickly, turning back to the TV and groping for the remote.

"Really?" Montgomery's eyes widened at the new information. Gossip—even here, among these people—was juicy.

"Look, it just didn't work out, okay?" he muttered, pretending to fix the screen format.

"Oh my gosh—did you guys *do it*? Is that what happened?"

"Hey. Monty. Shut your freaking trap and watch the elf, okay?" the geek growled, hitting *play*. "You're watching a movie you hate to impress your football-playing BF. Ix-nay on the relationship advice-ay. When I want *pom-pom* advice, trust me, I'll go straight to you."

"'Monty,'" the cheerleader said, giggling a little. "I kind of like that."

LUNCH BREAK

"So, how's your...*secret project* going?" Susan stage-whispered across the table. Montgomery kicked her under it. Her best friend was sitting *right next* to Ryan, who, breaking convention, was not as dumb as a football player could be. He had already questioned the unmarked bootleg in her purse—something she didn't usually carry with her cell phone, makeup, and tampons.

Ryan wasn't paying attention, though; he was shoveling the second of a trio of cheeseburgers into his mouth, the juices dribbling around to his chin. It would stain his white shirt with permanent greasy smears.

"It's going well," she said casually, as if it was about something for history class. She studied her limp salad. Then she cleared her throat and got Ryan's attention by tapping him with her fork. "Hey, there's a making of *Star Wars* special on tonight, on the History Channel."

"Yeah?" Ryan said, surprised. He swallowed quickly. "For real? How'd you hear about it?"

"I don't know.... Maybe you could come over and we could do

our homework and *watch* it." Which was really a way of saying "do our homework and *make out while we 'watch it.'* " It certainly got his attention.

"Oh, you can't," Susan said, pouting. "There's Reese's party tonight. You two have to come."

"I don't know...." Montgomery said unenthusiastically.

"Well," Ryan said, torn.

"Come on! I'm going to wear my new top, the one with the *zip-down*," Susan said flirtily, wheedling Ryan.

"Hey," Montgomery warned, surprised at her friend's forwardness.

"You know I'm just kidding," Susan said, backing down immediately. "I was just giving some added incentive."

"Hmm." Montgomery reached over and stole one of Ryan's fries, biting it in half, hard.

SF TV: THE SCIFI CHANNEL VS. PBS AND
THE MAJOR NETWORKS

After practice Montgomery took the bus over to Ellen's house for what would be, barring some wonderfully cataclysmic event, an incredibly boring afternoon.

The lone female member of Team Geek promised she would start slowly, beginning with socially acceptable nerd TV (*Lost, Heroes, Smallville, Buffy the Vampire Slayer*), then easing into the more commonly known serious sci-fi with a series of old- and new-school matchups (*Dr. Who* 1–8 vs. *Dr. Who* 9 and 10, *Stargate SG1* vs. *Atlantis*, old *Battlestar* vs. new *Battlestar*), ending with a very brief foray into the hardcore geek-but-not-forgotten (*Max Headroom, Misfits of Science, Friday the Thirteenth*, plus some sort of Canadian–Luxembourgian Dracula series).

Despite herself, the cheerleader was a little intrigued to see

Ellen's house. She had to admit that this little extracurricular project was interesting at least in how it revealed the personal lives of
people she hadn't really given a wet slap about before.

She could hear the shouting before she even rang the bell.

"Oh, they're upstairs," Mrs. Ellen's-Mom said with a smile, as
if nothing was wrong, or she was deaf.

Montgomery mounted the very-normal, very-family wooden
staircase with a growing sense of dread. At the top, at the end of
the hall, inside a door covered with pictures of stars and space
things (and *very* old stickers of unicorns), was exactly the sort of
scene she was afraid she was walking into.

Mr. Ellen's-Dad was yelling. Ellen was standing as calmly as
she could, a thin trickle of a tear along the outside of her cheek.
She was obviously trying not to see the cheerleader standing there,
but quickly wiped her face, embarrassed.

"Oh, and there you go, *crying* again," her father screamed, noticing her gesture. "For heaven's sake, why can't you be more like your
hero—what's his name? Schmock? Spock? Something stupid? The
one with no emotions. Why do you have to be *so emotional* about
everything? You're just like your freaking grandmother…crying over
everything. Are you going to *cry* when an employer yells at you?"

Montgomery looked down at the floor and gave a small cough.

"What? Oh, you must be Montgomery," he said, calming down
immediately.

But whatever small token he was paying to social decency
failed against an urge he just couldn't resist. He immediately
turned back to his daughter.

"Look at her—why can't you be more together, like her? *She*
looks like someone who's going to college! Not wasting her time
with stupid online games! Nice to meet you," he added, striding
angrily down the hall.

"Hey," the cheerleader said after a moment, with a twisted,
understanding little smile.

"Hey," Ellen said back, sniffling, wiping her nose with the back of her hand. Everything was silent in the house. Dust fell; it was hard to tell where Ellen's father had gone. Montgomery could tell that though they were from opposite worlds, at that one moment the two girls understood each other completely: What had just occurred *totally sucked*.

The cheerleader noticed Ellen's outfit with sadness: the tucked-in T-shirt printed with a weird, garish logo, the boy jeans that were actually cut for a boy, the cracked leather belt, the sneakers with duct tape and pins. Not slobby *or* punk enough to make any statement other than "lame." Oh, Ellen was going to college. She was super-smart.

She just wasn't going to interview well.

"Um. I don't really feel like watching TV. Here," Ellen finally said.

"No problem," Montgomery said easily. But she found herself a little disappointed.

Weird.

Here was just the sort of wonderful act of God she was hoping to preempt the afternoon of *très* boring geekery—she could be at Ryan's in forty-five minutes if she raced—and now she sort of felt cheated.

She stole a quick glance around and behind Ellen, trying to take in as much of the room as she could before she left. It was similar to Mica's, but different in a few key, girly areas. A box of tampons. Some stuffed animals. Paisley bedclothes.

A constellation of plastic painted spaceships— *star*ships—drifting from the ceiling.

On her desk was an explosion of things incongruous to the rest of the room: piles of neatly-folded cloth, measuring tape, diaphanous fluff, cones of thread. There wasn't a sewing machine or anything else crafty in sight save a neatly organized set of model paints.

"Sorry you came over," Ellen muttered, kicking her toe.

"We could go see a movie or something," Montgomery found herself suggesting. "Is there anything science fictiony out? You could coach me through it."

"Nothing good," Ellen sighed. "But…I'll see anything. Bad comedy. Crapulent thriller. Explody spies. Anything except for something dumb and chicky."

"*The Sweet Smell of Success* is playing at the Art House," the cheerleader suggested hesitantly.

Ellen gave her a look somewhere between surprise and respect. "A classic, huh? Okay. Yeah. Sure. That'd be great."

The two girls regarded each other for a second, suddenly realizing that they had somehow just agreed to go see an (almost) normal movie together, almost normally. Almost like friends.

"All right. We're outta here," Ellen said, grabbing her wallet, fleeing the touching moment.

"And maybe we could go to the mall afterwards," Montgomery suggested with a grin.

"What, is this the cheerleader-turns-the-geek-into-a-beauty montage?" Ellen growled.

"No," Montgomery retorted, "this is the surprising cheerleader-picks-up-her-asthma-prescription expositional scene…

"…and maybe we'll just pick you out a new pair of pants. Just one," she added mischievously.

ALL TOGETHER NOW

Technically, it was video-game night. Which meant Mica. But it was hosted at Ezra's, because he had the aforementioned biggest-baddest TV and greatest number of game systems. *Taught* by Mica, because he was the expert. Section-led by David, because he was also pretty qualified, and more importantly, wanted to play.

Chaperoned by Ellen because Montgomery refused to go to Ezra's ever again unless she was along.

The Trekspert was downstairs getting snacks out of the pantry with the host while David, Mica, and Montgomery lounged around Ezra's bedroom. David sat sort of upside down on the—king-sized—bed, legs up on the wall as if the extra blood rushing to his brain would help. Mica was upright at the computer, logged into the massive multiplayer fantasy rpg of the moment. There were bowls of M&M's and pizza bagels everywhere.

It was...surprisingly pleasant. Low-key.

Montgomery perched on a stool next to Mica, trying to pretend to care as he made a character for her, then showed her how to bash a level-one goblin.

"See, look! Now you're level two!" he said proudly, indicating the willowy elf-thing on the screen that had hair and eyes sort of like the cheerleader.

"Yay," she stated flatly. "What now?"

"Now we go get you some new armor, because you can wear light leather. And a helm, and some boots..."

"Wait, what? We're going shopping for new clothes? In this game? Are you serious? Can I choose different kinds?" She leaned closer into the screen, putting her hand on Mica's shoulder to get a better look. If he noticed, or enjoyed it, he didn't let on.

"Dig the cheerleader loving the virtual shopping. Too much." David cracked up, his last laugh sounding unfortunately very porcine.

"Oh my gosh," the cheerleader said, turning around slowly in her stool. "You snorted. You *actually snorted*."

"I'm a geek, whatever, like you're always calling us," he said, shrugging.

"Hey, Pom-Pom, you were just getting excited about buying a *pink shield* for your game character," Mica pointed out.

"Okay, okay, phasers down, everyone," she said, putting her hands up. "Let's just get back to work."

Ezra and Ellen were just entering the doorway, mini-eggrolls and drinks in hand.

"Did she just say what I thought she said?" Ezra asked, amazed.

"By George, I think she's got it," Ellen said with a smile.

FINALS

"What are you so stressed out about?" Ryan asked, not looking up from his phone. He was deeply texting.

"I want to be completely prepared for the conven—uh, this *big test*, and oh...never mind." Montgomery wore her big comfy sweatshirt and fat jeans, which were normally great for studying in but for the fact that her boyfriend found the outfit unbearably sexy. Tonight, however, he didn't even seem to notice. Unusual for him, but lucky for her.

"Mmm," Ryan chuckled at something someone sent him. For a while there were no sounds other than the tapping of his keypad and the turning of notebook pages.

"I'm really glad you're going to Locacon with me," Ryan mentioned, not looking up from his phone. "That's awesome of you."

"Really?" Montgomery glowed in the praise. She squeezed his arm and lay her head back on his shoulder. He patted her knee.

"Hey, what do you call the vampire who makes someone a vampire? Like, the vampire daddy?" she asked dreamily.

"Sire," Ryan answered without looking up.

Then he looked up.

"Wait, what?"

"Nothing," the cheerleader said quickly.

"Um, I don't know what to say," Montgomery said honestly.

David, Ellen, Ezra, and Mica stood before her—accidentally in descending order of height—dressed in, well, what she supposed they thought was formal. Ezra wore a jacket and tie, both of which were flashy, expensive, and ridiculously out of place in high school. David wore a jean jacket with all of his pins on it. *All* of them.

(They made, Montgomery was sort of delighted to realize she knew, a kind of scale-mail armor over his chest.)

Mica wore a vintage T-shirt that was printed to look like a tuxedo, but had a real carnation pinned to the fake lapel. Ellen wore a skirt. And a sweater. And what looked like Ferengi ears. For someone who apparently didn't know the first thing about makeup, she had done a spectacular job blending the prosthetic into her own skin.

Ezra cleared his throat. Pompously, of course. "On this day we would like to formally congratulate you on achieving the rank of *graduate* proto-geek...."

"Sub-lieutenant commander," Ellen corrected.

"Monty the Grey," Mica suggested with a grin.

"Level Four Cleric," David stated matter-of-factly.

"Why cleric?" Ellen asked, surprised.

"It seemed like the most scholarly, least violent of all the other kinds of classes. Think of her as a student-monk," David explained.

"Makes sense," Mica nodded.

"PEOPLE!" Ezra said, exasperated. "As I was saying. Today we are gathered here to formally congratulate you. Your hard work and near-endless toil have finally accomplished what you set out to do...."

"Good job, Monty," Mica said, ignoring him. He stepped out of line and kissed the cheerleader on her cheek. She was surprised by the casualness of his socially-appropriate action; he neither blushed nor tried to turn it into something else.

And then he handed her a little figurine of an elf. Blond hair. Legolas, probably. Maybe Haldir.

No, it definitely looked a little Orlando Bloomy.

"You can put it on the shelf next to your *American Idol* posters," Mica suggested with a mischievous smile.

"Nice paintwork," David said enviously. "Um, this is from me. It's like a diploma."

He handed her a scroll with a lot of calligraphy on it, and a bright, big-eyed picture of herself. As kind of a blond Japanese cheerleader.

"Did you draw this yourself?" Montgomery asked, trying not to sound like a mom. It was actually quite good. Maybe she would even frame it.

"Yeah, and *inked* and *colored* it, too," he pointed out.

"And from me, something to *inspire* you," Ezra said grandly, holding his hand out with a flourish.

Montgomery was expecting something ridiculous, expensive, and shiny, an embarrassingly lavish gesture.

What she got was a ball of fluff.

"A tribble?" she asked, confused.

"Don't girls love them?" Ezra asked, also confused.

"*Thirty years ago*, maybe," Ellen snorted, rolling her eyes. "Here, this is from me. For all of the thousands of bad guys in your life." She gave a meaningful look to Ezra. Then she smugly held up a case.

Montgomery popped the catches and opened the top.

"Oh, my gosh," she said.

Inside was a single piece of sharpened wood.

"MR. POINTY!" she screamed in delight.

"You gave Buffy's weapon...her stake...to the *cheerleader*," David said with a whistle. "Sheer genius."

"Ohhhhh, sweet," Mica said with admiration.

"Nice," Ezra said grudgingly.

"I win," Ellen said happily.

"Thanks, you guys, all of you," Montgomery said, clutching the stake to her heart. She felt an actual tear forming. "I thought this was going to be horrible. But it wasn't. Much. Sort of. You guys made it a lot of fun. I'm going to miss you. You most of all, Scarecrow," she sniffed loudly, pointing at Ellen.

But her eyes darted over to Mica.

He smiled quietly back.

THE CON

"Where is she? Do you see her yet?" David whispered. He was crouched down behind Mica and Ezra, who were sharing a pair of binoculars. All three were hiding behind a shelf of books at *The Neverending Story*'s booth. Mica wore a pith helmet.

"No — wait, there's Ryan and Reese...there she is!" Ezra said excitedly.

"What's she doing?" David whined.

"They're by the Knight's Arms. She's...she's picking up a d'k tahg."

"Let me see!" Mica grabbed the glasses. "No, it's too small, you moron. That's totally a Klingon throwing knife, or maybe B'Etor's...."

"Oh, come on, look at the blood gutter...."

David tapped them on the shoulders. "Guys, where'd she go?"

◦

"Hey, Montgomery."

"Oh my gosh, *Ellen*!"

The cheerleader's eyes popped out of her head. So did Ryan's.

The geek girl was in a yellow and black iridescent catsuit, holding a mask with what looked like giant pointy ears. An iridescent red-black cape hung from her shoulders, matching her boots.

She looked, in a word, great.

"Ellen Epstein?" Ryan said, backing up to get a better look. He was grinning in shock. "Really? You look *hot*."

Montgomery gave him a quick frown.

"Ellen, you really do look great," she said honestly. "You should..."

"What, wear this more often?" Ellen said with a giggle. "Have you seen the guys around? They promised to escort me to the masquerade."

"Oh, yes. Dumb, dumber, and dumbest are 'hiding' over there," Montgomery said dryly, pointing at the bookseller's stall. Three awkward shadows ducked down. "Who are you supposed to be, anyway?"

"Who cares?" Ryan said.

"Um, Kathy Kane? Batwoman? From the sixties? I'd better put the mask back on before Kim sees me without it. She spent *weeks* working on it. She'll kill me," Ellen said, fitting the unwieldy thing on. Ryan kept staring.

It should have been a little triumph for the geek. The quarterback was obviously drooling over *her*, and ignoring his pretty little cheerleading girlfriend.

But Batwoman hopped nervously from one foot to the other, obviously looking for an escape.

"You should *totally* do spandex more often," Ryan said, circling around her to get a better look.

"RYAN!" Montgomery growled.

"Hey, guys!" a perky voice said. A *completely* inappropriately cheery and busty vampire skipped up to them, tossing her raven-black hair and cheap capelet over her shoulders.

"Susan?!" Montgomery demanded.

The other cheerleader gave her a pouty smile that was not at all impeded by fangs. "My idiot brother loves this stuff. I told Mom and Dad I'd chaperone."

She batted glittery eyelashes at Ryan, whose eyeballs couldn't decide which costumed girl to look at.

THE INEVITABLE CLIMAX

When you're a cheerleader, even an unusual cheerleader who seeks knowledge beyond her normal ken, you're still bound by cheerleader laws. One of which is that everyone in the school knows gossip about you and yours *before* or *exactly at the same time* as you.

So in a high school of less than five hundred students, if a "celebrity"—say, a quarterback—and another "celebrity"—say, a cheerleader *not* his girlfriend—hook up at a party, someone is going to notice.

And immediately tell, text, and generally spill to everyone he or she knows.

Montgomery's posse of ponytailed cheerleaders were obviously trying to protect her from *something* the next day, escorting her from class to class even more closely—and nervously—than usual.

Or maybe they were trying to protect someone else.

"Oh, dude," David said sympathetically in passing, waving to Montgomery from the other side of the hall. "I'm so sorry. After all that, all the stuff you went through. What a jerk."

"What?" she asked, stopping. A crowd began to gather. Murmured voices rose: why were these two talking to each other? And about something besides science homework?

Ryan was coming from the other way.

The cheerleaders tried to get her walking again.

"Um? Ryan and Susan?" David said, thinking she might just be confused. If *he* knew, surely every other person at the school knew. Someone must have told her. "At the party at Shaniqa's place? Wow, did I get it wrong?"

"WHAT?!" Montgomery spun around to face Ryan.

Everyone in the hallway was silent, waiting.

"YOU!" she screamed, near-incoherent with rage. "YOU—"

What Montgomery said next was unimportant. It could have been a thousand different things. She could have called him a *"tin-plated dictator with delusions of godhood!"* She could have gone with the classic *"scruffy-looking nerf-herder!"* She might have chosen, appropriate to the situation, *"gods-cursed TOASTER frakker!"*

But in the end it was unimportant what *exactly* she said.

Because the entire population of Springfield High heard Montgomery K. Bushnell use an insult so geeky, so extreme, that there was no doubt in any other stealth geek's mind what she was.

One of them.

She pushed David out of the way.

"Excuse me, I've got a vampire to slay," she growled, looking for Susan and Mr. Pointy.

THE DÉNOUEMENT

She managed to make it all the way through school, the drive home, and up to her room before crying. It began messily: a chin shake, a couple of coughs, several quick sniffs. She didn't *want* to cry. She wanted to stay angry, or forget about it entirely.

Like an addict looking for a fix, she pawed through her neat shelves for something that would stop the pain.

Breakfast at Tiffany's. Casablanca. Doctor Zhivago. Sabrina....

Montgomery chose *Sabrina* (the Audrey Hepburn one, of

course), figuring the scene with the eggs would at least make her smile.

She delicately opened the DVD and snapped out the disk, holding it by the edges as if it were glass. She took it into her brother's room (he had the upstairs TV) and put it in, then sat on the floor, hugging her knees.

Tears coursed down her cheeks. Her lips moved silently as the story began:

"Once upon a time... on the North Shore of Long Island, some thirty miles from New York..."

The sobbing began for real. She took a deep gulp of air—

—and then realized something.

"Oh my gosh." Her eyes went beautifully wide with cheerleadery surprise.

She jumped up and grabbed her phone, stabbing at numbers. Not even bothering to pause the movie.

"Hello?" A grumpy female voice picked up from the other end.

"I GET IT!!!" Montgomery shouted. "I GET IT!"

"Um, what?" Ellen asked, obviously holding the phone away from her ear.

Montgomery paced back and forth, excited. "I get it! The spaceships and the quoting lines and memorizing stupid details about High Elvish and arguing over pronunciations! Before I thought you were all weird for the sake of, you know, just being weird.

"But I GET IT NOW! You just *really* love it. It's where you go to. Who you turn to. It's your... your *home*."

"Ah," Ellen paused, obviously torn between a sarcastic response and a grown-up one. "Yes," she decided.

There was a moment's silence as the cheerleader wiped her nose, reveling in her revelation.

"Wait, 'you'?" Ellen suddenly asked. "'*You*' just really love it? Not 'we'?"

"What?" Montgomery asked, confused. "Oh. Right. Yes. Not we. I mean, me. I mean, I don't love it, the elves and stuff, no."

"Even after all this time? We didn't convince you at all?"

Montgomery sighed. "I...*appreciate* your passion. Now. And I think I can even appreciate some of the more...easily accessible...aspects of science fiction and fantasy. But I don't love it the way you guys do. I just don't hate it anymore."

"Oh," Ellen said, thinking about it.

"But I like *you* guys," the cheerleader pointed out. "Just not the stuff you like."

"Well, I guess that's something," Ellen decided. She paused. "Um. I heard about Ryan...and, uh, David and what happened in the hallway, and you finding out, and...um, everything that was sucky. Um, sorry."

"Thanks. It *was*. Sucky." Montgomery sniffed. She was quiet for a moment, sad. And then she thought of something. "Hey. The girls are going to come over tonight and, you know, just hang with me for a while. Support circle. I'd...I'd really like it if you came, too."

"You want me to come over and hang out with a bunch of cheerleaders?" Ellen asked carefully, making sure she heard right.

"With my *friends*," the cheerleader corrected. "My *other* friends."

Ellen paused, letting the significance of the statement sink in.

"I don't know," she finally said. "I appreciate the offer, but your *other friends* might not."

Montgomery thought about it. Ellen was right; it was a little early for such a sudden culture clash. At least half her "other friends" had tormented Ellen and *her* friends at some point in their twelve long years of going to school together.

"But, um, if you want to go to the mall or something, maybe, Saturday, I could let you pick out some makeup for me," Ellen offered. It obviously took a lot out of her.

"Okay, it's a date," Montgomery paused. "Hey, do you think you could invite Mica along?"

"*What?* Oh, no," the other girl groaned. "No. No, no, no, no..."

"Jealous much?" the cheerleader quipped.

"Horrified, more. On a level I can't even put into words. Like—cosmic horror. I don't suppose you've read *The Call of Cthulhu*, have you?"

"Yes," Montgomery answered proudly. "Yes, I have."

Tracy Lynn is the pseudonym for Elizabeth J. Braswell. Elizabeth was born in the United Kingdom, to her great surprise. When her parents returned to the United States, she stowed away in their baggage (mega geek points if you know who I stole this from). She is the author of *Snow* and *Rx*, and *The Nine Lives of Chloe King* as Celia Thomson, as well as numerous Disney Pirates of the Caribbean books.

Geek creds, in no particular order:
Favorite SF: old school. Favorite authors: Sturgeon, Bradbury, Clarke, Moore, Ian McDonald. Favorite movie: *Blade Runner*. Favorite Doctor: Fifth. Growing to love the Tenth. Favorite quote: "Where are we going? Planet 10!"

Knows pi to 12 digits. Majored in Egyptology. Met husband at Star Trek convention. They were there as professionals: he published the Star Trek books, she produced Star Trek video games. Produced video games for ten years. Was on the math team, debate team, and in the Latin club…first story ever published was in *Amazing Stories* magazine. Can recite most of the *Hitchhiker's Guide to the Galaxy* by heart.

You can find the rest of the Five Rules of Girls at www.themessydesk.com and write her at tracy@tracy-lynn.com.

DEFINITIONAL CHAOS
by scott westerfeld

I wanted a mission, and for my sins the ConCom gave me one.

It was the usual chaos: everyone on the Convention Committee thought someone had wired the money. Nobody had. Eighty-four thousand dollars, due to the convention hotel two weeks ago. The owner was threatening cancellation, which really *would* be a problem: seventeen thousand stormtroopers, Browncoats, pirates, quidditch players, and Dr. Who sidekicks wandering the streets, plotting revenge on whomever had left them roomless.

The money was ready to go, but the hotel owner demanded cash now, delivered to her winter home in forty-eight hours. A crazy thing to want, but maybe the money was headed straight into drugs or political contributions—she was down in Florida, after all. That's what you get for dealing with family-owned hotels instead of the soulless Sheratons and Marriotts of this world: personality, chaos.

But I wasn't complaining. Like I said, I needed a mission. Even if it meant missing that weekend's Stargate SG-1 marathon, I was ready to go.

The call came at noon; my berth on Amtrak's Silver Star was booked for 3:25. An hour later I'd digested a handful of aspirin, showered, and packed, and was pulling my Walther PPK/S 380ACP (of German manufacture, not the post-war Manurhin production run) from its original cardboard box. I set to work with the (also original) finger-looped cleaning rod, bringing both the Walther and my Taurus PT138 to a dull shine. I decided that the Luger my dad gave me for acing my SATs was overkill, but I cleaned it, too, just for luck.

Let's get one thing clear: my gun collection wasn't the only reason the Convention Committee had chosen me. Just as important was my alignment, consistent across every system known to gamingkind. Whatever the common good needed, lawful or not, I was willing to do it. I was the only person for the job.

Or so I thought, until I saw Lexia Tollman waiting with the ConCom, bright-eyed, green-haired, and grinning like the devil. She was wearing the leather Peacekeeper jacket I remembered her always wanting, and it looked good on her.

"What's *she* doing here?"

The ConCom shuffled their feet, staring at the floor. One ventured, "We figured you'd need some company."

"Hey, Temptress Moon," Lexia said. "How's it going?"

I flinched at the sound of my old Mayhem name. Stats spilled across my mind: Temptress Moon had been a neutral good Paladin of Balance, Fourteenth Echelon, with a Voice of Barding and a persistent aetheric life-link. Practically divine, almost unkillable.

Almost...except for an obscure resurrection-blocking poison distilled from the bark of the Tree of Vile Tidings. Administered by my then girlfriend. For fun.

"You've got to be kidding," I said.

The ConCom collectively hemmed and hawed, pretending they hadn't expected any unpleasantness. As if Lexia's betrayal of me wasn't legendary on the Mayhem boards.

"We can't have you going alone," one said. "Not with that much money. We know it's a little...awkward, but Lexia's the only one who could go on such short notice."

I nodded slowly. She'd always hated *Stargate*.

"You're armed, after all," another spoke up. "And she's not."

"You're sure of that?" I said.

They all turned to stare at her.

I sighed. "Let me guess, she *said* she wasn't."

Lexia rolled her eyes, but pulled off the Peacekeeper jacket, its plastic snaps clicking between her fingers. She tossed it to me, kicked a small backpack across the floor in my direction, then turned slowly in place. All she wore now was a black T-shirt and a pair of jeans, too tight to hide a weapon. She'd been working out, I noticed.

I rifled the backpack: wallet, cell phone, another black T-shirt, and a bottle of my favorite vodka. The bottle made my mouth dry for a moment; I'd promised the ConCom to stay sober on the way down.

Then I saw the pair of handcuffs labeled: *Remember these, T-Moon?*

My stomach flipped, but I didn't let anything show on my face, just zipped the backpack up and searched the jacket. Nothing but two Amtrak tickets and pocket lint.

The public address crackled and screeched, then told us that the Silver Star was pulling up on Track One.

I could have told the ConCom *no* right then, gone back to my apartment for forty-eight solid hours of jonesing Jaffas and dodgy Dial-Home Devices. But suddenly my own DHD was out of order. Maybe it was just the chance to break out some +2 firepower in the real world. Or maybe something twisted inside me wanted to be trapped on a train with the woman who had killed me.

Lexia saw me hesitate. She smiled and yanked a black leather briefcase from one of the ConCom.

"I'll carry the treasure." Her tongue flickered across her lower lip. "Just like old times."

I gave the ConCom one last glare, then followed her to the platform, preparing myself for twenty-seven hours of angst and nerves and the dredging of long-buried anger. Not the mission I'd expected, not at all. But at least this way one worry was gone....

No way would I fall asleep on the way down to Florida.

○

Our roomette aboard the Silver Star was not Amtrak's finest. The size of two London phone booths stuck together, it smelled bluely antiseptic, like the water in an airplane toilet.

We settled into the two seats, facing each other, our ankles almost touching. Lexia instantly rebelled against the small space, flicking on and off the lights, discovering cup holders and coat hangers concealed in the walls. She fiddled with the small table beside her until it unfolded, astonishingly, into a toilet. Hence the blue smell.

I set the briefcase on the floor and rested my feet on it. When the station outside began to slide away I relaxed a little, feeling safer in motion. But Lexia was hovering now, fussing with her backpack up on the luggage rack.

"Sit down," I said.

"And fasten my seatbelt? This isn't a plane, T-Moon."

"Lucky thing, too." I breathed deep to feel the reassuring pressure of the PPK's holster against my chest, the Taurus strapped to my ankle. Guns and planes don't mix, so when carrying briefcases full of cash, slow and steady wins the race.

As long as slow and steady stays locked and loaded.

The conductor knocked on the door, asking for our tickets, and Lexia started fucking with him. She asked how long till New York City, and he sputtered until she laughed and admitted we were on the right train, headed down to Miami. She chattered as he punched and tore along perforations: asking questions about the "sleeping arrangements," half-flirting, pretending she and I were lovers who'd just been in a fight, sowing confusion.

Once he was gone, Lexia slid the roomette's door shut, locked it, and drew the blind that hid us from the corridor. She finally settled in the seat across from me, staring out the window.

But twenty seconds later she was bored, nudging the briefcase with one foot. "Maybe we should look inside."

"Forget it."

"Don't you want to see what fifty-seven thousand dollars looks like?"

"Eighty-four."

"Whoa, that's a lot. Thanks for telling me."

I cleared my throat. Score one for Lexia.

"What if it's not all there?" she said. "What if one of the Con-Com borrowed some? Shouldn't we count it?"

She reached for the case, and I lashed out with one steel-toed boot. She jerked back her hand, nursing two fingers between her lips. "Ow."

"I didn't touch you."

"It's the thought that counts." She played dejected for another moment, then her eyes brightened again. "Seriously, though, the case felt too light. It made a clunking noise, like there's a brick inside. Pick it up yourself."

"We're not. Opening. The briefcase."

"They didn't say we couldn't. So why not?"

"Because I can't imagine anything worse than being stuck in a tiny roomette with you and piles of *someone else's cash*!"

I shouted the last three words, which seemed to still the train noise for a moment, and her eyes grew manga-sized. Tears flickered with the shadows of passing trees. "You don't trust me, Temptress Moon?"

"Well spotted. You are, in fact, the last person I'd trust."

"Really? Why?"

"Because you're vain and self-centered and you do pointless, destructive things for fun. You're chaos personified."

She smiled. "Flattery *this* early in the journey, Temptress Moon?"

"Quit calling me that."

Lexia leaned back, propping her feet up on the briefcase. "Oh, so that's what this is about? You miss your little paladin girl?"

"*Miss* her? It took me two years to level her up, then gather all the artifacts I needed for that life-link!"

"But immortal is boring, T-Moon, and anyway, you enjoy grinding." She nudged the briefcase again. "Did you hear that? There's a brick in there, I swear."

"Quit fucking with the case. Quit *looking* at it. I'm not letting you do to the ConCom what you did to me, okay?"

"A blatantly false comparison," she said. "I quite like the ConCom, and I *hated* little miss Temptress Moon."

I turned away and stared out the window. The backyards of people poor enough to live next to train tracks flashed past—weedy lawns and broken cars. "It was the Voice of Barding, right? Because it gave her a higher charisma than you?"

"I didn't give a shit about that crappy Voice of Barding," Lexia said. "It was your tepid alignment."

I hissed out a slow breath through clenched teeth, feeling the dull twinge of old wounds. Here it was, said aloud at last: the underlying conflict of those last months of our relationship, in game and out.

"Neutral good is not tepid," I said. "It's the only real good, beyond the rigidity of law or the self-indulgence of chaos."

She rolled her eyes. "Beyond relevance, you mean. Goodness all alone is just an abstraction. Where's the *story* in neutral good?"

"Ever heard of Robin Hood? There's a story for you."

"Not this farko again." She sighed. "Dude steals from the rich and gives to the poor. That's *definitional* chaotic good."

I shook my head, the old arguments rising inside me, one hand scrawling on an invisible whiteboard as I spoke, drawing an alignment matrix in the air. . . .

𝔊𝔬𝔬𝔡   𝔞𝔫𝔡   𝔈𝔳𝔦𝔩

𝔏𝔞𝔴	LAWFUL GOOD	LAWFUL NEUTRAL	LAWFUL EVIL
𝔞𝔫𝔡	NEUTRAL GOOD	TRUE NEUTRAL	NEUTRAL EVIL
𝔆𝔥𝔞𝔬𝔰	CHAOTIC GOOD	CHAOTIC NEUTRAL	CHAOTIC EVIL

"Robin Hood isn't chaotic at all," I said. "The Merry Men aren't a bunch of fuckwits—they're an organized group with a strict internal code. And when King Richard, the *lawful* frickin' leader, comes back from the Crusades, Robin Hood restates his loyalty to the crown! He's for the greater social good, whether achieved lawfully or chaotically. That's *definitional* neutrality."

Lexia leaned forward, crashing through the invisible whiteboard. "But when King Richard comes back, the story *ends*! Robin Hood becomes just another monarchist suck-up. It's only when he's embracing his inner chaos that he's worth putting in a story. He's probably waiting for the next evil sheriff to take over so he can start up another guerilla campaign."

"Um, *citation needed*. In the actual, not-made-up-by-you story, Robin Hood isn't pining for chaos at the end. He gets elevated to the nobility and lives happily ever after." I raised my hands, balancing left palm and right. "And that's because he's neutral good: happy inside *or* outside the system."

She grabbed my wrists and pulled them out of balance. "Cite this: All that Earl of Huntington crap doesn't appear until the late fifteen hundreds, after a century of proto-Disneyfication. In the early tales, Robin Hood's a frakking *May Day character*."

I rolled my eyes. "Oh, great. Are we back to that semester you got all Marxist in AP History?"

"Not *that* May Day, the chaotic pagan one where they dance around the phallus. And however you try to neuter him, Robin Hood still robs from the rich—not the tax-hiking rich or the sheriff-aligned rich, *any* rich will do—and gives to the poor. And that is some pretty fucking chaotic social engineering." She paused and frowned, her face only inches from mine. "Hey, are we in kissing frame?"

I pulled away from her grasp, sinking back into my seat, my gaze dropping from hers. I saw fresh Celtic squiggles on her arms, and more muscles than I remembered. But despite tattoos, workouts, and green-streaked hair, Lexia hadn't changed much in the last year. This close, she still smelled the same.

I turned to the scenery blurring past. "Nice time to glorify stealing, when we're babysitting eighty-four grand of someone else's money."

"Nice time to change the subject." Lexia stood up, stretching. "Shit, I need a drink."

One hand on my shoulder, she pulled her backpack down from the luggage rack, its straps flailing around my head. I heard the top of the vodka bottle spin—a sharp sweetness spread across the roomette's antiseptic smell.

She took a long drink, then sat and offered me the bottle. The liquid sloshed languidly with the train's motion, and the glass frosted with condensation; she must have packed it straight from the freezer. Tempting, but I shook my head.

Everything she'd said so far made me trust her even less.

"You think *you're* Robin Hood, don't you?"

She shrugged. "We share an alignment, him and me. Delicious chaotic goodness."

"Hardly," I said. "He's neutral good. And you, my dear, are chaotic neutral."

She turned to watch the scenery, shaking her head. "You still don't know why I killed you, do you?"

"To bring chaos to the established order?" I said. Back then, almost unkillable, Temptress Moon had *ruled* in Mayhem. A cold, pale queen whom all had feared, even as they loved her. "And for fun, I suppose. Not much *good* came of it, certainly. From the message boards I've read, Mayhem's been a slaughterfest since she died."

"Mayhem a slaughterfest. What a tragedy." Lexia took another drink. "Perhaps we're laboring under different definitions of good."

I shook my head. "Don't take the easy way out, Lexia. Murdering your boyfriend doesn't count as good under any moral framework. And neither does stealing this money."

She looked down at the case, a smile forming on her lips. "Well, that's one way to illuminate the issues under discussion."

"What is?"

"Why not define our alignments in terms of this mission." She kicked the briefcase. "For example, why did the ConCom call upon you, Mr. Famously Neutral Good, instead of getting someone *lawful*?"

"That's obvious," I said. "Lawful good also takes the money to its rightful owner, but he won't bring a gun across state lines. He follows the laws of the land, even if that risks getting robbed."

"Fair enough. So what does lawful evil do?"

I leaned my head against the window. The glass was cool, pulsing with the rhythm of the tracks. "That one's trickier. If I'm lawful evil, I can't break my word, but I don't want any *good* to come of my actions." I chewed my lip for a moment, in no hurry to answer—we had about twenty-six hours to go, after all. "So I promise to take the money down to Miami, but in ambiguous terms, like one of those contracts with the devil. So I steal it and use the proceeds to start an evil cabal—a well-organized one with a strict internal code."

Lexia shook her head. "Two problems. One: eighty-four grand doesn't buy a lot of minions these days, so your cabal is small and lame. Two: the ConCom is composed entirely of aspies with level-twenty powers of nitpicking. Before they hand over any money, they make your lawful-evil ass swear to an ironclad agreement to deliver it."

I shrugged. "So I deliver the money, but then convince the hotel owner to use it in a scheme to foreclose on several orphanages. All very legal."

"Much better."

I closed my eyes for a moment, seeing the invisible whiteboard again. "Okay, Lexia, you do true neutral."

"That's easy: true neutral takes the money to Tijuana, has a draz of a time on someone else's dime." She raised a hand to ward off my protest. "Unless, of course, we're talking *druidic* neutrality. In which case she steals the money and gives it to the Florida Marlins." She snorted. "Because balance is everything."

"You always did find balance boring, didn't you?"

"Except when it's falling apart, T-Moon. Chaotic neutral goes to you."

"No way," I said, "I did the first two, and you're the chaotic neutral one in this roomette."

"I'm chaotic good, you fuckwit." She took a drink. "But *were* I chaotic neutral, I'd start by taking this train in the wrong direction. And when I get to New York, I take the briefcase to Grand Central Station at rush hour, pop the latches, and fling it all oh-so-high into the air." She gestured with the vodka bottle, which sloshed with delight. "Then I watch that lovely dance ensue."

I closed my eyes for a moment, visualizing it. The afternoon light flickered through the trees like a movie projector on my eyelids. "Wow, not bad. And you say that's not your natural alignment?"

"Of course not." She smiled. "I'm all about the greater good."

"Yeah, right." I opened my eyes and looked at the vodka bottle. "No poison in that bottle, I assume?"

She took a long drink, then held it up for me to check: The level had definitely gone down.

I reached for the bottle, which was as cold in my hand as a can of frozen orange juice. I took a sip, then a real drink. A little was okay, as long as I didn't get too far ahead of her.

"You do chaotic evil," she said.

"Whoa. So many choices." I took another drink. "Steal the money, obviously...and then go through the Miami phone book and pick eighty-four random names, hiring a hit man to kill each one."

"For a thousand bucks apiece?" She laughed and pulled the bottle away. "Those are some pretty cheap hit men."

"All the better. Think how many innocents my cut-rate hit men will kill in their chaotic, unprofessional way." I pulled the bottle back and took Swig Number Three, having decided to count my drinks. "So do chaotic good, if that is your real alignment. You steal the ConCom's money and give it to the poor?"

She shrugged. "That's a bit bland."

"But you said Robin Hood was full of *story*!"

"*Story* is sticking a cocked arrow in some rich bastard's face.

So what's the modern equivalent of that? How about I borrow the money and buy a couple of Stinger missiles, then shoot them at Rupert Murdoch's Learjet." Lexia sighed. "But I'm probably getting too sane for that, now that I'm all graduated and shit. Helping the ConCom fill downtown with seventeen thousand costumed geeks seems chaotic enough for me."

She stared past me at the speed-blurred trees, her voice falling off a bit, and pulled the bottle back from me.

I frowned. Maybe Lexia did look a little saner, staring out the window like that, her hand tight around the vodka bottle's neck. Almost philosophical.

I drank, counting Swig Number Four. The dining car was opening in an hour, and food would clear my head. But no more swigs after this one. It was going to be a long night of staying awake and watchful. Even if Lexia had grown too sane for shoulder-fired missiles, this was still the girl who had poisoned me. . . .

I frowned, looking down at the bottle in my hand.

"What's the matter?" she said.

"I just realized: You haven't had any since I took my first drink. What's up with that?"

"Not thirsty anymore."

I tried to hold her gaze, but my eyes dropped to the bottle again. My stomach flipped. "Quit fucking with me."

"I'm not fucking with you, Temptress Moon. You're being paranoid."

"With you around, paranoia is an entirely reasonable state of mind."

She sighed. "Well . . . maybe I *did* sneak something into that bottle just before I handed it to you. And that's why I haven't drunk any since."

I swallowed, my throat suddenly dry.

"That's why your head's muzzy," Lexia went on. "And that dizziness creeping up on you? A precursor of worse things."

I swallowed again, glaring at the bottle. The view was shooting past at top speed now, but the ride felt as smooth as if we'd stopped moving, the train resting on the track like a turntable needle on a spinning disk.

"Maybe the slightest hint of disassociation?" she said, leaning closer. "As if none of this is real?"

I shook the bottle. "What the fuck did you put in here?"

"Sucker!" Lexia leaned back, laughing. "You feel dizzy, T-Moon, because we're drinking eighty-proof liquor on an empty stomach in a speeding train. And you feel disassociated because you're a frakking geek, and we *always* feel disassociated."

I clenched the bottle neck as tight as a club, then sighed. "Don't *do* that shit, Lexia." My mouth was insanely dry, so I took another drink. "I might shoot you."

"You need to relax." She held out her hand. "I'll make you a deal. One more swig each, then we'll go get microwave pizzas from the café car."

I gave her the bottle, and Lexia held it steady for a moment, marking the level with one finger. Then she drank hard and measured it for me again — she'd knocked half an inch off. She handed it back. "Come on, wimp."

"Okay. But pizza next." I drank deeply.

When I was done, I capped the bottle and put it on the floor. The rattle of the train had settled into me, melding into my dizziness. I could feel the vodka in my veins, taking the edge off everything. Suddenly the briefcase full of cash under my feet didn't seem so unnerving — it was just an object I had to take somewhere — and Lexia didn't seem so dangerous.

I breathed out a slow sigh.

But she was staring at me.

"What?"

"That should be enough to put you down," she said quietly.

I rolled my eyes. "Didn't we already play this game?"

She stared out the window. "Yes, but I cheated last year. This time we both drank the same poison."

"Fuck off," I said. But her words were making my head spin again. I needed pizza.

She kept talking. "I put the roofies in there the moment the ConCom called. Figured you'd join me for a drink sooner or later."

The train lurched, and both of us grabbed our armrests. Shit, I really *was* feeling disassociated now. But only because Lexia was fucking with me.

"You drank a lot more than I did," I insisted. "Plus, I outweigh you by ten pounds."

"Yeah, but I use those things to get to sleep these days." She yawned. "So I have at least an even chance of waking up first."

I shook my head, trying to clear it. But red spots were drifting into the roomette now, hovering at the edges of my vision.

Shit. She'd really done it.

I reached for my Walther. "You won't wake up if I shoot you."

Lexia laughed. "But you're about to pass out, T-Moon. Not a good time to commit murder."

The roomette was really spinning now. I gritted my teeth and pulled the pistol out. "Maybe, but if you're dead you can't take the money."

She stared down the barrel and smiled. "And when my conductor pal finds my body in here, that briefcase full of cash just might be considered evidence. The ConCom's screwed, even if they eventually prove it's theirs."

I blinked away spots, trying to think. But the rattle of the train was tangling the situation. How had I been so *stupid*. Poisoned twice by the same woman!

Finally the gears in my brain caught, and I waved the Walther at her. "Your handcuffs, put them on."

"Ah, yes, the handcuffs." She shook her head, her words slurring now. "I have other plans for those."

"Get them out or I'll shoot you!"

"We already covered that." She settled back into her seat. "Why not take a fifty-fifty chance of waking up before me? You might get the money and save the con. Flip of the coin, roll of the die. I think that's the properly neutral good thing to do. Me? I'm going to sleep."

I watched in horror as she made a pillow of her Peacekeeper jacket, settling in for a long night. My brain was shutting down fast now, the red dots spreading into a roomette-filling haze, my fingers going numb around the Walther's grip. The rattle of the train grew louder, crowding the worry, fear, and anger from my mind....

I got my gun back in its holster just before the darkness came.

Temptress Moon rose up the wall of the Keep, her cloak of weirding blending with the shadows. Her fingers slipped into cracks and crannies, her split-toed boots tickling the ancient stones as she climbed. Iron watch-birds flitted past unseeing, their clockwork insides rasping like a potter's wheel.

She reached a window, slipped through. Inside should have been utter darkness after a sky crowded with two full red moons, but set in Temptress Moon's eyes were jewels of persistent vision, and the room sprang to life, every corner sharpened with their facets.

She stared at her victim on the bed, pausing to listen to his breath, slow and steady. He was naked, his arms ribboned with tattoos, hair streaked with green, the bedclothes coiled around him.

The jewels in her eyes revealed hexes of protection scattered on the floor, and she danced closer, like a child making a game of not stepping on cracks and discolored tiles.

Beside his bed, Temptress Moon hesitated. They'd built this Keep together, having slain the glass dragon whose teeth made the rose window of its chapel. Bare-handed they'd strangled the dire wolf whose skull lay in its flagstone, and carpeted the great hall with their bear-killing expeditions in the north. Uncountable creatures fought side by side; it was a shame it had to end like this.

But she drew the long knife anyway.

She raised it high, the marks of old magic shining on its blade. But suddenly the room splintered, her vision fracturing like a spun kaleidoscope, the floor rolling underfoot. Waves of nausea and dizziness pounded against the walls of the world, a roar filling her head like the rumble of a train.

Her victim rolled over and smiled up at her.

"Shouldn't have drunk that vodka," he said. "What were you *thinking*, Temptress Moon?"

She tried to answer, but her mouth was full of ashes.

○

Waking up was slow and winding. My head pounded, and my tongue seemed to have expanded to the size of a turkey leg. Something was kicking me, and I grunted at it.

"There you are." Lexia's voice.

I forced my eyes open and she came into focus, my Walther PPK/S in one hand, the briefcase in the other.

"Crap," I murmured. The sun flickered through the trees outside—in the east, morning already. I'd been out for more than twelve hours.

My arms and legs were tingling, the life squished out of them. As I tried to sit up, metal bit into my left wrist. Lexia's handcuffs rattled, attached to the armrest.

"*Crap!*" I cried.

"No yelling, now. I don't want to have to shoot you."

I glared at her, considering screaming for help. But Lexia had been willing to drug me last night, even to drug herself. Risking a bullet to test that chaotic resolve didn't seem like a great bet.

Besides, with my head throbbing like this, yelling was a painful prospect.

"Why are you still here?" I said. "Why aren't you at Grand Central throwing money at people?"

She pushed stray hairs away from her face. "Just woke up. Haven't had a chance to get off, but we'll be in Jacksonville in a few minutes. Besides, we never did get a last kiss the first time I poisoned you."

Lexia was holding the Walther too casually; I considered making a grab for it. But the pins and needles in my legs were fading, and suddenly I felt the Taurus PT138 holster strapped to my ankle....

My expression must have changed.

"What?" she said. "Those handcuffs bringing back fond memories?"

I shook my head slowly. "No, it's just that I finally won the argument."

"In what sense?"

"This proves you're not chaotic good. You're not anything but self-interested."

She squeezed the handle of the briefcase. "You don't know what I have planned for this money, T-Moon."

"Alms for the poor?" I made a fist with my right hand, trying to wake it up. The outskirts of a small town were flitting past the window—Jacksonville getting closer.

"More interesting than that." Lexia smiled. "A little social experiment. You'll find out sooner than you think."

"Can't wait." I shook my right hand, forcing blood back into the fingers.

The train began to brake, and more tracks sprang into being alongside ours, coursing like serpents around us. We were almost at the station.

Lexia stood, keeping the Walther leveled at me. She lifted the briefcase. "No shouting till the train pulls out, or someone might get hurt."

"I'd rather catch you myself, which I will." I narrowed my eyes, flexing my fingers. "Sooner than you think."

She smiled, pushing the gun into one jacket pocket, her hand still closed around it. "We'll see who catches what, T-Moon."

The train had almost stopped, the platform empty outside. Lexia probably could have gotten away, even if I'd started yelling.

But it wasn't going to come to that. The moment she turned to slide the door open, I reached down and drew the Taurus.

"Don't go, Lexia."

"Sorry, but I —" Her voice caught when she saw the gun.

She let the door slide shut behind her and leaned against it. I could see the Walther pointed at me from inside her jacket pocket.

"Now *this*," she said with a smile, "is getting chaotic."

◦

We sat there, face-to-face in our roomette, northern Florida passing by.

"I keep telling you," she said. "I don't *have* the key. I left it at home."

"Bullshit, Lexia." I yanked at the handcuff. "Where is it?"

"But I wasn't planning to let you go. And obviously it's to my tactical advantage not to have the key. Didn't you search me?"

I frowned. I didn't remember seeing any key, but wouldn't it have been stuck in the handcuffs?

"And anyway," she said. "Why would I let you have it?"

"Because otherwise I'll shoot you!"

"Bang, bang, bang," she retorted. "Just shot you back before I died. And my gun's way bigger."

"They're *both* my guns, I'd like to point out. I bet you don't even know how to flick the safety off."

"Bet you I do," she sing-songed, then glanced out the window. "Listen, we'll be pulling into Palatka, Florida, at 8:18. We need to get this squared away before then."

"Squared away?"

"Like, what do you want?" She thumped the briefcase. "Forty percent?"

"No, I want all one hundred percent of it—delivered to the rightful owner!"

She sighed. "Yeah, like *that's* going to happen."

We glared at each other for a while. Adrenaline had taken the edge off my roofie-and-vodka hangover, but I needed desperately to piss. I couldn't help but wonder if Lexia's handcuffs would let me close enough to the squalid folding toilet. Maybe the threat of an attempt would make her produce the key.

But I needed to hold on to my last shreds of dignity.

We sat there for long minutes, staring at each other. Either one of us could have started shooting, and the other would've been too late to retaliate. But that's the reality of standoffs with guns, I suppose. If anybody really wants to pull the trigger, it happens right at the beginning.

And there was something elegant in the balance about this situation, something I didn't want to break.

Finally, southern swamp-Gothic houses began to whip by: the outskirts of Palatka.

"Unlock this handcuff," I pleaded. "Hand me back the gun, and that'll be it. We can even take the money down together, if you want."

"No," she said.

"Why do you keep *doing* this stuff to me?" I said.

She leaned back into her chair and sighed. "You mean, why did I kill poor Temptress Moon?"

I nodded. In a funny way, that first betrayal mystified me more than this one. There hadn't been eighty-four thousand dollars at stake back then.

"That's simple," she said. "Everyone asked me to."

"*What?*"

She leaned closer, her chest a foot from the barrel of my Taurus. "The game's called *Mayhem*, T-Moon! But with you controlling everything, there were never any atrocities to avenge! Your meddling goodness made it boring, sucked all the mayhem out of it. In that narrative framework, killing you *was* the greater good. Boyfriend or not."

My jaw dropped open. "But nobody ever said—"

"Everyone *hated* Temptress Moon," she shouted. "People were begging me to kill you for months! I tried arguing with you, wiping out your minions, anything to get you unstuck from that lame alignment." She shook her head sadly. "I'm still trying."

I sat there, the gun in my hand wavering for the first time.

"But you just can't let the balance go, can you? Maybe if I make it easy on you." She stood and dropped the Walther on her seat. "This is my stop. Give my regards to Miami."

She took a step toward the door, briefcase in hand.

I blinked, looking at the discarded Walther on the empty seat across from me, then at the gun in my own hand. Why had she...?

"Wait," I said softly.

Lexia shook her head, put her hand on the latch.

I raised the gun. "Stop!"

She rolled her eyes. "Or you'll shoot me?"

"*Yes!*"

"An interesting possibility," she said, and slid the door open.

She was really walking out with eighty-four thousand dollars of the ConCom's money—the community's collective good faith in currency form. I couldn't let this happen.

I pointed the pistol at her leg....

Click.

Lexia turned back to me, smiling now. "Thought I wouldn't remember your ankle holster, T-Moon? I remember every one of your stupid guns."

I flung myself forward as far as the handcuff allowed, grabbing the discarded Walther from Lexia's seat and pointing it at her.

"Click, click, click," she said.

I wavered for a moment, the gun right in her face, then sighed. Didn't bother pulling the trigger, just dropped the gun on the floor.

"So this whole standoff thing," I said. "It was just so I wouldn't yell for help?"

The train was braking hard now, a ragged concrete platform sliding past. Not a cab in sight in this tiny station. How did she plan on getting away? I could call for the conductor now, but somehow the screams didn't come to my throat.

Lexia sat down across from me, reached a hand into her pocket. "Don't be silly, T-Moon." She pulled out a handcuff key. "Like I said, it was an experiment."

The cuff snapped open, and she took my wrist and began to massage it.

"But it's all over now."

I blinked. "So the money...?"

"Goes to Miami. Like I said: chaotic good really wants those seventeen thousand costumed geeks gathering downtown. I just needed a little quality time with my old boyfriend."

I coughed. "*Quality* time? You drugged me, handcuffed me, forced me to decide whether to shoot you or not!"

She shrugged. "Chaotic quality time. But it's all for the good."

So...yes, we took the eighty-four grand down to the hotel owner, who turned out to be more pleasant in person. Just a big fan of punctuality. She served us tea on her veranda, wearing a floral sundress that was all the colors of linoleum.

The convention went on as scheduled, the downtown streets full of stormtroopers, Browncoats, pirates, quidditch players, and Dr. Who sidekicks, along with fresh new ranks of unkillable cheerleaders and Guitar Hero characters.

Not to worry, chaos marches on.

And...no, we didn't get back together, if you thought that's where this was going. Are you nuts? Lexia's fucking crazy.

In any case, her scheme had never been about rekindling our love. It was simply her own very chaotic version of that goodbye kiss we'd never shared.

But one old flame was relit by the trip: I started playing Mayhem again. Anonymously, for now, long hours of grinding every day. And I'm not some lame-ass neutral good paladin this time, but a creature much more interesting. A chaotic evil assassin of the Iron Clan with a cloak of weirding, jeweled sight, and two specialties in climbing. I'm currently questing for the legendary Knife of No Doubt.

You see, my assassin doesn't want to stay anonymous forever. One day she plans to visit the keep that Lexia and I built together, climb in through that window, and reintroduce herself to an astonished world.

Frakk neutrality. Revenge *will* be mine.

Scott Westerfeld still owns the original trio of staple-bound D&D rulebooks, purchased when he was twelve, roughly the same time he went to his first fannish event: a Famous Monsters convention in New York City. Since then he's designed computer games, composed twelve-tone music, learned Esperanto, and ridden in a zeppelin. The geekiest thing he's done lately was to devise a tactical combat system for steampunk ironclads played with Lego miniatures.

He is the author of the Uglies and Midnighters series, and the novels *So Yesterday*, *Peeps*, and *The Last Days*. But his next trilogy will be far geekier: *Leviathan*, an alternate-history, Edwardian-biotech, living-airship extravaganza set in 1914, coming Fall 2009.

I am totally going to kill my bio teacher with an ax.

My best friend has no idea I hooked up with her boyfriend this weekend.

Look at these pictures of the party we had while Mom and Dad were out of town.

Here are the step-by-step instructions on how I cheated on my SATs.

I think I might be Otherkin.

I NEVER
by **cassandra clare**

The moment Lisle walks up to the front door, swinging her duffel bag determinedly over her arm, I have the strangest urge to grab her arm and tell her to get back in the car with me, that we should drive home and not come back. That this whole meetup thing is a bad idea. That I want to go home.

But the moment is brief and passes, and besides, Lisle would never listen to me anyway. She's already ringing the doorbell of the condo, over and over, a manic grin on her face. I can hear the harsh buzz of the bell as it echoes over and over inside. I glance around. The condominium is one of several dozen fake chalet-style structures scattered up and down the side of a grassy hill. A lake sparkles distantly under the gray winter sun. The air is cold and I shiver, wondering what the hell I'm doing here.

At last, the door is opened by a middle-aged woman with curling brown hair streaked with gray. She is stocky, wearing jeans and a baggy sweatshirt with the face of a wolf airbrushed onto the front. She drips silver pendants: pentagrams, Hands of Fatimah, Stars of David, and ankhs dangling from her neck, a sort of decorative spiritual grab bag.

"Well, hello there," she says, putting her hands on her hips. She has a distinct British accent. "And you are...?"

"Jane," I say, and then when Lisle's elbow jams into my ribs, "Catherine Earnshaw."

"Oh, right, you're one of the book people." She smiles, extends a hand. "Xena, Warrior Princess. This is my place."

Xena, Warrior Princess? The kickass chick with the breast-plates? This woman resembles someone's weirdo aunt, or an elementary school art teacher, the kind who's always telling you to "feel" the paintings.

Lisle is grinning. "I'm Faith," she says. "The Slayer."

"Then I'd better let you in before you start slaying!" The woman laughs like she's said something uproariously funny, and stands aside. "You can drop your bags in the first bedroom on the left. Everyone's in the living room."

We drop our bags as ordered in a small, plain bedroom with a king-size bed. The bed is covered in bags; I balance my duffel gingerly on top of a backpack covered in Invader Zim buttons. Lisle is already stripping off her sweater to reveal her black halter top and studded belt. She looks hot, enough to get me worried. I didn't really bring any special clothes, just jeans and T-shirts. But then, all that Ben has seen of me so far is my left eye, my hands, and my feet in sandals. It's hard to live up to that sort of mystery.

Lisle grabs my hand. "Come on."

The hum of voices hits us before we reach the living room. It's as big as promised, with a balcony overlooking a green lawn that slopes down to the lake. There's a granite island separating the living room from the kitchen, and lined up on it are all sorts of bottles—all sorts of booze, and some soda-pop mixers. Xena, Warrior Princess, is behind the island, mixing drinks into plastic cups. Everyone else is sprawled out all over the living room, and of course I recognize no one. One thing I can say: no one looks like their online icons. There are two skinny girls seated uncomfortably on a couch, staring at each other, and a bunch of college-age-looking boys sprawled around a low table on the floor, rolling dice and arguing in loud voices. There are older people, too: a woman with glasses, knitting in a chair. She's wearing a T-shirt that says THE HAMSTER OF DOOM RAINS COCONUTS ON YOUR PITIFUL CITY. Some teenage girls with long hair are playing cards at a round table. They look up as Lisle and I come into the room, then look down again, obviously uninterested.

I feel suddenly so uncomfortable that I'm almost dizzy. It's like I crashed a party where I don't know anyone, a party I shouldn't have been invited to in the first place. Everyone's wearing these long, color-blocked scarves, too, even inside. I rack my brain. Was I supposed to bring one? Is it a Game thing?

"Huh," says Lisle, looking around. She has that expression, an expression I know. It's "Where are the cute guys?" I'm briefly, meanly pleased that she feels uncomfortable, too, before I realize that Lisle's never uncomfortable. She just feels cheated of the cute guys that are her due. "Well, everyone's not here yet," she says to no one in particular. Then she grabs my hand, and hisses in a stage whisper: "Is one of these guys Ben?"

"I have no idea," I say with a jolt of shock, realizing that of course I don't know. The image of Ben I carry around in my head is just that, an image in my head. He could look like anything at all. He could be one of the bearded guys at the table. I stare at them in horror.

"Like some welcome drinks?" Xena, Warrior Princess, is standing at our elbows, holding two red plastic cups. She frowns at me and Lisle. "You are eighteen, right?"

"Yep," Lisle agrees cheerfully. I wonder if anyone's going to tell Xena, Warrior Princess, that the legal drinking age in the U.S. is twenty-one, not eighteen. But no one says anything. I take one of the cups and stare down at the murky brown mixture.

"It's vodka and diet chocolate soda," explains Xena. "Sorry I don't have any real soda—I'm on Atkins. But I sent some of the guys out to get mixers, so we should have them soon."

I nod and drink some of the brown mixture. It's the worst thing I've ever tasted.

Xena claps her hands together. "Okay, everybody! Roll call. Faith and Catherine, everyone. Everyone, Catherine and Faith." In quick succession we are introduced to Sherlock Holmes, Neo and Trinity from *The Matrix*, Luke Skywalker, G'Kar, Starbuck (the boy), Starbuck (the girl), Edward Elric, Dracula, Lana Lang, Kenshin, Modesty Blaise, and Hazel, who is apparently a rabbit from *Watership Down*. I breathe a little sigh of relief—no Heathcliff yet.

The two girls on the couch introduce themselves to us belatedly as Jack and Ennis from *Brokeback Mountain*, which makes Lisle snort. I remember their torrid journal posts and passionate online protestations of love. They don't look so torrid now—they're sitting as far as they can get from each other on the couch, wearing identical panicked expressions.

The doorbell rings and Xena goes to answer it. When she returns, she's trailed by two teenage boys carrying grocery bags. Both are about the same height, both have dark hair.

But I know Ben immediately. When we were first getting acquainted online, we sent flirty photos of ourselves to each other—I'd take a picture of my elbow and send it to him, and he'd respond with a photo of just his left eye, or the curve of his ear. I couldn't have put a picture of his face together in my mind, but I knew he had a scar on his right thumb, and a spray of freckles across one cheek, light as powder dust. Looking at him now, I know him by the curling hair at his temples, like ivy curling up at the corners, just like in the photos he sent me. I recognize the shape of his hands, the blue of his eyes. Now that the rest of him is filled in around the edges I am amazed—he looks just like I thought he would.

I barely notice the boy who's with him. He has dark hair, too, and glasses, and is skinnier than Ben, more what I imagine a nerdy online role-player to look like. He hoists his bag. "Snacks and mixers," he says. "Where should we put them?"

Ben starts to look over in my direction. And that's it—I'm out of the room, my feet carrying me down the hallway, so fast that I'm practically running. Running from what? I have no idea. I duck into a bathroom, almost slamming the door behind me. I turn the sink on and grab handfuls of icy water, splashing them up over my burning face. The bathroom is gross, too—the floor is sticky, and powder from burned incense covers the counter, though the air still smells like mold.

"Jane? Jane!" Lisle bangs on the door, her voice filled with anxiety. "Jane, are you okay?"

I suppose I should appreciate that she's come to find me, but instead I just feel more humiliated than ever. I slide down the wall until I'm sitting on the sticky, wet linoleum, and put my face in my hands.

○

I should take this moment to point out that me playing Catherine Earnshaw in a massive online multiplayer game was Lisle's idea in the first place. It would never have occurred to me, mostly because I don't use the computer that much—or at least, I didn't. It was Lisle who was crazy about the Game. Lisle and I had been friends for so many years that I'd forgotten when we'd met. She lived next door to me and was just always there, like a sister more than a friend. She annoyed me like a sister might, too. Especially since she'd become completely addicted to her online journal. She had a fair number of people logging on to read the rambling thoughts and massive multi-chaptered Buffy fanfiction she posted on her site, Pretty When You Blog. To be totally honest, Lisle isn't that great a writer. She never seems to be able to streamline her thoughts into any sort of logical shape, and she doesn't care about spelling or capitalization either. But she has a really cute icon of herself in a black corset top up on the page, which on the Internet is better than being able to spell.

It was because of her other blogger friends that she wound up being in the Game. There are lots of role-playing games online, but the Game is the most famous because it's so huge. The idea behind the Game is that every player picks a character from a book, TV show, movie, video game — anything, as long as it's a character a fair number of people can be expected to recognize. Every character gets a journal, and the ability to message other characters. The idea is that everyone in the Game is trapped in a huge castle together, where they live and eat and sleep and interact with each other. In theory, they're trying to get out of the castle, but nobody pays much attention to that part of the Game. Mostly they flirt and fight. And you're not supposed to interact exclusively with people from your own fictional "universe," which is why you get Alice in Wonderland hanging out with Indiana Jones and Lolita hooking up with Conan the Barbarian.

"It's a total mindfuck," Lisle explained when she first joined it. She was into the Game fairly early and got to pick the character she wanted — Faith, in her case. She'd been obsessed with *Buffy the Vampire Slayer* since we were about ten years old and first watched it together and she'd declared that she was Buffy. Later she decided she was Faith, because Faith had the dark hair. Lisle had been a crazed fan of a lot of things since, but nothing else seemed to have the staying power of *Buffy*.

Lisle quickly struck up an online love triangle with the brothers from *Supernatural*. (Lisle likes it when boys fight over her.) She never seemed to take it too seriously, but she was online constantly, messaging them, exchanging photos, and giggling. She got caught up in all the backstage dramas of the Game, always telling me who'd deleted their journal recently in a fit of pique, who was trolling who, and who had hooked up with who behind who's back.

It drove me crazy. For years, every day after school and on the weekends I'd gone by Lisle's house and hung out with her in her bedroom. We used to sprawl on the floor and watch movies together. (Lisle wanted to watch *Legend* and *Alien* and I wanted to watch black-and-white classics. We compromised on Merchant Ivory costume dramas, because she liked the boys with the English accents.) Once the Game started, all I did was lie on Lisle's bed and watch while she typed on her computer. She could sit there for hours, literally, without ever looking up. Every few seconds I'd hear that "pong" noise that meant someone was sending her an online message. After a while I felt like every time I heard it was another punch in the face.

Finally, I cracked. I joined the Game because it was either that or move and find a new best friend. Lisle was so excited that I was going to play in the Game with her, she practically cried. "I'll play if I can be Catherine Earnshaw," I told her, thinking of my favorite fictional character in my favorite book of all time, *Wuthering Heights*. I didn't think I'd get her — Cathy is such a great character, and her love story with Heathcliff is so intense, someone was sure to be playing her already.

But no one was. Lisle was practically dancing while she set up my journal for me and showed me how to message other players within the game interface. But there was one big problem: no one was playing Heathcliff, and a Cathy with no Heathcliff is like a bike with no wheels. I made a few journal entries about how life on the moors was dull and how I wished something exciting would happen and about how the heather was growing plentifully this season. I figured I must have the most boring Game journal ever.

Sometimes other characters would come into my journal and try to interact with me. Lisle bopped by occasionally and pinged me with messages; Draco Malfoy tried to start up a chat, and when I wasn't responsive, left some nasty comments in my journal and departed. Sherlock Holmes pinged to ask if I'd seen an enormous dog on the moors, and since I do love *The Hound of the Baskervilles* I considered e-mailing him back, but wound up being too shy. Lisle was disgusted with me and declared me a failure at the Game—and, it was strongly implied, at life.

And then there was Ben. He didn't tell me his real name at first, of course. I logged into my Game account one day and there it was: a note that I'd been added by a new character: Heathcliff. And a message in my inbox. I opened it, expecting it to be of the "What up UR kewl and Kute!" variety, but it wasn't. It was a love letter from Heathcliff to Cathy. And it was beautiful.

Even though it was addressed to Cathy, and not to me, and was from someone I'd never met, it made me cry. I sat there crying while I read it and feeling stupid but sort of not caring that I felt stupid. It was a letter about that sort of amazing, total love you always hope someone will feel for you someday, that obliterating passion that makes everything else in the world not matter. It didn't use any of the words from the book, but it still sounded like the Heathcliff who said about Cathy: *I cannot live without my life! I cannot die without my soul.* The letter talked about how his soul would wander the dark moors forever, in purgatory until I—or Cathy, really—came down to speak with him once again.

I wrote back. How could I not write back to that? It felt like someone had reached right into my chest and zapped it with forty-thousand volts. When he messaged me, I stayed up all night, fingers flying over the keyboard. When I was messaging Ben, I was

Cathy. He was Heathcliff. I could smell the air out on the moors, feel the cold, the loneliness, the excitement.

It was weeks before Ben even told me his real name, and then I was sort of shocked, a little bit, that he had one and that it was so ordinary. I felt a sort of terror—what if he was just completely ordinary in every way? But then, no one ordinary could write those letters, those messages. I asked him for a photo of himself, and he sent me elliptical pictures he took with his phone camera, just a piece of himself at a time: an eye here, a hand there, the side of his chin. I sent the same sort of pictures back, standing in the quad at school taking pictures of my painted toes in sandals. And the weird thing is that I felt like Cathy when I was doing it, even though Cathy lived hundreds of years before cell phones and text messaging. But I felt wild and flirty and free, just like her.

I thought Lisle would be pleased, but she seemed sort of annoyed about it. After all, she kept telling me, the point of the Game was to interact with everyone, and I only interacted with Ben. I didn't know any of the gossip she knew, and I still stared at her blankly when she talked about who was a drama queen and who was a sock puppet and who had deleted whose journal. Plus I'd been mean to Draco Malfoy, who was a friend of hers. Still, she told me she "shipped" me and Ben together, whatever that meant, and she kept trying to think of ways for me to meet him. Which, since he lived like two states away, didn't seem very likely.

But then Xena suggested the meetup. She had a condo out by a lake, she said, with a timeshare, and nobody was ever there in the winter. Why shouldn't she host a party for the East Coast members of the Game? Anyone who wanted could come and crash on the floor, as long as they were eighteen years old. "We're going," Lisle told me, with a manic gleam in her eye.

"But we're not eighteen."

"That's what the Internet is for. Lying about your age," she said, punching out a YES WE ARE GOING message into her AIM messenger box. "Besides. Ben's going to be there."

I sank down on her bed, gripping a pillow between my hands, which had gone suddenly numb. "He is?"

Lisle turned around and grinned at me. After that, it was just a matter of lying to our parents about visiting Lisle's older sister Alice at college, and we were gone. We drove up in Lisle's yellow Datsun with the radio on, Lisle singing her head off and me quietly freaking out with every mile marker we passed. *I'm going to see him*, my mind said, over and over. I heard his name in the soft grind of the wheels on the asphalt, the crunch of old snow. *Heathcliff. Heathcliff.* Then we were at the condo and Lisle was jumping out of the car, slamming the door behind her with a short, decided bang.

Ben.

⚬

"Jane!" The door thuds under my back. Lisle must be kicking at it with her feet. "Jane, open the goddamned door!"

"FINE!" I yell back. I get to my feet and yank the door open and there's Lisle, looking actually pretty Faith-like since her face is screwed up in rage and her hair's sticking up.

"Jesus Christ, Jane." She grabs me by the shoulders. "I thought you were trying to drown yourself in the bathtub in there. What's wrong with you?"

"Nothing. I'm fine."

She glances toward the living room. "Is it Ben? But—he's cute. Hot, even."

"I know."

She smirks a little. "So now you're freaked out."

"Yeah. I mean—I don't know." I shrug angrily. "I wish you hadn't run out after me. It makes it look like something's really wrong."

Lisle takes my arm. "We'll tell everyone you got carsick," she says, "and you totally had to puke. How's that?"

I pull away, brushing past her and into the living room. The energy in the room has gone up, maybe thanks to Xena's disgusting drinks. People are laughing and chatting, sitting on the floor and on the arms of chairs. There are bags of chips and snacks all over the floor, torn open, with people passing them around and munching, crumbs flying while they talk.

Ben's in the kitchen, a row of bottles lined up in front of him, a cocktail shaker in one hand. Jack and Ennis are leaning on the counter while he mixes them drinks, giggling and flirty. Now that they're both standing up I can see how tall and skinny they are. They almost look alike.

Ben's friend has taken my place on the couch. He has a fat book open on his lap—a graphic novel, probably. I can see the brightly colored drawings from here.

"What is he doing?" I whisper to Lisle, my eyes on Ben.

"Xena said he promised to be bartender, so—he's bartending." She shrugs. "Look, I'll go see what's going on with him. You wait here."

I perch on the edge of the couch while Lisle edges into the kitchen past the gay cowboy girls. I'm sitting next to a group of some of the kids I got introduced to earlier. I can't help but listen in on their conversation, since they're practically shouting—arguing about who makes a better starship captain, Captain Kirk or Captain Picard. Kirk, says the guy who introduced himself as John Connor, is clearly the better captain, because he was the youngest captain ever in Starfleet and Picard wasn't. Besides, Kirk is more virile and "manly."

"Oh, please. He shouldn't get points for being a horndog," snaps Trinity. "Kirk was sexist and misogynistic."

"He was a product of his time," points out G'Kar mildly.

"What time is that? The future?" Trinity hoots, and everyone else joins in. Hazel leans forward in her chair, her knitting dangling.

"I think you're all forgetting that both of them pale in comparison to the greatest captain of all time," she announces. "Captain Adama."

"Whoa, a BSG throwdown." Neo nods respectfully. He looks nothing like Keanu Reeves, of course, but is instead a chunky boy with slicked-back hair and a bright polyester shirt; I can't be sure if he's wearing it ironically or not. "Intense, intense."

I stare at them, mystified. I have no idea what they're talking about or how I could possibly join in. And I can't help the feeling that if I tried to, I'd be about as welcome as ants at a picnic. There's a whole language here and I don't speak it.

"It's a dorkument," says a voice at my elbow. "Your first?"

I turn and stare. The boy who came in with Ben has put his book aside and is looking at me curiously. He has what I've always thought of as a "sharp" face: bony, slightly angular, with high cheekbones. His eyes, a warm hazel, soften the harshness. He is cute, though not in an obvious way like Ben is. Maybe he'd be good for Lisle? I glance over at her, but she's still in the kitchen, showing Ben and the others how to make pie.

"A dorkument?" I echo. "What's that?"

"It's an argument between dorks meant to clarify some finer point of geek culture," the boy explains. "They've sort of grown out of the long-held comics tradition of arguing about which superhero could beat up which other superhero. You know: who would win in a fight, Batman or Superman? Alien or Predator? They made a whole movie about that last one."

"I think I missed it."

PAULSON, CHANCE SUMMER

Unclaim : 8/14/2020

Held date   : 8/3/2020
Pickup location : Cedar Mill Library

Title   : Geektastic : stories from the
nerd herd
Call number   : YA GEEK
Item barcode   : 33614038571799
Assigned branch : WCCLS Courier

Notes:

"Not a geek?"

"Right," I say, and then realize I've said the wrong thing. His eyebrows go sproinging up like rubber bands.

"Not a geek?" he says. "I know how much time you've spent messaging with Ben online. Not a geek?"

"There's nothing geeky about messaging people," I protest. "It's just a form of communication. That's like saying telephone calls are geeky."

"It's geeky when you're pretending to be a fictional character while you're doing it," he says. "There's nothing about being someone from a book, even a classic book, that makes you less geeky than someone from a movie. Or a TV show. Or whatever."

"Or whatever?" I'm starting to get mad, which hardly ever happens. "So what are you, then? Who do you play?"

"Mr. Kool-Aid," he says without missing a beat.

"Mr. Kool-Aid? You mean the big red pitcher from the old commercials? The one who bursts through the wall and says 'Hey kids, who wants Kool-Aid'?"

"Yep."

"Wow." I'm not even trying to keep the sarcasm out of my voice. "So what drew you to that character particularly? Were you just really thirsty one day?"

"Mr. Kool-Aid spreads happiness and joy through the world. He's a party guy. I like that."

I snort. "No offense, but you don't really seem like a party guy."

"And you don't really seem like a geek," he says, "and yet you are one." So we're back to that. "Besides," he adds, "people aren't always like the characters they play online."

"Do you mean me?" I blink at him, and then, suddenly, realize what he actually means. I feel my face flush. "Or do you mean Ben? Are you saying he's not like his online character?"

Noah holds his hands up. "Look, I'm not saying anything like—"

"I want to go back to the house," I say, and turn around abruptly. I can hear Noah calling my name but I'm already hurrying up the path to the condo, the cold wind stinging my eyes.

◦

After the fresh air, the smell in the living room hits me even more intensely. It's equal parts booze and BO. Everyone's sprawled on the floor in groups — Ben is in the middle of a crowd of girls, one of them Lisle. There are bags of chips open on the floor and someone's torn open a packet of M&M's and scattered them everywhere. M&M's sit melting on the coffee table in bright green, red, and blue pools of spilled booze. The effect is pretty and gross at the same time.

Ben doesn't seem to see me come in, so I go over and sit back down on the couch next to Jack and Ennis, who still aren't talking to each other. The boys who were arguing about Captain Kirk before are now arguing about some particular point of their role-play game. "But you can't be an anthropomorphic bat," Luke Skywalker is explaining patiently to Sherlock Holmes. "This isn't a monster campaign."

Xena, Warrior Princess, claps her hands together loudly, silencing the room. "Okay, we're all here now, so how about some icebreaking games? Charades?"

Oddly, the idea appeals to me. In Victorian times, before there were TV and video games and the Internet, people were always doing things like playing charades and putting on amateur theatricals to amuse themselves. I figure nobody else will be into the idea and get ready to look like I'm not interested either, when Jack pipes up that we should act out scenes from movies and TV shows and see if everyone can guess what they are.

"And books," I say before I can stop myself.

96

Jack blinks at me. "What?"

"And scenes from books," I say, and add, "You know, *Brokeback Mountain* was a book. Before it was a movie."

"Actually," says Noah, coming in through the door, "it was a short story." Cold has reddened his cheeks and his eyes are bright behind the glasses. He grins at me while he hangs up his jacket, but I don't smile back.

"I know that!" Jack looks furious.

"I think charades are a good idea," Lisle says hurriedly, standing up and brushing crumbs off the legs of her skinny jeans. "I'll go first."

Lisle hurries up to the front of the room and starts acting out a scene I know perfectly well is from *Buffy*. Big shock there. I slink lower in the sofa, then feel a tap on my shoulder. It's Ben.

"Come on," he says, jerking his head toward the hallway. "No one will notice."

Like I care if they do notice. I'm up and off the couch so fast I feel like I ought to leave smoking tracks behind, like the Road Runner. Lisle is acting out Buffy's death from the fifth season of the show, toppling into the void as I follow Ben down the corridor and into one of the beige bedrooms off it. I close the door behind me and turn to face him. I have to lean against the door a little because I feel weak in my knees. He's so handsome right now, his eyes startlingly blue under all that dark hair.

"You all right?" Ben asks. "You looked a little weird in there, like maybe you felt sick."

"No," I say. "No, I'm all right."

He looks at me more closely. "You're not upset with me, are you?"

"No, it's just—" I swallow hard. I can't believe I'm even going to say this. I would never normally say this to a boy. But Cathy would. Cathy always said exactly what she thought. "I thought we'd get to talk alone, just you and me."

"I know. I told you, I promised—" He gives a shrug, a lop-sided smile. "Anyway, I'm here now." He moves over to me, puts his hands on my shoulders. "I know, I'm the reason you came here, right?"

"Well…" His cockiness is unbelievable; but then again, it's just like Heathcliff to be that way. Online, that arrogance he could imitate so perfectly made me laugh, made my heart race. In person, it's sort of—annoying. Maybe because I'm not so sure he's just imitating someone else anymore. "Lisle's the reason I came."

"Right, sure." He has his face in my hair, is nuzzling my cheek through it, my neck. His hands slide down to my waist, then back up again. I don't want to do this right now—I want to talk, the way we talked online, the way we could talk about anything and everything. My mind races, trying to think of a topic to distract him, and meanwhile his hands race up my shirt, his fingers clamping down on the clasp of my bra.

"Stop that." I push him away.

"Cathy—"

I suddenly wish he wouldn't call me that. But that seems unfair—I never minded him calling me Cathy online. I liked it, even. But it's weird to have him look me right in the face and say it. Like he's looking at me, but not seeing me. He presses up against me, harder. He says her name again, in a breathy voice. "Cathy."

There's a loud banging on the door. Ben jumps, banging me in the chin with his shoulder, and we move apart. I'm pulling my shirt down as the door opens. It's Noah, framed in the hallway light. "Xena wanted to know where you were," he says. "She wants everyone in the living room. We're playing I Never."

Ben raises an eyebrow at Noah; he's giving him that look, that look boys give each other when they're trying to communicate that they just got some action. Noah doesn't look very happy. "Duty calls, I guess."

Everyone in the living room is sitting in a big circle now, with bottles of booze in the middle, and shot glasses lined up. I squeeze in next to Lisle as Xena explains that I Never is a drinking game. We go around the circle and each person makes a true statement starting with the words 'I never,' like 'I never have been to the Ice Capades.'" Then everyone who has been to the Ice Capades has to drink. That way you find out what everyone in the room has done. "It's an icebreaker," Xena explains. "Now, who wants to start?"

The statements start off pretty tame— "I've never flown in an airplane"—"I've never broken the speed limit"—and practically everyone has to drink to those. I'm happy to find out that whatever's in my shot glass doesn't contain diet chocolate soda. When it's Lisle's turn, she grins wickedly. I can tell she's pretty drunk already—she's listing to the side like a damaged sailboat, her hair extensions trailing. "I've never worn a rubber chicken suit," she announces, and takes a big swig from her glass. She's such a show-off—just because she once spent the summer working as the mascot at El Pollo Loco.

After a second, everyone else breaks up laughing, too. Suddenly people are yelling out I Nevers. I never kissed someone in a moving car. Made out on a plane. Had sex in a plane bathroom. Fooled around in public. All the statements are about sex now, and I hold my drink nervously, twirling the stem of the glass between my fingers. I have hardly anything I'd drink *for*, and even if I did I wouldn't do it in front of all these people, these strangers.

I'm watching Ben out of the corner of my eye, seeing when he drinks. It's a lot of times. He has his hand on Lisle's knee. After a few minutes she brushes it aside.

"I've never slept with two guys at once," announces Xena, chortling, and takes a big drink. Everyone's suddenly quiet. Only the thoughtful-looking woman with the knitting gazes serenely into the distance and takes a small sip from her cup. I wonder what that means? Maybe she slept with two guys, but she only did it once? Xena seems to notice everyone staring at her, and shrugs. "What? I'm polyamorous!"

Noah is looking down at the ground, clearly trying not to laugh. It's Lisle who speaks into the silence, as usual. "I've never," she says slowly, "gotten turned on while I was role-playing online with someone."

She drinks, slowly and deliberately. She's looking around the circle as she does it, like she's flirting with everyone at once. There's a low rustle of nervous giggles. Then Jack, looking across the circle at Ennis, drops her chin and takes a drink. And now the others are drinking, tipping their cups back, and I look over at Ben and he's drinking, but not looking at me while he's doing it. Lisle nudges my side and I know she wants me to drink, but I'm frozen, holding my stupid plastic cup and thinking: Turned on? Really? Is that what was going on with us, with me and Ben? Here I thought we had this amazing thing, this connection where we could talk about anything, this connection that was special. But maybe we were just like all the other billion jerks online using the Internet and anonymity to get their rocks off.

I wobble to my feet, feeling dizzy and sick. In the bathroom, I splash water on my face—my cheeks are bright red, my hair escaping out of its ponytail and sticking to my cheeks. I'd like to think I look wild and untamed, like Cathy, but I know I don't. I just look sweaty and a little insane. I tell myself I have to get back in there and sit next to Ben. Claim my place.

I push my way back into the living room, where the I Never game is still in full flow. People are hooting and screaming with laughter while they drink, and the room stinks like vodka. I look around for Ben, but he isn't there. My gaze lights on Lisle instead. Her eyes dart away from mine, quickly, toward the hallway. Lisle can never help herself. She's a terrible liar; her body language always gives her away.

Halfway down the hall Jack is standing in front of a closed door, her face puffy. She's pounding on it. "Ennis," she says. "Ennis, open up."

"You know," I say, "I bet her name isn't actually Ennis."

Jack scowls at me. "They're in there together, you know," she says, and there's real spite in it. I guess she doesn't like me much, but then why would she? I reach past her, twiddle the doorknob. "It's just stuck," I say, and without thinking, I push it open, hard.

Light floods into the bedroom, where Ben and the girl whose name I only know as Ennis are sitting on the bed, their arms around each other, their faces mashed together. Seeing people kiss in real life is never like it is in movies, is my first thought. My second thought is that I feel like I'm going to throw up. Again.

"Ennis!" cries Jack dramatically. Her eyes are huge, but I have the feeling she's not so much upset as enjoying the drama of the moment.

Ben and the girl jump away from each other guiltily, but their hands are still touching. The girl—I can't think of her as Ennis—shakes her head. "Oh, Jack," she says. "Really."

Jack makes a snuffling noise, but I don't stick around to see what she says to her friend—if they are even friends anymore. I'm heading out of the bedroom as fast as I can go.

Halfway down the hall something clamps around my wrist. I'm spun around to face Ben, who's glowering down at me, not looking very sorry at all. "Look, Cathy," he says. "Sorry if you're upset, but it's a game. It's *the* Game. We're just having fun."

But that's just it. I'm not having fun. "Let go of my wrist, Ben."

He lets go, a scowl passing across his handsome face. "Look, I'm sorry if I'm not exactly like some character in a book—"

"See, that's just it," I say, realizing the truth while I'm speaking it. "You are just like Heathcliff." And he is. Heathcliff was a self-ish, rotten bastard, really. He didn't care about anyone but him-self, and maybe Cathy. And I'm not Cathy, which doesn't leave anyone for Ben to care about, except, maybe, himself.

◦

My bags are still in a huge pile on the bed, tangled up with a dozen other people's belongings. I grab the bright green strap of my duf-fel and start hauling it free. I have no idea where Lisle is or what she's doing, or how I'm going to get out of here without her or her car. Maybe I'll take a taxi. Maybe I'll walk to the nearby highway and hitchhike.

"Jane." It's Noah in the doorway, looking rumpled and wor-ried. "What are you doing?"

"What does it look like? I'm leaving. I'm out of here." I jerk hard on the strap. It breaks off in my hand. "Shit."

"You don't have to go." He comes up beside me and puts his hand on my back, his fingers tracing circles between my shoulder blades. It's not at all the way Ben touched me: this is gentle, reassuring. My nausea starts to ebb, at least to the point where I can glance over at Noah without feeling like my stom-ach is about to shoot up into my throat. He's looking at me with concern.

"I don't have to. I want to. I don't belong here."

"Look, these people —" he gestures toward the door "— the people in the living room, you might not feel like you have a lot in common with them, but they're nice people. Who cares if they like science fiction and fantasy and you don't? The main reason they're here is because they love a character enough to want to be that person sometimes. Isn't that true for you, too?"

"It wasn't Cathy I loved," I said, throwing the broken strap down on the bed. "It was—oh, never mind. He's your friend; you'll just defend him."

"Ben might be my friend," Noah says carefully, "but he's not perfect. I know that."

A light flicks on in the back of my mind. "You were trying to warn me about him," I said. "Earlier, out by the lake—weren't you?"

"Er." Noah looks like a trapped rat. "I was just saying that maybe he wasn't exactly like you thought. People are some-times—different—than they seem online."

"Why would he even come to this?" I whisper. I know I shouldn't ask, but I can't help it. "If he didn't even want to see me?"

Noah looks at the floor, the wall, anywhere but at me. "I can tell you what he told me. He said meetups like this were always full of lonely, geeky girls who go online looking to hook up. He said he was certain to score with someone. Probably you, but if not you...someone."

"Probably me?" My voice is still a whisper and even the whis-per hurts. In books, no one ever says "It's probably you." It's always "It's only you" or "It's always been you." Not "It's probably you."

"I'm sorry." And Noah does look sorry, truly.

"I don't get it." I shake my head. "The things he wrote me, online, in e-mail—how could the kind of guy who goes to a party to take advantage of girls he thinks are lonely and pathetic be the same kind of guy who writes things like that?"

"Because," Noah says, very slowly, "he didn't write those things. I did."

"You wrote them?" I stare at him. "All those letters—those messages—everything?"

"Not the messages. That was Ben. Just the letters."

I want to not believe it, but I can't help thinking about how I always thought the messages sounded like they were in a different voice than the letters, that it was never quite the same, that Ben would never say the same amazing things in IM or chat as he would in the letters he sent. But I always thought that it was just because his prose required time and polish. Now I know better.

"So you lied to me," I say. "You knew Ben never wrote those letters and you didn't say anything about it. Probably because you knew that if you did, you'd be screwing him out of his chance to score with some lonely, geeky girl." My eyes are burning.

"I didn't lie to you," Noah protests. "I just—" He breaks off. "Okay, fine. I lied to you. But I didn't mean to."

I suddenly feel very tired. "Just go away, Noah."

He looks as if he wants to say something else, but he doesn't. With a sigh, he turns and leaves, shutting the door gently behind him.

I look down at my bag, the broken strap, and even my bones feel aching and exhausted. I want to creep into a hole and die, but since I know that's not going to happen, I do the next best thing. I get onto the bed and burrow in among the bags, pushing them up and aside until I've made a little crawl space for myself, a hidden cave where no one can find me. I curl up under the bags and fall asleep.

●

A loud banging wakes me up. I pop up from among the bags to see that the doorknob is jerking back and forth like someone's yanking on it desperately. Before I can get to my feet the door bursts open and G'Kar staggers in. He takes one look at me and streaks past me into the bathroom, where I can hear him throwing up.

Light is streaming in through the windows and I realize with some surprise that it's morning. Strange that no one came in at any point during the night looking for their bags. Or maybe they did and I slept right through it. My head is aching and I wonder if I'm hungover. I've never been hungover before.

I fight my way out from among the bags and go looking for Lisle. Once I'm in the living room I realize why nobody came looking for their bags last night. Everyone's sprawled out asleep on chairs, on the sofas, or on the floor. I don't see Ben or Noah or Lisle anywhere, but standing there in the doorway looking at the passed-out crowd I realize that I'm not thinking about what a bunch of weirdos these people are. What I'm thinking is that this looks like the morning after a party where people had fun.

I find Lisle eventually in the bathroom, asleep on the floor. She's not alone, either. Neo and Trinity are both with her, Neo's arms around her waist. She has her hand on Trinity's shoulder. Looks like Lisle will be drinking a lot more at the next I Never game.

Back in the living room, I pick my way across the sprawled bodies to the kitchen. Doritos are melting into soggy puddles in pools of spilled soda. The whole room smells sour. I grab a towel and a shiny green bottle of Comet and go to town on the mess.

Cleaning always helps me clear my mind. I'm humming under my breath and scrubbing when Jack comes into the room, red-eyed and with her hair in a tangled mess. She eyes me like I'm a bomb that might go off. "Is there anything to eat?"

I think about snapping at her, telling her off for asking me, like I would know. But for some reason Noah's voice is in my head, saying, *These are nice people. You might even like them.*

I put the sponge down and turn to face her. "I was thinking about making pancakes," I say. "But it depends if we have the ingredients."

She pulls open the refrigerator door and nods. "There's actually a lot of food here. Milk, eggs..."

"Great." I wipe my soapy hands on a towel. "Do you want to help?"

She hesitates a moment, and then smiles. "Sure."

Cooking is the other thing that helps me clear my mind. I'm a whirlwind, cracking eggs, mixing batter, throwing the towel over my shoulder. Jack is laughing as she watches me. She looks pretty when she laughs, less sullen and scary. She's wearing a pair of tiny hoop earrings with zigzag patterns etched into the metal, and I realize with a funny jolt that I have the same earrings at home.

"Pancakes. Awesome." Lisle appears, draping herself over one of the bar stools. She reaches out and sticks a finger in the batter. "Yum."

"Ew. Unsanitary!" I swat her away with the corner of the towel.

Jack hands her a bag of the chocolate chips I was about to dump into the batter. "Here. Eat these." She gives me a conspiratorial grin.

The kitchen is filling with good, warm smells, the smell of comfort and breakfast. I feel weirdly fine, even though I ought to be miserable. I see Ben file into the room, rumpling his hair, a scowl on his face. Ennis trails in behind him, looking vaguely embarrassed. I glance over at Jack, who's blushing, so I hand her a bowl of batter and a spatula. "Mix!"

She mixes, looking grateful to have something to do. Ben looks over at me and then away, sauntering toward the patio doors, Ennis following him like a puppy. I know I ought to feel jealous, heartbroken, all those other things. But I don't. I never really liked Ben. I just liked the person I thought he was.

I liked the person who wrote those letters.

As if on cue, Noah comes in. He doesn't saunter, just gives me a look through his hair and ambles over to the couch, where he parks himself behind his graphic novel. I don't have time to think about him, though, because Xena's suddenly here, clanking her jewelry and clapping her hands. "Pancakes! Fantastic! Thanks so much, Cathy!"

106

I don't bother to correct her about my name when she reaches out and hugs me. It's a squishy hug, but kind of nice. The kitchen is half-full of people now, chattering, grabbing glasses, setting the table. Everyone seems appreciative of the pancakes. I realize Noah was right. These are nice people. I look over at him on the sofa, but he's hiding behind the pages of his book like they are a curtain.

I even have fun at breakfast, with everyone laughing and chattering. We don't have maple syrup, so people sprinkle sugar and smear jam on their pancakes — "Like they do in France!" Lisle announces, scattering sugar everywhere.

When the meal is over, I start carrying stacks of plates into the kitchen. Everyone's in there, bumping, jostling, and pushing, but it's a friendly sort of crowding. Jack is over by the sink, running hot water, wrist-deep in soap suds. "Oh, no you don't," she says, taking the plates from me with a soapy hand. "You shouldn't have to clean. You cooked, you set the table, you didn't even have a mimosa...."

"You cooked, too," I point out. "And I *already* have a hangover."

"This will be the best thing for you, then," she says, picking up a glass filled with champagne and orange juice. "Besides — you have somewhere else you should be. Don't you?"

She's looking out toward the deck, through the big glass doors. Noah is out there, sitting on the wooden railing, staring out toward the lake. I look back at Jack, who is smiling.

"Go on," she says, handing me the glass, which I take without thinking. "We can wash up without you."

I mouth "thanks" at her, and go. The air out on the porch is cold and sharp as an ice sliver. Noah has his feet braced against the lower railings and is looking at me warily, as if I might be about to throw my drink in his face. His hair is messy, his eyes bright hazel behind his glasses. "Look," he says, before I can open my mouth, "if you came out here to ask me why I'm still here, it's because Ben wanted to stay for breakfast. But we're leaving right after."

"That's not why I came out here." I stare down at my drink, which is the pale orange color I associate with Tang and orange candies. "I want to know why you wrote those letters. In the first place. Did Ben ask you to?"

Noah glanced up toward the sky, the heavy clouds overhead. "He didn't ask me to. I wrote them for a class project. Write in the voice of a literary character. I left them out on my desk and Ben must have found them. It wasn't until a while later that I found out he was using them online—with you."

"How did you find out?"

"He told me. Ben's never ashamed of anything he does. It's just his way." Noah shrugged. "He thought I'd think it was funny."

"And did you?" Something cold hits my cheek and slides down my neck; it's starting to rain. "Think it was funny?"

"No," Noah says shortly. "He showed me all the e-mails between him and you, and trust me, I didn't think what he was doing was funny. But I did really like your letters, Jane. I liked the way you wrote. I liked the things you wrote." He still isn't looking at me. "I know. Stupid. But I started looking forward to your letters. Ben would forward them to me and I'd write the responses. And because you were responding to my letters, I felt sort of like you were writing to me. That was why I wanted you to walk down to the lake with me. Because I felt like I knew you."

My head is spinning. "So you never were Mr. Kool-Aid?"

He shrugs. "Ben gave me an account on the Game eventually. I just wanted it so I could read your journal entries. I picked Mr. Kool-Aid because I figured I'd never actually have to do anything. No one wants to interact with Mr. Kool-Aid, trust me."

I know I should be mad, but I'm not. I feel strangely relieved. It all makes sense now—why Ben's letters didn't sound anything like his instant messages. Why when I met him, I felt absolutely nothing, no connection at all, but when I met Noah—

"You should have told me," I say.

Rain is pattering down on the deck, turning the wood dark brown. Noah's hair is stuck to his cheeks and forehead in black swipes. "Why? It wasn't me you came here to see. It was Ben."

"That's not true." I take a step forward. "The person I wanted to meet was the one who wrote those letters. That was all I ever cared about."

I'm vaguely aware that there are faces pressed to the glass doors behind me, watching us, but I realize I don't care. Noah is shivering inside his wet jacket, rain running down his face. He looks at me like he doesn't believe me.

I look down at the glass in my hand. Rain is mixing with the alcohol, diluting the orange color. "I never," I say, very carefully, "yelled at someone because they told me something I didn't want to hear, even though it was the truth."

I lift the glass and take a drink out of it. Rainwater and oranges and champagne. When I lower the glass, Noah is staring at me.

"I never," I say again, "made a totally stupid mistake about who it was I really liked, and only realized it when it was too late."

I drink again. I feel a little dizzy, but it isn't from the mimosa. The rain has diluted the alcohol so I hardly taste it. He's sitting completely still, just watching me. I can feel my heart pounding, wondering if I have the nerve to say it, the last thing I want to say to him.

I do. "And I never," I say, "wanted you to kiss me, right now."

I lift the glass and drink the rest of it, fast. A second later Noah jumps down off the railing, his boots splashing up water from the deck. He comes over and puts his hands on my shoulders. I can see Lisle behind the glass doors, giving me the V for victory sign with her fingers. Ben is standing beside her, scowling.

109

"You mean it?" Noah says, water running off his eyelashes. "You want me to kiss you?"

"Cathy never says anything she doesn't mean," I tell him. "And neither do I."

His kiss tastes like rain. When he lets me go, he's grinning. "I'd tell you I've never kissed anyone like that before," he says, "but I think we're out of drinks."

He tightens his arms around me as I laugh. Someone behind the glass door whistles—I think it's Jack—and I know they're laughing and cheering for us, and I don't even mind that I just met all these people and don't even know their real names. It's nice. I know they're cheering because it just feels right—however strange it might seem—Catherine Earnshaw and Mr. Kool-Aid, kissing in the rain.

Cassandra Clare is the *New York Times* bestselling author of *City of Bones, City of Ashes,* and *City of Glass. City of Bones* was a 2007 *Locus* Award finalist for Best First Novel. She is also the author of the upcoming YA fantasy trilogy The Infernal Devices. She lives in Brooklyn, New York, with her boyfriend and two cats. She is also the author of the extremely geeky online Lord of the Rings parody *The Very Secret Diaries.*

Try not to throw up.

Try not to profess your undying love. Don't sleep with them. Don't ask them to sign your ass.

Do not recite a blow-by-blow account of a famous scene.

Do not tell them everything they did wrong in that one scene on page 63 because you think it will make you seem smart.

THE KING OF PELINESSE
by m. t. anderson

It was not until the final moon had risen over Brondevoult, lighting the carnage with its spectral dweomer, that Caelwin, called the Skull-Reaver, saw that the battle was won, the anthrophidians defeated, so he could at last lower his incarnadined blade and cease his work of destruction. The enemy was vanquished; Caelwin and his hired barbarian swords might at long last storm the basalt citadel. They rushed through the obsidian gates, shrieking with beserker rage, the white knights of Pelinesse behind them, bearing up the oriflamme of the swan and scythe, and the bus reached Portland, and Caelwin stormed up the stone steps and found the Princess of Yabtúb chained beside a cauldron, prepared for some fell thaumaturgic distortion, and he said, "I am Caelwin, called the Skull-Reaver, and I have been sent by the King of Pelinesse to bear you hence," and she regarded him with astonishment, and I got off the bus and went into the station in the dark of the night to wait until the 6 AM up Route 1.

I lay down on one of the benches with my bag under my head and *Tales of Marvel* open on my stomach. I closed my eyes hard and tried to doze. I knew my mom was looking for me, and I felt real bad, but I couldn't call her until I reached Boothbay Harbor. If I called too soon, the police at home could call the operators and trace the call back up the coast and then next thing I knew,

115

they would be showing up to have a little talk with me, you know, saying, "Jim? You must be Jim. Jim, why don't you come with me. Your parents are real worried about you, Jim," saying stuff like that, but walking toward me with their hands out. So I couldn't call my parents. I tried not to think about it. I just curled up right there on the bench and rolled up the magazine in both hands and held onto it and I wondered what *thaumaturgic* meant and I guess I finally fell asleep.

Just after six I caught the first bus of the day to Boothbay Harbor and I sat with my knees up against the back of the seat in front of me, and an eldritch beast, a-glitter with the ichor of Acheronian pits, strayed into the ceremonial chamber, the Princess meeped in her wyvern-wing corset, and Caelwin, called the Skull-Reaver, unsheathed again his mighty broadsword, so fatal to foes, and hacked at the monster's serpentine coils while the goring tail whipped around him, spiked like caltrops. The pines went by the windows, and I looked out, and my face haunted the woods. There were purple salt marshes and lots of mist.

"The Baron's Ambuscade," *Tales of Marvel*, vol. 3, no. 6 (June 1937). "The Weird of Caelwin, Skull-Reaver," *Tales of Marvel*, vol. 4, no. 2 (February 1938). Both uncollected. "Gloom Comes to Parrusfunt," *Tales of Marvel*, vol. 4, no. 8 (August 1938), the first Caelwin yarn with all the mythology worked out, the gods of Ur-Earth, etc. *Song of the Skull-Reaver* by R. P. Flint, 1945, collecting all the stories that appeared in *Tales of Marvel* and *Utter Tales* from 1938 to 1944, with an alternative version of "Lords of Pain" (originally from *Utter Tales* #6), in which the gem doesn't fall into the chasm and the Visigoths have a stronger German accent.

"The Serpent-Men of Brondevoult," *Tales of Marvel*, vol. 15, no. 10 (October 1949). The latest in the saga. "You are a brute," murmured the Princess, putting her small hand upon his oiled arm, "but yet you are strangely to my taste." Caelwin, called the Skull-Reaver, pulled her to him, and drew aside her velvet loincloth to reveal, as it said, *the gem of her womanhood*, and she yielded to him, melting in his clay-red arms. I was half-asleep and it was like I could see her, and she looked real good, with her wyvern corset ripped open and "the pale parentheses pressed into soft breasts by the iron brassiere, now cast aside" (and there were dark nipples — she groans and beckons — the clank of mail), and the bus stopped and I looked up and saw Wiscasset out the window but I realized I couldn't shift my knees off the back of the seat in front of me because one leg had gotten embarrassing. I hoped we wouldn't reach Boothbay Harbor very soon.

"Kid? Can you get your knees out of my back?"

No. No, I couldn't.

"They're trash," said my mother, and she dumped them into the garbage. She said, "You know who reads these things? Soldiers. And prisoners in the state pen."

I shouted at her to stop and I couldn't believe she was just wrecking them, and I wanted to grab her hand to stop her but I knew she'd smack me. She was pouring bacon grease all over my collection. I told her no but she just kept going.

"Do you see this grease? I don't want to hear anything else about R. P. Flint or his god-damned barbarian."

I told her it was ten dollars' worth. I said, "I been collecting those all over!"

"I'm telling you, Jimbo. Prisoners in the state pen. You know why they're in there? Robbing little bakeries and groping the Campfire Girls."

I kept on yelling at her and she stood there with her stupid arms folded and said, "That's the kind of company you're keeping."

I got off the bus in Boothbay Harbor. I looked around the bluffs and out toward the sea. It was a little town with old captains' houses and lobster fishermen. I put my hands in my pockets and went to find breakfast. I was real hungry. I read two more pages of the R. P. Flint story while I ate toast and eggs. I spread the pages real neatly so I didn't get jelly on them.

I realized there was no way my mom and pop could stop me now, so I found a phone and told the operator my town and my number, and they connected me, with all the clicks going down the coast. My mom answered and she'd been crying, I could tell, and I felt kind of sorry, but I thought I shouldn't feel sorry, and she asked me, "Are you all right? Where are you? Are you all right, sugar?" I said I was okay, and I told her I was in Boothbay Harbor. I thought that would really get her.

She didn't understand at first. She just said, "Where?"

So I said, "In Boothbay Harbor," again, and "Maine," and then she figured out what I was talking about and realized what I was doing and started to say I was being stupid, and not to make a fool out of—so I hung up and walked out.

I had looked up the address on a map, and I had drawn a little version of it on a piece of school paper. It didn't look like it was far. I walked out of the town center, and along a road that led past ridges of some kind of needly tree, like pines or firs or spruce. I don't know the difference between them. A couple of years ago, I tried to find out the differences from a book, but all the pictures looked exactly the same. The seagulls were crying out over the islands.

It took me forty-five minutes to walk to the house. It wasn't near the ocean. It was in an ugly, uneven field, and the bushes around it had grown up with elbows. It wasn't a very big house, but the name on the mailbox was Flint, painted in yellow, so I went up on the porch and knocked. There was no sound for a while, and I thought maybe no one was home, which would be stupid, but then someone moved. Whoever it was only moved a little. Then they said, "Who is it?" and I didn't know what to say, so I didn't answer.

"Who is it?" called R. P. Flint.

"I'm," I said, "I'm a person knocking on your door."

There were footsteps inside the house, and the door opened.

R. P. Flint was not as tall as I thought he would be. He was kind of short, but he was *wiry of limb like the thieves of Mortmoor.* He had a little mustache, and his hair was finger-combed and clutched. He was dressed kind of like a writer, in a silk bathrobe, but also just in his boxer shorts, which kind of made me embarrassed. He had a lot of black hair on his chest, which also hadn't been combed.

"Hi," he said. "You have a package or something?"

I shook my head. I didn't know what to tell him. A car drove by on the dirt road below.

R. P. Flint nodded. He said, "You are a disciple of the Skull-Reaver."

I said, "I have the. I have all the issues. I had them."

"Come inside," said R. P. Flint.

I went in. I was real nervous. There wasn't much in the house, just a few lamps and a desk and a sofa that someone had slept on, and some tin dishes. There was a map of the Age of Caelwin tacked up to the wall. It was done in blue pen on typing paper. The cover from *Utter Tales* no. 15 was pinned beside the window, showing Caelwin, called the Skull-Reaver, stomping on ooze.

"Welcome to my lair. This is where it all begins," said R. P. Flint, knocking on the desk. "It's just a little desk, made of wood, but boats are just little things made of wood, and they can transport you to foreign lands."

I stared at him and at the map of the Age of Caelwin, and I felt completely stupid, just like my mother'd said.

"You may wonder about me," said Flint. "I'm from Ohio. I write out my first drafts in blue pen—always blue—then I type them. I roll up my sleeves when I write, because I really dive into my world. I'm up to my elbows in sediment."

I was feeling real confused. He was right in front of me. He was looking at my face.

I pointed my foot at a wicker chair, and I asked if I could please sit down.

He said, "Kid, I've got Caelwin tied to a pillar, with a pterodactyl shrieking and coming to feast its unholy beak upon his numbles."

I went over to the wicker chair anyway and sat. I stared at the floor. I felt very weak.

There he was, right in front of me.

"Hey, pal," said R. P. Flint. "I've really got to get back to the typing." I didn't stand up. R. P. Flint smiled and he said, "I'm thinking maybe instead of a pterodactyl, a giant vampire bat. Which one do you think would be better? Here's your chance, pal. Prehistory in the making."

I told him, "You're having an affair with my mother."

For a long time after that, neither Mr. Flint or I moved any. I was sitting there with my hands on my legs. Mr Flint picked up a root beer bottle from his desk and rolled it between his hands.

"Or had," I said.

R. P. Flint scratched at the stubble on his lower lip with his teeth. He asked, "What's your, you know, name?"

I told him, "Jim Hucker."

R. P. Flint nodded. He stuck his finger into the neck of the bottle and popped it back out. "Swell," he said.

I said apologetically, "You used a vampire bat in 'The Worm-Born of Malufrax.'"

Slowly, Mr. Flint swung the bottle back and forth, his finger trapped in its mouth. Finally, he admitted, "Sure. But that was a normal-sized vampire bat. This would be huge."

Two months before, I found a letter in our mailbox. It was from "R. P. Flint, Author," and the address was in West Boothbay Harbor, Maine. The envelope was handwritten.

I ran into my parents' bedroom, where my mother was smoking, and I said, "Mom, you got a letter."

"Great," she said, and she took it.

"Who's it from?" I asked, knowing.

She looked at the return address. "Oh, Jesus," she said.

"It's from Maine," I said. I knew there couldn't be two R. P. Flint, Authors, of West Boothbay Harbor, Maine. "Who's it from?" I asked.

"No one."

"Is it someone you know?"

"It's someone I went to high school with."

"You went to school with R. P. Flint?"

"Yes." She started to leave the room.

I said, "He's the most amazing writer. I read him all the time. Everyone thinks he's the best. You know him? Actually?"

"Sure. I know him. Never mind."

"You know R. P. Flint?"

"I went to high school with him. He was called Dickie."

"I can't believe you really went to school with him."

"Someone had to."

I asked, "What's he like?"

"Can we not talk about this?"

"Can I meet him?"

"No."

"Can you get him to sign an autograph?"

"Forget it."

"Can I see the letter?"

"No."

"Mom, he's my favorite."

"You're never meeting him."

"You don't understand."

She yelled, "*No*, Jim. *You* don't understand, see?" She whacked the door frame so hard I jumped. She stared at me, real angry. She said, "I never want to hear his name again." She walked out of the room, slamming the door after her.

Then there I was, stuck alone in my parents' room, like it was my room.

The next day, I sat on the sofa reading the tales of Caelwin, called the Skull-Reaver. I held up the cover of the magazine clearly. My mom watched me but she didn't say anything. At dinner I brought up an interesting question from one of the R. P. Flint stories — if you were falling down a bottomless pit, would you die by some kind of altitude sickness or by starving to death? — and my mother said she didn't want to hear another word about those stupid codpiece-and-saber stories, and my dad frowned, real uncomfortable, like he knew the name R. P. Flint, Author, better than he should, but he didn't want to talk about it.

I left the magazines and the book around the house so that no one could ever forget about R. P. Flint, but the arguments between my mother and father were never about that, they were always about the car or the rug or the weekend. Watching my parents closely like a gumshoe, I noticed how my mother always said angry, mean things about everything my father did and how my father came home from work as late as possible and looked hurt into his soup. I tried bringing up R. P. Flint one more time at dinner, and my mother told me his stories were for perverts, and asked me whether I'd ever noticed that all of those serpents rearing up and dragons to be ridden and those huge swords wielded in battle perhaps were kind of symbolic, and whether they might be the kind of thing that men who were worried about themselves would read to make themselves feel better. That made me angry because she knows R. P. Flint is one of my favorites so I said that he was the greatest author I had ever read, and she went up to my room and grabbed all my issues of *Utter Tales* and *Song of the Skull-Reaver* and she poured bacon grease all over them.

What I didn't think about until later was that she knew a lot about R. P. Flint's stories — about the swords and the dragons — and she knew where I kept my copies.

122

Not too long after, I found another letter from R. P. Flint, recently arrived, this one torn up in eighths and in the living room wastepaper basket. I took it up to my room and put it on my desk and I fit it together. Then I read it all.

Dick Flint said he was glad he and my mom had met again and how beautiful she was. He talked about the *rhapsody of entry* and my fingers felt numb on the paper. Mr. Flint talked about how doing that with her made him feel young again, and we can't let a good thing die, honey, and then a lot about her breasts in the hotel room and lying naked while the evening fell, before she had to skedaddle *like a nymph, I'm telling you, viewed by some burly hunter espying her through a thicket in the gloaming. O, the radiant copse*, etc.

I just stared at the letter for a long time. It told a story of a world in which even the falling light on telephone wires was beautiful, and a man and a woman were in love, and it had sat torn up in eighths in a wastepaper basket in a room with two plants and three vases and a painting of horses.

I went downstairs.

My mother was polishing in the kitchen.

I went in and sat down.

My mother kept on polishing.

Finally she looked at me. "What's wrong?" she asked.

I couldn't say anything. I shrugged.

"Well, why have you been crying?" she asked.

"You're cheating," I said.

"What am I doing?"

I didn't want to repeat it so I kept quiet.

"Don't twizzle up your legs like that," she said. "It's just like your father. Don't twizzle them up. It's pathetic."

I said, "You had an affair."

She was surprised. She stopped polishing for a minute. "Who told you that?" she asked me. "Have people been talking?"

I didn't say anything. She kept asking me questions. I didn't tell her a word.

Finally, she said, "All right. Fine. That's the past."

"When?"

"During the war. And your father's no saint. Don't twizzle up your legs."

"I'm not twizzling up my legs."

"I mean when you wrap them around each other," she said. "You have to claim the chair as your own. Spread out a little. You sit like nothing in the world belongs to you."

"Well, you threw away all my magazines."

"Forget the stupid magazines."

"Tell me about the, you know, affair."

"I will not tell you a word. Neither your father or me wants to talk about it."

"I want to know about the affair. Tell me what happened in the affair."

"Stop saying 'affair.'"

She wouldn't talk about it. My dad came home pretty soon after that. At dinner, my mother started crying. She slammed the salad across the table and walked out.

My father tried not to move, like he was terrified.

I watched them both.

My dad, he watched the table.

A few days later, without telling anyone, I got on the bus for Maine.

"They're stuck inside their little houses," said R. P. Flint as we walked past cottages on the bay. Mr. Flint and I were going for some grub and a man-to-man. Mr. Flint cupped his hands around his mouth and repeated loudly, "STUCK INSIDE THEIR LIT-TLE HOUSES." He told me, "When people say, 'I don't get out much anymore,' they don't just mean out the door. They mean outside their own skin. They're sewed up in their hides. They're trapped in there. Kid, they need to go out on the town. They need to take their spirit out on a date." He cupped his hands around his mouth again. "YOU NEED TO GO STEADY WITH YOUR SOUL."

He was wearing a normal white shirt and a plain suit and I wondered whether that was what he had been wearing when he espied my mother through a thicket in the gloaming and they went to a hotel.

Flint asked, "Is she coming up?"

"Who? Mom?"

"Sure, your mom."

"I don't think so. I didn't tell her I was coming. I just called before I walked to your house. She only just found out I was here."

"I haven't seen her in a while. Is she still the fairest vixen to ever sweep across a glade?"

I shrugged, thinking: *the gem of her womanhood.*

"Let me tell you something that won't cost you a nickel. A great love is necessary for a great art," Mr. Flint explained.

I told him I didn't write or anything.

"But you have a lyrical soul," he said. "I can see it. People don't understand you. But that's because you haven't spoken yet. I mean, spoken in the voice that echoes off cliffs and mountaintops." He grabbed my arm and stopped the two of us from walking. He said, like a prophet, "You will speak in that voice, ere long."

I didn't know what he was talking about, and I didn't want to look at his eyes. I wanted to keep walking. But Mr. Flint wasn't letting go. I figured he was waiting for something but I didn't know what he wanted. Maybe thanks or something. So I said, "Thanks."

Mr. Flint let go of my arm and smiled and we kept walking toward the village. The water was real quiet in the bay. Some lobster boats drifted out between the isles. It was a bright day, and the wind blew over the church steeples and the warehouses on the docks.

I asked Mr. Flint whether he ever got lonely up in Maine.

"Why's that?"

"I thought writers lived in New York or Hollywood. And they had all kinds of friends who are other writers and movie stars."

"I've stripped my life down," he told me. "I don't need much. I have all the company I want to keep right in here." He shot himself in the head with his fingers. "People don't understand about the need to live simply. They make appointments all day. They even schedule their own deaths. The first time they'll have freedom to really be themselves is when they no longer exist. But up here, there's nothing but me and the sky. A million billion stars."

I looked out where the sun glanced along the harbor and I could kind of see what Mr. Flint meant. It looked heroic, with all the ocean and the coves and their pines. Everything seemed big.

That's one of the things I love about R. P. Flint's stories: They make the land feel huge. Even though they're set on an ancient, strange Earth, there's the feeling of a huge America in them. They have the pioneer spirit. The sea with the fishermen, and the fields of wheat to the west. *The frigid north, where roams the wolf, and the sands of the desert south.* The white marble cities and the little farms lost in the hills.

Looking out at the sea, I felt something cosmic in the nation and older than the settlers.

And I guess maybe that's what he'd made my mother see, how huge everything was, and I pictured them standing in some high place, and for a moment they looked out on the world together, the height of space, and maybe they felt like they were falling through it, but holding each other.

A lobster boat was puttering near to the shore. Men in rubber pants pulled up their traps. There was wood smoke in the air, which is a smell I like. We kept walking. I scuffed the dirt in streaks with my heels. I looked at Mr. Flint and I thought, *the rhapsody of entry*, and then I didn't say any more.

A few minutes later, we reached the luncheonette. We got a table.

"I'm buying," said Mr. Flint. "It's a celebration."

I got fried chicken. Mr. Flint got the Reuben sandwich. I picked the skin off the fried chicken. I like the breading, but not the skin. The skin is too wet and bumpy. I stacked little pieces of the broken breading on top of the meat. That way I could eat just the breading.

Mr. Flint announced, "The white knights, formerly Caelwin's allies, catch him and try to mate him with the inferior, watery beauties of Pelinesse. Those are no women for Caelwin — fine ladies taken up with needlepoint and the gentle arts. Weaving. Giggling in their snoods. He will not go to stud to improve the bloodlines of those anemic decadents."

"In the new story?"

"The wizard Arok-Plin, thirsty for the blood of the young nations of the north, seeks him, too, riding out of the desolate lands of Vnokk. He wishes to use Caelwin's life-strength in an amulet that will give him the power to melt metal with his very gaze. How do you like that? Would you like to have such an amulet?"

I shrugged. "I don't know what I'd really do with it. I mean, you can bust metal with stuff now and I never need to."

"Ah. Right." He nodded.

I was just trying to answer truthfully, but now I could see Mr. Flint was a little hurt about me not liking his amulet. So I said, "I have about every Caelwin story you ever wrote." He still didn't say anything, so I asked him, "How did you get such a big imagination?"

"By never ordering from the menu of life, except à la carte. By letting my own heart beat so strong that my body jumps to its rhythms. Do you understand?"

I nodded. But then I thought about it and I said, "You ordered a lunch special."

"I like the pickle."

"I mean, you didn't order a separate side. You just got the Reuben basket."

"I don't have anything against fries. What's got into you?"

"I thought à la carte meant you ordered everything separate."

"I wasn't talking literally. Don't be a chump. Anyway, why are you stacking up all your fried on your chicken after you just pulled it off?"

"I just like the fried."

"That's disgusting."

"I don't think so."

"I'm the one who has to watch it."

I said, "Tell me about my mother."

R. P. Flint got a look on his face that was either worried or angry, and he chewed real slow and hard, chops full.

Now I couldn't bear to look at him, so I played with the paper placemat instead. I rolled a corner of it around the handle of my fork.

"How are you boys doing here?" the waitress said. "Still working?"

"I am always working, kindly Ruby," said Flint. "So long as breath and mind persevere."

"You were going to write a sonnet about me on my apron," she said.

"Sure. I'm a couplet short of a quatrain. Think of something that rhymes with 'carbonation.'"

"This should be good."

I offered, "Inflammation."

"Real cute," said Ruby about me.

"Ain't he the bee's knees?" said Flint, wriggling a finger.

"Your nephew?"

128

"Sort of."

I explained, "He had an affair with my mother."

The waitress looked at Mr. Flint with a friendly kind of disgust and then said, "Prince Charming. Excuse me. I have a date with a side of mashed."

When she was gone, Mr. Flint told me, "I wish you hadn't said that. You can't just say things like that."

"It's true. If you didn't want people to say it, you shouldn't have done it."

Mr. Flint chewed again.

I said, "So?"

"So what?"

"So you knew her in high school."

Mr. Flint took another bite of his Rueben. He wiped pink sauce off his lips with his napkin. He half-shrugged and said, "Okay. We knew each other in high school."

"Did you date her then?"

"Did I...? No, not really. Not what you could call 'date.' You know, this is a colliding of worlds. You here. One world runs into another one." He sucked at his teeth. "Think about this: I could have Caelwin stumble on an electrical citadel. With a field of static energy like a veil of light and a buzzing sound. And in the citadel could be some creatures from another planet with ray-guns and all. But I'm worried how it would be, with a sword yarn mixing with a space yarn. What do you think?"

"You're... You aren't answering."

"You haven't asked any question."

"When did you see her again?"

He shook his head. "I don't want to talk about this, pal."

"But now I asked a question."

"She's a gorgeous woman, your mother. You must know that. If she's ever in the dumps, you've got to tell her that. Tell her people think she's gorgeous. You've got to make a woman realize how they delight men's eyes. Because otherwise they all think they have lousy figures or bad hair."

"You're not answering."

"I don't have to answer a thing. Your mother is a delicious woman. That's all you've got to know. Do you have to go to the john?"

"No. Why?"

"Because you have your legs all screwed up like that."

"Sorry," I said, and unwound them. I told him that my mother always says I need to sit like I'm willing to take up more room.

"She's not wrong," he said. "She's a smart woman, your mother. Smart as well as beautiful. It's one of the great mysteries that people take up different amounts of room. I mean, you think of, for example, a guy like me, normal sized, and a short little guy, let's say he's five two or something. We both have these thoughts and these feelings, but mine extend through more of the universe. More of the universe is made up of me. No matter how big his thoughts are, when it comes down to it, more of space is not him — and more of it is boiling with R. P. Flint. It's a question of how much you fill. Isn't that funny?"

"Where was the hotel?"

"You don't let up."

"I read your letter."

"You read my goddamn letter."

"She tore it up."

Mr. Flint wiped his mouth with his napkin, creased it into a square, and threw it down on his plate. "Look, kid, you've met me. Here we are. That's it. Now you know me. You're done. We're right in town. Let me give you change for the bus. You go back home and tell your mother I'm here whenever she wants to come up and see me." He stood up. "Get up. I'm paying. You need to use the john."

"I don't. That's just my legs."

"You have a long trip ahead of you."

"I'm not leaving."

"Why? What do you want to learn?"

That stumped me. I didn't answer.

"What do you want to learn?"

I didn't have anything to say.

Mr. Flint took his coat from the hook on our booth and he put it on and the moment was passing. He said, "I've got to go. Our hero is tied to a pillar, about to be gored by a pterodactyl."

"You said it might be a bat."

"I just said that to make conversation. That's the stupidest goddamn idea I've ever heard in my life."

"No stupider than a pterodactyl."

"A pterodactyl has a beak. It can rend, like the heaven-sent eagle that disemboweled Prometheus. A vampire bat would just crawl all over him and, I don't know, nibble."

"Things that crawl can be awful."

"Are you getting cute?"

I didn't understand him. He was trying to get past me to the door.

I tried to say something, but Mr. Flint held out his hand and interrupted me. "It was nice meeting you. Real nice. A pleasure."

I shook his hand.

I said, "I'm not going."

"What do you want?"

"I want to know what it was like."

"Laying your mother?"

"Don't you say that."

"I can't tell you anything."

"Why not? Where did you meet? What did she say to you? What did she tell you about my pop?" I asked him. "What did she say about me?"

Mr. Flint looked stumped. He pressed his thumbs hard against the table edge and watched them whiten. He lifted his hands and put them in his pockets.

"Jesus," he said. "I need a beer."

"What did she tell you?"

Mr. Flint picked up the bill and took out his wallet and thumbed through it until he had enough money. He put the money down on top of the bill. "You have a quarter?" he asked me.

I wasn't giving him any change.

"Look," said Mr. Flint, in a different kind of voice, "I haven't seen your mother since high school."

I put my hands in my underarms. I didn't say a word. Mr. Flint snorted and frowned.

"It's true," he said. "That's how it really is. I write her letters, she never writes back."

"I read the letter. You said that you met her in a hotel."

"I didn't."

"I read it."

"I know I wrote that. Okay? But I didn't meet her."

"You said in a hotel. At least once. Maybe more."

"Can we get out of here?" he asked, looking around quickly. "These people aren't really that interested in their meatloaf."

We went outside. A few cars drove past. I had my coat on.

"You said in a hotel," I pressed.

"Christ."

"I'm just telling you what you wrote in ink."

"Women"—Mr. Flint looked gray—"women like some romance in their life. They like it when a man talks to them from outside the wee world of lawns, you know what I mean? The little china tea-set world. So I wrote your mother some letters."

I said, "They weren't true. The letters."

I think Mr. Flint started to shake his head, but then he stopped. His head was getting lower on his shoulders. He was staring at the metal railing. He looked up quickly at my mouth, and he explained, "Women need some romance. I know how to lavish romance. It's what they love."

"You haven't seen her in twenty years."

He said, "I knew her in high school. She was the most beautiful…She was…You know how it is. I couldn't get her out of my head. So a few years ago I found out where she was and I wrote to her and asked what she was doing. She never wrote back, so I wrote again, and it just became this sort of—you can think of it like a novel. Okay? It became a story I was telling her."

"She said it was true."

"Then she's nuts."

"She said you had an affair during the war."

"Maybe she did."

"So?"

"With another man. At least, not with me. I don't know. But I can promise you: not with me. I'd be dancing to the moon in gingerbread slippers if it was me."

"So you never went to a hotel and there was never an evening on the telephone wires and the rhapsody of entry."

"Jesus. Some things you write don't sound so good when they're read back to you." He squinted in the sun and his mustache slanted. He said, "No. Really. I made it all up."

I didn't know what to believe. I asked him, "She was beautiful in high school?"

"There was no girl like her. Cross my heart." R. P. Flint kept ducking his head. He said, "Kid, you can be proud." He punched me on the arm, and it was like a little brother pretending to be an uncle. "Okay?"

I nodded. I guessed there was nothing else to know. More cars went past. I couldn't think of any more questions.

"Let's go down to the docks," said R. P. Flint, "and watch the boats come in."

We went down the street, which was steep, to the pier. Fishermen were carrying crates up ramps. They yelled things to each other. For a while, R. P. Flint and me sat there side by side.

We couldn't see the ocean from where we were sitting—just

the harbor—but the swells drew up and lay down the seaweed. The sky was as blue as a stupid postcard, and the islands were as green as islands. Mr. Flint smoked a cigarette like he wished it was a pipe.

I said, "So you just write her letters?"

Flint blew a stream of smoke, which wavered as he nodded.

"How long have you been writing her?"

"Can we not, you know, talk about this?"

I stopped talking so I wouldn't bother him. He was the one who kept talking.

"You think I'm a drip," he said.

I told him I didn't.

He said, "People might say so, but I've got…I told you: A man needs a great passion for a great art. For me, it happens to be your mother. I worship her as the paragon of women. The paragon. It doesn't matter whether she cares. You know what? I'm like the knights in the old medieval stories. She's my courtly lady. I ride into battle with her favor on my crest, okay, and it doesn't matter whether she ever even stoops to kiss me. I remain faithful until the end. Whatever may come."

"She tears the letters up," I said.

He hardly moved his head.

I faced back forward. On one of the boats, some men were playing cards. There was a breeze sometimes, and they held down the discards with their fists.

Mr. Flint was blushing and he kept staring out at the islands.

He was thinking about awful things. Just watching the seagulls. I felt bad, so I told him, "I liked the pun on Boothbay."

"Hm?" said Mr. Flint.

"Yabtúb," I said. "The Princess of Yabtúb."

"Oh," said Mr. Flint. "Yeah. That's not a pun. It's just backwards."

"In the story, is the place Yabtúb supposed to be like Boothbay Harbor?"

"No."

"The opposite of Boothbay?"

"No."

"Like Boothbay backwards?"

"No. It's nothing like Boothbay."

I nodded. We sat for a minute. I told him, "You could have called it Robrah Yabtúb."

He nodded. "Sure. I could've."

He stood up and kicked at the pier. He told me, "I'm going back to my house now. I've got some writing to do."

Ten feet under my shoes, the sea grew and shrank.

"All right?" said Mr. Flint. "It was really nice to meet you." He smiled at me, even though I could tell it wasn't a real smile. Mr. Flint held out his hand again like he had in the luncheonette. "It's been a pleasure. A real pleasure."

I stood up and I dusted off my pants and I shook R. P. Flint's hand. I said politely that it was good to meet him.

"I'm sorry," he said. "I know this isn't what you were expecting."

I shrugged. "It's not what you were expecting, either," I said.

R. P. Flint nodded. "You're a great kid, pal." He smiled, and this time it was for real. I smiled back. The sun was bright and we were both squinting. He said, "What's your name again?"

I told him, "Jim."

"Jim what?"

I stared at him. For a second he didn't realize what he'd said.

I said, "The same as my mother's. You write to her."

"Oh, sure," he said.

"So."

"So, it's…"

"Hucker."

"Of course, Jim. I know." He fumbled with the air. "All right. Great. Good-bye," he said quickly, and walked away as fast as he could.

I watched him. He moved as fast as a crab on the beach.

He hadn't known her name. He had no idea. None. He walked up the hill.

I just stared at him. I stood there and watched him go up the road and I wondered how many women Mr. Flint was writing to. I bet there was a list. Probably a monthly calendar, and he went through them all by date. Maybe Mr. Flint wrote to a lot of the women who were girls at his high school. I pictured their legs, their arms in front of Dickie Flint still, white hands sorting cards, writing "DANCE" in block letters, slim fingers held up to answer questions about Uruguay, pale socks twirling past his pimpled face, his slack, stupid mouth where he sat at his desk, scratching his lower lip with his upper—and maybe there were others, too, other women he thought about alone—the teller at Mr. Flint's bank, the typists at *Utter Tales*, Ruby at the luncheonette, who knows?—and he wrote his dirty letters in which he loved each one like no one else had ever loved him before, and in each envelope, the future was just beginning, a new future with just him and this girl, and she and he were going to meet in some courtyard with a fountain and wine and flutes, and Mr. Flint was never alone.

That was all. He walked away, trying not to look back at me, because he knew what I was thinking. Then he was gone, around a corner, and I went up and waited for three hours for the next bus back to Portland.

On the bus, Caelwin, called the Skull-Reaver, returned to do battle with his erstwhile ally, the King of Pelinesse, that he might seize the scepter of that benighted realm, but I couldn't fix my eyes on the page because the darkness was starting to fall over the salt marshes and towns.

Mr. Flint, I guess, was back at his house. Hunched over, drinking root beer, sleeves rolled up, one lamp. Doing his evening's work. I pictured him reading out the best passages to himself in a voice as swollen as opera, about the breasts and the thighs; and there they were; all of them, like women in a sunken kingdom, sitting in his garden with seaweed waving around them, there in his undersea court, his *consorts*, yielding up *the gem of* etc., and etc., and etc.

I decided I would have to phone my mother from Portland. I would have to tell her I was okay and I guess I'd have to ask her who she really'd had the affair with, and probably there'd be more stories after that. All the stories of parents that I couldn't even hardly imagine, all the things that happened to people in houses and hotels in this world, on this Earth, on this stupid Earth.

Caelwin was riding to the north, his demesne expanding; and on the bus, I stared at my own reflection in the window, my own twined legs, until evening came, and all that was left was specks; and then my traces grew so tiny I could not even be seen.

M. T. Anderson's satirical science fiction novel *Feed* was a finalist for the National Book Award and winner of the *LA Times* Book Award; his Gothic historical novel *The Astonishing Life of Octavian Nothing, Volume One*, won the National Book Award and the *Boston Globe/Horn Book* Award. He has also written music criticism, picture books, and stories for adults. For many years, he was fiction editor of *3rd bed*, a journal of experimental poetry and prose.

As this story suggests, Anderson was (and continues to be) a fan of old fantasy pulp: Robert E. Howard, H. P. Lovecraft, Jack Vance, and Clark Ashton Smith. Acting as a Dungeon Master for a D&D campaign in his early teen years taught him most of what he knows about creating narratives. As he sees it, an interest in fantasy drives right to the heart of what it means to be a geek: someone who admires barbarians, but who has to avoid swordplay due to really bad asthma.

Rotting smell. (Check to make sure not merely poor hygiene.) **Zombie**

Wrapped in gauze. (Make sure not facial treatment and bathrobe.) **Mummy**

Can see through them. (Make sure not standing in movie theater.) **Ghost**

Fangs. (Make sure not just making out.) **Vampire**

Digs body free from grave. (We really have no alternate explanation for this one.) **Who cares? Kiss your ass good-bye.**

THE WRATH OF DAWN
by cynthia and greg leitich smith

"Where's the dry cleaning?" Mom demands as she opens my bedroom door. "You know your father—"

"*Step*father," I say. My mom married him eleven months, two weeks, and four days ago. Worse, he came with a prissy daughter who's a couple of years older than me and two obnoxious sons who're a few years younger. I'm outnumbered, and, as if that's not bad enough, we also had to move to their house.

"—needs his gray suit for a client meeting tomorrow morning."

I notice the Colonel himself hasn't deigned to grace me with his presence (no, he doesn't sell fried chicken—he's a retired Marine who works as a security consultant).

As Mom's rant goes on, I minimize the Web page on my PC so she won't catch a glimpse of the bare-assed fan art beside the *Underworld* fic I'm reading.

"You know, Dawn, your sister—"

"*Step*sister," I put in. Megan. The athletic one. She of the chemical blondness. The one whose boyfriends have heavy brow-ridges and square jaws. "Megan took the car before I could run errands."

"You should have told her you needed it," Mom replies, because it's important that everything be my fault.

I don't point out that I tried but Megan ignored me. I don't

141

point out that even if I hadn't told her, *she* could've asked me before taking off.

Mom crosses her arms. "You know, it wouldn't hurt you to give her a chance. This adjustment hasn't been easy for Megan, either."

I don't say it, but it bothers me when Mom takes her side. The thing is, I did try in the beginning. When our parents announced their engagement at the Olive Garden, I told Megan in the ladies' restroom that it was hard for me, too. Out of nowhere, she starts yelling at me that I don't know anything and that my visiting my dad at his apartment in Round Rock is totally different from her visiting her mom's grave in Smithville.

Of *course* it's different. I get that — I got it then — but Megan's treated me like a lesser species ever since. Like how she always calls my room "the guest room." And how she always foists little-brother-babysitting duty on me because I have "no life."

I offer up a theatrical sigh. "Poor Megan!"

"You're grounded," Mom says as she exits.

I don't bother to shrug. To Mom, "grounded" means not going out, but doesn't include 'net, cell, or DVD restrictions. By this weekend, she'll have moved on to another of my allegedly fatal flaws, and it's not like I've got plans on the average Tuesday night.

When Mom leaves, I shut the door behind her. Then I bring my browser back up on screen and begin checking RSS feeds. I read this story about a sixth grader in Wyoming who's trying to get a new word accepted into *The Unauthorized Dictionary of the Klingon Language*. It's kind of cute, so I comment *Qapla!* Then I happily spend the next hour on the readergirlz boards at MySpace.

My mood is ruined again when Megan bursts into the room.

"You could knock," I say without turning around.

"Sorry," Megan replies. Then she says the most shocking thing imaginable: "Want to come with me tonight to the Buffy Sing-Along?"

142

Megan knows I want to go. I've been talking about it for weeks. And she's just come from speaking to Mom. She's clearly toying with me.

I shake my head. "Thanks to you, I'm grounded." I swivel in my desk chair. "Wait. *You're* going?"

Megan is not into anything remotely interesting. Her tastes are simple. She watches "reality" television. Worse, she wants to be *on* reality television. Last week, the Colonel practically pissed a kidney stone when she mentioned driving to San Antonio to audition for *So You Want to Marry a Movie Star?*

"Ryan's working the sing-along tonight," Megan replies. "We're going out after."

Ah, Ryan. The second and blander of her great loves. Like her, he rows a skinny boat backward and is into other sports that involve grunting and spandex.

I do have to admit, though, that he's pretty much gorgeousness personified. His only physical defect is the beginning of what promises to be a severe case of male-pattern baldness.

"He'll be bald by twenty-two," I say.

"Who cares what he'll look like at twenty-two?" She winks like we just shared a moment, which we did. But I don't think we got the same thing out of it.

"This involves me...why?" I ask, getting back to the Slayer.

Megan's smile turns brittle. "For reasons I don't understand, Ryan's cousin Eric will be joining us, and we need someone to keep him out of our way."

I'm in no mood to babysit again. "Waterloo doesn't allow kids under ten."

Megan steps daintily through the maze of paperbacks and graphic novels on my floor, brushes imaginary lint from my black comforter, and sits, addressing me in the same tone she might use with a cocker spaniel. "I'm not asking you to babysit, Dawn. I'm setting you up on a blind date."

I make a half-laugh, half-barfing noise. "No."

Megan lifts her French-manicured nails, examining them. "It won't kill you. He's not a troll, and he's into the same geeky stuff you are."

I minimize the screen again. "Like?"

"Like, like *Buffy*!" she replies, glancing at my posters. "*Star Trek! Batman!* Comic books, and…" Her gaze lingers appreciatively on Hugh Jackman's Wolverine.

Despite myself, I'm tempted. I adore Buffy. Well, actually, I like Buffy. I adore Willow and Tara, and I think their love ballad is the most romantic…Wait. Even if Eric is cool and it didn't mean spending a whole evening with Megan… "I'm still grounded."

"Carol says it's okay so long as you're with us," Megan replies, standing.

I hate it when she calls my mom "Carol," and I'm positive the "date" aspect is going to suck. Still, it *is* Buffy. "Fine, I'm in," I say. Then I add, "But you're paying for everything."

◉

The doorbell rings at seven sharp. I rush to the door. Fortunately, the twins don't realize a world exists beyond their latest video game, and the Colonel isn't here to indulge in his usual tactic when a boy comes over (giving him the third degree while ostentatiously cleaning his Winchester thirty-ought-six on the living room coffee table).

"Um, hi," Eric says.

He's a little over six feet tall, skinny, generally symmetrical, has fewer than the average number of pimples and a full head of hair. He's also wearing blue jeans and a green button-down oxford shirt, which is kind of boring and does nothing to set off my black sleeveless T, black tiered knit skirt, and combat boots.

144

Still, I've seen worse.

"Told you he was borderline cute," Megan murmurs as she comes down the hall. Brushing by, she adds, "I asked Daddy to lay off his whole intimidation-by-firearms shtick."

I take that in as she leads me out the front door to a minivan with fake wood paneling. We live in Austin, so I walk around to look at the bumper stickers: THE WHEATGRASS PRESERVA-TION SOCIETY. SAVE OUR SPRINGS. Number three is the universal negative symbol crossing out the name *Wesley*.

I take shotgun (Megan for once is happy to ride by herself, lower profile, in back). And as Eric backs out of the driveway, I ask, "Wesley Wyndham-Price or Wesley Crusher?"

Eric hits the brake and glances at me. "Oh, Crusher. I'm sure you'll agree that Wesley Wyndham-Price was less than outstand-ing in his early *Buffy* appearances—"

"Though he made Giles seem more buff—"

"Granted, but in any case, he dramatically improved on *Angel,* whereas Wesley Crusher started out bad and went downhill. No redeeming qualities whatsoever."

"Sure there were," I say, undaunted. "Redeeming qualities, that is." I try to recall if there's a single episode of *Star Trek: The Next Generation* in which Wesley Crusher is not annoying. Okay, maybe I'm a tad daunted.

I have to admit it, though. Megan was right. Eric's not a troll.

Glancing at his MapQuest printout, Eric begins reverse engi-neering his way out of the neighborhood. A moment later, he shoots me that supercilious look of the über-geeky. "Well?"

An instant later I have the answer. I take a breath to ensure there's no smugness in my voice. "He's not Dr. Z."

"Who?"

"Starbuck's kid. You know, Starbuck from *Battlestar Gallactica.*"

"She—"

"*He*," I interrupt. "*He* has a kid. In the original series." Which I used to watch with my dad on the only surviving Betamax videotape player this side of eBay. "Actually, it was *Galactica 1980*."

Eric looks at me like I've turned into a Fyarl demon and swerves just in time to avoid a bicyclist.

I've established enormous geek cred.

"A spin-off," I say. "Probably the single worst example of the child-genius motif in science fiction history. *Much* worse than Wesley Crusher." I'm actually enjoying myself now. "Dr. Z always had this weird white glow about him, practically an aura, which I suppose was how people could tell he was a genius." I fiddle with my seat belt. "Well, that and the fact that Commander Adama genuflected every time he saw him."

"La, la, la," Megan sings from the back, sounding bored but amused.

I'd half forgotten she was back there.

Eric does the smart thing and ignores her. "Yeah, the kid-genius thing is bad, but it pales next to the previously unknown, never-mentioned pseudo-sibling who appears suddenly out of nowhere."

"Fascinating," Megan mutters, checking her lipstick.

"Most prevalent on family sitcoms," Eric adds, "but also frequent and problematic in speculative fiction."

"Well, yes, there's Dawn," I say, trying to keep the irritation out of my voice. As we slow, stuck in traffic, I add, "Believe me, I know. I bear the burden of her name."

A lot of people have issues with Buffy's sister. But kleptomania aside, Dawn always tried to be one of the good guys. And every once in a while she was really brave.

"Are you familiar with the usenet group alt.dawn. die.die.die?" Eric asks. At my nod, he announces, "I founded it."

I give him a long, considering glare and try to decide if he's trying to piss me off or whether he just doesn't have any social skills.

146

"Look, Dawn Summers was thematic," I tell him. "Summers blood. Saving the world, again. It made sense. Besides, it's not like those monks asked Dawn if she wanted to be transformed from a ball of energy into Buffy's little sister."

"Oh, my God!" Megan interrupts with a bark of laughter. "No wonder neither of you can get dates by yourselves."

"Honestly," I say, "was Dawn really all that bad?"

"She whines," Eric replies. "All of the pseudo-siblings whine."

"Not Tim Drake Robin," I shoot back, although, to be fair, he didn't start out as Dick Grayson's sibling (or Bruce Wayne's son) per se.

"Jason Todd Robin?"

"He deserved to die," I admit. I hold my breath, worried Eric will counter with the abomination that was Spock's half-brother, Sybok. Even I don't have a defense for that.

A light changes, and we're moving again.

"Why do you two know all this?" Megan asks.

I glance over my shoulder. "Who won the third *American Idol*?"

As we turn into the parking lot, she says, "That's different. It's popular."

◉

Waterloo Cinema isn't like other movie theaters. The auditoriums have great stadium seats with long tables secured in front of each row. Even better, they have actual waiters who serve food and drink during the film itself.

We take in the crowd and settle into our seats about five minutes before the show starts. I'm oddly pleased by how packed the theater is. How *popular* the show is, even after all this time.

As we sit down, we're given bottles of soap bubbles, plastic vampire teeth, and cigarette lighters.

Megan examines hers like they're the unclean symbols of a mysterious, foreign, and possibly dangerous culture.

She gives up when her boyfriend Ryan takes our orders—Greek salad with chicken for Megan, burger and fries for Eric, a flaming chocolate bomb for me.

I ignore my stepsister's look of horror as a cheer rises and the overture begins.

○

It's an interactive show. When Tara serenades Willow, we blow magic bubbles. When Buffy walks through the fire, we raise our lighters high.

And we sing. We sing along.

Except when Dawn appears on screen. At the urging of the host, the audience boos, hisses, and glories in attacking her (even though it was Xander who summoned the tap-dancing demon in the first place). You can't even hear the soundtrack.

Megan looks baffled.

Eric, though, has to be the loudest person in the building. "Go away, Dawn!" he shouts, cupping his hands over his mouth like a megaphone. "Loser!"

Very mature. He's definitely trying to piss me off. Who the hell does he think he is? What makes him think he's so cool, anyway?

Besides, it's not just my *name* he's jeering. It's every newbie, every little sister who wasn't there before. It's the lesser sibling...the one blamed for everything...my God, it's *me*.

Not that anyone else seems to care.

"Get off the screen!" shouts the guy behind me.

"Screw you, Dawn!" screams a girl down in front.

"Die, Dawn, die!" someone yells from down the aisle.

At that, I decide I've had it. I've had it with Eric. I've had it with Megan. I've had it with everything. I'm frustrated. I'm furious. And I'm wired on sugar.

I drop my spoon and wipe chocolate from my lips.

I duck beneath the long table in front of my row and run to the stage, snatching the wireless microphone from the host on my way.

"You can't do that!" Ryan exclaims, snagging my arm.

"Get the hell out of my way," I say, enunciating carefully, "or I'll tell Colonel Green you deflowered his daughter in the backseat of your Volvo last fall after the A&M game."

Ryan turns pale—brow ridge, square jaw and all, and for the first time, he really sees me. "Okay."

"I need the stage."

"Okay," he says again, backing away.

As I block the screen, the hisses and boos grow louder, and for a moment, I'm blinded by the projector light. Then I'm in the spotlight.

"My name is Dawn!" I shout into the microphone, and my voice sounds loud, louder than I expected. Loud enough to be heard over the soundtrack.

"Your name is Dawn." I go on, in an only slightly more sane tone, realizing as I say it that metaphor isn't my best hope.

"So what if she's awkward? So what if she whines about her sister? Are you honestly telling me that you have *never* whined?"

●

The crowd's reply? More jeers, laughter, and a possible death threat from a man wielding a quesadilla.

"Come on!" I try again. "A lot of people didn't like Wesley in the beginning. A lot of people didn't like Tara in the beginning."

I scan the crowd again. The hardcore *Angel* fans are listening now. The Willow–Tara 'shippers, too.

"We've all been like Dawn," I argue. "We've all felt out of place. Sure, here, *here*, you belong. Here you're among your own. But what about out there?"

"Out there, people like her" — I point to Megan — "look down on you, judge you, and scorn you. She isn't even here for *Buffy*! She's here for her waiter-boyfriend!"

Is it working? It's not working. Is it? No. Only a few heads are nodding.

I'm not sure what I was expecting. I don't know what I was thinking. My sugar high has worn off.

"We must stand together!" I raise my fist, defiant. It's my last, best shot to convince them. "We must embrace our inner Dawn!"

Silence. Gaping, lonely silence.

It feels like the end of the world.

Just as I'm ready to hand off the mic and slink away, Megan stands and begins to clap. Slowly at first, but loud. Really loud. She looks me in the eye, then gives a small nod and a knowing, appreciative smile.

Like we're sisters or something.

In the next moment, Eric is standing beside her. And he's cheering, too.

Then Megan offers up this amazing two-fingers-in-her-mouth piercing whistle. I didn't even know she could do that. It's gloriously non-prissy. It's fantastic!

That's when it happens. Maybe it was my argument. Maybe it was my scary zeal. Whatever the reason, as soon as Megan whistles, the crowd is on its feet.

They're blowing bubbles. They're raising their lighters high.

They're cheering through their fangs...

For Dawn Summers, for themselves and each other, for every sibling who got tossed into a situation beyond her control.

For me.

And for my sister, who whistles again...

Once more with feeling.

Greg Leitich Smith channeled his student days at a math-science magnet high school into the Peshtigo School novels *Ninjas, Piranhas, and Galileo*, which won a Parents' Choice Gold Award, and *Tofu and T. rex*, both published by Little, Brown. Greg has long been a fan of *Star Trek*, although he was disappointed as a child when he found out it was fiction and that we had only recently made it to the moon. The starship *Enterprise* (NCC-1701E) adorned his wedding cake. (The actual ceremony, alas, was not performed in Klingon.) His Web site is www.gregleitichsmith.com.

Cynthia Leitich Smith is the author of *Tantalize*, which was a Borders Original Voices selection and a New York Public Library Book for the Teen Age, and its companion novel, *Eternal*. *Blessed*, a third book set in the universe, and a *Tantalize* graphic-novel adaptation are in the works. Cynthia also has written several YA short stories and award-winning books for younger readers. She teaches in the MFA program in Writing for Children and Young Adults at Vermont College. Back in the day, Cynthia and her husband Greg made a twice-weekly ritual out of each all-new *Buffy: The Vampire Slayer* or *Angel* episode and are now addicted to the comic adaptations. They both speak fluent "Scooby." Her Web site is www.cynthialeitichsmith.com.

How to CHEAT Like A NERD

MATH

Create complicated computer program to hack school computer and change every answer to "A."

Cost: Bribe to janitor for school computer password, bribe to your cousin to have the IP come from his home computer.

Time: Three weeks to two hours depending on your computer skill.

SCIENCE

Reanimate dog to eat homework.

Cost: Emotional scars. Grave-digging at the pet cemetery is no picnic.

Time: Could be a long wait for a lightning bolt to hit your house.

ENGLISH

Write own novel to write book report on.

Time: November (NaNoWriMo)

Cost: Your sanity

PHYS ED

Hologram of self playing dodgeball.

Time: Whole summer

Cost: $1,000,000

HISTORY

Build time machine.

Cost: Dad's lab entry card to secret government project he's working on.

Time: Don't worry about it, you've got all the time in the world!

QUIZ BOWL ANTICHRIST
by david levithan

I am haunted at times by Sung Kim's varsity jacket.

He had to lobby hard to get it. Nobody denied that he had talent—in fact, he was the star of our team. But for a member of our team to get a jacket was unprecedented. Our coach backed him completely, while the other coaches in the school nearly choked on their whistles when they first heard the plan. The principal had to be called in, and it wasn't until our team made Nationals that Sung's request was finally heeded. Four weeks before we left for Indianapolis, he became the first person in our school's history to have a varsity jacket for quiz bowl.

I, for one, was mortified.

This mortification was a complete betrayal of our team, but if anyone was going to betray the quiz bowl team from the inside, it was going to be me. I was the alternate.

I had been drafted by the coach, who also happened to be my physics teacher, because while the four other members of the team could tell you the square root of the circumference of Saturn's orbit around the sun in the year 2033, not a single one of them could tell you how many Brontë sisters there'd been. In fact, the only British writer they seemed familiar with was Monty Python—and there weren't many quiz bowl questions about

Monty Python. There was a gaping hole in their knowledge, and I was the best lit-boy plug the school had to offer. While I hadn't read that many of the classics, I was extraordinarily aware of them. I was a walking CliffsNotes version of the CliffsNotes versions; even if I'd never touched *Remembrance of Things Past* or *Cry, the Beloved Country* or *Middlemarch*, I knew what they were about and who had written them. I could only name about ten elements on the periodic table, but that hardly mattered—my teammates had the whole thing memorized. They told jokes where "her neutrino!" was the punch line.

Sung was our fearless leader—fearless, that is, within the context of our practices and competitions. Put him back into the general population and he became just another math geek, too bland to be teased, too awkward to be resented. As soon as he got the varsity jacket, there was little question that it would never leave his back. All the varsity jackets in our school looked the same on the front—burgundy body, white sleeves, white R. But the backs were different—a picture of two guys wrestling for the wrestlers, a football for the football players, a breast-stroker for the swimmers. For quiz bowl, they initially chose a faceless white kid at a podium, probably a leftover design from another school's speech-and-debate team. It looked as if the symbol from the men's room door was giving an inaugural address. Sung didn't feel this conveyed the team aspect of quiz bowl, so he made them add four other faceless white kids at podiums. I was, presumably, one of those five. Because even though I was an alternate, they always rotated me in.

I had agreed to join the quiz bowl team for four reasons.

(1) I needed it for my college applications.

(2) I needed a good grade in Mr. Phillips's physics class for my college applications, and I wasn't going to get it from ordinary studying.

(3) I did get a perverse pleasure from being the only person in

a competitive situation who knew that Jane Eyre was a character, while Jane Austen was a writer.

(4) I had an unarticulated crush on Damien Bloom.

An unarticulated crush is very different from an unrequited one, because at least with an unrequited crush you know what the hell you're doing, even if the other person isn't doing it back. An unarticulated crush is harder to grapple with, because it's a crush that you haven't even admitted to yourself. The romantic forces are all there — you want to see him, you always notice him, you treat every word from him as if it weighs more than anyone else's. But you don't know why. You don't know that you're doing it. You'd follow him to the end of the earth without ever admitting that your feet were moving.

Damien was track-team popular and hung with the cross-country crowd. If he didn't have a problem with Sung's varsity jacket, it was probably because none of the other kids in our school defined him as a quiz bowl geek. If anything, his membership on the team was seen as a fluke. Whereas I presumably belonged there, along with Sung and Frances Oh (perfect SATs, tragic skin) and Wes Ward (250 IQ, 250 lbs) and Gordon White (calculator watch, matching glasses). My social status was about the same as a water fountain in the hall — people were happy enough I was there when they needed me, but otherwise they walked on by. I wish I could say I was fine with this, and that I found what I needed in books or food or drugs or quiz bowl or other water-fountain kids. But it sucked. I didn't have the disposition to be slavishly devoted to popularity and the popular kids. And at the same time, I was pretty sure my friends were losers, and barely even friends.

When we won the States, Sung, Damien, Frances, Wes, and Gordon celebrated like they'd just gotten full scholarships to MIT. Mr. Phillips was in tears when he called his wife at home to tell her. A photographer from the local paper came to take our picture and I tried to hide behind Wes as much as possible. Sung had his jacket by that time, its white sleeves glistening like they'd been made from unicorn horns. After the article appeared, a couple of people congratulated me in the hall. But most kids snickered or didn't really care. We had a crash-course candy sale to pay for our trip to Indianapolis, and I stole money from my parents' wallets and dipped into my savings in order to buy my whole portion outright, shoving the crap candy bars in our basement instead of having to ask my fellow students to pony up for such a pathetic cause.

Sung, of course, wanted all of us to get matching varsity jackets to wear to Nationals. Damien already had a varsity jacket for cross country that he never wore, so he was out. Frances, Wes, and Gordon said they were using all their money on the tickets and other things for Indianapolis. I simply said no. And when Sung asked me if I was sure, I said, "You can't possibly expect me to wear that." Everybody got quiet for a second, but Sung didn't seem fazed. He just launched us into yet another practice.

If there were four reasons that I'd joined the quiz bowl team, there were two reasons that I stayed on:

I had an unarticulated crush on Damien Bloom. (These things don't change.)

I really, really liked beating people.

Note: I am not saying *I really, really liked winning*. Winning is a more abstract concept, and in quiz bowl, winning usually meant having to come back in the next round and do it all again. No, I liked *beating people*. I liked seeing the look on the other team's faces when I got a question they couldn't answer. I loved their geektastic disappointment when they realized they weren't good enough to rank up. I loved using trivia to make people doubt themselves. I never, ever missed an English question—I was a fucking juggernaut of authors and oeuvres. And I never, ever attempted to answer any of the math, science, or history questions. Nobody expected me to. Thus, I would always win.

The hardest were the scrimmages, where we would split into teams of three and take each other on. I didn't have any problem answering the questions correctly — I just had to make sure not to gloat. The only thing keeping me in check was Damien. Because around him, I wanted to be the good guy.

If I had any enthusiasm for Indianapolis, it was because I assumed Damien and I would be rooming together. I imagined us talking all night, me finding out all about him, bonding to the point of knowledge. I could see us laughing together about the quiz bowl kids from other states who were surrounding us in their quiz bowl varsity jackets. We'd smuggle in some beers, watch bad TV, and become so comfortable with each other that I would finally feel the world was comfortable, too. This was strictly a separate-beds fantasy... but it was a separate-from-the-world fantasy, too. That was what I wanted.

The closer we got to Indianapolis, the more I found myself looking forward to it, and the more Sung became a quiz bowl dictator. If I'd thought he was serious about it before, he was beyond all frame of reference now. He wanted to practice every day after school for six hours — pizza was brought in — and even when he saw us in the halls, he threw questions our way. At first I tried to ignore him, but that only made him YELL HIS QUESTIONS IN A LOUD, OVERLY ARTICULATED VOICE. Now anyone within four hallways of our own could hear the guy in the quiz bowl varsity jacket shout, "WHO WAS THE LAST AMERICAN TO WIN THE NOBEL PRIZE FOR LITERATURE?"

And I'd say, much lower, "James Patterson."

Sung would blanch and whisper, "Wrong."

"Toni Morrison," I'd correct. "I'm just playing with ya."

"That's not funny," he said. And I'd run for class.

It did, at least, give me something to talk to Damien about at lunch. I accidentally-on-purpose ended up behind him on the cafeteria line.

"Is Sung driving you crazy, too?" I asked. "With his pop quizzes?"

Damien smiled. "Nah. It's just Sung being Sung. You've gotta respect that."

As far as I could tell, the only reason to respect that was because Damien was respecting it. Which, at that moment, was reason enough.

The afternoon, though, wore me down. Sung got increasingly angry as I was increasingly unable to give him a straight answer.

"WHAT WAS JANE AUSTEN'S LAST FINISHED NOVEL?"

"Vaginas and Virginity."

"WHO IS THE LAST PERSON IAGO KILLS IN *OTHELLO?*"

"His manservant Retardio, for forgetting to change the Brita filter!"

"WHAT HAPPENS TO THE LITTLE MERMAID AT THE END OF HANS CHRISTIAN ANDERSEN'S *THE LIT-TLE MERMAID?*"

"She turns into a fish and marries Nemo!"

"Fuck you!"

These were remarkable words to hear coming from Sung's mouth.

He went on.

"Are you trying to sabotage us? Do you WANT to LOSE?"

The other kids in the hall were loving this—a full-blown quiz bowl spat.

"Are you breaking up with me?" I joked.

Sung turned bright, bright red. Which is not easy for an Asian American math geek to do.

"I'll see you at practice!" he managed to get out. Then he turned around and I could see the five quiz bowlers on the back of his jacket, their blank faces not quite glaring at me as he stormed away.

When I arrived ten minutes late to our final pre-Indianapolis practice, Mr. Phillips looked concerned, Damien looked indifferent, Sung looked both flustered and angry, Frances looked flustered, Gordon looked angry, and Wes looked hungry.

"Everyone needs to take this very seriously," Mr. Phillips pronounced.

"Because there are small, defenseless ponies who will be killed if we don't make the final four!" I added.

"Do you not want to go?" Sung asked, looking like I'd just stuck a magnet in his hard drive. "Is that what this is about?"

"No," I said calmly, "I'm just joking. If you can't joke about quiz bowl, what can you joke about? It's like mime in that respect."

"C'mon, Alec," Damien said. "Sung just wants us to win."

"No," I said. "Sung *only* wants us to win. There's a difference."

Damien and the others looked at me blankly. This was not, I remembered, a word-choice crowd.

Still, Damien had gotten the message across: *Lay off.* So I did for the rest of the practice. And I didn't get a single question wrong. I even could name four Pearl S. Buck books besides *The Good Earth*—which is the English-geek equivalent of knowing how to make an atomic bomb, in that it's both difficult and totally uncool.

And how was I rewarded for this display of extraneous knowledge? At the end of the practice, as we were leaving, Mr. Phillips offhandedly told us our room assignments. Sung would be the one who got to room with Damien. And I would have to share the room with Wes, the gargantuan hobbit.

On the way out, I swear Sung was gloating.

If it had been up to Sung, we would have had the cheerleading squad seeing us off at the airport. I could see it now:

Two-four-six-eight, how do mollusks procreate?
One-two-three-four, name the birthplace of Niels Bohr!

Then before we left, as a special treat, Sung would calculate the mass and volume of their pompoms. Each one of the girls would dream of being the one to wear Sung's letter jacket when he came back home, because that would make her the most popular girl in the entire sch —

"Alec, we're boarding," Damien interrupted my sarcastic reverie. The karma gods had at least seated us next to each other on the plane. Unfortunately, they then swung around (as karma gods tend to do, the bastards) and made him fall asleep the moment after takeoff. It wasn't until we were well into our descent that he opened his eyes and looked at me.

"Nervous?" he asked.

"It hadn't even occurred to me to be nervous," I answered honestly. "I mean, we don't have to win for it to look good on our transcripts. I'm already concocting this story where I overcome a bad case of consumption, the disapproval of my parents, a terrifying history of crashing in small planes, and a twenty-four-hour speech impediment in order to compete in this tournament. As long as you overcome adversity, they don't really care if you win. Unless it's, like, a real sport."

"Dude," he said, "you read way too much."

"But clearly you don't know your science enough to move across the aisle the minute I reveal my consumptive state."

"Oh," he said, leaning a little closer, "I can catch consumption just from sitting next to you?"

"Again," I said, not leaning away, "medicine is your area of expertise. In novels, you damn well can catch consumption from sitting next to someone. You were doomed from the moment you met me this morning."

"I'll say."

I wasn't quick enough to keep the conversation going. Damien bent down to take an issue of *Men's Health* out of his bag. And he wasn't even reading it for the pictures.

I pretended to have a hacking cough for the remaining ten minutes of the flight. The other people around me were annoyed, but I could tell that Damien was amused. It was our joke.

We were staying at the Westin in Indianapolis, home to the Heavenly™ bed and the Heavenly™ shower.

"How the hell can you trademark the word *heavenly*?" I asked Wes as we dumped out our stuff. We were only staying two nights, so it hardly seemed necessary to hang anything up.

"I dunno," he answered.

"And what's up with the Heavenly™ shower? Am I really going to have to take showers in heaven? It hardly seems worth the trouble of being good now if you're going to have to wear deodorant in the afterlife."

"I wouldn't know," Wes said, making an even stack of the comics he'd brought on the bedside table.

"What, you've never been dead?"

He sighed.

"It's time to meet the team," he said.

Before we left, he made sure every single light in the room was off.

He even unplugged the clock.

The competition didn't start until the next morning, so the evening was devoted to the Quiz Bowl Social.

"Having a social at a quiz bowl tournament is like having all-you-can-eat ribs and inviting a bunch of vegetarians over," I told Damien as the rest of us waited for Sung and Mr. Phillips to come down to the lobby.

"I'm sure there are some cool kids here," he said.

"Yeah. And they're all in their rooms, drinking."

Some people had dressed up for the social—meaning that some girls had worn dresses and some boys had worn ties, although none of them could muster enough strength to also wear a jacket. Unless, of course, it was a varsity quiz bowl jacket. I saw at least five of them in the lobby.

"Hey, Sung, you're not so unique anymore," I pointed out when he finally showed up, his own jacket looking newly polished.

"I don't need to be unique," he scoffed. "I just need to win."

I pretended to wave a tiny flag. "Go, team."

"All right, guys," Gordon said. "Are we ready to rumble?"

I thought he was being sarcastic, but I wasn't entirely sure. I looked at our group—Sung's hair was plastered into perfect place, Frances had put on some makeup, Gordon was wearing bright red socks that had nothing to do with anything else he was wearing, Damien looked casually handsome, and Wes looked like he wanted to be back in our room, reading *Y: The Last Man*.

"Let's rumble!" Mr. Phillips chimed in, a little too enthusiastically for someone over the age of eleven.

"Our first match is against the team from North Dakota," Sung reminded us. "If you meet them, scope out their intelligences."

"If we see them on the dance floor, I'll be sure to mosey over and ask them to quote Virginia Woolf," I assured him.

The social was in one of the Westin's ballrooms. There was a semi-big dance floor at the center, which nobody was coming close to. The punch was as unspiked as the haircuts, the lights dim to hide everyone's embarrassment.

"Wow," I said to Damien as we walked in and scoped it out. "This is *hot*."

I almost laughed, because Damien had such a look of social distress on his face. I could imagine him reassuring himself that none of his other friends from home were ever going to see this.

"The adults are worse than the kids," Wes observed from over my shoulder.

"You're right," I said. Because while the quiz bowlers were

mawkish and awkward, the faculty advisors were downright weird, wearing their best suits from 1970 and beaming like they'd finally gone from zero to hero in their own massively revised high school years.

Either out of cruelty or obliviousness (probably the former), the DJ decided to unpack Gwen Stefani's "Hollaback Girl." A lot of the quiz bowlers looked like they were hearing it for the first time. From the moment the beat started, it was only a question of whose resolve would dissolve first. Would the team captain from Montana start break dancing? Would the alternate from Connecticut let down her hair and flail it around?

In the end, it was a whole squad that took the floor. (Later I would learn it was the home-state Indiana team, who may have felt more comfortable at the Westin.) As a group, they started to bust out the moves—something I could never imagine our team doing. They laughed at themselves while they danced, and it was clear they were having a good time. Other kids started to join them. And then Sung, Frances, and Gordon plunged in.

"Check it out," Wes mumbled.

Gordon was doing a strut that looked like something he'd practiced at home; I had no doubt it went over better in his bedroom mirror than it did in public. Frances did a slight sway, which was in keeping with her personality. And Sung—well, Sung looked like someone's grandfather trying to dance to "Hollaback Girl."

"This shit really *is* bananas," I said to Damien. "B-A-N-A-N-A-S. Look at that varsity jacket go!"

"Enough with the jacket," Damien replied. "Let him have his fun. He's stressed enough as it is. I want a drink. You want to get a drink?"

At first I thought he meant breaking into the nearest minibar. But, no, he just wanted to head over to the punch bowl. The punch was übersweet—like Kool-Aid that had been cut with Sprite—and as I drank glass after glass, it almost gave me a Robitussin high.

"Do you see anyone who looks like he's from North Dakota?" I asked. "Tall hat? Presence of cattle? If so, we can go spy. If you distract them, I'll steal the laminated copies of their SAT scores from their fanny packs."

But he wasn't into it. He kept checking texts on his phone.

"Who's texting?" I finally asked.

"Just Julie," he said. "I wish she'd stop."

I assumed Just Julie was Julie Swain, who was also on cross-country. I didn't think they'd been going out. Maybe she'd wanted to and he hadn't. That would explain why he wasn't texting back.

Clearly, Damien and I weren't ever going to get into the social part of the social. He had something on his mind and I had nothing but him on my own. We'd lost Wes, and Sung, Frances, and Gordon were still on the dance floor. Sung looked like it was a job being there, while Gordon was in his own little world. It was Frances who fascinated me the most.

"She almost looks happy," I said. "I don't know if I've ever seen her happy."

Damien nodded and drank some more punch. "She's always so serious," he agreed.

The punch was turning our lips cherry-red.

"Let's get out of here," I said.

"Okay."

We were alone together in an unknown hotel in an unknown city. So we did the natural thing.

We went to his room.

And we watched TV.

It was his room, so he got to choose. We ended up watching *The Departed* on basic cable. It was, I realized, the most time we had ever spent alone together. He lay back on his bed and I sat on

Sung's, making sure the angle was such that I could watch Damien as much as I watched the TV.

During the first commercial break, I asked, "Is something wrong?"

He looked at me strangely. "No. Does it seem like something's wrong?"

I shook my head. "No. Just asking."

During the second commercial break, I asked, "Were you and Julie going out?"

He put his head back on his pillow and closed his eyes.

"No." And then, about a minute later, right before the movie started again, "It wasn't anything, really."

During the third commercial break, I asked, "Does she know that?"

"What?"

"Does Julie know it wasn't anything?"

"No," he said. "It looks like she doesn't know that."

This was it, I was sure — the point where he'd ask for my advice. I could help him. I could prove myself worthy of his company.

But he let it drop. He didn't want to talk about it. He wanted to watch the movie.

I realized he needed to reveal himself to me in his own time. I couldn't rush it. I had to be patient. For the remaining commercial breaks, I made North Dakota jokes. He laughed at some of them, and even threw in a few of his own.

Sung came back when there were about fifteen minutes left in the movie. I could tell he wasn't thrilled about me sitting on his bed, but I wasn't about to move.

"Sung," I told him, "if this whole quiz bowl thing doesn't work out for you, I think you have a future in disco."

"Shut up," he grumbled, taking off the famous jacket and hanging it in the closet.

We watched the rest of the movie in silence, with Sung sitting on the edge of Damien's bed. As soon as the credits were rolling, Sung announced it was time to go to sleep.

"But where are you sleeping?" I asked, spreading out on his sheets.

"That's my bed," he said.

I wanted to offer Sung a swap—he could stay with Wes and talk about polynomials all night, while I could stay with Damien. But clearly that wasn't a real option.

Damien walked me to the door.

"Lay off the minibar," he said. "We need you sober tomorrow."

"I'll try," I replied. "But those little bottles are just so pretty."

He chuckled and hit me lightly on the shoulder.

"Resist," he commanded.

Again, I told him I'd try.

Wes was in bed and the lights were off when I got to my room, so I very quietly changed into my pajamas and brushed my teeth.

I was about to nod off in my bed when Wes's voice asked, "Did you have fun?"

"Yeah," I said. "Damien and I went to his room and watched *The Departed*. It was a good time. We looked for you, but you were already gone."

"That social sucked."

"It most certainly did."

I closed my eyes.

"Good night," Wes said softly, making it sound like a true wish. Nobody besides my parents had ever said it to me like this before.

"Good night," I said back. Then I made sure he'd plugged the clock back in, and went to sleep.

The next morning, we kicked North Dakota's ass. Then, for good measure, we erased Maryland from the boards and made Oklahoma cry.

168

It felt good.

"Don't get too cocky," Sung warned us, which was pretty precious, since Sung was the cockiest of us all. I half expected "We Are the Champions" to come blaring out of his ears every time we won a round.

Our fourth and last match of the day — the quarterfinals — was against the team from Clearwater, Florida, which had made it to the finals for each of the past ten years, winning four of those times. They were legendary, insofar as people like Sung had heard about them and studied their strategies, with some tapes Mr. Phillips had managed to get off Clearwater local access.

As usual, even though I was the alternate, I was put on the starting lineup. Because Clearwater was especially known for treating the canon like a cannon to demolish the other team.

"Bring it on," I said.

It soon became clear who my counterpart on the Clearwater team was — a wispy girl with straight brown hair who could barely bother to put down her Muriel Spark in order to start playing. The first time she opened her mouth, she revealed their secret weapon: She was British.

Frances looked momentarily frightened by this, but I took it in stride. When the girl lunged with Byron, I parried with Asimov. When she volleyed with Burgess, I pounced with Roth. Neither of us missed a question, so it became a test of buzzer willpower. I started to ring in a split-second before I knew the answer. And I always knew the answer.

Until I did the unthinkable.

I buzzed in for a science question.

Which Nobel prize winner later went on to write The Double Helix *and* Avoid Boring People*?*

I realized immediately it wasn't Saul Bellow or Kenzaburo Oe.

As the judge said, "Do you have an answer?" the phrase *The Double Helix* hit in my head.

169

"Crick!" I exclaimed.

The judge looked at me for a moment, then down at his card.

"That is incorrect. Clearwater, which Nobel prize winner later went on to write *The Double Helix* and *Avoid Boring People?*"

It was not the lit girl who buzzed in.

"James *D.* Watson," one of the math boys answered snottily, the D sent as a particular *fuck you* to me.

"Sorry," I whispered to my team.

"It's okay," Damien said.

"No worries," Wes said.

Sung, I knew, wouldn't be as forgiving.

I was now off my game and more cautious with the buzzer, so Brit girl got the best of me on Caliban and Vivienne Haigh-Wood. I managed to stick *One Hundred Years of Solitude* in edgewise, but that was scant comfort. I mean, who didn't know *One Hundred Years of Solitude?*

Clearwater had a one-question lead with three questions left. And it ended up that the last questions were about math, history, and geography. So I sat back while Sung rocked the relative areas of a rhombus and a circle, Wes sent a little love General Omar Bradley's way, and Frances wrapped it up with Tashkent, which I had not known to be the capital of Uzbekistan, its name translating as "Stone City."

Usually we burst out of our chairs when we won, but this match had been so exhausting that we could only feel relieved. We shook the other team's hands—Brit girl's hand felt like it was made of paper, which I found weird.

After Clearwater had left the room, Sung called an emergency team meeting.

"That was too close," he said. Not "congratulations" or "nice work."

No, Sung was pissed.

He talked about the need to be more aggressive on the buzzer, but also to exercise care. He said we should always *play to our strengths*. To make a blunder was to *destroy the fabric of our entire team*.

"I get it, I get it," I said.

"No," Sung told me, "I don't think you do."

"Sung," Mr. Phillips cautioned.

"I think he needs to hear this," Sung insisted. "From the very start of the year, he has refused to be a team player. And what we saw today was nothing short of an insurrection. He broke the unwritten rules."

"*He* is standing right here," I pointed out. "Just come right out and say it."

"YOU ARE NOT TO ANSWER SCIENCE QUESTIONS!" Sung yelled. "WHAT WERE YOU THINKING?"

"Hey—" Damien started to interrupt.

I held up my hand. "No, it's okay. Sung needs to get this out of his system."

"You are the *alternate*," Sung went on.

"You don't seem to mind it when I'm answering questions, Sung."

"We only have you here because we have to!"

"That's enough," Mr. Phillips said decisively.

"No, it's not enough," I said. "I'm sick of you all acting like I'm this English freak raining on your little math–science parade. Sung seems to think my contribution to this team is a little less than everyone else's."

"Anyone can memorize book titles!" Sung shouted.

"Oh, please. Like I care what you think? You don't even know the difference between Keats and Byron."

"The difference between Keats and Byron doesn't matter!"

"None of this matters!" I shouted back. "Don't you get it, Sung? NONE OF THIS MATTERS. Yes, you have knowledge—but you're not doing anything with it. You're *reciting* it. You're not out curing cancer—you're *listing the names of the people who've tried to cure cancer.* This whole thing is a joke, Captain. It's *trivial.* Which is why everyone laughs at us."

"You think we're all trivial?" Sung challenged.

"No," I said. "I think *you're* trivial with your quiz bowl obsession. The rest of us have other things going on. We have lives."

"You're the one who's not a part of our team! You're the outcast!"

"If that's so true, Sung, then why are you the only one of us wearing a fucking varsity jacket? Why don't you think anyone else wanted to be seen in one? It's not just me, Sung. It's all of us."

"Enough!" Mr. Phillips yelled.

Sung looked like he wanted to kill me. And at the same time, I knew he'd never look at that damn jacket the same way again.

"Why don't we all take a break over dinner," Mr. Phillips went on, "then regroup in my room at eight for a scrimmage before the semifinals tomorrow morning. I don't know who we're facing, but we're going to need to be a team to face them."

What we did next wasn't very teamlike: Mr. Phillips, a brooding Sung, Frances, and Gordon went one way for dinner, while Wes, Damien, and I went another way.

"There's a Steak 'n Shake a few blocks away," Wes told us. Clearly, he'd done his research.

"Sounds good," Damien said.

I, brooding as well, followed.

"It was a question about books," I said once we'd left the hotel. "I didn't realize it was a science question."

"Crick wasn't that far off," Wes pointed out.

"Yeah, but I still fucked it up."

"And we still won," Damien said.

Yeah, I knew that.

But I wasn't feeling it.

Damien and Wes saw I was down and tried to cheer me up. Not just by getting my burger and shake for me, but by sitting across from me and treating me like a friend.

"God, there are a lot of fat people in Indiana!" Wes exclaimed.

"They're probably looking at you and saying the same thing," Damien replied.

Wes smiled and shook his head. "I know, I know." Then he ate his three cheeseburgers.

"So how does it feel to be the Quiz Bowl Antichrist?" Damien asked in a mock-sportscaster voice, holding an invisible microphone out for my reply.

"Well, as James *D*. Watson said, I'm the motherfuckin' princess. All other quiz bowlers shall bow down to me. Because you know what?"

"What?" Damien and Wes both asked.

"One of these days, I'm going to be the *goddamn answer* to a quiz bowl question."

"Yeah," Wes said. "'What quiz bowl alternate murdered his team captain in the semifinals and later wrote a book, *Among Boring People*?'"

Damien shook his head. "Not funny. There will be no murder tonight or tomorrow."

"Do you realize, if we win this thing, it's going to come up on Google Search for the rest of our lives?" I said.

"Let's wear masks in the photo," Wes suggested.

"I'll be Michelangelo. You can be Donatello."

And it went on like this for a while. Damien stopped talking and just watched me and Wes going back and forth. I was talking, but mostly I was watching him back. The green-blue of his eyes. The side of his neck. The curl of hair that dangled over the left corner of his forehead. No matter where I looked, there was something to see.

I didn't have any control over it. Something inside of me was shifting. Everything I'd refused to articulate was starting to spell itself out. Not as knowledge, but as the impulse beneath the knowledge. I knew I wanted to be with him, and I was also starting to feel why. He was a reason I was here. He was a reason it mattered.

I was talking to Wes, but really I was talking to Damien through what I was saying to Wes. I wanted him to find me entertaining. I wanted him to find me interesting. I wanted him to find me.

We were done pretty quickly, and before I knew it we were walking back to the Westin. Once we got to the lobby, Wes magically decided to head back to our room until the "scrimmage" at eight. That left Damien and me with two hours and nothing to do.

"Why don't we go to my room?" Damien suggested.

I didn't argue. I started to feel nervous — unreasonably nervous. We were just two friends going to a room. There wasn't anything else to it. And yet … he hadn't mentioned watching TV, and last time he'd said, "Why don't we go to my room to watch TV?"

"I'm glad it's just the two of us," I ventured.

"Yeah, me, too," Damien said.

We rode the elevator in silence and walked down the hallway in silence. When we got to the door, he swiped his electronic key in the lock and got a green light on the first try. I could never manage to do that.

"After you," he said, opening the door and gesturing me in.

I walked forward, down the small hallway, turning toward the beds. And that's when I realized — there was someone in the room. And it was Sung. And he was on his bed. And he wasn't wearing his jacket. Or a shirt. And he was moaning a little.

I thought we'd caught him jerking off. I couldn't help it—I burst out laughing. And that's what made him notice we were in the room. He jumped and turned around, and I realized Frances was in the bed with him, shirt also off, but bra still on.

It was all so messed up that I couldn't stop laughing. Tears were coming to my eyes.

"Get out!" Sung yelled.

"I'm sorry, Frances," I said between laughing fits. "I'm so sorry."

"GET OUT!" Sung screamed again, standing up now. Thank god he still had his pants on. "YOU ARE THE DEVIL. THE DEVIL!"

"I prefer Antichrist," I told him.

"THE DEVIL!"

"*THE DEVIL!*" I mimicked back.

I felt Damien's hand on my shoulder. "Let's go," he whispered.

"This is so pathetic," I said. "Sung, man, you're *pathetic.*"

Sung lunged forward then, and Damien stepped in between us.

"Go," Damien told me. "*Now.*"

I was laughing again, so I apologized to Frances again, then I pulled myself into the hallway, where I doubled over with more laughter.

Damien came out a few seconds later and closed the door behind us.

"Holy shit!" I said. "That was hysterical!"

"Stop it," Damien said. "Enough."

"Enough?" I laughed again. "I haven't even started."

Damien shook his head.

"You're cold, man," he said. "I can't believe how cold you are."

"What?" I asked. "You don't find this funny?"

"You have no heart."

This sobered me up pretty quickly. "How can you say that?" I asked. It made no sense to me. "How can you, of all people, say that?"

"What does that mean? Me, of all people?"

He'd gotten me.

"Alec?"

"I don't know!" I shouted. "Okay? *I don't know.*"

This sounded like the truth, but it was feeling less than that. I knew. Or I was starting to know.

"I do have a heart," I said. But I stopped there. I couldn't tell him what was inside it. Because I still wasn't sure of myself. The only thing I was sure of was that he wouldn't want to hear it.

I could feel it all coming apart. The collapse of all those invisible plans, the appearance of all those hidden thoughts. I couldn't let him see it. I had to get out of there.

I bolted. I left him right there in the hallway. I didn't wait for the elevator—I hit the emergency stairs. I ran like I was the one on the cross-country team, even when I heard him following me.

"Don't!" I yelled back at him.

I got to my floor and ran to my room. The card wouldn't work the first time, and I nervously looked at the stairway exit, waiting for him to show up. But he must've stopped. He must've heard. I got the key through the second time.

Wes was on his bed, reading a comic.

"You're back early," he said, not looking up.

I couldn't say a thing. There was a knock on the door. Damien calling out my name.

"Don't answer it," I said. "Please, don't answer it."

I locked myself in the bathroom. I stared at the mirror.

I heard Wes murmur something to Damien through the door without opening it. Then he was at my door.

"Alec? Are you okay?"

"I'm fine," I said, but my voice was soggy coming out of my throat.

"Open up."

I couldn't. I sat on the lip of the tub, breathing in, breathing out. I remembered the look on Sung's face and started to laugh. Then I thought of Frances lying there and felt sad. I wondered if I really didn't have a heart.

"Alec," Wes said again, gently. "Come on."

I waited until he walked off again. Then I opened the door and went into the bedroom. He was back on his bed, but he hadn't picked up the comic. He was sitting on the edge, waiting for me.

I told him what had happened. Not the part about Damien at first, but the part about Sung and Frances. He didn't laugh, and neither did I. Then I told him Damien's reaction to my reaction, without going into what was underneath.

"Do you think I'm cold?" I asked him. "Really—am I?"

"You're not cold," he said. "You're just so angry."

I must've looked surprised by this. He went on.

"You can be a total prick, Alec. There's nothing wrong with that—all of us can be total pricks. We like to think that just because we're geeks, that means we can't be assholes. But we can be. Most of the time, though, it's not coming from meanness or coldness. It's coming from anger. Or sadness. I mean, I see fat people, and I just want to rip them apart."

"But why do I want to rip Sung apart?"

"I don't know. Because he's a prick, too. And maybe you feel if you rip apart the quiz bowl geek, no one will think of you as a quiz bowl geek."

"But I'm not a quiz bowl geek!"

"Haven't you figured it out yet?" Wes asked. "Nobody's a quiz bowl geek. We're all just people. And you're right, what we do here has no redeeming social value whatsoever. But it can be an interesting way to pass the time."

I sat down on my bed, facing Wes so that our knees almost touched.

"I'm not a very happy person," I told him. "But sometimes I can trick myself into thinking I am."

"And where does Damien fit into all this, if I may ask?"

I shook my head. "I really have no idea. I'm still figuring it out."

"You know he likes girls?"

"I said, I'm still figuring it out."

"Fair enough."

I paused, realizing what had just been said.

"Is it that obvious?" I asked Wes.

"Only to me," he said.

It would take me another three months to understand why.

"Meanwhile," he went on, *"Sung and Frances."*

"Holy shit, right?"

"Yeah, holy shit. And you know the worst part?"

"I can't imagine what's worse than seeing it with my own eyes."

"Gordon is totally in love with Frances."

"No!"

"Yup. I wouldn't miss practice tonight for all the money in the world."

We all showed up. Mr. Phillips could sense there was some tension in the room, but he truly had no idea.

Frances was wearing Sung's varsity jacket. And suddenly I didn't mind it so much.

Gordon glared at Sung.

Sung glared at me.

178

I avoided Damien's eye.

When I looked at Wes, he made me feel like I might be worth saving.

Amazingly enough, during practice we were back in fighting form, as if nothing had happened. I felt like I could admit to myself how much I wanted to win. And, not just that, how much I wanted our team to win. More for Wes and Frances and Gordon and Damien than anything else.

After we were done, Damien asked me if we could talk for a minute. Everyone else headed back to their rooms and we went down to the lobby. Other quiz bowl groups were swarming around; those that hadn't made the semifinals were taking it for what it was—a night where, for a brief pause in their high school lives, they were free from any pressure or care.

"I'm sorry," Damien said to me. "I was completely off base."

"It's okay. I shouldn't have been so mean to Sung and Frances. I should've just left."

We just sat there.

"I don't know why I did that," he said. "Reacted that way."

It would take him another four months to figure it out. It would be a little too late, but he'd figure it out anyway.

We lost in the semifinals to the Des Moines School for the Blind. I knew from the look Sung gave me afterward that he would blame me for the loss for the rest of his life. Not because I missed the questions—and I did get two wrong this time. But for destroying his own invisible plans.

Looking back, I don't think I've ever hated any piece of clothing as much as I hated Sung's varsity jacket for those few weeks. You can't hate something that much unless you hate yourself equally as much. Not in that kind of way.

It was, I guess, Wes who taught me that. Later, when we were back home and trying to articulate ourselves better, I asked him how he'd known so much more than I had.

"Because I read, stupid," was his answer.

We lost in the semifinals, but the local paper took our picture anyway. Sung looks serious and aggrieved. Gordon looks awkward. Frances looks calm. Damien looks oblivious. And Wes and me?

We look like we're in on our own joke.

In other words, happy.

All of the science facts in **David Levithan's** story had to be found and/or checked on the Internet. The English facts came from his head. Take out the Internet part, and you pretty much have a summation of his academic career from kindergarten through college.

David's books include *Boy Meets Boy*, *The Realm of Possibility*, *Are We There Yet?*, *Marly's Ghost*, *Wide Awake*, *Love is the Higher Law*, and (with Rachel Cohn) *Nick & Norah's Infinite Playlist* and *Naomi & Ely's No Kiss List*. His next book is a collaboration with John Green, entitled *Will Grayson, Will Grayson*.

He still remembers who wrote *Cry, the Beloved Country*, but has completely forgotten how to work a sine or a cosine.

181

How to Cosplay with Common Household Objects

Grandma might have a surprising assortment of blue wigs.

Don't overlook the kitchen.

Dad's closet can be fun, too.

Bathroom is not just a place to get clean.

And who knows what you'll find in the garage?

THE QUIET KNIGHT
by garth nix

"No going out till you've split that wood, Tony. All two tons, you hear?"

Tony looked up from lacing his outdoor boots and made a gesture to indicate he'd already done the job. His father understood the sign, but he still went outside to check, returning a few minutes later as Tony was finishing winding the lace around the top of his left boot.

"When did you do it?"

Tony held up five fingers and curled back his forefinger, to make it four and a half.

"Four thirty? This morning before school?" his father exclaimed. "You're crazy, son. But good for you. You must have chopped like crazy."

Tony nodded. He *had* chopped like crazy. He'd enjoyed it though, crossing the lawn to the shed, the frost cracking under his boots. It had been cold to start with, and quite dark under the single lightbulb swaying on its lead high above his head. But as he'd swung the blockbuster, split the wood and stacked it, he'd gotten hot very quickly, and the sun had come up bright and strong.

"What is it tonight? Basketball practice?"

Tony nodded again, and shrugged on his backpack. It was a full-on hiker's backpack, not a school satchel or day bag. He carried it everywhere outside school, notionally for all his sporting equipment, and his father had gotten used to it long ago and didn't inquire about what was actually inside.

"Considering how much practice you do it's a wonder you guys never win a game," said his father. He'd been an all-round athlete in his youth, and he couldn't help but needle Tony a little about his lack of sporting success. He didn't come to the games, either, not for the last few years. He didn't like being with the other dads when Tony's team didn't win. He was also too busy. Though they lived on a farm on the outskirts of the city, it was a hobby farm, a tax deduction and sideline interest for his dad, who was a senior executive in some shadowy government intelligence outfit. Tony's mother and younger sister lived on the other side of the city, almost an hour's drive away. He spent some time with them, but not much. He preferred the farm, even though it took him forty minutes to get to school on the bus.

Tony settled his pack, then mimed turning a car key to his dad.

"You want to borrow the monster again?"

Tony nodded.

"You know, it wouldn't hurt you to talk to me."

"Sorry," mumbled Tony. His voice was low and scratchy. It sounded like a rough scrubbing brush being drawn across broken stones. He'd accidentally drunk some bathroom cleaner when he was little, and it had burned his throat and larynx. His mother had blamed his father for it, and his father still blamed himself. "Can I borrow the car?"

"Of course. Be careful. No drinking after practice. None at all, you hear?"

Tony nodded. He looked old enough that he could easily pass for legal drinking age. He stood six foot four in bare feet, and took after his father in both his heavy build and an early onset of dark stubble on his face. He didn't plan on drinking and he wasn't going to basketball practice anyway.

186

He took the keys to the farm truck. His father moved as if to hug him, but didn't follow through. Tony waited stolidly, ready to hug if that was what was required to get the keys.

"Okay. I'll see you later. I'll be in my study, working till late. Check in when you get home."

Tony nodded and walked out into the cool, near-freezing air of the night.

The backpack held his armor, belt, helmet, and mask. His foam-wrapped PVC pipe boffer sword was in a sack in the tray of the truck. Tony checked to make sure it was still there. His dad hardly ever used the truck and practically never looked in the back, but a good knight always checks his weapons before venturing to battle.

That night's game was being held in the usual place, the old wool shed and farm buildings on Dave Nash's family property. Dave was a big mover and shaker in LARP circles; he'd been involved in live-action role-playing for more than twenty years. He was in his forties, heavier and slower than in the old pictures and videos Tony had seen. He was still a tough fighter, though he mostly ran the games rather than participating in them.

Tony parked the truck off the road a half mile from the Nash property, edging it well behind a fringe of trees. It was a rural road, and not much traveled, but there would be other LARP gamers heading along it later and he didn't want them to spot him or the vehicle.

It took him ten minutes to get his armor on. First there was the athletic supporter and the padded undergarment, which were easy enough. It was the thigh-length hauberk made of thousands of steel rings that was the hassle. It was a lot easier if you had help to lace the back up, but he'd worked out a method using a long leather strap and a lot of wriggling about.

He didn't change his boots, but tied on a pair of gaiters that disguised them so they looked more medieval. The hauberk was long enough to protect his thighs, but he strapped on converted ice-hockey armor to his knees and shins. It was painted black and looked okay, at least it would in the partially lit game that would occur tonight.

Tony's helmet was fairly basic. Unlike the hauberk, which he'd bought with the unwitting assistance of his mother, he'd made it himself in Dave's workshop with a lot of help. It was modeled on a classic Norman nasal-bar helmet and went on over a padded lining and a mail coif, which also protected his neck.

With almost everything on, Tony added the final unique touch: a half-mask of beaten gold (actually gold paint over tough plastic) that covered his face from his chin to just below his eyes. It locked onto the nasal bar and the sides of the helmet and was perforated so he could breathe. And talk, if he wanted to do that.

All armored up, Tony tested his movement, jumping, springing, lunging and stepping back. Everything was on right and tight, so he strapped on his belt and put on his leather gauntlets. Last of all he took up his sword, practiced a few test swings and cuts, then laid it at rest on his shoulder.

There was a beaten track made by the sheep along the inside of the barbed wire fence that paralleled the road some ten yards in. Tony had made a rough stile when he first started going to the LARP sessions a few years before, just a log up against a corner post that he could run up and jump down on the other side. He checked that, too, before he went over. It would be very embarrassing to break a leg out here alone, in full armor. . . .

As he always did, Tony stopped at the edge of the roadside trees to observe who was waiting outside the woolshed, before he went on. The woolshed itself was huge, a vast barnlike relic of bygone days when two hundred shearers had worked inside, shearing several thousand sheep a day. Dave Nash had partitioned it up inside with moveable walls and scenery like a theater so he could arrange all kinds of different scenarios. The LARP group used the paddocks outside as well as the smaller buildings. For evening games like this one, they always chose a night when the moon was full. It wasn't up yet, so all the exterior lights were on, including the big floodlights at the front of the woolshed. They lit up the bare dirt field in front that was used as a car park.

There were half a dozen cars there now, parked as far from the woolshed as possible, in the half-dark so they wouldn't detract from the atmosphere. Tony recognized all but one of them. Seeing a strange car made him cautious, so he carefully scanned the group around the front steps of the woolshed.

Dave Nash was standing there, wearing his wizard's robes, which meant he would be the gamemaster and not an active participant. Next to him were the twins, Jubal and Jirah, equipped and dressed as elven scouts in green and tan leather, with their boffer long swords at their sides. They didn't have their bows. Dave didn't allow even boffered bows, since he'd nearly lost an eye a few years before. Other groups did use them, and Jubal and Jirah were fine archers, even with the very light draw bows used in LARP.

Besides Jubal and Jirah, there were five regulars Tony knew, all of them already geared up in armor from Dave's Orc armory, with an array of foam-core axes, halberds, and other polearms. Their latex masks and helmets were stacked on the steps. No one put them on until they had to. It got very hot and sweaty very quickly fighting in a latex mask. But it looked good.

That meant the strange car belonged to the two people Tony didn't know. A girl he guessed was around his age, who wasn't wearing armor, but a serviceable dress of red and gold, square-cut around the neck. She had a lute on her back and a reed pipe through the gold cloth belt she wore, so she was clearly a bard.

The boy at her side was younger and had the same dark but slightly strange good looks as the girl, so Tony guessed they were brother and sister. He wore leather trousers, a leather brigandine coat and a leather cap that was a bit like a WWI aviator's helmet.

Two long daggers were thrust through broad loops on his belt. Boffer weapons didn't scabbard very easily. The foam cladding made them bulky but was of course essential to not getting hurt.

Dave walked up to the top step, tapping his way with his six-foot oaken staff that was tipped with a Cyalume chemical light. He turned at the top and spread his arms wide.

"Are all who would essay tonight's adventure present?"

"Aye!" called the people around the steps.

Tony hesitated, then strode forward toward the light, stamping his feet as he walked so he made more noise.

"Ah, the Quiet Knight approaches!" declaimed Dave, a smile flitting across his face. He was the only one who knew who Tony actually was, and he respected the confidence. "You are welcome, as always, Sir Silent."

Tony saluted with his sword, and went to stand off to one side, near but not close to Jubal and Jirah.

"We have two newcomers, recently moved to our fair realm," said Dave. "Sorayah the Bard, and Horace the Halfling Rogue. Welcome, Sorayah and Horace."

Sorayah was cute, Tony thought, and she and Horace were definitely sister and brother. They had the same nose and eyes, and probably the same ears, though it was hard to tell, as Horace had stuck artificial hairy ears over his own.

"Tonight we seek to find a passage through the ancient tunnels of Harukn-Dzhur," said Dave. He nodded at the orcs, who picked up their masks and helmets and walked off to one of the entrances around the side of the woolshed. "If we can but find a way, we may escape those who have pursued us from the wilds...."

Tony listened carefully as Dave set up the scene. "Tunnels" meant that Dave would have spent the last week rearranging the walls and lowering the temporary ceilings inside the woolshed, and there would be lots of close combat, with only enough light for safety. Dave liked strobe lights, too, and color effects for magic, and he had a lot to work with, since he'd bought all the old lighting gear, sets, and props when the city had condemned the Alder Street Theater.

"We begin with the long crawl through the zigzag way," intoned Dave. "Horace, will you scout a little way ahead? Not too far, mind. Ten feet, no more."

"Aye," said Horace. He drew his daggers and moved to the door.

"Sir Silent, if you would follow, and Sorayah behind you," said Dave. "I task you with protecting the Bard, for she wears no armor, and we will need her magic and her song in times to come. I will follow, and Jubal and Jirah will guard our rear."

Sorayah came over to Tony and curtsied, inadvertently giving him a good look down the front of her dress.

Tony bowed back. He was glad she couldn't see him blush.

"I thank you for your protection, gallant knight," she said. He liked her voice. It sounded cool and pure, and she had the trace of some foreign accent that sounded real, not like it was put on for the game.

He bowed again, and led the way up the steps. Horace was lying on his stomach, listening at the gap in the bottom of the door. As Tony approached, he stood up and slowly opened it. There was darkness within, but slowly a weak red light blossomed, revealing a narrow passage no more than three feet high.

"The long crawl!" hissed Dave. "Let the adventure begin!"

◦

Tony didn't get home till just before midnight, his curfew time. It had been a great game, one of the best, and the others had stayed behind to have a drink and chat around the fire, wrapped in the cloaks from a long-ago Alder Street production of *Henry V.*

191

Tony had wanted to stay too, to talk to Sorayah, and it wasn't the curfew that stopped him. It was his inability to talk. He knew that as soon as he opened his mouth and she heard his hoarse crow-voice her face would show scorn, or even worse, pity. He didn't want that. She respected him as the Quiet Knight; they had enjoyed playing their parts; it was best to keep whatever they had in the game.

Tony laughed at himself for thinking such stupid thoughts. Whatever they had! They didn't have anything. He'd protected her in the game, sure enough, and had taken bruises enough to show for it, including the one across the back of his left hand that was coming up purple and brown. But that didn't mean anything in real life. He didn't even know her real name, or where she lived, or anything.

Tony was sore and his arms and legs were very stiff the next morning. Splitting two tons of wood for the potbelly stove and later fighting for four hours was way too much, too much even for a blindingly hot shower to totally remedy. His bruises had come up as well, on his hand and forearms and the back of one leg. He applied anti-inflammatory cream to the worst of them, but didn't take a painkiller.

The bus trip to school was normal. Tony sat two-thirds of the way to the back, alone as always, with the hood of his sweatshirt pulled up over his head. He was big and mean-looking enough that the bullies and the petty annoyers left him alone, but since he didn't talk, no one else interacted with him, either. In fact, most of them, including the bullies, were afraid of his dark, hooded presence, though he didn't know that.

He spent the time looking out the window, wondering what the hell he was doing with his life. There was one more year of school to get through, which he could do. His grades were good, better than anyone ever expected from a silent ox. But he had no friends. Not real friends. Dave was the closest to a real friend that he had, but Dave had a family and a job and was just being kind to a kid.

Tony supposed he could be friends with Jubal and Jirah. They went to the same school, though they were a year behind. They had lots of friends, too, gamers and fantasy freaks and alternative drama types. That was the trouble. Tony already felt he was an outcast. A disguised outcast, to be sure. He looked normal enough. No one in the street would ever know he that he had a weird voice and liked to dress up and play pretend fighting.

If he revealed himself to Jubal and Jirah as the Quiet Knight, they probably would welcome him as a friend, and he could hang out with their friends. But everyone would know he was a real weirdo. Besides, if he had friends they'd expect him to talk....

What would the Quiet Knight do? Tony asked himself. *Not talk, that's for sure. He'd just get on with things, in his own quiet way....*

The bus stopped outside the school. Tony waited for everyone to get out, then slowly followed, steeling himself for another day of trying to minimally answer questions. The teachers usually didn't push him too much now, not after a long trial with one particular English teacher a few years before, which had ended with Tony still stubbornly refusing to deliver a speech, his father raging in the principal's office, and the teacher requesting a job transfer to another school.

The usual stream of student foot traffic filled the front drive, most of them heading for the main doors, with knots of people here and there delaying the inevitable. Tony strode through them, his mind on last night's game. Younger students scattered out of his way without him noticing. He didn't know that he was a legend to the lower years, his reluctance to talk transformed into a story of backwoods tongue mutilation and bloody revenge. Even if the backwoods in question were only ten miles past the outer suburbs.

There was a small commotion just before the doors, to the

left of the front steps in the blind spot that was hidden from the security cameras out front and the gaze of the teacher on door duty. There often was something going on there; it was a favorite spot for some casual bullying or lunch money shakedowns. Tony never paid much attention to this kind of thing. It never happened to him.

This time, he stopped. Two students were being terrorized by five of the spoiled brat girls, the ones who liked to think they were rough and tough and had some kind of gang readily identifiable by infected eyebrow piercings without the studs (since the school wouldn't allow it) and expensive leather jackets bought by their daddies and driven over to rough them up.

The two students being tormented were Soraya and Horace. Soraya was wearing another medieval-style dress, this time in dark yellow. She looked good, but totally out of place at school. Horace, though in jeans and a T-shirt, still had on the stupid hairy ears. Two of the self-proclaimed bad girls were holding Soraya back with difficulty; two more were holding Horace, and the five-eyebrow-piercings leader, whose name was Ellen, was trying to tear the ears off Horace.

"They're stuck on; he can't get them off!" Soraya shouted. She shook off one of the girls and swung at Ellen, but there were too many of them and she was dragged back.

"Stop! Let him go!"

A baseball cap was shoved in Soraya's mouth, muffling her shouts. She kept struggling, kicking back at her captors' knees. Horace was trying to bite his enemies, tears of pain welling up as his real ears were twisted every which way.

Tony saw Soraya's frantic gaze as she looked every which way for help. But her gaze swept across him and then she was bundled farther back into the shadow of the stairs.

He'd been invisible to her. Just another student who wasn't going to help, who didn't want to get involved, or cross Ellen and her gang.

It wasn't just her and her half-dozen girls. There were their boyfriends as well, most of whom were bad-tempered second-string jocks who weren't good enough to focus all their energy on sports.

Tony stopped for what felt like ages, but could not have been longer than a second. Then he continued on up the steps, crashing through several slower students.

I can't intervene, he thought. *She's in a medieval dress. He's got hobbit ears on. They won't really hurt her. . . .*

He stopped before the doors as another thought struck him like a blow to the heart.

What would the Quiet Knight do?

Tony turned about and pulled back his hood before taking a very deep breath. The students coming up the stairs parted like the red sea as he stood there, taking another breath, sucking in the air as if he were taking in strength.

I must do it, he thought. *And I will talk to her, even if she does laugh.*

He ran down the stairs. Students sprang aside and dragged their friends out of his path and turned to watch as Tony picked Ellen up and lifted her over his head and then gently but very firmly deposited her on the steps.

"Sit," he ordered. Ellen gulped and sat on the step, and Tony turned to the other girls.

"Let them go."

His voice was as peculiar and scratchy and variably pitched as ever, but coming immediately after lifting their leader above his head, incredibly effective. The bad girls released Soraya and Horace and backed away.

"They are under my protection," rasped Tony. "You will never even talk to them again, understand?"

The bad girls nodded.

"Go to class," added Tony. He stabbed a finger at Ellen. "You, too. And keep your mouths shut."

Ellen stood, and for a moment Tony thought she might do something. But she turned away and went up the stairs, with her minions hurrying after her.

Tony turned back to Soraya, and the words that had so gloriously issued from his mouth failed him. She smiled and curtsied. He looked up and blushed and averted his gaze to Horace, who shrugged and rubbed his ears.

"Super glue, all right?" said Horace. "So it was a bad idea. It goes with being called Horace in the first place. Stupid parents. They can't organize laundry either or my sister—"

"Thank you again, Sir Silent," interrupted Soraya, with a quelling glance at her brother. She stepped closer to Tony, and looked up at him. He thought that it would be very easy to rest his chin upon her silky head and draw her close.

Tony tried to ask her how she knew who he was. No sound came out, but his puzzled frown was clear enough.

"Your eyes are very distinctive," said Soraya. "And the bruise on your arm."

Tony nodded slowly, and gulped again. He was making a fool of himself, he knew, and he felt an incredibly strong compulsion to back away, to pull his hood up and just disappear.

But he wanted to stay, he wanted to talk, and so he fought against the urge to run.

"My name really is Soraya, by the way."

Tony cleared his throat. Soraya waited patiently, smiling, looking straight into his eyes. The world faded away around them as Tony gulped at the air again and searched for the words that he knew he had to say.

"Tony," said the Quiet Knight at last. "My name is Tony."

Garth Nix is the bestselling and award-winning author of more than seventeen novels, several role-playing magazine articles and scenarios, and an unpublished journal of the five-year Dungeons and Dragons campaign he ran between the ages of 11 and 16. A keen role-player in his student years, Garth was involved in running very large "free-form" role-playing events in the late 1970s and early 1980s in Australia, including the creation of a starport for 250 role-players in a school assembly hall. Long ago he also used to fight duels with PVC pipe swords while wearing a motorcycle helmet and several old leather coats that didn't provide much protection but did slow everything down. Garth is also deeply interested in computers, the weather, military history, strategy and role-playing games, fantasy and science fiction, and many other highly geektastic subjects. Garth is married, with two children, and lives near a beach in Sydney, Australia.

What Your Instrument Says About You

Flute: If you're a girl, the boys find it hot. If you're a boy, the boys still find it hot.

Tuba: No one ever messes with you. You are the bouncer of band.

Piano: What you really want to do is write your own songs.

Guitar: You sleep with everyone else in band.

Drums: No one thinks you know what you're doing even though you know more music theory than they do.

Triangle: This doesn't look as good on your college application as you think.

EVERYONE BUT YOU
by lisa yee

I had never seen the ocean, Ohio being a landlocked state, when suddenly I found myself adrift on an island. My mother was terrified of water, but even more scared of being poor. That's why she agreed to marry Mr. Hunter. He was the answer to her prayers—although he didn't look like an angel or Jesus, or any of the assorted saints she was constantly making deals with. No, Mr. Hunter looked like an old man on the verge of dying, which was exactly what he was.

◎

"Felicity, you're nuts not to be thrilled," Natalie Catrine kept screaming. "To leave Ohio for Hawaii—that's like living a dream!"

I was thrilled, at first. Yet the closer our move date, the more unsure I became. Leaving my friends would be hard. Everyone in Asher (population 5,728) knew my name and who I was. There, it didn't matter that I was poor. Lots of kids were poor, so it was no big deal. Like having hazel eyes, or bleached blond hair from a box, or a brother who was mentally ill, it was just part of who you were.

Known for my indomitable school spirit, I was voted Asher High Miss Pep for two years in a row and on track to snag it again. But it was my baton twirling skills that got me in the local newspaper almost as often as Mrs. Harvey's tree-climbing English setter. As head majorette, I lead our well-rehearsed team of eight twirlers. I even designed our red spangled uniforms.

We debuted our new look on Nigel Franklin Day. He was the star of that cheesy cable TV reality show, *Nigel, Nigel, Are You Listening?* When the City Council learned he'd be passing through Asher on his way to Columbus, they decided to give him the key to the city. The whole town turned out. If anyone was disappointed when Nigel Franklin failed to materialize, the mood changed the minute I kicked off the parade with the Asher High Band behind me.

Twirling meant the world to me. From my pointed toes, all the way up to my straight arms and proper free hands, my form was flawless. Plus, my vertical and horizontal two-spin was legendary. Every football and basketball half-time finale ended with me tossing the baton in the air as the crowd would yell, "Whoooooooooooa." This continued until my baton made its downward descent and I reclaimed it, whereupon the crowd would shout "Nelly!" and a cheer would erupt.

○

On my first day at Kahanamoku Academy I woke up early. I was excited to make new friends. Maui's tropical weather made my perm frizzier than it already was, so I elected to wear my hair in French braids and adorned them with blue and yellow ribbons (my new school colors). To complement this, I wore matching sky-blue eye shadow. I considered wearing my Miss Pep sweater, but didn't want to appear boastful, so instead I brought my lucky baton to school. That baton won me more twirling awards than I could count. It was the baton I was holding when I was named Miss Pep, and it was the baton I gripped every time Mom and I got kicked out of our apartments for not paying the rent.

At Asher, the majorettes were never without their batons. Carrying one was the sort of status symbol girls could aspire to.

Mrs. Smith, our principal, once likened them to security blankets. Though it was true that my baton did make me feel better, I also had ulterior motives for bringing it to Kahanamoku. Even though it was mid-semester, I hoped to talk to the band director about securing a spot as a majorette. My twirling skills were a surefire way to propel me into the popular group.

"There's no band?" My mouth hung open. I had specifically made an appointment to see Headmaster Field to discuss band.

He ran his hand though his unruly gray hair and offered me a sad smile. "Not this year, Francis," he said apologetically.

"Felicity," I corrected him. Headmaster Field's office was full of photos of him shaking hands with well-coiffed people wearing nice suits. My father was fond of nice suits, which was probably why he never had enough money for child support. "Was there a band last year?" I sputtered.

Headmaster Field shook his head again. "We're more of an academic school than a sports one. Our sports program was, er, cancelled last year ago due to the, er, well, the abuse of—" I followed his gaze as he looked out at a blue jay that had alighted on the windowsill. Finally, Headmaster Field turned his attention back to me. "The University of Hawaii gives a full athletic scholarship to one high school baton twirler each year!"

We both brightened at the idea of this, but our smiles soon faded when I pointed out, "I won't be a high school twirler since Kahanamoku Academy doesn't have a band. Besides, I don't need a scholarship. My stepfather can pay for college."

"True, true." Headmaster Field nodded and absentmindedly began to twirl his pen. "You're paying full tuition here. We like that. Well, perhaps you can practice baton on your own? You know, sort of like independent study, except without grades or the credit." This idea seemed to please him. As he made note of it in my file, the blue jay and I studied each other from opposites sides of the glass.

"What about clubs?" I finally asked. I had been president of the French club (*mais oui!*) back at home.

"Clubs?" Headmaster Field asked, raising his bushy eyebrows.

"Yes, clubs," I said again. I wondered if he was hard of hearing. Mr. Hunter wore a hearing aid. "I'd like to know about the clubs here."

Headmaster Field tapped his pen on the desk, then said, "We don't have a lot of clubs, but Felicity, why don't you start one?" His eyes lit up. "Yes, you could start one and I would be your sponsor. What club should we have? Do you play backgammon?"

"No."

"Pity," he said, letting out a sad sigh. "Well, is there anything else I can help you with?"

I hesitated. "Um, this may sound weird, but I am having trouble understanding some of the other kids."

He laughed, murmured something about teenagers being so confusing, then admitted that he himself was often flummoxed by his students.

"No, no," I tried again. "I mean I can't understand their speech. It's like they speak another language. You know, like Portuguese."

"Ah!" Headmaster Field cried. "That's not Portuguese, that's pigeon." He went on to explain that Hawaiians often slipped into what was called "pidgin" English, a very casual way of talking that set the locals apart from the tourists. For example, "How is it?" would be "howzit?" And "would you like to go to dinner" would be "wanna goda dinna, huh?"

Great. As if moving from Asher to Maui weren't hard enough. Now there was a language barrier.

○　　·

Before we met Mr. Hunter, we lived in what seemed to be an endless series of dark, cramped apartments. Because of my brother, there was never enough money. Carl was expensive. We were always looking for ways to save a dollar or two. Sometimes, like when my mother had to perm my hair at home or when we ate spaghetti for a week, I'd blame Carl. Afterward, I always felt bad and would apologize to my brother and Henry, the stuffed monkey who was his constant companion.

Our minister once told me, "Felicity, it's not Carl's fault, or your parents'. You must not blame them."

Okay. So, if it wasn't Carl's fault, and it wasn't my mother's or my father's, then whose fault was it? One time, when Mom was pregnant, I ran to give her a hug. Only I was going so fast I knocked her down. Maybe I hurt the baby. Maybe that's why his brain was damaged. Maybe all our family's sorrows were because of me.

My mother became a nurse so she could look after my brother. But as he got older, it got harder. Carl would spit out food. He'd wail and cry, and so would she. Even though he had the IQ of a one-year-old, my brother was bigger than both of us. After Carl broke Mom's nose for the second time, he went to live in a special needs home. I remember his first night. At my mother's urging, I kissed him and then waved good-bye. Carl, thinking it was a game, gave me one of his big sloppy kisses and made Henry wave back to me. He didn't know he wouldn't be coming home.

Even with Carl safely tucked away, my father couldn't deal with my brother. It troubled him that his son would never be the man he was. So Dad left us for some woman he met at Rotary. That's how Mom and I came to be poor and on the run from landlords.

I'd love to say that Mom and Mr. Hunter "met cute" like those romantic comedies she is so fond of. Only, that's not quite how it happened. During a first-class flight back from New York, Mr. Hunter had a stroke and the plane was forced to land. An emergency room nurse was credited with saving his life. On the day he checked out, Mr. Hunter proposed to her and Mom accepted.

Mr. Hunter's house was unlike anything I had ever seen

before. In the bathroom, metal grip bars were next to the toilet. A plastic chair sat in the master bedroom shower. All the light switches were down low, so Mr. Hunter wouldn't have to get out of his wheelchair to reach them.

The house was sprawling and flat with smooth blond wood floors. Sliding glass doors opened silently onto lushly landscaped grounds, where blue jays, something rare in Asher, adorned the trees. There was a view of the ocean from almost every room. The house was gorgeous and it didn't cost us anything. Well, it didn't cost any money.

Old and frail, Mr. Hunter's face was pocked and wrinkled and the color of sand. When he coughed, which was often, phlegm or blood, or both, stained his handkerchief. He shook violently, and when he was not in his wheelchair he hunched over, leaning on his carved wooden cane, or my mom, for support.

But Mr. Hunter was good to my mother. Unlike my father, he never beat her, he never called her a mean name or even raised his voice to her. In return, she gave him youth and companionship and, in the end, love.

◦

Despite going solo at lunch, I was determined to make friends at my new school. I didn't let the fact that I was being ignored deter me. Sure, it was something I was unaccustomed to, but I could understand why. No one knew what I had to offer—but that was about to change.

I took a deep cleansing breath, put on my best majorette smile, and, as I strolled down the halls, I twirled. Nothing too fancy, I didn't want to show off. To my surprise, the more I twirled, the more people ignored me. Well, not everyone.

With the athletic program suspended, there was a new sport. It involved former athletes grabbing my baton, tossing it to each other, and then hurling it over the balcony like a javelin. After two days of this I left my lucky baton at home.

I need to take a moment to describe my peers at Kahanamoku Academy. At least a third of the kids seemed to be native Hawaiians or at least some version of Asian, and a third were white, and a third I couldn't tell. With about two hundred students in each grade, the school was twice the size of Asher High. The girls had a sheen to them like they had just slipped off the pages of a glossy fashion magazine.

In Asher, I didn't dare leave home without concealer, foundation, powder, blush, liner, shadow, eyebrow pencil, mascara, lip liner and two lipsticks (to get my signature color). Yet the strange thing about the Kahanamoku girls was that they appeared to go without makeup, and still looked beautiful. They didn't seem to sweat, either. And modesty certainly wasn't an issue with them considering that their clothes consisted of little more than short shorts and tiny tops that looked like underwear.

The boys resembled ads for Sun & Surf Suntan Oil. Muscled and supremely confident, they carried themselves like athletes without the letterman's jackets. One boy in particular had the looks of a movie star, the build of an Olympic athlete, and the swagger of someone who has never doubted himself. He was so handsome it hurt to even look at him. Kai Risdale was like the sun, with the other planets orbiting around his fiery glow.

At the risk of being blinded by his beauty, I stared. Everyone else stared at Kai, too, except for the few scholarship students who mostly kept their heads down and clutched their books tight to their chests like armor. Perhaps it was. They couldn't afford to get hurt. Without a scholarship, the privilege of attending Kahanamoku was over eighteen thousand dollars a year.

If in Asher, Ohio, I was considered pale, in Maui I was a ghost. I was peppy at a school where the less pep you had, the more popular you were. Everything was so confusing. The cool kids at Kahanamoku seemed to do nothing more than stand around. Whereas at Asher, the only time people stood still was for the morning flag salute.

At the end of the week things finally started to look up. I was about to head home when Kai brushed past me. With ease, he hoisted himself onto the pedestal where the bronze statue of Duke Kahanamoku stood bare-chested and ready to surf. Duke, the legendary Hawaiian surfer and namesake of the school, was akin to God on the islands. As Kai leaned on the statue I could see that his biceps rivaled Duke's. I shut my eyes and wondered what it would be like to be held in Kai's arms. My eyes fluttered open when I heard Kai cry, "C'mon, everyone, party at my house!"

A cheer filled the air and what appeared to be the entire student body started to follow Kai. Not to be left out, I ran to catch up. A party! This would be my first Hawaiian party and I was intent on showing everyone how fun I could be. In Asher, I was known for being something of a party animal. At Natalie Catrine's sweet sixteen, I was dared to—and did—eat three cupcakes without using my hands.

Suddenly Kai stopped and I almost bumped into him. He smelled like coconuts. "Where do you think you're going?" he asked.

I looked around before I realized he was talking to me. "To the party?" I said, making it sound like a question. Being this close to Kai made me feel faint.

He smiled for the benefit of those watching and then answered, "That's funny, because no one invited you."

My face was on fire. "But," I stammered, "you said, 'everyone, party at my house.'"

"Yes, I did say that," Kai mused agreeably. He had flecks of brown in his green eyes. "But what I meant was everyone but you."

Laughter filled the air, and even though it pained me, I joined in. According to the Miss Pep mission statement, "Asher High School's Miss Pep is always peppy, even in the face of adversity."

If I had thought things couldn't get any worse, I was wrong. I had tried to befriend the scholarship students, but they eyed me with suspicion once it was discovered that Justin Hunter of Justin Hunter Electronics was married to my mother. Yet our newfound money wasn't enough to buy my way into the popular group.

In an attempt to fit in, I toned down my blush and switched to a waterproof mascara since the humid weather made my makeup melt. I stopped putting ribbons in my hair, and although I didn't wear short shorts or skimpy tank tops, I did go sleeveless quite often. I even tried to swear like the popular kids by throwing the occasional "damn" into my sentences. Once I even said "bitch," though I instantly regretted it.

One day Kai cornered me by my locker. "Hey, you, what's your name?"

It didn't matter that I had been at school for almost two months, or that the teachers often called on me in class, or that anytime Headmaster Field saw me he'd say, "How are you today, Felicity?"

"So what's your name?" Kai asked again, this time leaning in so close I could smell cigarettes on his breath. My heart raced. His friends looked bored.

It had occurred to me that maybe Kai was testing me. Or joking, the way the boys at Asher High did when they were flirting. Back home, I had 1.5 boyfriends. The first, Don Connelly, was in band. If you saw him strut and play the trumpet, you'd understand what the attraction was. We were named His and Her Asher High Sophomore Spirit leaders during football kickoff week last year. Don and I dated for three months, but there was never any true spark between us. Plus, I never liked it that he tucked in his sweaters.

The .5 was Jeremy Hall. Since we were both major *Sound of Music* (Do-Re-Mi!) and Julie Andrews fans, we started hanging out. Before we knew it, we were an item. This came as a surprise to us, since the other thing we had in common was that we both had a huge crush on Kyle Kincaid, the actor from that musical where rival schools are pitted against each other in a battle of the bands on Mars. If only Jeremy hadn't been gay. I think we could really have had something special.

My name is Felicity," I told Kai cautiously.

"What was that?" Kai said, even though I had taken the care to enunciate clearly. "Felicity."

"Interesting name," he said, toying with my hair. "Fellatio?" Kai boomed, "I've never met a girl named *Fellatio* before."

"It's FELICITY," I said loudly, trying to mask the sound of my heart beating furiously. "Felicity. F-e-l-i-c-i-t-y."

"Fellatio?" Kai repeated as his entourage howled. "Isn't that the technical term for oral sex?"

After weeks of being ignored, suddenly everyone knew who I was. Only, instead of saying, "Hi, Felicity!" or "Loved your routine, Felicity!" the Kahanamoku students would shout, "Hellooooo, Fellatio!" Sometimes the girls would chide their boyfriends, but then they would crack up, too.

I had turned into one big joke.

As the rest of the year wore on, the fellatio wordplay wore old. By then everyone had taken to calling me BJ, the slang for blow job, which I discovered when I looked it up in the *Oxford American Dictionary*, was the slang for fellatio. Even though I would have preferred to be called Felicity, BJ was at least a compromise I could live with.

At home, whenever Mom asked about school, I'd just say, "It's great!" I didn't want to worry her. She was having trouble adjusting, too. With Carl settling into Celebration Residential Center, my mother now took care of Mr. Hunter, who was falling apart even faster than I was.

I visited my brother every day. We'd sit and talk for hours. Well, I'd sit and talk for hours. Carl would listen, or at least I liked to think he did. It was hard to tell how much Carl comprehended. Just when you thought you were breaking through to him, he'd fall asleep or fling himself out of his wheelchair, or throw his plush monkey across the room. Once he even tossed Henry out the window. If it hadn't been for a Good Samaritan down below, Henry might have been lost forever.

The six-hour time difference made it difficult to call to my friends back home — most were busy with their twirling and school activities. And when I did talk to Natalie Catrine and the rest, they refused to hear that I was miserable. They were more interested in the white-sand beaches, Maui's current temperature, and Mr. Hunter's big house.

"Paradise," Natalie Catrine would murmur. "Felicity, you're living in paradise."

One day as I walked home, I spotted a tour bus near the waterfall. I didn't believe it at first, but sure enough, there was Mrs. Cardiff, from the dry cleaner back in Asher! She was the last person I would ever think would travel to Maui. Mrs. Cardiff was shading her eyes with one hand and fanning her face with the other. I hardly recognized her — she must have put on eighty pounds.

I raced over and before I could stop myself I was sobbing, telling Mrs. Cardiff about my poor sad life. When I got to the Fellatio part, I could see the fear in her eyes. That's when a skinny pale man in shorts with a leather fanny pack cinched tightly around his waist stepped in and said, "Beatrice, is this girl bothering you?"

Only then did I realize I wasn't talking to Mrs. Cardiff at all. Instead this was just some fat version of someone I once knew. I apologized profusely as she scurried back to the safety of the bus.

After school and on weekends, when most of the kids headed to the beach, I pushed past them in the other direction. My skin burned easily, and as a rule I stayed away from the shore except at dusk when the water looked the prettiest and the sun was kinder. It was cool inside the library, and I would spread my homework out under the approving eye of Mrs. Yamashiro the librarian who, like me, looked like she rarely ventured outdoors. The musty smell of the books was the sweet perfume I preferred to the strong sea air or the mockery of the students who hung around Kahanamoku to socialize, score drugs, or have sex.

In less than four months, I had morphed from golden girl to invisible girl, the former Felicity, Fellatio, BJ, and who now was not called anything at all because none of the other students even noticed her. Or if they knew me, it was only as the weird girl who had tried to impress everyone with her baton. It pained me to even think about it. Was this how my brother felt, I wondered? In Maui, whenever I took Carl out in public, little kids gawked and all others pretended not to see him. It wasn't that way back home. There, the only person who pretended that Carl didn't exist was my father.

Occasionally, I'd spy a fellow Kahanamoku student, but they always averted their eyes, especially if Carl was howling or making the loud moaning sounds that signaled he was happy. With no one to hang out with I threw myself into my studies. I was determined to get into a good college. At Asher High I had wanted to prove to everyone that I was someone. At Kahanamoku I needed to prove it to myself.

When third quarter reports came, I was pleased, although not surprised, to discover I had gotten all A's. With several students within earshot, Headmaster Field congratulated me with unbridled enthusiasm. My feeling of pride quickly dissipated when he turned to congratulate Kai, whose report card apparently mirrored mine.

I took in a sharp breath that felt like a stab to the heart. Kai never studied, turned in his homework, or aced any exams. "How can this be possible?" I said out loud.

Danny, one of the scholarship students from my AP English class, slammed his locker shut and shook his head. For a brief moment our eyes met. Then he turned away.

At Asher High every good grade was earned. Here at Kahanamoku Academy it seemed that actual work didn't factor into the GPA. I hated Kai, and hated myself even more for not being able to stop thinking about him. Ever since I had spied him surfing one afternoon, Kai had worked his way into my dreams. His body was the definition of perfection, and as his surfboard cut through the water, it appeared as if the Hawaiian sun and surf had materialized solely for his benefit.

That afternoon, I bypassed the library in favor of the Golden Goodness Bakery, where I bought a big bag of malasadas, the Hawaiian version of donuts. I carried the brown paper sack to the park that lined the shore across the street. As I bit into a malasada, I savored the taste of the sweet balls of fried dough rolled in sugar. Carl loved these and I made sure to save some for him. In the months that I had lived on Maui, my skin no longer burned an angry red thanks to the natural adjustment of my pigment and SPF 80 sunscreen. The warm weather did wonders for my mother and brother, too. Everyone had taken on a healthy glow, except for Mr. Hunter, who appeared to be fading.

Carl clapped and set Henry aside when he saw me. "You do know how much I love you, don't you?" I asked. Carl merely smiled and moaned as he motioned for another malasada. It was only when the bag was empty that Carl picked up Henry and retreated into his silence.

His doctors always said that he didn't understand much. Yet Carl always knew when I was leaving. "It's okay," I'd say, wiping away his tears. "I'll be back tomorrow, silly. You know that." Then I'd kiss him and wave good-bye.

As we entered the last quarter of my junior year, I started going to the park every day and began twirling once more. When my baton flew high in the air, so did I. It made me happy.

One day when I was practicing I spotted a familiar group of boys. When they got close, I had trouble focusing and dropped my baton. Kai and I reached for it at the same time. "Give it to me, BJ," he whispered in a low growl that made me want to swear and swoon at the same time. I despised myself for that.

With his cronies looking on, Kai tried to yank the baton from my hand, but I hung on tight. He loosened his grip and before I could think, I grabbed the baton and whacked him on the head.

Instantly, the laughter stopped.

Novice twirlers get hit on the head all the time and seldom sustain injury. Of course, none of this mattered to Kai. His eyes narrowed as he hissed, "You're lucky I don't hit girls."

I held my baton like a baseball bat, ready to strike again. "Shove it, Kai," I shot back. "You're lucky I don't hit girls, either."

Kai blinked his long eyelashes as if unsure of who or what I was. Then, he slowly reached toward me. I stood frozen, determined not to flinch. "BJ, you're all right," he said, tousling my hair.

His laughter gave the others permission to laugh, too.

As I watched Kai and his pals stroll away, I wasn't sure what had just happened. In my confusion, I hardly noticed the giant gecko standing nearby. He waddled up to me and in a muffled voice said, "That was really something."

"Excuse me?" Maybe I was the one who had been hit with the baton. The gecko handed me a brochure. "Auntie Alea's Authentic Hawaiian Luau?" I read out loud.

The gecko nodded and then said, "Help me get this head off, will you? It's like Hades in this costume."

It was a struggle, but finally I was face-to-face with an elderly Hawaiian gentleman. Despite his being in a lizard costume, he had a regal bearing. His skin was dark and smooth and his brown eyes glistened, like he knew a secret. "My name's Jimmy Chow and I'm Alea's second cousin," he said. "I've been watching you. You're amazing. Have you ever twirled fire?"

"I can twirl anything," I told him.

"We could use someone like you," Jimmy mused. He was almost as old as Mr. Hunter, only wiry and full of energy. "Help me get my head back on; there's a tour bus I have to meet. But first, promise me you'll call Alea. Be sure to say Jimmy sent you."

On Jimmy's recommendation, and three auditions later, I became the only female and the youngest baton flame twirler at Auntie Alea's Luau. Sure it's a tourist attraction, but aren't we all tourists at some point? I was also the only haole. *Haole*. That's Hawaiian for white person. Shortly after, I had another name change, but this time I didn't protest. Auntie Alea christened me *Kalani*. It means heaven and sky.

Auntie Alea's felt like home. She treated everyone like family. On my first day I was pleasantly surprised to find Danny from my AP English class working as a waiter. "The tips are really good," he explained. "I'm saving up for college." His black hair was thick and wavy and he had freckles trekking across his nose bridge. "Plus, Auntie Alea lets me study when it's slow."

Danny and I would study together during our breaks, and later on our days off. Eventually we'd just hang at the beach or visit Carl. Danny introduced me to some students at Kahanamoku who I had never noticed before. I guess I had been too busy staring at what I thought were the popular kids, when really they were the jerks.

Not too long ago, Kai and his friends came in for the luau waving their fake IDs. At first they didn't recognize me in my grass skirt and green bikini top. It had been over a year since I had first landed on the island. I had toned down my makeup and stopped perming and dyeing my hair, letting it go back to its natural auburn color. It's just easier, plus Danny thinks I look best with my hair straight. I had also learned to chill out, something I was incapable of doing back in Asher.

The boys hooted and whistled when I first stepped onstage, and when Kai finally figured out who I was he shouted, "Hey, BJ, wanna get lei-ed?"

I was about to tell him off when my music cued up. So instead, I glared at him and lit my batons on fire. When I heaved them into the night sky, it silenced any snide remarks that were still floating around. Instantly, Kai and his ilk turned into nothing more than faces in the crowd, with their necks turned upward and their mouths hanging open, waiting to see what I would do next. Finally, when my routine was over, they stood up and cheered with everyone else in the audience.

After the show, as I was downing a bottle of water, Kai strutted backstage. "BJ, you were great!" He swayed when he spoke. Kai reached toward me and twirled my hair as he looked deep into my eyes and whispered, "Wanna join me for a private party at my house?" He was asking me to be with him? There was a time when this would have meant the world to me.

For a moment I felt flush, until the stench of whiskey and cigarettes on his breath brought me back to reality. Then out of the corner of my eyes, I noticed Danny coming toward us with his fists clenched. I motioned for him to stop and turned to face Kai. "What's my name?"

"BJ," he said as he blinked slowly.

"What's my name?" I asked again.

Kai broke into a lazy smile and winked. "It's Felicity. You're Felicity. That's who you've always been."

I smiled back and leaned in so that my lips were practically brushing his cheek. "You got that right, asshole," I said. Then I emptied my water bottle over his head and pushed him aside so I could get ready for my second show.

As I walked toward Danny he held up his hand and without breaking my stride we high-fived.

My mother was able to bring Mr. Hunter and Carl to the luau one night, shortly before Mr. Hunter died. Auntie Alea gave them the best table and Danny waited on them like they were royalty. When I was onstage Mr. Hunter cheered so loud that he had a coughing fit and everyone stared. Mom tenderly calmed him down, and I could see how much they meant to each other.

Carl clutched Henry and sat mesmerized during the entire show. If you didn't know his history, he almost seemed normal. Before he left each of my coworkers took off their leis and placed them around his neck. Barely visible under all the flowers, Carl moaned with delight and we all laughed and clapped along with him.

"You guys are great," I said, choking up.

Jimmy hugged me and said, "Kalani, your brother is our brother, too."

Not long after that, I went back to Asher, Ohio. I stayed with Natalie Catrine, who proudly showed me her Miss Pep trophy. Though I had a great time, it just wasn't the same. Everyone had changed so much. Or maybe they hadn't. Maybe it was me. I never realized how hard it had been to be so peppy and that all that pep had been weighing me down.

I saw my father while I was in town. Was it true, he wondered, that we had come into a fortune? I told him it was just a rumor. Not once did he ask about Carl.

I was so happy to return to Maui.

It was hard leaving Auntie Alea's at the end of summer. I had been one of four Kahanamoku Academy valedictorians, the others include Samantha Tsui, a girl I had never heard speak until she gave a killer speech during graduation, Kai Risdale, whose family generously donated the new auditorium, and Danny Kaleho, my boyfriend.

Danny earned a scholarship to NYU, and even though we both knew the time would come when we'd go our own ways, it still hurt. He left first. Danny was eager to get off the island and get on with the rest of his life. I, on the other hand, was reluctant to leave.

"Felicity, you have to go," my mother insisted. "I'm grounded here and so is Carl, but you can go places. Do this for us."

Thanks to Mr. Hunter, my education is paid for and I attend Rogers College in Southern California. Even though they have an impressive majorette squad, I elected not to participate. Twirling had taken up so much of my life that I wanted to see what more there was. Besides, I left my lucky baton behind. It was a last-minute decision.

My mother had brought Carl to the airport to see me off. As he slumped in his wheelchair, tourists maneuvered their suitcases around us, pretending we didn't exist. I knelt down on the sidewalk as I struggled to explain to Carl why I had to leave. But he would hear none of it. He had been increasingly agitated, having lost Henry a week earlier. As my brother began to scream and swat the invisible demons that had been hiding, the people who had been trying so hard to ignore us stopped and stared.

"Carl, Carl, look!" I had to shout to get his attention. "Look at me, Carl!"

I began to twirl my baton and Carl grew quiet. I put everything into my routine—high kicks, trick moves, even stuff I learned from Auntie Alea's. Everything. When I was done, the crowd cheered and Carl moaned with delight. He held out both hands and reached for my baton, but I held on tight. Yet he kept motioning for it, until we were both on the verge of tears.

Finally, I gave in.

When I handed my baton to him, I knew I was never getting it back.

"It belongs to you now," I assured my brother as I held him tight. "It's yours."

Then I kissed him and waved good-bye.

In high school, **Lisa Yee** was a member of the varsity debate team, honor society president, and the student rep of the California Scholarship Federation's State Board. In an act of total geek rebellion, Lisa would cut class to go to the library. And once, during science, she threw her fetal pig over the balcony to see what would happen when it landed on someone. She never got caught and was later named Physiology Student of the Year.

Lisa's been a TV writer/producer, written jingles, and penned menus for Red Lobster. The winner of the prestigious Sid Fleischman Humor Award and Thurber House Children's Writer-in-Residence, her books include *Millicent Min, Girl Genius*, *Stanford Wong Flunks Big-Time*, and YA novel *Absolutely Maybe*. Lisa's Web site is www.lisayee.com, and her blog is www.lisayee.livejournal.com.

Wash and change your clothes. For the love of all that is holy.

Stay hydrated and remember to eat. Low blood sugar will make you weep at inappropriate moments.

Get some sleep. It will keep you from seeing things that aren't there. By the way, that monster to your right is actually there.

Bring spending money. Otherwise you will spend all your food money on the original shirt Captain Kirk wore when he made out with Uhuru (you are such a stud).

Make sure your costume has breathing vents.

SECRET IDENTITY
by kelly link

Dear Paul Zell.

○

Dear Paul Zell is exactly how far I've gotten at least a dozen times, and then I get a little farther, and then I give up. So this time I'm going to try something new. I'm going to pretend that I'm not writing you a letter, Paul Zell, dear Paul Zell. I'm so sorry. And I *am* sorry, Paul Zell, but let's skip that part for now or else I won't get any farther this time, either. And in any case: how much does it matter whether or not I'm sorry? What difference could it possibly make?

So. Let's pretend that we don't know each other. Let's pretend we're meeting for the first time, Paul Zell. We're sitting down to have dinner in a restaurant in a hotel in New York City. I've come a long way to have dinner with you. We've never met face-to-face. Everything I ever told you about myself is more or less a lie. But you don't know that yet. We think we may be in love.

We met in FarAway, online, except now here we are up close. I could reach out and touch your hand. If I was brave enough. If you were really here.

Our waiter has poured you a glass of red wine. Me? I'm

223

drinking a Coke because I'm not old enough to drink wine. You're thirty-four. I'm almost sixteen.

○

I'm so sorry, Paul Zell. I don't think I can do this. (Except I have to do this.) *I have to do this.* So let's try again. (I keep trying again and again and again.) Let's start even farther back, before I showed up for dinner and you didn't. Except I think you did. Am I right?

You don't have to answer that. I owe you the real story, but you don't owe me anything at all.

Picture the lobby of a hotel. In the lobby, a fountain with Spanish tiles in green and yellow. A tiled floor, leather armchairs, corporate art, this bank of glass-fronted elevators whizzing up and down, a bar. Daddy bar to all the mini-bars in all the rooms. Sound familiar? Maybe you've been here before.

Now fill up the lobby with dentists and superheroes. Men and women, oral surgeons, eighth-dimensional entities, mutants, and freaks who want to save your teeth, save the world, and maybe end up with a television show, too. I've seen a dentist or two in my time, Paul Zell, but we don't get many superheroes out on the plain. We get tornadoes instead. There are two conventions going on at the hotel, and they're mingling around the fountain, tra la la, tipping back drinks.

Boards in the lobby list panels on advances in cosmetic dentistry, effective strategies for minimizing liability in cases of bystander hazard, presentations with titles like "Spandex or Bulletproof? What Look Is Right for You?" You might be interested in these if you were a dentist or a superhero. Which I'm not. As it turns out, I'm not a lot of things.

A girl is standing in front of the registration desk. That's me. And where are you, Paul Zell?

The hotel clerk behind the desk is only a few years older than me. (Than that girl, the one who's come to meet Paul Zell. Is it pretentious or pitiful or just plain psychotic the way I'm talking about myself in the third person? Maybe it's all three. I don't care.) The clerk's nametag says Aliss, and she reminds the girl that I wish wasn't me of someone back at school. Erin Toomey, that's who. Erin Toomey is a hateful bitch. But never mind about Erin Toomey.

Aliss the hotel clerk is saying something. She's saying, "I'm not finding anything." It's eleven o'clock on a Friday morning, and at that moment the girl in the lobby is missing third-period biology. Her fetal pig is wondering where she is.

Let's give the girl in line in the hotel lobby a name. Everybody gets a name, even fetal pigs. (I call mine Alfred.) And now that you've met Aliss and Alfred, minor characters both, I might as well introduce our heroine. That is, me. Of course it isn't like FarAway. I don't get to choose my name. If I did, it wouldn't be Billie Faggart. That ring any bells? No, I didn't think it would. Since fourth grade, which is when I farted while I was coming down the playground slide, everyone at school has called me Smelly Fagfart. That's because Billie Faggart is a funny name, right? Except girls like Billie Faggart don't have much of a sense of humor.

○

There's another girl at school, Jennifer Groendyke. Everyone makes jokes about us. About how we'll move to California and marry each other. You'd think we'd be friends, right? But we're not. I'm not good at the friends thing. I'm like the girl equivalent of one of those baby birds that fall out of a nest and then some nice person picks the baby bird up and puts it back. Except that now the baby bird smells all wrong. I think I smell wrong.

225

If you're wondering who Melinda Bowles is, the thirty-two-year-old woman you met in FarAway, no, you've never really met her. Melinda Bowles has never sent late-night e-mails to Paul Zell, not ever. Melinda Bowles would never catch a bus to New York City to meet Paul Zell because she doesn't know that Paul Zell exists.

Melinda Bowles has never been to FarAway.

Melinda Bowles has no idea who the Enchantress Magic Eight-ball is. She's never hung out online with the master thief Boggle. I don't think she knows what a MMORPG is.

Melinda Bowles has never played a game of living chess in King Nermal's Chamber in the Endless Caverns under the Loathsome Rock. Melinda Bowles doesn't know a rook from a writing desk. A pawn from a prawn.

○

Here's something that you know about Melinda Bowles that is true. She used to be married, but is now divorced and lives in her parents' house. She teaches high school. I used her name when I signed up for an account on FarAway. More about my sister Melinda later.

Anyway. Girl-liar Billie says to desk-clerk Aliss, "No message? No envelope? Mr. Zell, Paul Zell?" (That's you. In case you've forgotten.) "He's a guest here? He said he was leaving something for me at the front desk."

"I'll look again if you want," Aliss says. But she does nothing. Just stands there staring malevolently past Billie as if she hates the world and everyone in it.

226

Billie turns around to see who Aliss is glaring at. There's a normal-looking guy behind Billie; behind him, out in the lobby, there are all sorts of likely candidates. Who doesn't hate a dentist? Or maybe Aliss isn't crazy about superheroes. Maybe she's contemplating the thing that looks like a bubble of blood. If you were there, Paul Zell, you might stare at the bubble of blood, too. You can just make out the silhouette of someone/something inside.

Billie doesn't keep up with superheroes, not really, but she feels as if she's seen the bloody bubble on the news. Maybe it saved the world once. It levitates three feet above the marble floor of the atrium. It plops bloody drops like a sink faucet in Hell. Maybe Aliss worries someone will slip on the lobby floor, break an ankle, sue the hotel. Or maybe the bubble of blood owes her ten bucks.

The bubble of blood drifts over to the Spanish-tiled fountain. It clears the lip, just barely; comes to a halt two feet above the surface of the water. Now it looks like an art installation, albeit kind of a disgusting one. But perhaps it is seeing a heroic role for itself: scaring off the kind of children who like to steal pennies from fountains. Future criminal masterminds might turn their energies in a more productive direction. Perhaps some will become dentists.

◦

Were you a boy who stole coins from fountains, Paul Zell?

◦

We're not getting very far in this story, are we? Maybe that's because some parts of it are so very hard to tell, Paul Zell. So here I linger, not at the beginning and not even in the middle. Already it's more of a muddle. Maybe you won't even make it this far, Paul

Zell, but me, I have to keep going. I would make a joke about superheroic efforts, but that would just be me, delaying some more.

Behind the desk, even Aliss has gotten tired of waiting for me to get on with the story. She's stopped glaring, is clacking on a keyboard with her too-long nails. There's glitter residue around her hairline, and a half-scrubbed-off club stamp on her right hand. She says to Billie, "Are you a guest here? What was your name again?"

"Melinda Bowles," Billie says. "I'm not a guest. Paul Zell is staying here? He said he would leave something for me behind the desk."

"Are you here to audition?" Aliss says. "Because maybe you should go ask over at the convention registration."

"Audition?" Billie says. She has no idea what Aliss is talking about. She's forming her backup plan already: walk back to Port Authority and catch the next bus back to Keokuk, Iowa. That would have been a simpler e-mail to write, I see now. *Dear Paul Zell. Sorry. I got cold feet.*

"Aliss, my love. Better lose the piercing." The guy in line behind Billie is now up at the counter beside her. His hand is stamped, like Aliss's. Smudgy licks of black eyeliner around his eyes. "Unless you want management to write you a Dear John."

"Oh, shit." Aliss's hand goes up to her nose. She ducks down behind the counter. "Conrad, you asshole. Where did you go last night?"

"No idea," Conrad says. "I was drunk. Where did you go?"

"Home." Aliss says it like wielding a dagger. She's still submerged. "You want something? Room need making up? Night-shift Darin said he saw you in the elevator around three in the morning. With a girl." *Girl* is another dagger.

"Entirely possible," Conrad says. "Like I said, drunk. Need any help down there? Taking out the piercing? Helping this kid? Because I want to make last night up to you. I'm sorry, okay?"

Which would be the right thing to say, but Billie thinks this guy sounds not so penitent. More like he's swallowing a yawn.

"That's *very* nice of you, but I'm *fine*." Aliss snaps upright. The piercing is gone and her eyes glitter with either tears or rage. "This must be for you," she tells Billie in a cheery, desk-clerk robot voice. It's not much of an improvement on the stabby voice. "I'm *so* sorry about the confusion." There's an envelope in her hand.

Billie takes the envelope and goes to sit on a sofa beside a dentist. He's wearing a convention badge with his name on it, and where he comes from, and that's how she knows he isn't a superhero and that he isn't Paul Zell.

She opens her envelope. There's a room key inside and a piece of paper with a room number written on it. Nothing else. What is this, FarAway? Billie starts to laugh like an utter maniac. The dentist stares.

Forgive her. She's been on a bus for over twenty hours. Her hair is stiff with bus crud and her clothes smell like bus, a cocktail of chemical cleaners and other people's breath, and the last thing she was expecting when she went off on this quest, Paul Zell, was to find herself in a hotel full of superheroes and dentists.

It's not like we get a lot of superheroes in Keokuk, Iowa. There's the occasional flyover or Superheroes on Ice event, and every once in a while someone in Keokuk discovers they have the strength of two men, or can predict the sell-by date on cans of tuna in the supermarket with 98.2 percent accuracy, but even minor-league talents head out of town pretty quickly. They take off for Hollywood, to try and get on a reality show. Or New York or Chicago or even Baltimore, to form novelty rock bands or fight crime or both.

But, here's the thing; the thing is that, under ordinary circumstances, Billie would have nothing better to do than to watch a woman with a raven's head wriggling upstream through the crowd around the lobby bar, over to the fountain and that epic bubble of blood. The woman holds up a pink drink, she's standing on tip-toes, and a slick four-fingered hand emerges from the bubble of blood and takes the glass from her. Is it a love story? How does a woman with a raven's beak kiss a bubble of blood? Paul Zell, how are you and me any more impossible than that?

Maybe it's just two old friends having a drink. The four-fingered hand orients the straw into the membrane or force field or whatever it is, and the glass empties itself like a magic trick. The bubble quivers.

But: Paul Zell. All Billie can think about is you, Paul Zell. She has the key to Paul Zell's hotel room. Back before she met you, way far back in FarAway, Billie was always up for a quest. Why not? She had nothing better to do. And the quest always went like this: Find yourself in a strange place. Encounter a guardian. Outwit them or kill them or persuade them to give you the item they've been guarding. A weapon or a spell or the envelope containing the key to room 1584.

Except the key in Billie's hand is a real key, and I don't do that kind of quest much anymore. Not since I met you, Paul Zell. Not since the Enchantress Magic EightBall met the master thief Boggle in King Nermal's Chamber and challenged him to a game of chess.

◦

While I'm coming clean, here's a minor confession. Why not. Why should you care that, besides Enchantress Magic EightBall, I used to have two other avatars in FarAway. There's Constant Bliss, who's an elfin healer and frankly kind of a pill, and there's Bear-hand, who, as it turns out, was kind of valuable in terms of accu-mulated points, especially weapons class. There was a period, you see, when things were bad at school and things were worse at home, which I don't really want to talk about, and anyway, it was a bad period during which I liked running around and killing things. Whatever. Last month I sold Bearhand when you and I were planning all of this, for bus fare. It wasn't a big deal. I'd kind of stopped being Bearhand except for every once in a while, when you weren't online and I was lonely or sad or had a really, really shitty day at school.

I'm thinking I may sell off Constant Bliss, too, if anyone wants to buy her. If not, it will have to be Magic EightBall. Or maybe I'll sell both of them. But that's part of the story I haven't gotten to yet.

○

And, yeah, I do spend a lot of time online. In FarAway. Like I said, it's not like I have a lot of friends, not that you should feel sorry for me, because you shouldn't, Paul Zell, that's NOT why I'm telling you all of this.

My sister? Melinda? She says wait a few years and see. Things get better. Of course, based on her life, maybe they do get better. And then they get worse again, and then you have to move back home and teach high school. So how exactly is that better?

And yes, in case you're wondering, my sister Melinda Bowles is kind of stunning, and all the boys in my school who despise me have crushes on her even when she flunks them. And yes, a lot of the details I fed you about my life, Billie Faggart's life, are actually borrowed from Melinda's life. Although not all of the details. If you're still speaking to me after you read this, I'll be happy to make up a spreadsheet of character traits and biographical incidents. One column will be Melinda Bowles and the other will be Billie Faggart. There will be little checkmarks in either column, or both, depending. But the story about shaving off my eyebrows when I was a kid?

That was true. I mean, that was me. And so was the thing about liking reptiles. Melinda? She's not so fond of the reptiles. But then, maybe you don't really have a chameleon named Moe and a tokay gecko named Bitey. Maybe you made up some stuff, too, except yeah, okay, why would you make up some lizards? I keep having to remind myself: Billie, just because you're a liar doesn't mean the whole world is full of liars. Except that you did lie, right? You were at the hotel. You left me the key to your room at the hotel in an envelope addressed to Melinda Bowles. Because if you didn't, then who did?

○

Sorry. This is supposed to be about me, apologizing. Not me, solving the big mysteries of the universe and everything. Except, here's the thing about Melinda, in case you're thinking maybe the person you fell in love with really exists. The *salient* thing. Melinda has a boyfriend. He's in Afghanistan right now. Also, she's super religious, like seriously born again. Which you're not. So even if Melinda's boyfriend got killed, or something, which I know is something she worries about, it would never work out between you and her.

And one more last thing about Melinda, or maybe it's actually about you. This is the part where I have to thank you. Because: *because* of you, Paul Zell, I think Melinda and I have kind of become friends. Because, all year I've been interested in her life. I ask her how her day was, and I actually listen when she tells me. Because, how else could I convince you that I was a thirty-two-year-old, divorced high-school algebra teacher? And it turns out that we actually have a lot in common, me and Melinda, and it's like I even *understand* what she thinks about. Because, she has a boyfriend who's far away (in Afghanistan) and she misses him and they write e-mails to each other, and she worries about what if he loses a leg or something, and will they still love each other when he gets back?

And I have you. I had this thing with you, even if I couldn't tell her about you. I guess I still can't tell her. Which is even weirder, I guess, than the other thing: how for so long I couldn't tell you the truth about me. And now I can't shut up about me when what I really ought to be explaining is what happened at the hotel.

Billie gets into an elevator with a superhero and the guy who blew off Aliss. The superhero reeks. BO and something worse, like spoiled meat. He gets out on the seventh floor, and Billie sucks in air. She's thinking about all sorts of things. For example, how it turns out she doesn't have a fear of heights, which is a good thing to discover in a glass elevator. She's thinking about how she could find a wireless café, go online and hang out in FarAway, except Paul Zell won't be there. She wonders if the guy who bought Bearhand is trying him out. Now that would be weird, to run into someone who used to be you. What would she say? She's thinking how much she wants to take a shower, and she's wondering if she smells as bad as that superhero did. She's thinking all of this and lots of other things, too.

"Now that's how to fight crime," says the other person in the elevator. (Conrad Linthor, although Billie doesn't know his last name yet. Maybe you'll recognize it, though.) "You smell it to death. Although, to be fair, to get that big you have to eat a lot of protein and the protein makes you stinky. That's why I'm a vegetarian." The smile he gives Billie is as ripe with charm as the elevator is ripe with super stink.

Billie prides herself on being charm resistant. (It's like the not having a sense of humor. A sense of humor is a weakness. I know how you're supposed to be able to laugh at yourself, but that's pretty sucky advice when everyone is always laughing at you already.) She stares at Conrad Linthor blankly. If you don't react, mostly other people give up and leave you alone.

Conrad Linthor is eighteen or nineteen, or maybe a well-preserved twenty-two. He has regular features and white teeth. He'd be good looking if he weren't so good looking, Billie thinks, and then wonders what she meant by that. She can tell that he's rich, although, again, she's not quite sure how she knows this. Maybe because he pressed the Penthouse floor button when he got on the elevator.

"Let me guess," Conrad Linthor says, as if he and Billie have been having a conversation. "You're here to audition." When Billie continues to stare at him blankly, this time because she really doesn't know what he's talking about and not just because she's faking being stupid, he elaborates: "You want to be a sidekick. That guy who just got off? The Blue Fist? I hear his sidekicks keep quitting for some reason."

"I'm here to meet a friend," Billie says. "Why does everyone keep asking me that? Are you? You know, a sidekick?"

"Me?" Conrad Linthor says. "Very funny."

The elevator door dings open, fifteenth floor, and Billie gets off.

"See you around," Conrad Linthor calls after her. It sounds more mocking than hopeful.

○

You know what, Paul Zell? I never thought you would be super handsome or anything. Don't be insulted, okay? I never cared about what you might turn out to look like. I know you have brown hair and brown eyes and you're kind of skinny and you have a big nose.

234

I know because you told me you look like your avatar. Boggle. Me, I was always terrified you'd ask for my photo, because then it would really have been a lie, even more of a lie, because I would've sent you a photo of Melinda.

My dad says I look so much like Melinda did when she was a kid, it's scary. That we could practically be twins. But I've seen pictures of Melinda when she was fifteen and I don't look like her at all. Melinda was kind of freakish looking when she was my age, actually. I think that's why she's so nice now, and not vain, because it was a surprise to her, too, when she got awesome looking. I'm not gorgeous, and I'm not a freak, either, and so that whole ugly duckling thing that Melinda went through probably isn't going to happen to me.

But you saw me, right? You know what I look like.

●

Billie knocks on the door of Paul Zell's hotel room, just in case. Even though you aren't there. If you were there, she'd die on the spot of heart failure, even though that's why she's there. To see you.

Maybe you're wondering why she came all this way, when meeting you face-to-face was always going to be this huge problem. Honestly? She doesn't really know. She still doesn't know. Except that you said: Want to meet up? See if this is real or not?

What was she supposed to do? Say no? Tell the truth?

There are two double beds in room 1584, and a black suitcase on a stand. No Paul Zell, because you're going to be in meetings all day. The plan is to meet at the Golden Lotus at six.

Last night you slept in one of those beds, Paul Zell. Billie sits down on the bed closest to the window and she even smells the pillows, but she can't tell. It's a damn shame housekeeping has already made up the room, otherwise Billie could climb into the bed you were sleeping in last night and put her head down on your pillow.

She goes over to the suitcase, and here's where it starts to get kind of awful, Paul Zell. This is why I have to write about all of this in the third person, because maybe then I can pretend that it wasn't really me there, doing these things.

The lid of your suitcase is up. You're a tidy packer, Paul Zell. The dirty clothes on the floor of the closet are folded. Billie lifts up the squared shirts and khakis. Even the underwear is folded. Your pants size is 32, Paul Zell. Your socks are just socks. There's a velvet box, a jeweler's box, near the bottom of the suitcase, and Billie opens it. Then she puts the box back at the bottom of the suitcase. I can't really tell you what she was thinking right then, even though I was there.

I can't tell you everything, Paul Zell.

Billie didn't pack a suitcase, because her dad and Melinda would have wondered about that. Fortunately nobody's ever surprised when you go off to school and your backpack looks crammed full of things. Billie takes out the skirt she's planning to wear to dinner, and hangs it up in the closet. She brushes her teeth and afterward she puts her toothbrush down on the counter beside your toothbrush. She closes the drapes over the view, which is just another building, glass-fronted like the elevators. As if nobody could ever get anything done if the world wasn't watching, or maybe because, if the world can look in and see what you're doing, then what you're doing has to be valuable and important and aboveboard. It's a far way down to the street, so far down that the window in Paul Zell's hotel room doesn't open, probably because people like Billie can't help imagining what it would be like to fall.

All the little ant people down there, who don't even know you're standing at the window, looking down at them. Billie looks down at them.

Billie closes the blackout curtain over the view. She pulls the cover off the bed closest to the window. She takes off her jeans and shirt and bra and puts on the Boston Marathon T-shirt she found in Paul Zell's suitcase.

She lies down on a fresh white top sheet, falls asleep in the yellow darkness. She dreams about you.

When she wakes up she is drooling on an unfamiliar pillow. Her jaw is tight because she's forgotten to wear her mouthpiece. She's been grinding her teeth. So, yes, the teeth grinding, that's me. Not Melinda.

It's 4:30, late afternoon. Billie takes a shower. She uses Paul Zell's herbal conditioner. She folds the borrowed T-shirt and puts it back in Paul Zell's suitcase, between the dress shirts and the underwear.

The hotel where she's staying is on CNN. Because of the superheroes.

For the last three weeks Billie has tried not to think too much about what will happen at dinner when she and Paul Zell meet. But, even though she's been trying not to think about it, she still had to figure out what she was going to wear. The skirt and the sweater she brought are Melinda's. They fit okay; Billie hopes they'll make her look older, but not as if she is *trying* to look older. She bought a lipstick at Target, but when she puts it on it looks too Billie Goes to Clown School, and so she wipes it off again and puts on ChapStick instead. She's sure her lips are still redder than they ought to be; she hopes no one will notice.

When she goes down to the front desk to ask about Internet cafés, Aliss is still on the front desk. "Or you could just use the business center," Aliss tells her. "Guests can use their room keys to access the business center. You are staying here, right?"

Billie asks a question of her own. "Who's that guy, Conrad?" she says. "What's his deal?"

Aliss's eyes narrow. "His deal is he's the biggest slut in the world. Like it's any of your business," she says. "But don't think he's got any pull with his dad, Little Miss Wannabe Sidekick. No matter what he says. Hook up with him and I'll stomp your ass. It's not like I want this job, anyway."

"I've got a boyfriend," Billie says. "Besides, he's too old for me."

Which is an interesting thing for her to say, when I think about it now.

Here's the thing, Paul Zell. You're thirty-four and I'm fifteen. That's nineteen years' difference. That's a substantial gap, right? Besides the legal issue, which I am not trying to minimize, I could be twice as old as I am now and you'd still be older. I've thought about this a lot. And you know what? There's a teacher at school, Mrs. Christie. Melinda was talking, a few months ago, about how Mrs. Christie just turned thirty and her husband is sixty-three. And they still fell in love, and yeah, Melinda says everyone thinks it's kind of repulsive, but that's love, and nobody really understands how it works. It just happens. And then there's Melinda, who married a guy *exactly the same age that she was*, who then got addicted to heroin, and was, besides that, just all-around bad news. My point? Compared to those thirty-three years between Mr. and Mrs. Christie, eighteen years is practically nothing.

The real problem here is timing. And, also, of course, the fact that I lied. But, except for the lying, why couldn't it have worked out between us in a few years? Why do we really have to wait at all? It's not like I'm ever going to fall in love with anyone again.

*

Billie uses Paul Zell's hotel room key to get into the business center. There's a superhero at one of the PCs. The superhero is at least eight feet tall, and she's got frizzy red hair. You can tell she's a superhero and not just a tall dentist because a little electric sizzle runs along her outline, every once in a while, as if maybe she's being projected into her too-small seat from some other dimension. She glances over at Billie, who nods hello. The superhero sighs and looks at her fingernails. Which is fine with Billie. She doesn't need rescuing, and she isn't auditioning for anything, either. No matter what anybody thinks.

For some reason, Billie chooses to be Constant Bliss when she signs onto FarAway. She's double incognito. Paul Zell isn't online and there's no one in King Nermal's Chamber, except for the living chess pieces who are always there, and who aren't really alive, either. Not the ones who are still standing or sitting, patiently, upon their squares, waiting to be deployed, knitting or picking their noses or flirting or whatever their particular programs have been programmed to do when they aren't in combat. Billie's favorite is the King's Rook, because he always laughs when he moves into battle, even when he must know he's going to be defeated.

○

Do you ever feel as if they're watching you, Paul? Sometimes I wonder if they know that they're just a game inside a game. When I first found King Nermal's Chamber, I walked all around the board and checked out what everyone was doing. The White Queen and her pawn were playing chess, like they always do. I sat and watched them play. After a while the White Queen asked me if I wanted a match, and when I said yes, her little board got bigger and bigger until I was standing on a single square of it, inside another chamber exactly the same as the chamber I'd just been standing in, and there was another White Queen playing chess with her pawn, and I guess I could have kept on going down and down and down, but instead I got freaked out and quit FarAway without saving.

Bearhand isn't in FarAway right now. No Enchantress Magic EightBall either, of course.

Constant Bliss is low on healing herbs, and she's quite near the Bloody Meadows, so I put on her invisible cloak and go out onto the battlefield. Rare and strange plants have sprung up where the blood of men and beasts is still soaking into the ground. I'm wearing a Shielding Hand, too, because some of the plants don't like being yanked out of the ground. When my collecting box is one hundred percent full, Constant Bliss leaves the Bloody Meadows. I leave the Bloody Meadows. Billie leaves the Bloody Meadows. Billie hasn't quite decided what she should do next, or where she should go, and besides it's nearly six o'clock. So she saves and quits.

The superhero is watching something on YouTube, two Korean guys breakdancing to Pachelbel's Canon in D. Billie stands up to leave.

"Girl," the superhero says. Her voice hurts to listen to.

"Who, me?" Billie says.

"You, girl," the superhero says. "Are you here with Miracle?"

Billie realizes a mistake has been made. "I'm not a sidekick," she says.

"Then who are you?" the superhero says.

"Nobody," Billie says. And then, because she remembers that there's a superhero named Nobody, she says, "I mean, I'm not any-body." She escapes before the superhero can say anything else.

○

Billie checks her hair in the women's bathroom in the lobby. Nothing can be done. She wishes her sister's sweater wasn't so tight. She decides it doesn't make her look older, it just makes her look lumpy. Melinda is always trying to get Billie to wear something besides T-shirts and jeans, but Billie, looking in the bathroom mirror, suddenly wishes she looked more like herself, forgetting that what she needs is to look less like herself. To look less like a fifteen-year-old crazy liar.

Although apparently what she looks like is a sidekick.

Billie doesn't need to pee, but she pees anyway, just in case, because what if later she really has to get up and leave the dinner table? You'd know that she was going to the bathroom, and for some reason this seems embarrassing to her. The fact that she's even worrying about this right now makes Billie feel as if she might be going crazy.

The maître d' asks if she has a reservation. It's now five minutes to six. "For six o'clock," Billie says. "For two. Paul Zell?"

"Here we are," the maître d' says. "The other member of your party isn't here, but we can go ahead and seat you."

Billie is seated. The maître d' pushes her chair in, and Billie tries not to feel trapped. There are other people eating dinner all around her, dentists and superheroes and maybe ordinary people, too. Costumes are definitely superheroes, but just because some of the hotel guests aren't wearing costumes, doesn't mean they're dentists and not superheroes. Although some of them are definitely dentists.

Billie hasn't eaten since this morning, when she got a bagel at Port Authority. Her first New York bagel. Cinnamon raisin with blueberry cream cheese. Her stomach is growling a little, but she can't order dinner yet, of course, because you aren't there yet, Paul Zell, and she doesn't want to eat the bread sticks in the bowl on the table, either. What if you show up, and you sit down across from her and her mouth is full or she gets poppy seeds stuck in her teeth?

People who aren't Paul Zell are seated at tables, or go to the bar and sit on bar stools. Billie studies the menu. She's never had sushi before, but she decides that she will order boldly. A waiter pours her a glass of water. Asks if she'd like to order an appetizer

241

while she's waiting. Billie declines. The people at the table next to her pay their bill and leave. When she looks at her watch, she sees it's 6:18.

You're late, Paul Zell.

Billie eats a bread stick dusted with a greenish powder that makes her lips burn, just a little. She drinks her water, and then, even though she went to the bathroom not even a half hour ago, she needs to pee again. She gets up and goes. Maybe when she comes back to the table, Paul Zell will be sitting there. But she comes back and he isn't.

Billie thinks: Maybe she should go back to the room and see if there are any messages. "I'll be right back," she tells the maître d'. The maître d' couldn't care less. There are superheroes in the hotel lobby and there are dentists in the elevator and there's a light on the phone in room 1584 that would flash if there were any messages. It isn't flashing. Billie dials the number for messages just in case. No message.

Back in the Golden Lotus no one is sitting at the table reserved for Paul Zell, six o'clock, party of two. Billie sits back down anyway. She waits until 7:30, and then she leaves while the maitre d' is escorting a party of superheroes to a table. So far none of the superheroes are ones that Billie recognizes, which doesn't mean that their superpowers are lame. It's just, there are a lot of superheroes and knowing a lot about superheroes has never been Billie's thing.

She rides up the glass-fronted elevator to Paul Zell's hotel room and orders room service. This should be exciting, because Billie's never ordered room service in her life. But it's not. She orders a hamburger, and when the woman asks if she wants to charge it to her room, she says sure. She drinks a juice from the minibar and watches the Cartoon Network. She waits for someone to knock on the door. When someone does, it's just a bellboy with her hamburger.

By nine o'clock Billie has been down to the business center twice. She checks Hotmail, checks FarAway, checks all the chat-rooms. No Boggle. No Paul Zell. Just chess pieces, and it isn't her move. She writes Paul Zell an e-mail; in the end, she doesn't send it.

When she goes upstairs for the last time, no one is there. Just the suitcase. She doesn't really expect anyone to be there. The jeweler's box is still down at the bottom of the suitcase.

The office building in the window is still lit up. Maybe the lights stay on all night long even when no one is there. Billie thinks those lights are the loneliest things she's ever seen. Even lonelier than the light of distant stars that are already dead by the time their light reaches us. Down below, ant people do their antic things, unaware that Billie is watching them.

Billie opens up the minibar again. Inside are miniature bottles of gin, bourbon, tequila, and rum that no one is going to drink, unless Billie drinks them. What would Alice do, Billie thinks. Billie has always been a Lewis Carroll fan, and not just because of the chess stuff.

There are two beers and a jar of peanuts. Billie disdains the peanuts. She drinks all of the miniatures and both normal-sized cans of beer. Perhaps you noticed the charges on your hotel bill.

◎

Here is where details begin to be a little thin for me, Paul Zell. Perhaps you have a better idea of what I'm describing, what I'm omitting. Then again, maybe you don't.

It's the first time Billie's ever been drunk, and she's not very good at it. Nothing is happening that she can tell. She perseveres. She begins to feel okay, as if everything is going to be okay. The okay feeling gets larger and larger until she's entirely swallowed up by okayness. This lasts for a while, and then she starts to fade in and out, like she's jumping forward in time, always just a little bit dizzy when she arrives. Here she is, flipping through channels, not quite brave enough to click on the pay-for-porn channels, although she thinks about it. Then here she is, a bit later, putting that lipstick on again. This time she kind of likes the way she looks. Here she is, lifting all of Paul Zell's clothes out of the suitcase. She takes the ring out of the box, puts it on her big toe. Now there's a gap. Then: here's Billie, back again, she's bent over a toilet. She's vomiting. She vomits over and over again. Someone is holding back her hair. There's a hand holding out a damp, cold facecloth. Now she's in a bed. The room is dark, but Billie thinks there's someone sitting on the other bed. He's just sitting there.

Later on, she thinks she hears someone moving around the room, doing things. For some reason, she imagines that it's the Enchantress Magic Eightball. Rummaging around the room, looking for important, powerful, magical things. Billie thinks she ought to get up and help. But she can't move.

Much later on, when Billie gets up and goes to the bathroom to throw up again, Paul Zell's suitcase is gone.

There's vomit all over the sink and the bathtub, and on her sister's sweater. Billie's crotch is cold and wet; she realizes she's pissed herself. She pulls off the sweater and skirt and hose, and her underwear. She leaves her bra on because she can't figure out how to undo the straps. She drinks four glasses of water and then crawls into the other bed, the one she hasn't pissed in.

When she wakes up it's one in the afternoon. Someone has left the Do Not Disturb sign on the door of Room 1584. Maybe Billie did this, maybe not. She won't be able to get the bus back to Keokuk today; it left this morning at 7:32. Paul Zell's suitcase is gone, even his dirty clothes are gone. There's not even a sock. Not even a hair on a pillow. Just the herbal conditioner. I guess you forgot to check the bathtub.

Billie's head hurts so bad she wonders if she fell over when she passed out and hit it on something. It's possible, I guess.

Billie is almost glad her head hurts so much. She deserves much worse. She pushes one of the towels around the sink and the counter, mopping up crusted puke. She runs hot water in the shower until the whole bathroom smells like puke soup. She strips the sheets off the bed she peed in, and shoves them with Melinda's destroyed sweater and skirt and all of the puke-stained towels under the counter in the bathroom. The water is only just warm when she takes her shower. Better than she deserves. Billie turns the handle all the way to the right, and then shrieks and turns it back. What you deserve and what you can stand aren't necessarily the same thing.

She cries bitterly while she conditions her hair. She takes the elevator down to the lobby and goes and sits in the Starbucks. The first time she's ever been inside a Starbucks. What she really wants is a caramel iced vanilla latte, but instead she orders three shots of espresso. More penance.

(I know, I find all of this behavior excruciating and over the top, too. And maybe this is a kind of over-the-top penance, too, what I'm doing here, telling you all of this, and maybe the point of humiliating myself by relating all of this humiliating behavior will only bring me even greater humiliation later, when I realize what a self-obsessed, miserable, martyring little drama queen I'm allowing myself to be right now.)

Billie is pouring little packets of sugar into her three shots of espresso when someone sits down next to her. It isn't you, of course. It's that guy, Conrad. And now we're past the point where I owe you an apology, and yet I guess I ought to keep going, because the story isn't over yet. Remember how Billie thought the room key and the bus ride seemed like FarAway, like a quest? Now is the part where it starts seeming more like one of those games of chess, the kind you've already lost and you know it, but you don't concede. You just keep on losing, one piece at a time, until you're the biggest loser in the world. Which is, I guess, how life is like chess. Because it's not like anyone ever wins in the end, is it?

Anyway. Part two. In which I go on writing about myself in the third person. In which I continue to act stupidly. Stop reading if you want.

○

Conrad Linthor sits down without being asked. He's drinking something frozen. "Sidekick girl. You look terrible."

All during this conversation, picture superheroes of various descriptions. They stroll or glide or stride purposefully past Billie's table. They nod at the guy sitting across from her. Billie notices this without having the strength of character to wonder what's going on. Every molecule of her being is otherwise engaged, with misery, woe, self-hatred, heartbreak, shame, all-obliterating roiling nausea and pain.

Billie says, "So we meet again." Which is, don't you think, the kind of thing people end up saying when they find themselves in a hotel full of superheroes. "I'm not a sidekick. And my name's Billie."

"Whatever," Conrad Linthor says. "Conrad Linthor. So what happened to you?"

Billie swigs bitter espresso. She lets her hair fall in front of her face. Baby bird, she thinks. Wrong smell, baby bird.

But Conrad Linthor doesn't go away. He says, "All right, I'll go first. Let's swap life stories. That girl at the desk when you were checking in? Aliss? I've slept with her, a couple of times. When nothing better came along. She really likes me. And I'm an asshole, okay? No excuses. Every time I hurt her, though, the next time I see her I'm nice again and I apologize and I get her back.

246

Mostly I'm nice just to see if she's going to fall for it this time, too. I don't know why. I guess I want to see where that place is, the place where she hauls off and assaults me. Some people have ant farms. I'm more into people. So now you know what was going on yesterday. And yeah, I know, something's wrong with me."

Billie pushes her hair back. She says, "Why are you telling me all this?"

He shrugs. "I don't know. You look like you're in a world of hurt. I don't really care. It's just that I get bored. And you look really terrible, and I thought that there was probably something interesting going on. Besides, Aliss can see us in here, from the desk, and this will drive her crazy."

"I'm okay," Billie says. "Nobody hurt me. I'm the bad guy here. I'm the idiot."

"That's unexpected. Also interesting. Go on," Conrad Linthor says. "Tell me everything."

Billie tells him. Everything except for the part where she pees the bed.

When her tale is told, Conrad Linthor stands up and says, "Come on. We're going to go see a friend of mine. You need the cure."

"For love?" This is Billie's lame attempt at humor. She was wondering if telling someone what she's done would make her feel better. It hasn't.

"No cure for love," Conrad Linthor says. "Because there's no such thing. Your hangover we can do something about."

As they navigate the lobby, there are new boards up announcing that free teeth-whitening sessions are available in Suite 412 for qualified superheroes. Billie looks over at the front desk and sees Aliss looking back. She draws her finger across her throat. If looks could kill you wouldn't be reading this e-mail.

Conrad Linthor goes through a door that you're clearly not meant to go through. It's labeled. Billie follows anyway and they're in a corridor, in a maze of corridors. If this were a MMORPG, the zombies would show up any minute. Instead, every once in a while, they pass someone who is probably hotel cleaning staff; bellboys sneaking cigarettes. Everyone nods at Conrad Linthor, just like the superheroes in the Starbucks in the lobby.

Billie doesn't want to ask, but eventually she does. "Who *are* you?"

"Call me Eloise," Conrad Linthor says.

"Sorry?" Billie imagines that they are no longer in the hotel at all. The corridor they are currently navigating slopes gently downward. Maybe they will end up on the shores of a subterranean lake, or in a dungeon, or in Narnia, or King Nermal's Chamber, or even Keokuk, Iowa. It's a small world after all.

"You know, Eloise. The girl who lives in the Plaza? Has a pet turtle named Skipperdee?"

He waits, like Billie's supposed to know what he's talking about. When she doesn't say anything, he says, "Never mind. It's just this book—a classic of modern children's literature, actually—about a girl who lives in the Plaza. Which is a hotel. A bit nicer than this one, maybe, but never mind. I live here."

He keeps on talking. They keep on walking.

Billie's hangover is a special effect. Conrad Linthor is going on and on about superheroes. His father is an agent. Apparently superheroes have agents. Represents all of the big guys. Knows everyone. Agoraphobic. Never leaves the hotel. Everyone comes to him. Big banquet tomorrow night, for his biggest client. Tyrannosaurus Hex. Hex is retiring. Going to go live in the mountains and breed tarantula wasps. Conrad Linthor's father is throwing a party for Hex. Everyone will be there.

Billie's legs are noodles. The ends of her hair are poison needles. Her tongue is a bristly sponge, and her eyes are bags of bleach.

There's a clattering that splits Billie's brain. Two wheeled carts come round the next corner like comets, followed at arm's length

248

by hurtling busboys. They sail down the corridor at top speed. Conrad Linthor and Billie flatten themselves against the wall. "You have to move fast," Conrad explains. "Or else the food gets cold. Guests complain."

Around that corner, enormous doors, still swinging. Big enough to birth a Greyhound bus bound for Keokuk. A behemoth. Billie passes through the doors onto the far shores of what is, of course, a hotel kitchen. Far away, miles, it seems to Billie, there are clouds of vapor and vague figures moving through them. Clanging noises, people yelling, the thick, sweet smell of caramelized onions, onions that will never make anyone cry again. Other savory reeks.

Conrad Linthor steers Billie to a marble-topped table. Copper whisks, mixing bowls, dinged pots hang down on hooks.

Billie feels she ought to say something. "You must have a lot of money," she contributes. "To live in a hotel."

"No shit, Sherlock," Conrad Linthor says. "Sit down. I'll be back."

Billie climbs, slowly and carefully, up a laddery stool and lays her poor head down on the dusty, funereal slab. (It's actually a pastry station, the dust is flour, but Billie is mentally in a bad place.) Paul Zell, Paul Zell. She stares at the tiled wall. Billie's heart has a crack in it. Her head is made of radiation. The Starbucks espresso she forced down has burnt a thousand pinprick holes in Billie's wretched stomach.

Conrad Linthor comes back too soon. He says, "This is her."

There's a guy with him. Skinny, with serious acne scars. Big shoulders. Funny little paper hat and a stained apron. "Ernesto, Billie," Conrad says. "Billie, Ernesto."

"How old did you say?" Ernesto says. He folds his arms, as if Billie is a bad cut of meat Conrad Linthor is trying to pass off as prime rib.

"Fifteen, right?"

Billie confirms.

"She came to the city because of some pervert she met online?"

"In a MMORPG," Conrad says.

"He isn't a pervert," Billie says. "He thought I was my sister. I was pretending to be my sister. She's in her thirties."

"What's your guess?" Conrad asks Ernesto. "Superhero or dentist?"

"One more time," Billie says. "I'm not here to audition for anything. And do I look like a dentist?"

"You look like trouble," Ernesto says. "Here. Drink this." He hands her a glass full of something slimy and green.

"What's in it?" Billie says.

"Wheat grass," Ernesto says. "And other stuff. Secret recipe. Hold your nose and drink it down."

"Yuck," Billie says. (I won't even try to describe the taste of Ernesto's hangover cure. Except, I will never drink again.) "Ew, yuck. Yuck, yuck, yuck."

"Keep holding your nose," Ernesto advises Billie. To Conrad: "They met online?"

"Yeah," Billie says. "In FarAway."

"Yeah, I know that game. Dentist," Ernesto says. "For sure."

"Except," Conrad says, "it gets better. It wasn't just a game. Inside this game, they were playing a game. They were playing *chess*."

"Ohhhh," Ernesto says. Now he's grinning. They both are. "Oh as in superher-oh."

"Superhero," Conrad says. They high-five each other. "The only question is who."

"What was the alibi again?" Ernesto asks Billie, "The name this dude gave?"

"Paul Zell?" Billie says. "Wait, you think Paul Zell is a superhero? No way. He does tech support for a nonprofit. Something involving endangered species."

Conrad Linthor and Ernesto exchange another look. "Super-hero for sure," Ernesto says.

Ernesto says, "Or supervillain. All those freaks are into chess. It's like a disease."

"No way," Billie says again.

Conrad Linthor says, "Because there's no chance Paul Zell would have lied to you about anything. Because the two of you were being completely and totally honest with each other." Which shuts Billie up.

Conrad Linthor says, "I just can't get this picture out of my head. This superhero going out and buying a ring. And there you are. This fifteen-year-old girl." He laughs. He nudges Billie as if to say, I'm not laughing at you. I'm laughing near you.

"And there I was," Billie says. "Sitting at the table waiting for him. Like the biggest idiot in the world."

Ernesto has to gasp for air he is laughing so hard.

Billie says, "I guess it's kind of funny. In a horrible way."

"So, anyway," Conrad says. "Since Billie's into chess, I thought we ought to show her your project. Have they set up the banquet room yet?"

Ernesto stops laughing, holds his right hand out, like he's stopping traffic. "Hey, man. Maybe later? I've got prep. I'm salad station tonight. You know?"

"Ernesto's an artist," Conrad says. "I keep telling him he needs to make some appointments, take a portfolio downtown. My dad says people would pay serious bucks for what Ernesto does."

Billie isn't really paying attention to this conversation. She's thinking about Paul Zell. How could you be a superhero, Paul Zell? Can you miss something that big? A secret as big as that? Sure, she thinks. Probably you can miss it by a mile.

"I make things out of butter," Ernesto says. "It's no big deal. Like, sure, someone's going to pay me a million bucks for some thing I carved out of butter."

251

"It's a statement," Conrad Linthor says, "an artistic statement about the world we live in."

"We live in a world made out of butter," Ernesto says. "Doesn't seem like much of a statement to me. You any good at chess?"

"What?" Billie says.

"Chess. You any good?"

"I'm not bad," Billie says. "You know, it's just for fun. Paul Zell's really good."

"So he wins most of the time?" Ernesto says.

"Yeah," Billie says. She thinks about it. "Wait, no. I guess I win more."

"You gonna be a superhero when you grow up? Because those guys are way into chess."

Conrad Linthor says, "It's like the homicidal triangle. Like setting fires, hurting small animals, and wetting the bed means a kid may grow up to be a sociopath. For superheroes, it's chess. Weird coincidences, that's another one. For example, you're always in the wrong place at the right time. Plus you have an ability of some kind."

"I don't have an ability," Billie says. "Not even one of those really pointless ones like always knowing the right time, or whether it's going to rain."

"Your power might develop later on," Conrad Linthor says.

"It won't."

"Well, okay. But it might, anyway," Conrad Linthor. "It's why I noticed you in the first place. Probably. You stick out. She sticks out, right?"

"I guess," Ernesto says. He gives her that appraising a cut of meat look again. Then nods. "Sure. She sticks out. You stick out."

"I stick out," Billie says. "I stick out like what?"

"Even Aliss noticed," Conrad says. "She thought you were here to audition, remember?"

Ernesto says, "Oh, yeah. Because Aliss is such a fine judge of character."

252

"Shut up, Ernesto," Conrad says. "Look, Billie. It's not a bad thing, okay? Some people, you can just tell. So maybe you're just some girl. But maybe you can do something that you don't even know about yet."

"You sound like my guidance counselor," Billie says. "Like my sister. Why do people always try to tell you that life gets better? Like life has a bad cold. Like, here I am, and where is my sister right now? She drove my dad up to Peoria. To St. Francis, because he has pancreatic cancer. And that's the only reason I'm here, because my dad's dying, and so nobody is even going to notice that I'm gone. Lucky me, right?"

Ernesto and Conrad Linthor are both staring at her.

"I'm a superhero," Billie says. "Or a sidekick. Whatever you say. Paul Zell is a superhero, too. Everybody's a superhero. The world is made of butter. I don't even know what that means."

"How's the hangover?" Conrad Linthor asks her.

"Better," Billie says. The hangover is gone. Of course she still feels terrible, but that's not hangover related. That's Paul Zell related. That's just everything else.

"Sorry about you know, uh, your dad." That's Ernesto.

Billie shrugs. Grimaces. As if on cue, there is a piercing scream somewhere far away. Then a lot of shouting. Some laughing. Off in the distance, something seems to be happening. "Gotta go," Ernesto says.

"Ernesto!" It's a short guy in a tall hat. He says, "Hey, Mr. Linthor. What's up?"

"Gregor," Conrad says. "Hope that wasn't anything serious."

"Nah, man," the short guy says. "Just Portland. Sliced off the tip of his pointer finger. Again. Second time in six months. The guy is a master of disaster."

"See you, Conrad," Ernesto says. "Nice to meet you, Billie. Stay out of trouble."

As Ernesto goes off with the short guy, the short guy is

saying, "So who's the girl? She looks like somebody. Somebody's sidekick?"

Conrad yells after them. "Maybe we'll see you later, okay?"

He tells Billie, "There's a get-together tonight up on the roof. Nothing official. Just some people hanging out. You ought to come by. Then maybe we can go see Ernesto's party sculptures."

"I may not be here," Billie says. "It's Paul Zell's room, not mine. What if he's checked out?"

"Then your key won't work," Conrad Linthor says. "Look, if you're locked out, just call up to the penthouse later and tell me and I'll see what I can do. Right now I've got to get to class."

"You're in school?" Billie says.

"Just taking some classes down at the New School," Conrad says. "Life drawing. Film studies. I'm working on a novel, but it's not like that's a full-time commitment, right?"

Billie is almost sorry to leave the kitchen behind. It's the first place in New York where she's been one hundred percent sure she doesn't have to worry about running into Paul Zell. It isn't that this is a good thing, it's just that her spider sense isn't tingling all the time. Not that Billie has anything that's the equivalent of spider sense. And maybe room 1584 can also be considered a safe haven now. The room key still works. Someone has remade the bed, taken away the towels and sheets in the bathroom. Melinda's red sweater and skirt are hanging down over the shower rod. Someone rinsed them out first.

Billie orders room service. Then she decides to set out for Bryant Park. She'll go watch the chess players, which is what she and Paul Zell were going to do, what they talked about doing online. Maybe you'll be there, Paul Zell.

She has a map. She walks the whole way. She doesn't get lost. When she gets to Bryant Park, sure enough, there are some chess games going on. Old men, college kids, maybe even a few superheroes. Pigeons everywhere, underfoot. New Yorkers walking their dogs. A lady yelling. No Paul Zell. Not that Billie would know Paul Zell if she saw him.

Billie sits on a bench beside a trashcan, and after a while someone sits down beside her. Not Paul Zell. A superhero. The superhero from the hotel business center.

"We meet again," the superhero says. Which serves Billie right.

Billie says, "Are you following me?"

"No," the superhero says. "Maybe. I'm Lightswitch."

"I've heard of you," Billie says. "You're famous."

"Famous is relative," Lightswitch says. "Sure, I've been on *Oprah*. But I'm no Tyrannosaurus Hex."

"There's a comic book about you," Billie says. "Although, uh, she doesn't look like you. Not really."

"The artist likes to draw the boobs life-sized. Just the boobs. Says it's artistic license."

They sit for a while in companionable silence. "You play chess?" Billie asks.

"Of course," Lightswitch says. "Doesn't everybody? Who's your favorite chess player?"

"Paul Morphy," Billie says. "Although Koneru Humpy has the most awesome name ever."

"Agreed," Lightswitch says. "So are you in town for the shindig? Shindig. What kind of word is that? Archeological excavation of the shin. Knee surgery. Do you work with someone?"

"Do you mean, am I a sidekick?" Billie says. "No. I'm not a sidekick. I'm Billie Faggart. Hi."

"Sidekick. There's another one. Kick in the side. Pain in the neck. Kick in the shin. Ignore me. I get distracted sometimes." Lightswitch holds out a hand for Billie to shake, and Billie does. She thinks that there will be a baby jolt maybe, like one of those joke buzzers. But there's nothing. It's just an ordinary handshake, except that Lightswitch's completely solid hand still looks funny, staticky, like it's really somewhere else. Billie can't remember if Lightswitch is from the future or the eighth dimension. Or maybe neither of those is quite right.

Two little kids come up and want Lightswitch's autograph. They look at Billie, as if wondering whether they ought to ask for her autograph, too.

Billie stands up, and Lightswitch says, "Wait a minute. Let me give you my card."

"Why?" Billie says.

"Just in case," Lightswitch says. "You might change your mind at some point about the sidekick thing. It isn't a long-term career, you know, but it's not a bad thing to do for a while. Mostly it's answering fan mail, photo ops, banter practice."

Billie says, "Um, what happened to your last sidekick?" And then, seeing the look on Lightswitch's face, wonders if this is not the kind of question you're supposed to ask a superhero.

"Fell off a building. Kidding! That was a joke, okay? Sold her story to the tabloids. Used the proceeds to go to law school." Lightswitch kicks at a can. "Bam. Damn. Anyway. My card."

Billie looks, but there's nobody around to tell her what any of this means. Maybe you'd know, Paul Zell.

Billie says, "Do you know somebody named Paul Zell?"

"Paul Zell? Rings a bell. There's another one. Ding dong. Paul Zell. But no. I don't think I do, after all. It's a business card. Not an executive decision. Just take it, okay?" Lightswitch says. So Billie does.

●

Billie doesn't intend to show for Conrad Linthor's shindig. She walks down Broadway. Gawks at the gawkworthy. Pleasurably ponders a present for her sister, decides discretion is the better part of harmonious family relationships. Caped superheroes swoop and wheel and dip around the Empire State Building. No crime in progress. Show business. Billie walks until she has blisters. Doesn't think about Paul Zell. Paul Zell, Paul Zell. Doesn't think about Lightswitch. Pays twelve bucks to see a movie and don't ask me what movie or if it was any good. I don't remember. When she comes out of the movie theater, back out onto the street, everything sizzles with lights. It's Fourth of July bright. Apparently nobody in New York ever goes to bed early. Billie decides she'll go to bed early. Get a wake-up call and walk down to Port Authority. Catch her bus. Go home to Keokuk and never think about New York again. Stay off FarAway. Concede the chess game. Burn the business card. But: Paul Zell, Paul Zell.

Meanwhile, back to the hotel, Aliss the nemesis has been lying in wait. Actually, it's more like standing behind a flower arrangement, but never mind. Aliss pounces. Billie, mourning lost love, is easy prey.

"Going to your boyfriend's party?" Aliss hisses. There's only one *s* in that particular sentence, but Aliss knows how to make an *s* count.

She links arms with Billie. Pulls her into an elevator.

"What party?" Billie says. "What boyfriend?" Aliss gives her a look. Hits the button marked Roof, then the emergency stop button, like she's opening cargo doors, one, two. Goodbye, cruel, old world. That bomb is going to drop.

"If you mean Conrad Linthor," Billie says, "That was nothing. In the Starbucks. He just wanted to talk about you. In fact, he gave me this. Because he was afraid he was going to lose it. But he's planning on giving it to you. Tomorrow, I think."

She takes out the ring that you left behind, Paul Zell.

Surely you've checked the jeweler's box by now. Seen the ring is gone. Billie found it in the bed sheets that morning when she woke up. Remember? I was wearing it on my big toe. All day long

257

Billie carried it around in her pocket, just like the business card. It didn't fit her ring finger.

I slipped it on and off, on and off, all day long.

Billie and Aliss both stare at the ring. Both of them seem to find it hard to speak.

Finally: "It's mine?" Aliss says. She puts her hand out, like the ring's a cute dog. Not a ring. Like she wants to pet it. "That's a two-carat diamond. At least. Antique setting. Just explain one thing, please. Why did Conrad give you my ring? You expect me to believe he let some girl carry my diamond ring around all day?"

"Yeah, well, you know Conrad," Billie says.

"Yeah," Aliss says. She's silent for another long moment. "Can I?"

She takes the ring, tries it on her ring finger. It fits. There's an inappropriate ache in Billie's throat. Aliss says, "Wow. Just wow. I guess I have to give it back. Okay. I can do that." She holds up her hand. Drags the diamond along the glass elevator wall, then rubs at the scratch it's left behind. Then checks the diamond, like she might have damaged it. But diamonds are like the superheroes of the mineral world. Diamonds cut glass. Not the other way around.

Aliss presses the button. The elevator elevates.

"Maybe you should go to the party and I should just go to bed," Billie says. "I have to catch a bus in the morning."

"No," Aliss says. "Wait. Now I'm nervous. I can't go up there by myself. You have to come with me. Except we can't act like we're friends, because then Conrad will suspect something's up. That I *know*. You can't tell him I know."

"I won't. I swear," Billie says.

"How's my hair?" Aliss says. "Shit. Don't tell him, but they fired me. Just like that. I'm not supposed to be here. I think management knew something was up with me and Conrad. I'm not the first girl he's gotten fired. But I'm not going to say anything right now. I'll tell him later."

258

Billie says, "That sucks."

"You have no idea," Aliss says. "It's such a crappy job. People are such assholes, and you still have to say have a nice day. And smile." She gives the ring back. Smiles.

The elevator opens on sky. There's a sign saying Private Party. Like the whole sky is a private party. It's just after nine o'clock. The sky is orange. The pool is the color the sky ought to be. There are superheroes splashing around in it. That bubble of blood floating above it, like an oversized beach ball. Tango music plays.

Conrad Linthor lounges on a lounge chair. He comes over when he sees Billie and Aliss. "Girls," he says.

"Hey, Conrad," Aliss says. Her hip cocked like a gun hammer. Her hair is remarkable. The piercing is in. "Great party."

"Billie," Conrad says. "I'm so glad you came. There are some people you ought to meet." He takes Billie's arm and drags her off. Maybe he's going to throw her in the pool.

"Is Ernesto here?" Billie looks back, but Aliss is having a conversation now with someone in a uniform.

"This kind of party isn't really for hotel staff," Conrad says. "They get in trouble if they socialize with the guests."

"Don't worry about Aliss," Billie says. "Apparently she got fired. But you probably already know that."

Conrad smiles. They're on the edge of a group of strangers who all look vaguely familiar, vaguely improbable. There are scales, feathers, ridiculous outfits designed to show off ridiculous physiques. Why does everything remind Billie of FarAway? Except for the smell. Why do superheroes smell weird? Paul Zell.

The tango has become something dangerous. A woman is singing. There is nobody here that Billie wants to meet.

Conrad Linthor is drunk. Or high. "This is Billie," he says. "My sidekick for tonight. Billie, this is everyone."

"Hi, everyone," Billie says. "Excuse me." She rescues her arm from Conrad Linthor. She heads back for the elevator. Aliss has escaped the hotel employee and is crouched down by the pool, one finger in the water. Probably the deep end. You can tell by her slumped shoulder that she's thinking about drowning herself. A good move: perhaps someone here will save her. Once someone has saved your life, they might as well fall in love with you, too. It's just good economics.

"Wait," Conrad Linthor says. He's not that old, Billie decides. He's just a kid. He hasn't even done anything all that bad, yet. And yet you can see how badness accumulates around him. Builds up like lightning on a lightning rod. If Billie sticks around, it will build up on her, too. That spider sense she doesn't have is tingling. Paul Zell, Paul Zell.

"Ernesto will be so disappointed," Conrad Linthor says. They're both jogging now. Billie sees the lit stair sign, decides not to wait for an elevator. She takes the stairs two at a time. Conrad Linthor bounds down behind her. "He really wanted you to see what he made. For the banquet. It's too bad you can't stay. I wanted to invite you to the banquet. You could meet Tyrannosaurus Hex. Get an autograph or two. Make some good contacts. Being a sidekick is all about making the contacts."

"I'm not a sidekick!" Billie yells up. "That was a dumb joke even before you made it the first time. Even if I were a sidekick, I wouldn't be yours. Like you're a superhero. Just because you know people. So what's your secret name, superhero? What's your superpower?"

She stops on the stairs so suddenly that Conrad Linthor runs into her. They both stumble forward, smack into the wall on the twenty-second floor landing. But they don't fall.

Conrad Linthor says, "My superpower is money." The wall props him up. "The only superpower that counts for anything. Better than invisibility. Better than being able to fly. Much better than telekinesis or teleportation or that other one. Telepathy. Knowing what other people are thinking. Why would you ever want to know what other people are thinking? Did you know everyone thinks that one day they might be a millionaire? Like that's a lot of money. They have no idea. They don't want to be a superhero. They just want to be like me. They want to be rich."

Billie has nothing to say to this.

"You know what the difference is between a superhero and a supervillain?" Conrad Linthor asks her.

Billie waits.

"The superhero has a really good agent," Conrad Linthor says. "Someone like my dad. You have no idea the kind of stuff they get away with. Fifteen-year-old girls is *nothing*."

"What about Lightswitch?" Billie says.

"Who? Her? She's no big deal," Conrad Linthor says. "She's okay. I don't really know much about her. She's kind of old school."

"I think I'm going to go to bed now," Billie says.

"No," Conrad Linthor says. "Wait. You have to come with me and see what Ernesto did. It's just so cool. Everything's carved out of butter."

"If I go see, will you let me go to bed?"

"Sure," Conrad Linthor says.

"Will you be nice to Aliss? If she's still up at the party when you get back?"

"I'll try," Conrad Linthor says.

"Okay," Billie says. "I'll go look at Ernesto's butter. Are we going to go meet him?"

Conrad Linthor levers himself off the wall. Pats it. "Ernesto? I don't know where he is. How should I know?"

●

They go into the forbidden maze. Back to the kitchen, and through it, now empty and dark and somehow like a morgue. A mausoleum.

"Ernesto's been doing the work in a freezer," Conrad Linthor says. "You have to keep these guys cold. Wait. Let me get it unlocked. Cool tool, right? Borrowed it from The Empty Jar. He's one of dad's clients. They're making a movie about him. I saw the script. It's crap."

The lock comes off. The lights go on. Before I tell you what was inside the freezer, let me first tell you something about how big the freezer is. It will help you visualize, later on. The freezer is plenty big. Bigger than most New York apartments, Billie thinks, although this is just hearsay. She's never been in a New York apartment.

What's inside the supersized freezer? Supervillains. Warm Gun, Glowworm, Radical!, Heatdeath, The Scribbler, The Ninjew, Cat Lady, Hellalujah, Shibboleth, The Shambler, Mandroid, Manplant, The Manticle, Patty Cakes. Lots of others. Name a famous supervillain and he or she is in the freezer. They're life-size. They're not real, although at first Billie's heart slams. She thinks: who caught all these guys? Why are they so perfectly still? Maybe Conrad Linthor is a superhero after all.

Conrad Linthor touches Hellalujah's red, bunchy bicep. Presses just a little. The color smears. Lardy, yellow-white underneath. The supervillains are made out of butter. "Hand-tinted," Conrad says.

"Ernesto made these?" Billie says. She wants to touch one, too. She walks up to Patty Cakes. Breathes on the cold, outstretched palms. You can see Patty Cakes's life line. Her love line. Billie realizes something else. The butter statues are all decorated to look like chess pieces. Their signature outfits have been changed to black and red. Cat Lady is wearing a butter crown.

Conrad Linthor puts his hand on Hellalujah's shoulder. Puts his arm around Hellalujah. Then he squeezes, hard. His arm goes through Hellalujah's neck. Like an arm going through butter. The head pops off.

"Be careful!" Billie says.

"I can't believe it's butter," Conrad says. He giggles. "Come on. Can you believe this? He made a whole chess set out of butter. And why? For some banquet for some guy who used to fight crime? That's just crap. This is better. Us here, having some fun. This is spontaneous. Haven't you always wanted to fight the bad guy and win? Now's your chance."

"But Ernesto made these!" Billie's fists are clenched.

"You heard him," Conrad says. "It's no big deal. It's not like it's art. There's no statement here. It's just butter."

He has Hellalujah's sad head in his arms. "Heavy," he says. "Food fight. Catch." He throws the head at Billie. It hits her in the chest and knocks her over.

She lies on the ice-cold floor, looking at Hellalujah's head. One side is flat. Half of Hellalujah's broad nose is stuck like a slug to Billie's chest. Her right arm is slimy with butter and food dye.

Billie sits up. She cradles Hellalujah's head, hurls it back at Conrad. She misses. Hellalujah's head smacks into Mandroid's shiny stomach. Hangs there, half embedded.

"Funny," Conrad Linthor says. He giggles.

Billie shrieks. She leaps at him, her hands killing claws. They both go down on top of The Shambler. Billie brings her knee up between Conrad Linthor's legs, drives it up into butter. She grabs Conrad Linthor by the hair, bangs his head on The Shambler's head. "Ow," Conrad Linthor says. "Ow, ow, ow."

He twists under her. Gets hold of her hands, pulls at them even as she tightens her grip on his hair. His hair is slick with butter, and she can't hold on. She lets go. His head flops down. "Get off," he says. "Get off."

Billie drives her elbow into his stomach. Her feet skid a little as she stands up. She grabs hold of Warm Gun's gun for balance, and it breaks off. "Sorry," she says, apologizing to butter. "I'm sorry. So sorry."

Conrad Linthor is trying to sit up. There's spit at the corner of his mouth, or maybe it's butter.

Billie runs for the door. Gets there just as Conrad Linthor realizes what she's doing. "Wait!" he says. "Don't you dare! You bitch!"

Too late. She's got the door shut. She leans against it, smearing it with butter.

Conrad Linthor pounds on the other side. "Billie!" It's a faint yell. Barely audible. "Let me out, okay? It was just fun. I was just having fun. It was fun, wasn't it?"

Here's the thing, Paul Zell. It was fun. That moment when I threw Hellalujah's head at him? That felt good. It felt so good I'd pay a million bucks to do it again. I can admit that now. But I don't *like* that it felt good. I don't like that it felt fun. But I guess now I understand why supervillains do what they do. Why they run around and destroy things. Because it feels fantastic. Someday I'm going to buy a lot of butter and build something out of it, just so I can tear it all to pieces again.

Billie could leave Conrad Linthor in the freezer. Walk away. Somebody would probably find him. Right?

But then she thinks about what he'll do in there. He'll kick apart all of the other buttervillains. Stomp them into greasy pieces. She knows he'll do it, because she can imagine doing the same thing.

She lets him out.

"Not funny," Conrad Linthor says. He looks very funny.

Picture him, all decked out in red and black butter. His lips are purplish-bluish. He's shivering with cold. So is Billie.

"Not funny at all," Billie agrees. "What the hell was that? What were you doing in there? What about your friend? Ernesto? How could you do that to him?"

"He's not really a friend," Conrad Linthor says. "Not like you and me. He's just some guy I hang out with sometimes. Friends are boring. I get bored."

"We're not friends," Billie says.

"Sure," Conrad Linthor says. "I know that. But I thought if I said we were, you might fall for it. You have no idea how stupid some people are. Besides, I was doing it for you. No, really. I was. Sometimes when a superhero is in a really bad situation, that's when they finally discover their ability. What they can do. With some people it's an amulet, or a ring, but mostly it's just environmental. Your adrenaline kicks in. My father is always trying stuff on me, just in case I've got something that we haven't figured out yet."

Maybe some of this is true, and maybe all of it is true, and maybe Conrad Linthor is just testing Billie again. Is she that stupid? He's watching her right now, to see if she's falling for any of this.

"I'm out of here," Billie says. She checks her pocket, just to make sure Paul Zell's ring is still there. She's been doing that all day.

"Wait," Conrad Linthor says. "You don't know how to get back. You need help."

"I made a trail," Billie says. All the way through the corridors, this time, she pressed the diamond along the wall. Left a thin little mark. Nothing anyone else would even know to look for.

"Fine," Conrad Linthor says. "I'm going to stay down here and make some scrambled eggs. Sure you don't want any?"

"I'm not hungry," Billie says.

Even as she's leaving, Conrad Linthor is explaining to her that they'll meet again. This is like their origin story. Maybe they're each other's nemesis, or maybe they're destined to team up and save the world and make lots of—

Eventually Billie can't hear him anymore. She leaves a trail of butter all the way back to the lobby. Gets onto an elevator before anyone has noticed the state she's in, or maybe by this point in the weekend the hotel staff are used to stranger things.

She takes a shower and goes to bed still smelling faintly of butter. She wakes up early. The bubble of blood is down in the lobby again, floating over the fountain.

Billie thinks about going over to ask for an autograph. Pretending to be a fan. Could you pop that bubble with a ballpoint pen? This is the kind of thought Conrad Linthor goes around thinking, she's pretty sure.

Billie catches her bus. And that's the end of the story, Paul Zell. Dear Paul Zell.

Except for the ring. Here's the thing about the ring. Billie wrapped it in tissue paper and sealed it up in a hotel envelope. She wrote "Ernesto in the kitchen" on the outside of the envelope. She wrote a note. The note says: "This ring belongs to Paul Zell. If he comes looking for it, maybe he'll give you a reward. A couple hundred bucks seems fair. Tell him I'll pay him back. But if he doesn't get in touch, you should keep the ring. Or sell it. I'm sorry about Hellalujah and Mandroid and The Shambler. I didn't know what Conrad Linthor was going to do."

○

So, Paul Zell. That's the whole story. Except for the part where I got home and found the e-mail from you, the one where you explained what had happened to you. That you had an emergency appendectomy, and never made it to New York at all, and what happened to me? Did I make it to the hotel? Did I wonder where you were? You say you can't imagine how worried and/or angry I must have been. Etc.

266

I'll be honest with you, Paul Zell. I read your e-mail and part of me thought, I'm saved. We'll both pretend none of this ever happened. I'll go on being Melinda, and Melinda will go on being the Enchantress Magic Eightball, and Paul Zell, whoever Paul Zell is, will go on being Boggle the Master Thief. We'll play chess and chat online, and everything will be exactly the way that it was before.

But that would be crazy. I would be a fifteen-year-old liar, and you would be some weird guy who's so pathetic and lonely that he's willing to settle for me. Not even for me. To settle for the person I was pretending to be. But you're better than that, Paul Zell. You have to be better than that. So I wrote you this letter.

○

If you read this letter the whole way through, now you know what happened to your ring, and a lot of other things too. I still have your conditioner. If you give Ernesto the reward, let me know and I'll sell Constant Bliss and the Enchantress Magic Eightball. So I can pay you back. It's not a big deal. I can go be someone else, right?

○

Or else, I guess, you could ignore this letter, and we could just pretend that I never sent it. That I never came to New York to meet Paul Zell. That Paul Zell wasn't going to give me a ring.

We could pretend you never discovered my secret identity. We could go on being Boggle the Master Thief and the Enchantress Magic Eightball. We could meet up a couple times a week in Far-Away and play chess. We could even go on a quest. Save the world.

We could chat. Flirt. I could tell you about Melinda's week, and we could pretend that maybe someday we're going to be brave enough to meet face-to-face.

But here's the deal, Paul Zell. I'll be older one day. I may never discover my superpower. I don't think I want to be a sidekick. Not even yours, Paul Zell. Although maybe that would have been simpler. If I'd been honest. And if you're what or who I think you are. And maybe I'm not even being honest now. Maybe I'd settle for sidekick. For being your sidekick. If that was all you offered.

Conrad Linthor is crazy and dangerous and a bad person, but I think he's right about one thing. He's right that sometimes people meet again. Even if we never really truly met each other, I want to believe you and I will meet again. I want you to know that there was a reason that I bought a bus ticket and came to New York. The reason was that I love you. That part was really true. I really did throw up on Santa Claus once. I can do twelve cartwheels in a row. I'm allergic to cats. May third is my birthday, not Melinda's. I didn't lie to you about everything.

When I'm eighteen, I'm going to take the bus back to New York City. I'm going to walk down to Bryant Park. And I'm going to bring my chess set. I'm going to do it on my birthday. I'll be there all day long.

◦

Your move, Paul Zell.

Kelly Link is the author of the collection *Pretty Monsters*, as well as *Stranger Things Happen* and *Magic for Beginners*. She lives in Northampton, Massachusetts, with her partner, Gavin J. Grant. Together they run Small Beer Press and produce the twice-yearly zine *Lady Churchill's Rosebud Wristlet* as well as co-edit the fantasy half of *The Year's Best Fantasy and Horror*. Link's stories have won the Nebula, the Hugo, and the World Fantasy Awards.

When she was in third grade, Kelly read the Lord of the Rings series eight times. Today she's a Katamari Damacy addict, and someone (Holly Black) is finally teaching her how to play D&D.

What Your Lunch Table Status Means:

Just Because You're a Geek Doesn't Mean You Don't Still Have to Choose a Lunch Table

THE BAND TABLE

What it says about your nerdiness: You have acne and good breath control.
Chic Geek points: 50—we all know what goes on at band camp, but those uniforms are mood killers.

THE THEATER STAGE CREW TABLE

What it says about your nerdiness: You can hang a light and look good in a headset.
Chic Geek points: 80—everybody loves someone who can make a sawhorse look like Juliet's balcony.

THE FANDOM TABLE

What it says about your nerdiness: You are loyal, dedicated, and a little bit eccentric. But you always have a lot of friends.
Chic Geek points: 75—no one knows if that person you met online or at the convention who you say is your boyfriend/girlfriend actually exists.

CHESS CLUB

GONE TO THE LIBRARY TO PLAY CHESS ON LUNCH BREAK

What it says about your nerdiness: You're a ruthless re-reader of *The Art of War*.
Chic Geek points: decreases depending on what board you are (first board: 75, second board: 65, etc.).

THE COMPUTER TECH TABLE

What it says about your nerdiness: You are friggin' smart but you puke when you talk to the opposite sex.
Chic Geek points: 99—one day you will be a millionaire.

FREAK THE GEEK
by john green

Right after our last class, Kayley and I are walking past the only bit of stone wall that survived the epic 1922 fire that nearly destroyed Hoover Preparatory School for Girls. Tragically, the school was able to reopen, which led inevitably to our matriculation at this god-awful place. The only redeemable facet of Hoover is Kayley herself, who is about the best BAOF one could ask for. (BAOF meaning, of course, best and only friend; it is the final frontier in friendship, the heady waters out past the Sea of BFF.)

So we're walking past the waist-high ruin of the wall, which everyone since 1922 has touched whenever walking past it—the wall has been touched so many times that it is worn down into an almost pleasant oval. Kayley walks past, spits in her hand, and rubs the wall. I laugh, and then don't touch it myself, not because I'm scared of Kayley's germs, but because I hate traditions.

Hoover Preparatory School for Girls has a number of profoundly stupid traditions—such as the singing-the-alma-mater-song-every-Thursday-at-lunch tradition, and the stand-when-your-teachers-enter-the-classroom tradition, and the everyone-has-to-wear-the-exact-same-uniform-so-that-no-one-will-be-able-to-tell-who-the-geeks-are-except-of-course-everyone-can-tell-who-the-geeks-are-because-geek-isn't-something-you-wear-it-is-something-you-are tradition.

As it happens, I think doing things solely because they were done in the past is absolutely idiotic. I suppose it shows respect to our teachers when we stand every time they come into the room, but you know what would show more respect? If the insolent students who have colonized this awful place paid attention in class. Or took notes.

⊙

Witness, for instance, seventh period: AP Physics. In the row before me, Amber and Nataley quietly discuss whose basically identical calf-length white socks are cuter. ("No, yours are," Amber whispers, when Dr. Halfrecht turns around to draw a diagram of how one can measure the speed of light. "No," Nataley mouths silently in response. "Yours are adorable.") Beside me, Amelia Lionel, the heir to the Wonder Bread fortune (really!), pretends to sip from a can of Coke. In fact, she is spitting tobacco juice into it. Dipping is cool here, for some reason, particularly if you are on the field hockey team, which Amelia is. The weirdest things get cool sometimes. This is why I have never taken a lot of stock in 'being' cool (as if popularity is something that inhabits you, permanently, a virus that overwhelms your immune system so completely that you cease to 'be' you; instead you have become cool). Sometimes I like things cool kids like. But I find it a little ridiculous to like ALL of the things that the cool kids like. I mean, dip? Really? All the tooth-staining power of coffee with the extra added bonus of mouth cancer? Thank you, but no.

274

The bell rings. We stand and wait as poor Dr. Halfrecht, who just wants to share the magic of physics with young people, shuffles out of the room, shoulders slightly hunched. He perks up a little when he sees Kayley, who actually likes physics, smiling at him, and then shuffles out the door.

So, yes. We are awash in a sea of traditions, and I hate them all. I like going to Hoover, because the only thing worse than having just a BAOF is being separated from her. I mean, Kayley is the badass I can never be, and if you can't be a badass, it is at least a privilege to hang out with one. Hoover is all right. But the incessant fetishizing of traditions? Unbearable.

And so when, just after Kayley spitrubs the stone, someone runs past Kayley and me and whispers "Freak the Geek," I am doubly pissed. First, I am pissed because Freak the Geek is a tradition. And second, I'm pissed because you only hear those words whispered to you when you are one of the geeks who are about to get freaked. I'm not ashamed that I love *Dr. Who*, or that I've read ten thousand pages of HP fanfiction online. I'm not even ashamed about my Pokémon addiction. (Okay, a little.) I like being a geek. But no one — not even the hard-core geeks who have g-e-e-k tattooed on their knuckles — wants to be one of THE geeks.

Kayley and I wheel around simultaneously, trying to identify the whisperer. But she's already several paces away, just a narrow-hipped body with a blond ponytail bobbing around. She could be any of us, really. And that's the idea, I guess: Freak the Geek is the one day each year when everybody at Hoover gets to be One of Us—except, I suppose, for Kayley and me. I feel weirdly embarrassed, like I've disappointed the universe by failing to claw far enough out of the social-caste basement to escape whatever humiliation awaits.

We know the drill, because we've seen geeks Freaked our freshman and sophomore years. The entire class gets together—at least everyone who is willing to participate in idiotic traditions, which is almost everyone—and on a chosen day in the second semester of junior year, they pick two geeks to Freak. Freaking takes various forms, of course: They might drag you by the ankles to the pond and throw you in, or they might egg your car with three hundred eggs. The Freaking always lacks cleverness, because—as previously noted—those doing the planning don't spend enough of their time engaged in academic pursuits. I mean, think of the Freaking opportunities physics provides!

○

Kayley and I don't say anything; we just take off sprinting toward my car. I figure it's our best chance. But when we get within view of the parking lot, I see fifty girls standing in concentric rings around my SUV. Each of them appears to be holding a gun. "Jesus, Lauren," she mumbles under her breath to me, "have they renamed it Kill the Geek?" One of them—honestly, they all look the same from this distance, but I think it might be this field hockey girl named Josie—raises her weapon toward us. It's a strange-looking gun, with a pink handle and an exceptionally long barrel. I'm pretty sure it doesn't shoot bullets, but even so I dive for the ground and cover my head. Kayley just stands there, and when I look up at her, she's shaking her head. "Paintballs?!"

she shouts. "Paintballs?! The whole world of mischief and malfeasance is available to you and you pick PAINTBALLS?! You disappoint me, ladies." I cover my head up and want to disappear, but I manage in a shaky voice to say, "You're an f'ing folk hero, K—"

The sound that interrupts me is not like a gunshot; it's just a loud puff of air. I'm watching from the ground: Kayley doesn't even flinch when a splatter of scarlet red paint bursts a foot away from her head against one of our campus's famed live oaks. I'm inclined to stay down, but Kayley reaches down and pulls on the collar of my school-provided itchy white blouse, and I rise. We take off running together, away from the parking lot toward the lacrosse practice field. I don't hear any more paintball firings as I race across Hoover Green. I want to run back toward the classrooms, because surely someone will help. I mean, the administration has no official policy on Freak the Geek because they love traditions too much to denounce any of them, but they wouldn't let this happen to us. But Kayley grabs me, steering me toward the woods. "We just need a teacher," I say. I can hear them behind me, some girl shouting, "Switch to automatic mode, Scarlet Ballers!" Kayley swivels around and starts running backward long enough to shout, "You call yourselves the Scarlet Ballers and *we're* the geeks?"

●

I hear a series of air bursts, and I turn back long enough to see how far away they are and the bright red explosions littering the ground behind of us. Kayley shouts, "Lauren, come on. Fast." We're almost across the lacrosse field now, a thick stand of trees before us, and the Freakers must have terrible aim or else paintball guns are hard to shoot, because the trees are soon riddled with abstract paintings in red, but nothing's hit me yet. Kayley's running just in front of me, crouching slightly, and I say, "Stay low,

277

stay low," and she says, "I know," and then finally we're in among the trees.

○

And here is our advantage: The Freakers might be in better physical shape than us, but no one knows these woods like Kayley and me. We've been walking around the hundreds of acres of forest on Hoover's campus for three years' worth of lunch periods. Both the food and the atmosphere at the cafeteria are unbearable, and anyway, we've never really gotten along terribly well with the girls who eat there—which is to say all of them. So as Kayley and I weave parallel paths through the trees and brush, a thick blanket of rotting leaves cushioning our every step, I can hear the voices of the Freakers grow more distant. I'm still half-running, which makes me fully out of breath. Still, my wits have recovered sufficiently to talk in complete sentences.

○

"I never really thought about it before," I tell Kayley as we simultaneously duck under a low-hanging oak branch, "but just the phrase 'Freak the Geek' is just hugely lame."

"Yeah," Kayley says. "True. It's almost like the name was thought up by a bunch of mustachioed purple-hued maltworms." Kayley likes using Shakespearean insults.

I get down on one knee in a flash to pull up my socks—a girl has to protect herself from poison ivy. *"Richard III?"* I guess.

"Henry IV," she says.

I nod. I can hardly hear the girls behind us anymore; I mostly just hear our breath coming fast and hard and the ground

278

scrunching beneath us. "Like, admittedly I am not an expert in slang," I say, "but isn't *freaking* usually kind of sexual?"

Kayley turns around to me and runs backward just long enough to say, "Example?"

"'Madam, I wish to freak your body.' Or, 'My heart desires to become freaky with you.'"

"Ha," says Kayley. She doesn't laugh much, but she ha's a fair amount. "Yeah, well, maybe that's what they want. Maybe that's why they picked the cutest girls in the junior class. Maybe they just want to slather us in paintball paint and then do unspeakable things to us." I laugh, but only for a syllable. I think Kayley is beautiful — oval face and big eyes and very curvy — and I think that I am marginally acceptable. I mean, there are no large-scale problems with me that I can detect, except for a general lack of vroom in the bust area and a nose that occupies a bit too much space. But no one would think of me as pretty at Hoover. Or even Kayley. Being pretty here involves so much more than just being pretty, and frankly I don't have time for it.

●

By the time we crest the hill, I can't even hear the Freakers anymore, and even though my Mary Janes are half-soaked, I feel good. I wish they hadn't picked us. There are plenty of unpopular people to go around — the drama kids who do the tech work, the girl who single-handedly runs the student newspaper, the girls who Kayley and I play Pokémon with in the student lounge during free periods — but if they had to pick us, at least they've picked BOTH of us.

We descend the other side of the hill, headed toward the cemetery where the school founder and her family are buried. My weight is way back on my ankles as I half-walk and half-slide down

279

the hill, dodging boulders and trees and the immense mounds of kudzu that have overtaken bushes twice as tall as me. We get down the hill much quicker than we got up it, and I know we're near the bottom when I hear Hoover Creek.

"The bridge," I say.

"Yeah, obviously," Kayley answers without looking back at me.

"Jesus, sorry," I say. The land flattens out and Kayley launches into full stride, and she gets way out in front of me, as if she feels compelled to remind me that she's faster than I am. But it doesn't matter—we're going to the same place. I watch her reach the dirt road that leads back to the stables, run parallel to it for a moment, and then dip her head down underneath the one-lane bridge that crosses over the creek.

Kayley and I had spent many lunches under the bridge—the cement outcropping lets us sit with our legs dangling over the water, which ran loud enough to muffle our voices to anyone walking or driving above, but quiet enough that we could always hear each other.

I reach the bridge a couple minutes later and sit down next to Kayley, who is staring into the water.

She doesn't say anything to me, so after a while, I tell her, "I feel kinda like an ork, hiding out under a bridge."

"A troll," she says, and then sighs. "You feel kinda like a troll."

"No, trolls are people. I don't feel like a person. I feel like an ork," I insist.

She sighs again, this time clearly annoyed. "Lauren," she says. "You're so stupid sometimes. Trolls are not people. Orks are not people. Only humans are people. Orks are from Tyrol folklore, and they live on mountains. Trolls live under bridges. And they have really long hair and big noses, and that's clearly what you mean when you say ork."

I reach over and put my hand on her shoulder and say, "Okay. Sorry. I meant trolls. Jeez, are you okay?"

280

"Yeah, Lauren, I'm splendid. Everyone in my entire class is trying to attack me with paintball guns, and I've officially been declared one of the two least-liked people in my peer group, and my best friend doesn't know crap about folklore, and I'm dirty and sweaty and gross and just *splendid.*"

"Well, you don't have to be bitchy," I say. "It's not my fault."

She says nothing.

"It's not my fault," I repeat, and she says nothing, and then smaller, I say, "You think..."

She takes that as a start. "I think that sometimes you can be a little...I don't know. Meek. And they prey on that. So they prey on us."

I just stand up and climb out from under the bridge. Maybe what bothers me so much is the thought that Kayley might be right, but mostly I'm just furious with her for even thinking that, let alone saying it out loud.

"Where are you going?" she asks.

"To the car," I say as I walk away. I'm talking so softly she probably can't even hear me. "All things being equal, I would rather be paintballed."

●

I'm walking for about thirty seconds when I hear Kayley's footfalls behind me. "I'm sorry," she says.

I wheel around. "You know, you're a total know-it-all. And it's incredibly rude sometimes; I mean, you're not perfect either, and you act like it's my fault but it's not my fault for being quiet or your fault for being a know-it-all. It's not your problem or my problem; it's their problem. They're the demented ones, not us, so don't take it out on me, because the only thing that holds anything together for me is having someone else on the Not Demented Team."

Kayley just nods, and then we stand there for a second, and then she hugs me. She says, "I'm sorry," and I can hear her crying in her voice a little, but then when we separate, she has her hands on my shoulders and says, "Back to the bridge for the trolls!"

We go back to the bridge and just listen to the water run. There is this phenomenon that Dr. Halfrecht taught us about in physics, about particle behavior, and I'm thinking about it while I watch the water rumble over the pebbles in the creek bed. When particles are suspended in water, they move around really weirdly, I guess, and one way to think of how they move around is that every time they run into another particle, they immediately forget everything about where they've been before. Fighting with Kayley is like this, thank God. We can completely forget our fights as soon as we run into each other in a not-fighty way, and I love that about her.

So after a minute, I say, "I still think trolls are people."

"They aren't human," Kayley answers, friendlier now.

"Right; I'm not saying they're human. I'm saying they're people."

"Dude," she says, "I think you have a completely insane take on what constitutes personhood. For starters, people are real."

"Oh, really? The Freakers strike me as pretty fake, but they're still people," I say.

"Ha," she says. "Fair enough. Would they were clean enough to spit upon, as the Bard would say, but they are people."

"And so are trolls."

"No," Kayley says, smiling. "Trolls are trolls; elves are elves; orks are orks; fairies are fairies."

"I would say that trolls and elves are definitely people. Elves have to be people, because interspecies sex is gross, and there's nothing gross about Aragorn getting it on with Arwen in *Lord of the Rings*."

"Is the kind of thing someone would say," Kayley scoffs, "if someone was basing their analysis on the movies, not the books. Doesn't happen in the books!"

"Wrong!" I say. The burden of meekness has lifted. "They get married in the appendices! It's a total symbol for the restoration of Numenor! Pwned!"

"We will have to continue this discussion," Kayley says, realizing her defeat, "at another juncture. For now, let us return to your car."

On the walk there, circling back around the other side of campus, we find other debates: Do zombies bleed blood? What happens if a zombie attacks a unicorn? How can mermaids hook up with seamen if they have no legs to spread? Princess or Toad? Dawn or May? By the time we make it to the car, in the gray twilight, I've forgotten our fight entirely in a way that the Freakers never forget their fights, because their fights are all they have. The Freakers have gone home, their cars all disappeared from the parking lot.

◉

There's a single lipstick-red splotch of paintball goo on the front grill of my car. It doesn't wash off for months, but I don't mind. It is not my scarlet letter. It's theirs.

John Green is the Printz Award–winning author of the novels *Looking for Alaska*, *An Abundance of Katherines*, and *Paper Towns*. He is also an unabashed fan of underappreciated role-playing games, most particularly Teenage Mutant Ninja Turtles: The Game.

How to Hook Up at the Science Fair

Wow her with your specimens

Put ribbons in your hair

Girls, remember: boys who wear glasses never make passes.
You're going to have to go first.

Hypothesize about the romantic dinners you could cook her on a Bunsen burner.

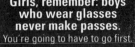

No matter how hot she is, don't go for the girl who made the volcano.

THE TRUTH ABOUT DINO GIRL
by **barry lyga**

Okay, follow me for a second: Guys are like dinosaurs.

We don't know much about dinosaurs. We know a lot, but not nearly enough. Just like with guys.

Of the twelve hundred or so genera suspected to exist, we've only discovered around three hundred and fifty. There are *huge* gaps in our knowledge. When you go to a museum or watch a movie and you see a dinosaur with a certain color pattern on its hide, that's just someone's speculation. It's informed speculation, sure, but it's still just guesswork. Because we don't *know*.

We're guessing what they looked like based on patterns imprinted on petrified mud. We conjure their motions from the interrelationships of their bones, figuring that if they fit together *this* way, then they must have moved *this* way.

We're guessing what they *sounded* like.

Roar.

It's the closest we can come to the sound.

Maybe *Grawr.*

But there's not much difference between the two, and still that's as close as we can come.

We know so much and we know nothing, absolutely nothing, nothing at all.

Again, like with guys.

•

I tried to explain this to Sooz. Sooz is my best friend.

Sooz is my *only* friend, really.

We were at Sooz's house, doing our homework in her room. Other kids were out doing things, but we had no after-school activities. It was early in our freshman year and I had tried to start a Fossil-Hunters Club, but there were no takers. Sooz wanted to join the art club because she's all about the art, but it was all poseurs, so she quit.

I was on the bed, reading. She was at her desk, madly sketching away. Part of her assignment was not using the computer. Which, to Sooz, is like saying, "Here. Draw this with your nose."

"First of all," I told her, "we know they definitely exist. We have proof of that."

"Duh."

"And then, well . . . for guys *and* dinosaurs, even though we have evidence of them and their habits, they're still a mystery to us."

"This is about Jamie," she said knowingly.

And it was.

Jamie Terravozza.

See, there were certain things I knew for sure. I knew that the dinosaurs lived from 65 million to 230 million years ago. I knew that Compsognathus was the smallest dinosaur ever discovered — about the size of a chicken. I knew that the theropods were the only dinosaurs to survive the entire Age of Dinosaurs — first on the scene, last to die off. I knew that predators evolved early stereoscopic vision to aid in the hunt and that Troodon had the highest brain-to-body-mass ratio of any dinosaur.

I knew that they shook the earth when they walked.

I also knew that I was in love with Jamie Terravozza.

He was a junior and on the baseball team, while I was a mere freshman, and a geek. But it didn't matter.

He sat across the aisle from me in biology. I felt out of place — it was all seniors and juniors in there because it's an advanced class and there I was, this freshman girl. A Compsognathus among Carcharodontosaurs.

I remember the moment when it happened, when I fell in love. One day Mrs. Knight asked us why animals never evolve with three limbs instead of four or two or six or eight. I raised my hand. I was the only one. I said, "Bilateral symmetry" as soon as she pointed at me. Zik Lorenz — another baseball player — chuckled and said, "What's this about bisexual?" My cheeks burned and everyone laughed but me. And then I noticed Jamie. He wasn't laughing either. He just rolled his eyes.

I couldn't believe it.

He flashed me a grin, then scribbled something on his notebook and slid it to the edge of his desk so that I could see it:

IGNORE HIM. HE'S AN IDIOT.

I loved him for that.

There were no other notes after that. Every time I went to answer a question, though — the too-smart freshman in a room of upperclassmen — he would nod his head a little bit, like it was okay.

God. *Love.*

The problem, of course, was that he had a girlfriend already: Andi Donnelly. A junior. Captain of the girls' soccer team. Drop-dead gorgeous in all the ways boys like.

Sooz sighed and threw down her pencil. "Coprolite!" she said. "This is just one big piece of coprolite."

(In second grade, I made the mistake of telling Sooz the scientific term for petrified dung.)

"Coprolite, coprolite, coprolite!" She crumpled up her paper.

"I suck. I have coprolite for brains. You do it." She threw the paper at me.

"No way. Uh-uh." I was a decent artist—you have to be, if you want to be a paleontologist, all of those bones and fossils to sketch while on a dig—but I was mechanical. I could draw something right in front of me, but I couldn't invent. I couldn't draw the pictures in my brain, the way Sooz could.

I looked at the piece she'd thrown at me. It was gorgeous. Just not up to Sooz's impossible standards.

She sighed again. "Who knew high school would be this hard?"

"What? It's not hard. We're both doing…"

"I mean guys," she said. "Jamie." She looked at me. "You know—dinosaurs."

·

The next day, sitting at lunch, Sooz read *A Song Flung Up to Heaven*. I read *Scientific American*. That was how we rolled.

"Apatosaur in the house," Sooz murmured.

I followed her gaze. Andi had sashayed into the lunchroom. Jamie followed, carrying two lunch trays. He always did that for her. I loved the way he balanced both trays so carefully, but casually, like it was nothing. His arms went all taut and on days when he wore short sleeves (like that day), I could see the tension in his biceps and their hardness.

He had a tattoo of a flaming baseball on his left arm, just below the cuff of his T-shirt. I saw it all the time in biology because he sat to my right and I looked at it all the time and it was like it was tattooed on my brain.

My bio notebook was filled with pages of me drawing that tattoo over and over again, applying my meager art skills to it as if it were a thigh bone from a brachiosaur found on a dig, and I was trying to capture it, pristine and perfect, before plastering it and shipping it off to a museum.

In the meantime, my sketches would be all the world would see.

Drawing that baseball, over and over...

"Apatosaur," Sooz murmured. "Apatosaur."

Her nickname for Andi. Apatosaurs had a terrible brain-to-body-mass ratio.

Jamie put Andi's tray down in front of her. Nothing on it moved at all. He sat down across from her after accepting a quick kiss on the lips that was gone before a teacher could say anything.

"Ugh," Sooz said. "Don't you just *hate* her?"

"No. I just want to be her."

And it was true. If I could be Andi, I would be the world's *greatest* Andi. I *adored* Andi — her hair, her body, her walk. Her clothes. She wore clothes effortlessly, like she just woke up every morning and her clothes flowed onto her body. The right colors, the right fit, the right style. I loved everything about her. She was perfect.

And, of course, she had Jamie.

Sometimes I imagined that she and Jamie weren't going out anymore. And Jamie and I started dating, and Andi was cool with it and we were all three great friends. Sometimes I imagined that she had *never* dated Jamie, that she was just this perfect girl without a boyfriend, and even though I had Jamie as *my* boyfriend, I was still friends with her, still nice to her, and I was never jealous if Jamie wanted to hang out with her alone because I trusted both of them.

"You need to get him out of your system," Sooz went on, snapping me out of my fantasy world. "It's weird. As long as we've been friends, you've always been single-minded. Dinosaurs, dinosaurs, dinosaurs, from Day One. Now you have this new obsession and I don't know how to deal with it. Get back to your lizards."

"They're not lizards. They're both from subclass Diapsida, but dinosaurs are archosaurs, while lizards are lepidosaurs. Two different things."

Sooz grinned. "I love when you do stuff like that. I have no idea if you're making it up or not, but it sure sounds good."

○

Of course, I wasn't making it up. None of it.

In kindergarten, when they asked what we wanted to be when we grew up, I said paleontologist. (Actually, I said, "plentyologist" because I couldn't quite wrap my mouth around it yet...but I could *spell* it.) By first grade, I had the pronunciation down pat. Enough so that a boy once accosted me on the playground while I was sitting off to one side, reading a dinosaur book. "You're not *really* a girl," he said. "Girls don't like dinosaurs."

I blinked. "What do you mean? Of course I'm a girl. I'm wearing *pink*." I pointed to my headband, just in case he didn't get it.

Third grade: A-plus for my paper on theropods. Eighth grade—just last year—won the science fair with my project showing the difference between ornithischian and saurischian hips. I built my models painstakingly over a month, using books and Web sites for reference. I made Mom drive me to the museum in Washington DC two weekends in a row so that I could talk to one of the paleontologists there. Dr. Marbury liked me and let me e-mail him pictures of the project in progress. I wouldn't let him help me, though. I had to do it on my own.

Dr. Marbury was so impressed with me that he said that—if my parents approved—he would take me on a dig with him. He had one scheduled for the summer of my junior year. I thought my eyes would pop right out of my skull. (Fortunately, that's biologically unlikely. It *does* happen, though.)

That was a year ago and I still stayed in touch with him and he still wanted to take me and, honestly, nothing else mattered. I didn't care that the other girls were getting into makeup and boys. I didn't care that I only had one friend. I didn't care that I wasn't glamorous or that I was what Mom called a "late bloomer." I didn't care that boys didn't think I was a girl. I didn't care about any of it. I saved my money and I didn't waste it on clothes or makeup or music from bands with hot guys in them or anything like that. Digs are expensive. I would need equipment. I would need *stuff.*

I didn't care what it cost or what I had to sacrifice to get there. I just wanted to go on a dig. I wanted to be there, to find the remains, to brush away the dirt and the sand, to gently pry from the earth the bones of its past.

To sketch them and make them immortal.

The Field Museum of Natural History in Chicago has one of the most complete T. rexes in existence, nicknamed Sue after the woman who found it. I just wanted a dinosaur nicknamed Katie—or even Katya.

That was all I wanted.

Until high school started.

Until Jamie.

Suddenly, I wanted something *else.* And I had no idea how to get it.

○

At her table, Andi got bored with food, apparently. She stood up and bounced a hacky sack from knee to knee, occasionally flipping up a foot to kick it up even higher. Everyone at her table watched and applauded. Even Jamie.

I am uncoordinated. If there is a piece of furniture in the room, trust me to stub my toe on it. I'm sort of like an allosaur or a T. rex—they could move somewhat quickly, but only straight ahead. The saurischian hip structure isn't designed to swerve from side to side, so they blundered in a straight line, sometimes changing direction by shifting their weight with their tails. But dodging? Sidestepping something? No way. Can't happen. It's just a fact of anatomy.

"Close your mouth," Sooz whispered to me. "You're chewing like a theropod." She picked up some of the lingo just from hanging out with me. Theropods were meat-eaters.

The lingo, but not the facts.

"Theropods didn't chew their food," I told her. "They didn't have crushing teeth like we do. Their teeth were for tearing. Like this." I demonstrated with my hamburger, attacking it with my front teeth, tearing off wads of meat and bread and growling.

Sooz looked at me in horror.

"See?" I told her, after I'd gotten it down. Grease and ketchup dripped down my chin. I wiped at it with a napkin. "They would just tear off chunks and then swallow them whole."

"Um, Katya, you're really loud...."

"They had these awesome teeth with serrated edges, called *denticles*—"

"Katya..."

"Testicles?" someone said much too loudly.

I looked over my shoulder. At the table behind us, everyone was laughing, mimicking the way I'd chomped my burger.

"She said they have *testicles* for teeth!" one of them howled.

"No, not testicles. Denticles. They were for—"

"Katya."

"What?" I turned back to her.

"Let it go."

I checked over my shoulder again. "I'm eating with my testicles!" one guy said in a mockingly nerdy voice, holding a French fry near his crotch.

"What am I going to do with you, Katya?" Sooz asked, and shook her head.

Only Sooz ever called me Katya. My real name is Katherine and everyone called me Katie, but Sooz said Katya was more exotic and claimed she would call me Katya for the rest of my life, even during the maid of honor's toast at my wedding.

"I'll never get married," I told her. "Guys don't like geeks."

○

"You know," Sooz said as we left the cafeteria, "it's okay to do the dinosaur stuff with *me*. I like it, even when I don't get it. But not everyone's like that."

"But dinosaurs are important! They ruled the earth for millions of years. When we study them, we can understand not just them, but also the way the world *was*, the way the world *changed*, maybe even what the world is changing *into*."

She gave me the special Sooz look, the one that meant I was talking too loud again. Sure enough, people around us were snickering, shaking their heads, rolling their eyes. A few junior boys tucked their arms up like velociraptors and staggered around like drunk birds.

"Any day," I said, more quietly, "we could wake up and there could be a discovery that could change everything. Right now, while we're standing here, there are bones, Sooz. Bones and other fossils, filed away in museums all over the world. They've been in the ground for millions of years and they've been sitting in the basement of some museum for ten years or more, but every single day, someone looks at one of them for the first time. And that could be the one that changes everything. We could hear about it on the news any moment. Isn't that amazing?"

"It is," she said, and she was sincere because she was Sooz and she got it. "It really is."

I didn't tell her the rest. The best part.

The news could come at any moment. Or years from now.

I could be the one to make it.

And then everyone would notice.

Everyone would love me and respect me.

○

"I don't get how you can *like* Andi," Sooz said later that day, at her house. "She's so mean. She once made so much fun of another girl that she went into the bathroom and cried for, like, an hour."

I filed that one away, another "mean Andi moment" brought to you courtesy of Sooz, who has an endless supply.

"Jamie likes her," I explained. "So there must be *something* to her, right? It's just biology. Attractive specimens are good by definition — they reproduce and they pass down their genes."

"This isn't *science*," Sooz said. "You're in *love* with the guy. She's your arch nemesis, not a science experiment."

But I just couldn't find it in me to hate Andi. I figured it had to be difficult to be her. There were all kinds of stresses that came with being Andi, things I couldn't understand because I was *not* her. She was beautiful and funny and athletic and popular and I was…

When I was a kid, I had a picture book about T. rex. It talked about how juvenile T. rexes probably hunted in packs, and there was an illustration of a bunch of them ganging up on a lizard, probably an ancestor of the crocodile, judging by the spine and the tail.

But it was weird. They weren't biting it or slashing at it or even *touching* it. They just surrounded the poor thing, which was slithering along the ground because it didn't have the proper hip and tail alignment to stand on two feet like the T. rexes did. And the lizard had…It had this look on its face. This long-suffering look of *Here we go again*. And the T. rexes were leaning in, almost like they were taunting the poor lizard, making fun of it.

I knew how that lizard felt. And I hated that. I hated that I felt that way because that made me think that maybe…Maybe I was a lizard. I didn't *want* to be a lizard. I wanted to be a dinosaur.

Andi was definitely a dinosaur. Sooz called her the apatosaur, but at least that's a dinosaur.

"She has a biological advantage," I told Sooz. "I need to figure out how I can get a biological advantage, make myself evolutionarily attractive."

She waggled her eyebrows. "Oh? Really?" Sooz was marginally more girly than me — she actually wore makeup.

"Maybe. I'm thinking about it."

That night, I went to my dad, simply because he's a male and, therefore, would probably have an opinion.

"Dad, am I pretty?"

He grinned. "Honey, you're the prettiest girl in the whole world."

Well, that wasn't helpful. He didn't even stop to think about it. When someone answers a question that fast, they're never telling the truth. I couldn't possibly be the prettiest girl in the world. That's just scientifically impossible. And what did I expect my dad to say? He's not going to look at me and say, "Well, sweetie, your mom and I have been talking about this since you were born and we're just sorry that we have such an ugly daughter, but we love you anyway and it's what's inside that counts."

Right.

In my room, I looked in the mirror. I took off my glasses. My reflection became a big blur. How could I know what I looked like without my glasses if I couldn't *see* without my glasses?

I squinted, scrunching up my face until I could make something out, but all I saw was my own scrunched-up face, which looked disgusting.

I checked my bank book. I'd been saving money forever—for the dig, for college. They're both way expensive. I could buy contact lenses, maybe some makeup...some new clothes....

That wouldn't totally drain my bank account. I would have money left over, but I would also have a new Katya to show off, a new, *evolved* Katya to attract Jamie, maybe.

Back to the mirror. I wished my boobs were bigger. Then it would be easy to get Jamie to notice me. I knew how *that* worked. I would just wear a button-down shirt with a couple of buttons undone and my boobs would work their magic boy-power. Maybe I needed a new bra. I could get one with padding in it, make everything stand up and stand out.

(Dinosaurs didn't have boobs. Dinosaurs didn't *need* boobs. Lucky dinosaurs.)

I thought about Andi, effortlessly juggling with her knees and feet. I thought of her lithe form in gym. Everything physical came so easily to her. She could head-butt a soccer ball in less time than it took me to realize there even *was* a soccer ball.

And Jamie loved her.

I had two things I thought of: dinosaurs and Jamie. Sometimes—like that night—the two merged in my dreams, and I was a T. rex hunting him down. Or he was hunting me (don't I wish!).

Predator and prey. Prey and predator.

The next morning, at breakfast, I guess I still looked depressed. Dad asked me what was wrong.

"I wish I was good at something, Dad."

He jerked his head like someone grabbed his hair from behind and pulled. "Honey! Why would you say that?"

I shrugged. "I don't know. Like baseball. Or soccer. Or something."

He said what he *always* says when I shake him up: "Maybe we should have held you back after all."

I have the dubious distinction of being the youngest freshman in school. Back when I went into kindergarten, I missed the cut-off by two days. My parents could have held me back and then I would have been the *oldest* freshman...next year. I would have never met Sooz, though, and that's a world I'd rather not contemplate. My parents—Dad in particular—think all of my ills stem from that decision they made a bunch of years ago.

"This isn't about *that*, Dad."

Dad said, "Everyone is good at something. Some people play baseball or football. Some people are musicians. You're good at dinosaurs."

Yeah, but dinosaurs wouldn't make Jamie fall in love with me. I already *knew* that.

You're not a girl, that boy said on the playground.

Dinosaurs are *neutered*. Dinosaurs are sexless.

(Well, not really. Dinosaurs were amniotes—they fertilized eggs internally, just like human beings. I wanted to be amniotic with Jamie, and I couldn't believe I just thought that with my dad right across the table!)

"Honey?" he said, because I'd drifted off.

"Nothing." God, what am I, a total slut or something?

But when I got on the bus, I still thought about it. Thinking about Jamie not just liking me or talking to me, but actually *kissing* me. And maybe more.

Did being a dinosaur geek have to mean being sexless? Did T. rex discoverer Sue have a boyfriend? Did anyone ever kiss Sue, out on a dig or down in some dark, musty museum basement? Passion among the catalogued artifacts of a dead world.

Sigh.

◉

On the way to homeroom, I kept my eyes down, watching my own feet. No footprints on school linoleum. A million years from now, if some future paleontologist tries to retrace the steps of the *geekus girlus*, she'll have no luck because there aren't any pathways to follow. Not like the dinosaurs. We take the fossilized imprints of their feet and string them together into "pathways," which we use to reconstruct the way they moved. Along with the skeletons, this allows us to figure out how they walked and how fast they could run. Like, T. rex had a sort of lumbering run/walk, with its feet staggered.

I watched my own feet and started to mimic the T. rex. They had to start slow because they were so big—it took them some time to build up to velocity, but then they could move at twenty-five, maybe even up to forty miles an hour.

This is how we learn. Indirectly. We can't observe them, so we observe what they left behind, and even though they left behind a lot, it's never enough. Never. So we keep looking. We never stop. Because it matters. It's *important*. They're extinct, yes, but they still have so much to teach us, if only we'd listen and learn.

I looked around me at the swarm of kids in the hallway. I felt so small in that moment. I knew I was the only one thinking anything even remotely related to dinosaurs or history or science. I was alone.

And I felt like that lizard, the one being hounded by the young T. rexes. Just little lizard me, slithering along on my belly and along comes a bunch of big, bad dinosaurs and they're going to take their time to eat me. They're in no hurry. You know why? Because I'm just a little lizard. I'm nothing. Less than nothing.

And I don't want that.

○

I had gym with Andi three days a week. I tried to be nice to her. I wanted her to like me. Maybe then I could learn how to be like her.

I thought about it this way: I knew the names of more than a hundred species of dinosaurs. I knew the order of the periods and epochs. I spent hours reading Gould and Barsbold and Bakker. I tried to understand both sides of the debate: warm-blooded or cold? Feathers or not? I taught myself how to *draw*, for God's sake, endlessly tracing bone patterns out of books, sitting in the museum for hours on end, sketching the fossils on display there. I sat in the backyard for entire *weekends*, chipping away at different kinds of rocks with three different hammers, testing them for the proper weight and hardness of steel. (A paleontologist's hammer is her most important tool—too heavy and you get tired using it too soon. Too light and it won't do you any good. Too soft and it'll fragment and poke your eye out. These things *matter*.)

I lived in eternal frustration. I didn't get it. I knew all of these things! I figured them out, sometimes on my own.

So why couldn't I figure out the qualities in Andi that attracted Jamie? Why couldn't I mimic them, improve on them? I was smart. This was one more science problem, a biology test set in real life.

Maybe that's crazy. But I couldn't help myself. I was desperate. I clung to the fantasy that—somehow—I could break up Jamie and Andi and yet be friends with Andi and make everyone happy all at once. There was no direct evidence that such a thing would work, but you know what? There's no conclusive evidence as to *exactly* what made the dinosaurs extinct, either. Maybe it was a comet hitting the earth. Maybe it was disease. There's a recent theory that bugs killed the dinosaurs. Tiny, insignificant insects. They weakened the dinosaurs enough that environmental factors were able to wipe them out.

Was that it? Maybe. We don't know. But we know it was *something* because they're definitely dead.

So maybe there *was* some way to live out my fantasy. Maybe I just hadn't figured it out yet.

But I had to. It was killing me.

I never knew that being in love was a physical thing. I never knew your body reacted. Like when I saw Jamie and my stomach felt like someone had tied lines to it and pulled it in ten directions at once. Or the way I became suddenly aware of myself, of my body, when I sat across the aisle from him in bio—the way I felt my hair and my eyelashes and my lips and my nose and every motion of my body as I breathed, hyper-conscious in every way.

But it didn't matter. Because one day it all became impossible.

That day was the worst day of my life. My own personal extinction-level event, right in the halls of high school.

I was leaving gym, following close to Andi. I did that whenever I could. Watching her. Listening. Trying to learn. Doing my research, like a good scientist.

But then, suddenly, Andi turned around, as if she'd forgotten something. Maybe she had. I don't know. All I know is this: The worst thing that could possibly happen, happened.

She bumped into me. Hard.

I dropped everything I was holding. Including my bio notebook.

Which fell, fluttering like a wounded bird, to the floor.

And landed spread open.

The reproductions of Jamie's tattoo.

That tattoo. Over and over and over again. Meticulous. Precise. Because that's the only way I knew how to draw.

I prayed that Andi wouldn't notice it. But her eyes dipped down.

I prayed that she wouldn't realize what it was.

Fat chance. Like I said—precise. It couldn't be anything but Jamie's tattoo.

Before she could say anything, I started babbling. I just couldn't stop myself. I was terrified and embarrassed and strangely giddy all at once.

"Please don't say anything. Andi. Please. Please. It's nothing.

It's really nothing. It doesn't mean...I would never try to take him away from you, really. Never."

Her eyes got wide and then she laughed. She *laughed*.

"Are you *serious*? Do you think I'm afraid of *that*? He doesn't give a shit about you. He needs you following him around like he needs a hole in his head."

"Actually, um, that can be useful." Oh my God! What on *earth*? Where was that coming from? "The theropods had holes in their skulls to make their heads more lightweight." *Shut up, Katie!* I begged myself. *Shut up!*

But I couldn't stop myself. I was on autopilot. It was like my brain and my mouth became disconnected and my mouth just kept on going.

"It's something of an evolutionary advantage for a large preda-tor to have at least one hole in its head, as a way of reducing drag when—"

"Hey!" she snapped. Her eyes scrunched and her brows came together and her mouth twisted into a scowl. Andi was suddenly the one thing I never thought she could be—ugly. It shocked me into silence. "Shut your little prissy, geeky mouth and listen to me, okay?

"Look, Dino Girl. There's, like, a natural order to things, okay? It's the way the world works. And girls like you do not get to go with guys like Jamie, okay? Especially when the guy is already with a girl like *me*. Do you get it? Did that get through your little lizard head?"

Dinosaurs aren't lizards! I wanted to shout. Just like spi-ders aren't insects or rabbits aren't rodents, you stupid piece of coprolite!

But I said—I shouted—nothing. I just stood there, pinned, frozen by her anger.

"Do you *get* me, Dino Girl?"

I thought about that lizard in the picture book. And wouldn't it just shock the living hell out of those T. rexes if it suddenly stood on up on its hind legs and roared and bit one of their heads off?

Impossible, of course. A physiological impossibility.

But I wasn't a lizard. I was a human being.

And yet...

And yet I stood there. And I said and I did nothing.

"I asked you a question, lizard brain!"

"I understand." My voice didn't sound like my own. It sounded like a very small girl who has just learned how to speak and is being punished by her parents.

Andi turned away, stepping on my notebook. She left an imprint of her shoe there, destroying two of my sketches. A pathway for the modern dominant girlosaur. What would a future paleontologist make of it?

○

I was proud of myself: I managed to scoop up my stuff and make it to the girls' bathroom before I burst into tears. I thought about the girl Sooz had told me about, the one Andi made cry in the bathroom for an hour. All she had done was make fun of her. Me? She had destroyed my soul. How long would I be in there?

Why did she have to be so mean? Why? All I wanted was a kiss. All I wanted was for a boy to like me. A special boy.

I locked the door to a stall in the corner and sat down, bringing my knees up to my chest. No one else was there, so I cried and cried and cried, but I don't think it would have mattered. I don't think I could have held it in even if the entire school had been sitting out there.

She was mean. Yes. But the worst part was that she was *honest.*

Like she said, he wouldn't like me. He would never love me. I was just a geeky girl who knew too much about dinosaurs.

No threat to her. Just a little lizard. The most pathetic example of prey—not even worth the time for a predator to hunt, much less eat.

○

I spent the rest of the afternoon in the bathroom. I just couldn't make myself leave. And when I left at the end of the day, I felt like everyone knew. Like Andi had texted everyone in school and sent instant messages and e-mails and then put up a Web page, just to make sure: "DINO GIRL LOVES MY BOYFRIEND! ISN'T THAT ~~CUTE~~ PATHETIC?"

Mom and Dad could tell something was wrong when I got home. I told them I had really bad cramps. They didn't believe me. I've always been a lousy liar.

But I stuck to my story anyway and went to bed early and lay there, replaying those horrible moments in my mind over and over.

I fell asleep praying for a sudden Ice Age that would just make all of us extinct.

○

The next day, I went to school prepared for the worst. I somehow anticipated posters of my face throughout the school, with the word "LOSER!" plastered over them in big fonts.

But no one said anything. No one did anything. No one even looked at me funny.

Andi hadn't told anyone. Maybe it wouldn't be as bad as I thought. Sure, I'd blown any chance of being friends with Andi, but at least no one would be making fun.... And maybe I could get past it. Maybe someday it would be the kind of thing Andi and I would laugh about. *Remember the time you tried to steal my boyfriend and I was mean to you?*

But then came biology. I panicked. Jamie. What if she told *Jamie?*

Somehow, that had been the furthest thing from my mind. I had been so concerned with Andi that I couldn't even make the leap to her telling Jamie about my crush on him.

Jamie sauntered into bio just before the bell.

My breath went out of me, entirely gone. I couldn't find any more. I was in a vacuum.

He sat down.

He was wearing a long-sleeve shirt, but he had the sleeves rolled up so that I could see the bottom of his tattoo.

The tattoo burned my eyes. I thought of those pages from my notebook, now carefully torn out and left at home, where they could no longer incriminate me—too late.

And then...

And then he rolled his sleeve down. Slowly. Like an after-thought. Like he was trying to be casual about it. He stared straight ahead while he did it, not looking at me.

She told.

She *told* him.

I wanted to die. I wanted to combust, to burn up and die right there, leaving nothing but the smell of fried hair and a black scorch mark on the chair and the desk and the floor.

I heard nothing throughout bio. It was my favorite class, my *best* class, but I heard nothing and when I looked at my notebook later that day, there was nothing on the page. Just the date, printed neatly like on the rest of the pages, and then nothing.

Same thing with my memory. Just a white space—a blank like my notebook—in my brain where the carbon cycle should have been.

I stumbled out of class. Jamie knew. He knew I was in love with him. She'd told him. I had lost everything.

She could have just walked away from me. She didn't have to be mean. If I wasn't a threat, she could have been kind and just walked away and never mentioned it to anyone, ever.

And that's the thing: She could have been *kind*. Why wasn't she? Why was she so mean? If you're not going to eat the prey, why smack it around? It just doesn't make *sense*.

I spent the day in my own little hell, trying to figure it out. Trying to figure out what she had to gain by it. If she was right, if Jamie would never be interested in me (and she *was* right—I knew it, and I knew it all along), then why hurt me like that? Why?

Just because she could? Just because she was a dinosaur? Just because *she* was a dinosaur and I was a lizard, predator and prey, and she *could*?

She could. That's what it came down to: She could do whatever she wanted just because she was Andi Donnelly, and there was nothing I could do about it.

And then...

And then, on the bus on the way home...

It hit me.

Like a comet.

It *hit* me:

The dinosaurs were more powerful, but the lizards *survived*.

Look around. They still exist. In forms almost identical to their dinosaur-age forebears. I could show you a salamander from the late Triassic and you would think, "Hmm, that looks like a salamander." You would recognize it right away. Because it survived and the dinosaur didn't.

They used to be prey, but they lived. They thrived, these lizards. Some of them are even predators now.

It's scientifically, biologically impossible for a lizard to evolve into a dinosaur.

But prey *can* become a predator. It happens all the time.

All the time.

◦

"Well, what are you going to do about her?" Sooz asked when I finally told her everything.

I couldn't believe it when I heard the words come out of my mouth:

"I'm going to destroy her."

◦

Sooz stared at me as I told her my plan. I waited. I was nervous. Had I gone too far?

Finally, she said, "It's about damn time."

And then she said, "That bitch. I swear to God…Finally. *Finally*, Katya."

I waited for her to get it all out.

"I hate her. Do you understand me? I *hate* her. And I've been sitting here while you talk about how *great* she is and how *wonderful* she is and it's been *killing* me. Because she's *not* great and she's *not* wonderful."

She took a deep breath.

"Do you remember that one story I told you about her?"

"Which one?" There were millions. Sooz was the editor of *The Compleat Crimes of Andi Donnelly*.

"About the girl. In the bathroom."

"Yeah. What about...oh." It hit me. "Oh, God. Sooz. Why didn't you tell me?"

"Because you were so in *love* with her, that's why! Because all you could talk about was how great she was and I didn't want to...I don't know. I don't know."

I hugged her. "I'm sorry. I'm really sorry, Sooz."

"Never mind. It's all over." She shuddered. "Let's kick her perfectly rounded ass."

So, Sooz was on board. Good. I needed her Photoshop expertise.

I would have to spend a little bit of the money I was saving. But if I was willing to do that before, for makeup, shouldn't I be willing to do it now, for revenge?

Maybe it was insane to take on Andi. She was bigger than me. She was more popular, more important.

But here's something every good paleontologist knows: Even the biggest die. Even the meanest get killed off by something that they can't see coming. Like a meteor. Or an insect.

What it comes down to is this: In this world, you're either predator or you're prey.

There are *many* ways that dinosaurs caught and killed their prey. Everyone thinks that T. rex or allosaur or whatever just ran out into the open air and chased the little guys and ate them up. But the truth is that most of the meat-eaters were ambushers. They lay in wait very carefully and then grappled their prey. Chasing after prey was useless — it consumed too much energy and left too great a chance that the predator would injure itself. Besides, a high-speed pursuit of a smaller, more agile creature isn't to your advantage when you can only move in a straight line.

So the big boys learned how to be patient. And stealthy. And to attack when least expected.

Like me.

Like a *paleontologist.*

Because you have to be patient to study dinosaurs. There are massive advantages to patience. On a dig, you can't just go ahead and rip up everything in your path in your quest for fossils. You'd just end up destroying what it is you're looking for. Fossils are *fragile.* They've been around for hundreds of millions of years and they won't react kindly to someone tearing them out of the ground.

So you take your time. You dig out the earth in teaspoons. You don't gouge the ground—you *brush* it away gently. You don't pound the rocks to release the knowledge within—you *chip* at them. Fragment by fragment. It's the patient work of centimeters.

It takes forever.

And once you've got the ground chipped and swept and brushed away, you have yet *another* long wait ahead of you. Maybe you want nothing more than to pull it up and marvel at it, but you can't. There are procedures.

Because once you isolate the fossil in the ground, you have to sketch it for the record and for cataloging. You sketch and take notes and then finally pull it up, but you can't enjoy it. No. Because you have to wrap it in plaster of paris, for protection. And pack it in a special crate. And send it off to a museum, where it will sit in a basement vault somewhere. It'll sit there for years until someone has the time (and the grant money) to pull it out and break open the plaster of Paris (again, carefully—patiently) and sit down to clean it and examine it and draw more sketches and officially decide what it is and where it belongs and everything else.

Years.

That's what I had waiting for me in my future. So I was ready. I was ready to be as patient as I had to be.

Someday, I'll be the world's greatest paleontologist. Because I am patient like nobody's business.

After three months, I began to lose faith in the "ambush theory" of predation. There's no way a meat-eater could or would wait so long for its prey.

I didn't have a choice, though. I had to wait for soccer season.

I had to wait for Andi to be in practice pretty much every day of the week.

So I waited. And waited.

On one of my gym days, I "accidentally" left my math book in the locker room after changing. I begged Mom to take me back to school for it.

We got there just as practice was ending. A stream of girls headed into the locker room.

Coach Kimball gave me an annoyed look, but Mom said, "She really needs this book. It'll just take a second."

Coach made me give her my cell phone first—cell phones aren't allowed in the locker room because of the cameras.

But no one noticed my new little credit card–size camera. That's because I hid it in an empty blush compact, with a hole drilled through for the lens. So I could hold it up and look like I was just looking in the mirror, but I was actually snapping pictures.

When I'm stressed—like I was in the locker room that day, surrounded by Andi's friends, all of whom just ignored me, thank God—I try to remind myself that over ninety-nine percent of all the species that have ever lived on earth are already extinct. So it's not like I matter. Or any of us. But on that day, I didn't care that my existence was just a blink of the universe's eye. I wanted

Jamie Terravozza. And if I couldn't have him, well, at least I could make sure that *she* couldn't, either.

●

Sooz giggled uncontrollably when she saw the pictures.

"This is serious," I told her. "Stop it."

"Sorry." But she kept giggling. "I'm just thinking of how it's gonna look when I'm done."

I had taken as many as I could, as quickly as I could. They were mostly pretty bad—*you* try taking a bunch of pictures through a tiny hole in a compact case while surrounded by girls who could notice you at any minute.

But there were two or three that weren't totally awful. Sooz took the best one and massaged it in Photoshop until it looked pretty good and then she did some more work. I watched her, impatient.

"That's it," I said. "It's done."

"Not yet," she said, focused on the screen.

An hour went by. "Come on, Sooz. It's perfect." I was practically dancing from foot to foot.

"It's nowhere near perfect. Shut up, Katya."

I spun around her room. I paced. I practiced my brachiosaur walk.

"Come *on*, Sooz!"

She grumbled a little and clicked the mouse a few last times. "Fine. Fine. Here."

I looked at the screen over her shoulder. "It's perfect. It's *beyond* perfect."

Sooz grinned. "How many should we print out?"

We waited. To have it all come out the next day would be too suspicious. *Someone* would remember me in the locker room.

So I waited. Again. Still lying in ambush. I've already pegged the prey — it just doesn't know it yet.

After two weeks, I pounced.

Brookdale awakened to a new poster on its telephone poles and newspaper boxes and bulletin boards. A new flier tossed in piles by the post office and the grocery stores and scattered all over the entrance to the high school.

It had taken us all night to walk around and do it. All night. Worth every last second of it.

I didn't even get five minutes of sleep, but I couldn't possibly miss school that day. Not and miss what everyone was talking about.

The image Sooz had mocked up.

Andi, half-naked from the shower in the locker room, drying her hip and leg, her torso completely revealed. Wet and gorgeous and totally unaware.

Sooz gave it atmosphere and mood. She Photoshopped out the locker room and Photoshopped in a sleazy hotel room we'd found online. And at the top:

DO YOU LIKE SEX? SHE DOES!!!!!

Under the picture: CALL ANDI! with her phone number and her address. And then:

TRUST ME — SHE LOVES IT!!! I KNOW FROM EXPERIENCE — COUNTLESS TIMES!!!!!

The first time I saw Andi that day, she was in tears. She was alone. She was rushing to the bathroom.

She probably tried to lie. She probably tried to say it wasn't her. But she *knew* it was. You can't hide that kind of knowledge from your expression, from your eyes. People can tell when you're lying.

Everyone in Brookdale knows what Andi's boobs look like now.

It was the talk of the school. I heard all sorts of rumors: She was a secret prostitute. (She and her best friend had had a three-some with a college guy from Pennsylvania.) She was an exhibitionist — she couldn't help it. It was an ex trying to get back at her. She was a nympho and couldn't help cheating on Jamie. It wasn't really her. (Then why did it *look* like her? Why was her phone number on it?)

◉

At lunch, I sat with my usual view of Andi's table. By then, the *real* story had spread throughout school: They were over. Period. For good. Zik Lorenz and Michelle Jurgens had heard the whole fight near the stairwell between third and fourth period.

What the hell is going on? Jamie yelled. *Everyone's saying you're a slut.*

It's not me! she protested.

It is you! It is! Jamie said.

Which clinched it. For everyone. After all, Jamie would definitely know what she looked like naked.

If it's not real, Jamie demanded, *how did they get a naked picture of you?*

What could she say to that? With the locker room Photoshopped out, how could she know *where* that picture had come from?

According to the grapevine, Andi had just broken down into tears again at that. I wished, oh, I wished I had been there to see it!

I watched at lunch instead.

I watched as Andi sat down at her table.

Jamie didn't sit with her.

In fact, *no one* sat with Andi.

Sooz flashed me the biggest smile I've ever seen. I resisted the urge to high-five her. Too incriminating.

But when I got up from the table, something amazing happened.

The earth shook with my footsteps.

It *shook*.

From now on, the earth would tremble in my wake.

And I knew. I knew what the dinosaurs sounded like.

They sounded like *me.* . . .

Barry Lyga was a geek long before it was cool to be a geek, back when being a geek meant getting beat up on a regular basis, as opposed to selling that cool new Web app you wrote to a Silicon Valley start-up and retiring at twenty-five. In his time, he's been a comic-book geek, a role-playing geek, a computer geek, and a sci-fi geek, though never a Trekkie, Trekker, or a Whovian, because he has his limits.

Barry is the author of *The Astonishing Adventures of Fanboy and Goth Girl* (called a "love letter and a suicide note to comic books"), *Boy Toy*, and *Hero-Type*. He's still a geek.

Theater Types

The Ingenue: You may be a wide-eyed freshman, but watch out. No one is as friendly as they seem.

The Character Actor: That poison ring isn't just for show. A little muscle relaxant and you'll be the star.

The Leading Lady: The part is yours for now, but there's always an understudy in the wings.

The Hero: Don't be too mad. We all know that's how you got the part last year.

The Villain: You may wear black and tie people to train tracks, but at least you're honest.

THIS IS MY AUDITION MONOLOGUE

by **sara zarr**

I wrote it.

I know we're supposed to pick something from a quote-un-quote known work such as something by Shakespeare or Chek-hov, or one of those photocopied monologues in the drama room, but I looked at them and honestly there's nothing that shows my range or says anything about who I am that will be memorable in any important way and that's what I need: to be memorable. Because, and I'm not trying to embarrass you, Mr. P, but you've had trouble remembering my name since I first started audition-ing freshman year. So obviously I need to take a new approach. Look at the audition form and look at my face: Rachel Banks. Not Rochelle, not Ruthie, not Melissa — I really don't understand where you got that last one, but you have called me Melissa at least three times in as many years.

So my goal here is to be memorable. And anyway I thought that if Candace Gibson is allowed to reenact a scene from *Napo-leon Dynamite* as her audition, then I can perform something that I wrote and is not just a total rip from a movie every single person at this school has seen fifteen times and can recite in his or her sleep.

We might as well get this out of the way now: I am going to go over the time limit. I beg you not to cut me off because I saw with my own eyes how Peter Hantz went overtime with that Sam Shepard thing, which was not even that brilliant. And all this introduction doesn't count against the time. It says on the form that your introduction doesn't count against the time.

I'm going to tell you a story here. One you already know, Mr. P, but I'll be including some facts and details for anyone in this room who may not have been there or in case I want to use this monologue again someday when I am finally auditioning out in the quote-unquote real world, as you are so fond of calling it when trying to alert us to the truth that our high school shenanigans will not be appreciated by professionals.

You can start timing me . . . now.

Scotty King got electrocuted while running the light board.

It sounds like a joke, I know, but I'm saying that he *got electrocuted*. While *running the light board*. I'm saying that he died, during the second act of *Miracle Worker* when Julie-Ann Leskowitz had gotten so good at playing blind, deaf, and dumb that she didn't stop her scene, even though the lights flashed and everyone heard the sizzling noise from up in the booth and Annie Sullivan stopped and said, "Oh my God, Scotty," because she knew about the leak in the auditorium roof and Scotty's belief that bare feet were good luck and we were having one of those late spring storms and there were puddles and drips everywhere, and she put it all together faster than any of us. And we stopped the show and people filed out, a lot of them not realizing what had happened and asking if they'd get a refund. Seriously, who asks for a refund for a seven-dollar high school play? I'm sorry, I'm still making it sound like a joke. You don't know this about me, since you've never taken the time to know anything about me, but I use humor that way. It relieves the tension. Unless someone is actually dead, like Scotty, in which case it just ends up sounding sick and insensitive.

You know all this already, of course, as it is in our very recent history. And, well, you were there and all. What you may not realize is that it was supposed to be me.

Now it doesn't sound like a joke. Now it sounds melodramatic, like I'm trying to get attention or turn the focus away from Scotty's tragedy on to me, who has suffered no tragedy other than spending the last few months walking around like a zombie, like a ghost, like I stole someone else's life and thinking if it had been me, would anyone have noticed?

One time I was at Adam Gunderson's house looking through the sophomore yearbook, and next to my picture someone wrote and I quote: *Look up ATTENTION WHORE in the dictionary and you'll see this pic*, and added like fifteen exclamation points. But I'm not. One, I'm obviously not memorable. Two, a performer does not an attention whore make. Not that I'm a performer. As you well know I've never gotten a part. I audition every single freaking time and this is the mistake I've made: I check the YES box.

On the part of the audition form where it says *In the event you are not cast in the play, would you be willing to work behind the scenes on this production?* I always put a checkmark in the YES box. Every time I see that question I think to myself:

Rachel, don't check yes. DO NOT CHECK IT!

And this time, I didn't. Because if I don't check yes, and I make myself memorable, maybe I'll get a part. Chances are that part will be Onlooker #8 in the third act or the maid who passes through the set with a feather duster twice, but I don't care. As I have tried over and over and over to figure out why I don't get even the crap parts no one wants, the only conclusion I come to is that you see I'm willing to be backstage so you give the parts to someone else, someone smarter who has checked NO.

This is an aside and should not count against my time: Are you really that desperate for backstage help? Can't you offer the job to some D-average jock who needs extracurriculars or community service or something?

What happens is the part of me that would rather mop up Julie-Ann's sweat or de-crust the greenroom furniture than not have anything to do with the play panics and I check YES. Yes, use me. Yes, abuse me. Yes, make me post call times in my own blood, I will do it. I will do it. These are not the thoughts of an attention whore. These are the thoughts of a person—me—who would do anything, anything to be in the general vicinity of this auditorium every single day, including weekends.

And no, Adam Gunderson and I are not dating. As everyone knows, he is with Candace. I simply happened to be in his bedroom looking through his yearbook on a stormy day last fall when the raindrops were hitting the window with sharp little *thap*s and we made popcorn and watched *Twelve Angry Men*.

Speaking of *Twelve Angry Men*, now there's a play we'll never be doing unless we get the asexual version of it, and *Twelve Angry Jurors* just doesn't have the same ring. The problem is there are too many girls at this school who think they want to be actresses. Actors, I guess, is what you're supposed to say now whether it's a guy or a girl. If I were a guy, I bet I'd have any part I wanted. I could have been King Lear *and* crazy Duke of Cornwall because as you will recall exactly two guys auditioned and then one dropped out because of baseball and that is why we ended up stuck with *The Glass Menagerie*, which, I'm sorry, is more than a little dated.

This is one way to make myself memorable: I can play dudes. I'd cut my hair and flatten myself out on top—not too challenging—and there are already people in this school who think I like girls. You may have read about it on the second floor bathroom wall. People make the assumption that just because I don't let guys grope me in the halls or dress in clubwear for school or spend fifteen hours straightening my hair and spackling on cosmetics I'm not a real girl. People are wrong about me, and someday soon these wrong people will know how very wrong they are when a certain person makes his feelings for me public. Not Adam Gunderson.

He's with Candace. The point is I would stuff a sock down there if I had to in order to get a part. Hillary Swank did it and got an Oscar, so wrong people can make fun of me all they want but they won't be laughing when I'm on *E! True Hollywood Story* and they are day-job-having single mothers.

Miracle Worker was supposed to be my big break. As I mentioned and as you can see, I do not have a lot going on in the cleavage department, which made me a perfect candidate to play Helen Keller. Look at me. I'm small and wiry, I fit the part. As usual, I completely blew the audition. Hence the trying-something-new-and-memorable ploy of writing my own audition, hoping it will help me relax (and it kind of is, now that I think about it) because I'm telling you, when I do the lines in my room and no one is watching, I'm so, so good and that isn't bragging.

Of course for *Miracle Worker* there were not *lines* per se, but I'm saying that in general when I practice in my room I'm Sarah Bernhardt, I'm Julie Harris, I'm Dame Judi Dench, for real. I practically made myself cry thinking about what it would be like to not be able to see *or* hear. Can you imagine? Then I get in front of you, Mr. P, and anyone else who might be in the room and I am so bad. So truly bad. Even I know how bad I am. If you were watching me and thinking: Does she know? Does she know how bad she is? The answer is yes, yes, I do. When there are lines, I say the wrong ones at the wrong time, in a total monotone, and I don't know what to do with my hands, and one time I drooled. I was staring at the page with my mouth sort of agape I guess, because I lost my place, and this string of drool, sparkling in the stage lights, oozed right out. Probably you recall.

This is why I check the YES box.

This is how I ended up running lights but not wanting to run lights because that's a job for people who are passionate about running lights, people such as Scotty King.

When I hand-picked Scotty to be my lighting assistant, my

intent was not to kill. Originally, he wasn't supposed to be running the board at all. Originally, he would have been my errand boy, my cue keeper, my clipboard peon. He was, after all, a freshman, and I think it goes without saying that you can't trust a freshman with a junior's job. Since I did lights for *Our Town* — and by the way please can we agree as an entire high school drama community to never ever do that play again? — it seemed like a good time to pass on some of my knowledge and experience. And also I didn't want to do the lights, I deeply and completely did not want to do them. What I wanted was to be onstage, but since that didn't happen I hoped that while Scotty took care of things I could spend a little more time with the actors and soak up some of their actory personalities because I really think sometimes the reason you don't cast me comes down to that: you don't see me as one of them. Even if I completely nailed an audition you would still see me as a backstage kind of a personality.

It's okay, I know I'm not like them. And since I'm not like them but I'm here anyway, I must be like a techie, right? Wrong! Ever since I checked my first YES box, I've been stuck in this limbo between techie and performer. Unlike the techies, I do not own seventeen different black T-shirts. I do not spend my weekends scouring yard sales for the perfect Agatha Christie ashtray or Oscar Wilde table lamp. I have never slept with a penlight around my neck. I do not know how to make iced tea look like single malt scotch. At the same time I know I'll never be one of those sparkling, chosen, beautiful oddballs that have The Second I Turn Eighteen I'm Moving to New York written all over them. I think too hard before I talk. I haven't considered how I look from all angles. I can't break into songs from *Spring Awakening* at the drop of a wool stocking. I have never dared to wear an item of clothing that strays from my jeans-and-cardigan comfort zone. It would never occur to me to wear a sequined tube top over a long-sleeved T-shirt and paired with a boho skirt. This is another reason I don't understand the attention-whore comment in Adam's yearbook. Maybe Candace wrote it.

What I'm saying is I know you don't know what to do with me. I understand. Which is why I put Scotty on the board and tried to spend a little more time with the Chosen, because I thought if I want to be an actor so bad maybe I could at least try to act like an actor acts when she's not acting. Fake it 'til you make it, as my brother says. I think he learned that in AA. Because most people do not look at Rachel Banks and think: Drama Nerd. Most people do not look at Rachel Banks and remember that Rachel Banks is her name, or even think she, I, could be friends with someone like Adam. Or that someone like Adam could care about me. And I'm not saying Adam, I'm saying *someone like* Adam. Someone who is having a hard time knowing where I fit in his life, the way you are having a hard time knowing where I fit in into the play. What do we do with the plain girl in the cardigan? you are thinking. One of these kids is not like the others, and why are we still letting her talk when she has gone way over the time limit? The funny thing is I thought drama would be a place where being not like the others was okay, but it turns out you have to be not like the others in a way that is exactly like the others who are not like the others.

This is why I'm not doing that stupid piece from *Butterflies Are Free* for my audition and instead am trying to tell you who I am because let me assure you, I will never be one of them. Not in the way you expect me to. For one thing I don't have that thing, that instinct that tells me about vintage tube tops and asymmetrical hair. But I know that doesn't matter, that someday some director, some boy, some anybody, will like me plain and in my cardigan and not be blind to me just because I'm not aggressively DIF-FERENT and not worry what his friends will think if they know how he feels about me and not leave me hanging while he decides will I/won't I/do I/don't I for a year and a half.

If I do this, if I leave this school and go on to study theater or go on auditions out in the real world and start getting parts, it's not going to be because I am oh so delightfully quirky and wear unmatched shoes and tiaras around town. It's going to be because I love it, and because I have paid my dues and been willing to check that YES box every time if only so that I can watch and learn and get out of here and finally become the real Rachel who will then go out and claim the parts that are out there waiting for me.

I will tell you what I have that the rest of these girls do not. Not Candace. Not even Julie-Ann. Passion. Passion deep down that is not just a passion for attention or a passion for being able to decide who gets to sit at the drama table in the cafeteria or a passion for cast parties. Do you know I've memorized every play we've done since I got to this school? I'm not talking about the parts I wanted. I mean the whole play. Every day I make Adam give me a cue from one of the index cards I've made. I don't even know what play it's from before he says it, but he gives me a cue and I know the next line. I just know it. You can test me, if you want, when we're done here.

Some might say I shirked my responsibilities by putting Scotty on the board at what you might call the last minute. But you're so wrapped up with what's going on onstage and you always talk about empowerment and ownership and I figured since you don't remember my name you wouldn't really care if it were me or Scotty or the Queen of Sheba actually running the board, while the other one of us stayed backstage on the headset. So I planned it for weeks without telling you, and showed Scotty what to do.

And I did give him the talk. You know the one.

Don't let anyone into the booth who doesn't belong there. Keep the booth clean. Light your own area carefully so there's no bleed. Don't do this, don't do that. Above all, do not enjoy a beverage anywhere near the board because you will get electrocuted and die. Until now, that part has been pretty much an urban legend. A scare tactic. The only way we'd die if we drank up there was if we spilled and ruined a piece of seven-thousand-dollar equipment, because you would personally kill us.

We never thought about other means of electrocution. Like spring storms and leaky roofs and the heretofore-unnoticed faulty wire on the board mixed with a freshman with a no-shoes habit and who really wasn't so skilled at multitasking let alone remembering your basic laws of electrothermal dynamics. I know it wasn't my fault. I know I don't have any real responsibility for Scotty's death, that it was a freak accident. But I can't help but think if it had been me up there things would have gone differently. I mean, I would have known that my bare feet in a puddle of water under a mass of power cords wasn't the best scenario. He seemed pretty capable, though, for a freshman. So instead, I took my place and stood in the wings, on the headset, probably looking like I was engaged in heavy duty communication with the booth, talking some techie jargon, when in reality my lips were moving to every line of every character in that play, something stirring deep in the pit of my heart the way it does every time the house lights go down and the stage lights come up and I want to be one of them—not for the attention but to be transported and remade and to say all the right things for a change, inside a life that has a script where you always know who you are and what's coming next.

And I also can't help but think Scotty's death was a sign, someone up there telling me:

Stop checking the YES box.

Stop being willing to stay behind the scenes when what you want is to be *in* the scenes.

Stop putting up with a boy's cowardly self, no matter how great he seems behind closed doors when no one is watching, because if he won't cast you in the part then you need to find a new play.

I've only got one more year and I've proved my dedication.

The fact that I'm even here auditioning after what happened

and the role I played in it just proves that I know the basic truth of plays and of life: that the show must go on. Even when it's hard to watch the show going on without you.

I'll take any part, I will, and if it's Onlooker #8 I will be the best Onlooker #8 this town has ever seen. But if you can't find a part for me I'm going to walk away. I'm not going to hang around in the shadows anymore. This time you'll remember my name.

Sara Zarr is the author of two critically acclaimed novels for young adults, *Sweethearts* and *Story of a Girl* (a 2007 National Book Award finalist). She has also contributed to the anthologies *Does This Book Make Me Look Fat?: Stories about Loving—and Loathing—Your Body,* and *Jesus Girls: True Tales of Growing Up Female and Evangelical.*

Sara exploded onto the theatrical scene in the role of a greedy bad girl in Linda Mar Elementary's original production, *Three for the Money.* She continued her career through high school as a passenger in *Anything Goes*, Theodosia in *Bone-Chiller!*, and Mollie in *The Mousetrap.* As an adult, she's appeared in *Alice in Wonderland*; *Oliver!*; *A Christmas Carol*; *Look Homeward, Angel*; and *Judevine*, and was a penlight-wearing stage crew member for many other shows. She met her husband while working backstage on a production of *Pinocchio.* Being married to him has been her favorite role to date.

The Best Ways to Stay Awake for Gaming*

Coffee hat

Portable ice bath

Shock-training dog collar

Toothpicks under fingernails

Cut-off eyelids

*These are also good for finals week.

THE STARS AT THE FINISH LINE

by **wendy mass**

2,563 DAYS AGO...

Three more kids until my turn, and I had no idea what I was going to say.

"Fireman!" Jimmy Anderson shouted.

The class laughed. Jimmy had nearly burned down the school last year lighting leaves with a magnifying glass.

"Race car driver!" announced Rick Atterly from two seats in front of me.

The class laughed again. Rick's dad owned the biggest tractor store in town. No wonder Rick wants to go faster than five miles an hour.

When it was Tabitha Bell's turn to respond, we all waited expectantly. No one knew anything about her except that she was smart. Really smart, like scary smart, and she had a funny name that I secretly repeated to myself when I couldn't fall asleep at night *(Tabitha Bell...Tabitha Bell)*. She walked into our fourth grade class two months ago, and suddenly I wasn't the smartest kid in the class anymore. For instance, I knew that Athena was Zeus's daughter, but Tabitha knew that Athena had sprung, fully grown, from the top of Zeus's head. I knew the temperature at which water boiled, and she knew the temperature at which atoms got so

cold they stopped moving. We were all waiting to hear what someone who could be anything in the world would choose as a career.

"Astronaut," Tabitha Bell said quietly, but firmly. "I'm going to
be an astronaut."

"Me, too!" I called out, surprising everyone, including myself.

"That's wonderful, Mr. Berman," Miss McIntire said, jotting a
note in her book. "I'm sure you'll both succeed."

Tabitha turned around in her seat. She narrowed her grass-
green eyes at me, sizing up my very soul. The youngest of six, I
was not used to being noticed so intently. I instinctively pushed
myself against the back of my seat. My flinch made the corners of
Tabitha's mouth twitch upwards. "Bring it on," she said with one
sharp nod.

We were nine years old, and the competition had begun.

·

The sun has risen and set 2,563 times since that day, and the two
of us have spoken exactly 238 words. That's, like, less than a five-
minute conversation. And those words were spread out over years.
224 of them were during our sixth grade science project where we
got stuck on the same team, two of them came from an accidental
brush in the hall in eighth grade that required a mumbled "Oops,
sorry," and the rest resulted from a request to pass a beaker of
liquid hydrogen in AP Chem sophomore year. In the beginning I
tried to be friendly, but she's never given me the time of day. Literally. I once asked her the time because my watch had stopped
and she wouldn't tell me. Stuff like this used to drive me crazy,
but now it's the end of our junior year and I'm used to it.

Since we're in every honors class together, I spend a lot of time
staring at the back of her head (even in high school we still sit
alphabetically). Honors English is about to start when Tabitha

walks in and heads to her desk. It takes me a few seconds to realize that instead of sitting down, she's standing next to *my* desk. In
fact, she's actually talking to me. This does not happen. I blink
and sit up straighter.

"How could you not have told me about this?" she demands,
waving an orange flyer in my face. "That's not fair!"

Okay, so just because Tabitha and I don't talk, that's not to
say we aren't aware of each other. We always know what grades
the other receives, what extracurriculars the other is involved in,
what accolades or awards we earn, how many laps around the field
we can do before getting winded. Getting into NASA requires being
in peak physical condition, an advanced degree in something like
astrophysics or aeronautical engineering, and that most mysterious
of qualifications—the "Right Stuff." Without saying a word, we
push each other to be our best in every area. We "bring it on" every
day. When I sit down to a test, I see Tabitha's face in my mind, her
eyes challenging me to beat her score. Before, I never cared much
about grades; I just enjoyed learning for its own sake. Because of her,
I now have straight A's and am pretty sure I can get a scholarship
to college, which my family never could have afforded otherwise.
Instead of practicing quadratic equations alone in my room, I'm
the treasurer of the junior class. And I owe all that to her.

The thing is, sometime over these same 2,563 days I probably should have told Tabitha I don't actually want to BE an astronaut. I get carsick on any road that isn't perfectly straight. I almost
fainted from fear on the Care Bears roller coaster at the county fair
when I was seven. The likelihood of me becoming an astronaut
and zooming into space at thousands of miles per hour and then
floating around at Zero Gravity is zilch. I know I should tell her
that she doesn't have to worry about me taking her spot at MIT,
but honestly, our wordless competition has made my life so much
better and I don't want it to stop.

So now she's waiting for me to form words, and I can't seem

to answer. Because here's the thing. Even though she annoys the you-know-what out of me, I still repeat Tabitha's name to myself in bed at night. And it's not because the melody of it (*Tabitha Bell...Tabitha Bell*) lulls me to gentle slumber. It's because I'm madly in love with her.

My feelings began in fifth grade, when she made a diorama of the Pantheon in Rome complete with statues of all the gods modeled out of Ivory soap. Then in seventh grade, when she constructed a wave pool in science class to show how all matter behaves both like a wave and like a particle, my heart started to flutter. Anyone who would try to explain quantum mechanics to seventh graders is a special girl for sure. But then last year she won the high school speech competition by talking for an hour about the existential meaning of Sisyphus pushing his rock up the hill every day. And that did it. From that moment on, I was hers. Or she was mine. Or something like that. Not that she knows, of course, considering how, you know, we don't talk at all.

"Peter?" she demands, all golden eyes and honey-brown hair and tank top. How am I supposed to ignore all that and just answer her?

I stall by glancing at the flyer. It's for the big Star Party the local astronomy club is hosting out in the desert next weekend. This year they're running an all-night Messier Marathon. My name is listed at the bottom as the Youth Advisor.

"I found this on the community board at the rec center," she says accusingly. "Why didn't you tell me you were involved with this?"

I finally find my voice. "It's not a secret," I tell her. "You know I'm into astronomy."

She stares at me like I have two heads. "No, I don't."

This surprises me. Perhaps she hasn't been paying quite as much attention to me as I've been paying to her all these years. I don't know what to say, so I stare down at the flyer. When I look back up, she inexplicably has a tear in the corner of her eye. It glistens on her lower lashes like a diamond. I redden and resist the strong urge to dab at it. She blinks quickly and it's gone. Her eyes narrow and she asks, "Can you tell me how much hydrogen gas the sun transforms into helium per second?"

"Um, no."

Tabitha tosses her book bag around the back of her seat and sits down, still facing me. "Well, I can. I know the exact orbits of the planets and the names of Jupiter's moons. But you know what?"

I shake my head. This conversation is very weird.

She exhales loudly and says, "I've never *seen* them. Any of them. I've never looked through a telescope in my life." She picks up the flyer and waves it at me. "When I saw your name on this I realized how stupid I'd been to ignore basic observational astronomy. Clearly *you* knew enough to study it. How can I expect to get into NASA if I don't know the difference between Cassiopeia and Andromeda? If I've never seen the Ring Nebula with my own eyes?"

Without waiting for an answer, she does something she's never done before. She touches me. Or, more accurately, she clutches my arm in a death grip. "You're taking me with you. I'm going to do that marathon, or whatever it is, and it's going on my college application."

I don't want her to know the effect her touch is having so I blurt out, "You don't even know what the marathon *is*?"

Her grip tightens in response. I can't help but squirm. "Okay, okay, I'll tell you. Charles Messier was a French astronomer at the turn of the nineteenth century. He made this list of deep-sky objects, you know, galaxies, nebula, star clusters. He was trying to find comets, and kept coming across these other things. So he started keeping a chart so other astronomers wouldn't confuse them with comets. For a few days in March each year, all 110 objects are visible sometime between dusk and dawn. So the idea of the Marathon is to find and identify all 110 objects on the list."

"Fine. Then that's what I'll do."

"Um, doing the marathon is really hard. Most people don't get everything. A good goal for a beginner would be a dozen or so."

Her grip tightens even more. "You don't think I can do it?"

I fear my circulation is being cut off. She's getting harder to love. "Look, finding deep-sky objects that are millions of light years away is hard enough. But going from one to the other in a race against the dawn, well, that takes a lot of practice, that's all. I've never done it, and I've been studying the sky since, well, for a long time." I might not want to fly in outer space, but I love looking at it. I recently took a picture of the Copernicus Impact Crater on the moon that is SO COOL that I hung it up inside my locker.

Tabitha releases my arm and I have to shake it to restore feeling in my hand.

She blows her hair out of her eyes. "I'll just practice then."

I point to the flyer. "It's in four days."

"Then that gives me three nights to practice," she replies matter-of-factly.

I want to tell her that even if she had three *months* it might not be enough time. Instead I ask, "Do you want me to help you?" Even as the words are out of my mouth, I know they are a mistake. Tabitha and I don't help each other. To admit we needed help was unthinkable. She glares at me and whips around in her seat, her long hair actually skimming my nose.

I know she's only talking to me now because she needs something from me, but I can live with that.

After all, her hair smells like strawberries.

◎

I gently place my telescope in the back of the purple VW van Tabitha borrowed from her uncle for the trip. My eyes land on the big box next to it and almost pop out of my head. "You've got to be kidding me! *That's* what you're bringing?"

Tabitha shuts the back of the van—barely missing my

fingers—and puts her hands on her hips. "What's wrong with it? It's a top of the line computerized telescope."

"Exactly!" I reply, following her around the side of the van. "You can't do the Messier Marathon with a GoTo! That's cheating!"

She climbs into the driver's seat and closes the door. I hurry around to the other side and slide in. I'm not sure how she became the one organizing this trip, but I should have expected as much. The ancient van groans and sputters, but finally starts. She pulls away from the curb in front of my house, the clutch grinding into second gear. It's going to be a long five hours.

"Using a computerized telescope isn't cheating," she insists, reaching behind her to pull a bag of pretzels out from the stash of healthy food she packed. She offers me some. I shake my head and pull out a Charleston Chew instead. I had frozen it in preparation for the drive, and it's still cold.

"You'll never pass the NASA physical if you eat like that," she says.

"That won't be for, like, *years* from now."

She shrugs. "Suit yourself."

I take a big bite off the end and take my time chewing. I don't want to antagonize her. But as much as the two of us have wanted to get ahead, we've never cheated. At least *I* haven't. I didn't even bring my equatorial mount because using the setting circles feels like cheating.

"Tabitha," I say as gently as possible, "don't you think it's cheating if you plug in the coordinates of each item on the list, and then wait for your telescope to "go to" them? Where's the challenge in that? How are you learning your way around the night sky?"

Instead of answering, she empties her bag of pretzels into her mouth, which I have to admit is impressive. Even the way she chomps on pretzels—crumbs and salt dotting her lips—is sexy. She swallows and says, "I've been doing some reading. The point of the Messier Marathon isn't to learn the night sky; the point is simply to see all 110 objects. How you find them doesn't matter."

Technically, she's right.

"Plus," she adds, "I only had three days to prepare. If *someone* had told me about this earlier, I would have been able to learn the major constellations and then maybe I'd have a chance with a regular scope. But since no one *told* me, I had to rent this one."

By sheer force of will—and the fact that I can see the outline of her bra through her thin white T-shirt—I don't answer. Instead, I say, "Why don't I just go over how things are going to work when we get there?"

"Oh, so now you're going to help me?"

I gnaw hard on my Charleston Chew so I don't say something I'll regret. *Focus on the bra strap, focus on the bra strap.* I gulp down half of my water bottle. "If you'd rather do it all on your own, be my guest."

"No, I want your help." She glances fleetingly in my direction. Our eyes meet for a second and even though she drives me crazy, my heart skips a beat.

So I explain how I've made a chart of when each object will rise and set, and how we have to find them in this precise order, or we'll miss them. I explain how the club chose this location because it has the clearest line of sight in all directions. Some objects will be very close to the horizon, and even a small hill could block out a whole galaxy. The fastest-setting objects—the spiral galaxies M77, M74, and M33, will be fighting the twilight, so they'll be really hard to see. And in the morning M30 will be the biggest challenge because it'll be practically dawn and it's only one degree above the horizon.

"We'll just use my scope," she says confidently when I've finished my little lesson.

I shake my head. "Nope. We can't use yours during twilight. We'll have to do those early ones the old-fashioned way."

She glances over again. This time she looks almost impressed.

340

"I got my Messier Certificate a few years ago," I explain. "That means I've seen all the objects on the list. Never in one night, though."

"So why do you want to do this, if you've already seen them all?"

Her question takes me by surprise. "Well, to be honest, it's the only thing I haven't done before."

"Huh? Doing the Messier Marathon is the only thing you haven't done before?" Her voice takes on a teasing tone, and for a second I feel naked.

I hurry to answer before my cheeks grow any hotter. "I mean, astronomy-wise of course. I've gone through all the observing programs that the Amateur Astronomy Association offers." I start ticking them off on my fingers. "I got my Sky Puppy pin when I was ten, my Lunar Club pin at eleven, my—"

She starts laughing. "I'm sorry, your *Sky Puppy* pin?"

I cross my arms over my chest. "Hey, don't knock the Sky Puppy. It took me a year to earn that one. You have to be able to point out fifteen constellations and find five deep-sky objects like the ones we'll be seeing tonight. Plus you have to be able to tell stories—like myths—about two of the constellations and how they got up in the sky. That's hard when you're just a kid."

"I'm sure it is," she says in mock seriousness.

I guzzle some more water and change the subject. "You brought everything I told you to, right? It gets really cold out there at night. Especially when you're mostly standing still."

She pushes her sunglasses up onto her head. "I know it gets cold at night, Peter. I've lived here eight years."

"Eight years, two months, three days." Wait, did I say that out loud? I sink down in my seat. *Please don't let me have said that out loud, please don't let me have said that out loud.* For a minute I think I've escaped, then the van swerves and I grab the side of the door.

"Why would you remember that?" she asks almost suspiciously.

I can't look at her. "Um, I just remember how long it's been since our, you know, *competition* started."

"Our competition?" she repeats.

Now I turn to stare, a tingly feeling creeping up my spine. "The whole 'bring it on' thing?"

Her brows furrow. "You mean, like the movie?"

She really doesn't remember. My mind races to all the things I've done over the past eight years because I thought I had to keep up with her. I can't believe it was completely one-sided. How could I have thought that someone like Tabitha would ever really care what I was doing? I'm such an idiot! I shiver even though it's warm in the van. A small choking sound escapes my throat.

"Hey, don't choke, dude," Tabitha says, handing me the water bottle I'd put on the seat next to me. "I'm just busting you! Of course we're in a competition. If it wasn't for you, I'd have seen that cheer-leading movie. Or maybe even have *been* a cheerleader. Or had a boy-friend. Or gone to parties. Or, like, done a single thing just for fun."

Relief floods through me, literally warming me up again. When my heart rate returns to normal, I say, "So just to get this straight, you're blaming me for all the things you didn't get to do? And to think I've been crediting you for all the things I *have* been able to do!"

She shrugs. "As my dad always says, that's what makes horse races."

"What does that even mean?"

"You know, if everyone thought the same way, they'd all bet on the same horse and where's the fun in that? Tonight will prove which one of us really has what it takes. Which of us belongs in the stars, and which on the ground."

"Does it have to be one or the other? Why can't we both get what we want?"

"Have you ever heard of two people from the same high school becoming astronauts?"

I scan my memory and shake my head.

342

She continues, her hands gripping the wheel so tight her knuckles whiten. "It's still harder for a woman. Did you know Judith Rosner got a perfect score on her SATs? That's what it's going to take for me."

This was probably as good a time as any to tell her she didn't have to worry about me taking her spot since I'm not planning on being an astronaut, but she's not done talking.

"Hey, listen. I only half meant it about resenting you for making me miss things. Just knowing you were trying to achieve the same thing made me work so much harder. It was worth missing a few stupid parties. So seriously, thank you for always breathing down my neck." She laughs. "And I mean that literally. Sometimes I could actually *feel* your breath on my neck in class."

I redden again. Darn that alphabetical order!

"One more year," she says, her usual look of determination on her face. "Then we'll go our separate ways. Me to MIT, you to, well, anywhere else!" She grins at me.

I grin back. If I tell her the truth now, she might not work so hard. I wouldn't want her to lose her focus senior year. So I lean back and enjoy the ride.

◦

Two hours later, we pull into the makeshift parking lot that is full of cars from states as far as Illinois. Our 31 degree latitude is worth driving for. Up north they wouldn't get to see everything.

"Hurry," Tabitha says, jumping out of the van. "We need to get a good spot!"

"I really don't think we need to worry." I wave my arm at the miles of open space.

But she already has her metal cart set up and is yanking at her scope.

"Hang on," I tell her, reaching over to help. "You have to be really gentle with these things. If a lens slips out of place, you're out of luck."

She steps back, and I push the scope back into the van. "Let's set up our station first, then get the scopes, okay?"

She salutes me. "Whatever you say."

"That's what I like to hear," I reply, swinging my backpack onto my shoulders. I stick the waterproof blanket and my sleeping bag under one arm, the two beach chairs under the other, and trudge after her. After making a wide circle, she plops down her stuff. "Here looks good to me."

We spread out the blanket and arrange the chairs. Reaching into my backpack, I line up a gray hooded sweatshirt, a battery-operated alarm clock, a bottle of Tylenol, four bottles of water, four cans of Coke, long underwear, four peanut butter/jelly/fluff sandwiches, a regular flashlight, a red-bulbed flashlight, extra C, AA, and AAA batteries, an assortment of eyepieces, a dew cap for the scope, a wool hat, my Marathon Observer's Logbook, my well-worn copy of Peterson's *Field Guide to Stars and Planets*, laminated sky charts, an extra pair of socks, my cell phone that probably wouldn't get a signal anyway, a foldable tripod, a pair of fingerless gloves, the digital single-lens reflex camera I'd spent a year of lawn-mowing money on, four granola bars, four apples, and a thermos to fill with hot chocolate later. I'm double-checking my battery supply when I notice Tabitha watching me. Suddenly, she grabs my now-empty backpack and starts frantically searching through it.

"Where is it?" she says, rummaging into its depths. She makes a big show of turning it upside down and shaking it. "It's got to be here somewhere!"

I snatch the knapsack. "What are you *looking* for?"

"The kitchen sink! You have everything else, so I figure it's got to be here."

"Wow, I didn't know you had such an outstanding sense of

humor." I carefully replace my supplies. "I hope you're as prepared as I am, or you're going to be mighty cold and hungry tonight."

She grabs the *Field Guide*. "At least I'll have good reading."

I grab it back. "Not if you don't have a flashlight."

"Of course I have a flashlight." She reaches into her bag and holds up a small white plastic flashlight with a picture of Hello Kitty on it.

"You're kidding me. Do you know how dark it's going to get out here? Darker than you've ever seen in your life. That thing doesn't look strong enough to shine more than three feet."

She frowns and turns it around in her hand. Then she grabs my red-bulbed flashlight before I can stuff it back in my bag. "I'll just use this one, then. You don't need two."

"As a matter of fact, I do. The red one is so you don't ruin your night vision. I'll use it to consult my charts once it gets dark."

"You mean, *we'll* use that one," she says, "to consult *our* charts."

I look up, surprised. "I thought you didn't want my help."

Her eyes darken. "Fine," she says, her voice clipped. "You're right." She turns on her heel and marches toward the tent marked BREAK STATION. I watch as she strikes up a conversation with a young couple setting up a huge coffee machine. Well, that probably could have gone better. I didn't say I *wouldn't* help her. I just thought she didn't want me to. She didn't have to storm off like that. She can be *so annoying*.

I busy myself by setting up my scope. I want to make sure it's completely cooled down by the time twilight arrives. I align the scope's finder and then calibrate my eyepiece. Tabitha still hasn't returned by the time I'm done, so I grab one of my sandwiches and wander around greeting people I know from the club. A big group of kids—mostly made up of Boy Scouts and Girl Scouts—ask for help setting up their telescopes. It's fun seeing all the different types. The troop leaders show me their plan of attack for the night and I make a few tweaks to it. By the time I get back to our blanket, probably another fifty people have arrived and their varying scopes are glinting in the last of the sun. It's such a big space that everyone has allowed a sizable distance between themselves and their neighbors. Tabitha is lying on her belly reading my Peterson's *Guide*. Why does her butt have to be so cute? It's hard to stay annoyed at a butt like that.

I tap her shoulder lightly. "Hey."

"Hey," she replies, not glancing up from the page.

"Um, sorry about before," I say, plopping down into one of the chairs. "I'm happy to help. You just never, um, asked before." I almost add how in order to ask me, she would have had to talk to me, but I don't want to start another fight.

"Maybe not," she admits. "But I'm asking now. I may be a little out of my league here. I mean, I don't know M30 from M29!"

I laugh. "That's easy. M29 is an open cluster, while M30 is a globular—"

She rests her hand on my ankle and says, "I'm serious."

I may never wash my ankle again. "Okay, we'll do it together," I manage to choke out.

Her shoulders visibly relax and she smiles, releasing her hand. "Cool. I was afraid you'd say no. I thought maybe you'd want to keep it off my college apps."

I can feel the memory of each individual finger imprinted on my leg. I wish she'd touch me again. I clear my throat and say, "No worries. I already have those other Observing Programs under my belt. I can share this one."

"That's right," she says with mock seriousness. "You're already a Sky Puppy. What can beat that?" She pops open a can of Coke (*my* Coke) and takes a long swig.

I pretend to be insulted. "Hey, the Sky Puppy has a long and honored past."

She laughs. "Maybe I should try to get *my* pin."

I pop open another of the Cokes. "Too late. You can only do it before you're ten years old."

"So I guess this is my only chance to get a pin in anything," she says, suddenly serious.

"Nah, there are lots of others."

She shakes her head, but doesn't reply. I wonder again why she's never studied astronomy before. It just seems like a strange subject to have overlooked by someone who wants to fly through space. I lean back to check out the sky. The sun has turned the horizon a deep orange-pink, which normally I would stop to admire. But now it's time to get focused. "There it is," I announce, eagerly pushing myself out of the chair. I can see others around me getting down to work, too.

"M74? Where? You can see it already?" Tabitha cranes her neck in all directions. "That wasn't so hard. One down, a hundred and nine to go!"

I laugh. "Not M74. Just the North Star. I need to use it to make the final alignments on my scope." A few minutes later, whoops and yelps fills the air. "Here we go!" I call to Tabitha. "Grab the logbook!"

"M74 this time?" she asks.

"Yup!" I swing around to the west until I find Aries. I follow it down into Pisces until I have the general area. Then I get behind the scope. I've found M74 before, but not at this time of year. It's a lot closer to the horizon now, which makes it even harder to find than usual. "Got it! Come look!"

Tabitha leans against my arm as she closes one eye and peers through the eyepiece. "That's it?" she asks, sounding a bit disappointed. "It just looks like a blob of stars."

I smile, using a pencil from my pocket to make a check on the first line of my log. "*You'd* look like a blob of stars at forty million light-years away."

"Wow. Our eyes just absorbed protons that are forty million years old. How cool is that?"

"No time to dwell on that now. Gotta find M77. That one's over *sixty* million light-years away. Wanna give it a try?"

She shakes her head. "It would take me too long. We'd get too far behind."

That's probably true. "Okay, I'll find this one, but you'll do the next one. That one's so easy we won't even need the scope." Once I find Delta Cetus, the closest star to M77, it only takes a minute to find the spiral galaxy. I show it to Tabitha, who admits it looks slightly less like a blob than the first one.

"At this rate, we'll be done before midnight," she says, and dramatically crosses it off on our list.

"Sorry, doesn't work that way."

"I know, I know," she says, rolling her eyes. "As the earth rotates, different objects come and go from view all night, blah blah blah."

"You're a fast learner," I tease.

"So true, so true. So what's the next one?" She looks down at the list. "M31, Andromeda Galaxy. You expect me to find that on my own?"

I stand as close as I dare (which is to say, close enough to smell her hair, but not close enough to feel it), and point out the five stars that form the *W* shape of Cassiopeia. Then I gently lift her arm. "Make a fist."

She looks doubtful, but does it. "Now move your fist so it's directly under the lower part of the W and hold it there." I get distracted for a second by the graceful way her sleeve slips down toward her shoulder, and I freeze up.

"Um, arm getting tired here," she says impatiently.

"Sorry." I hand her the binoculars. "Now look right below your fist and scan the area for a bright blob with faint light coming off both sides."

It takes a while for her to coordinate looking through the

binoculars without moving her fist out of position. Standing so close to her as darkness falls all around us is kind of making me breathless. Then I hear a sharp intake of breath from her. "I think I found it! Does it look kinda like a flying saucer?"

I smile, proud of her. "Yup, that's it. Congratulations. You now know how to find Andromeda and Cassiopeia! You're on your way!"

She lowers her fist and the binoculars, and beams at me. For a few long seconds neither of us moves. My heart starts beating crazily. The stars are coming out in full force now. I've never had a more romantic moment. Should I kiss her? "What are you waiting for?" she says.

She *does* want me to kiss her! What if my lips don't line up right with hers? What if we bang noses? She's waiting. I hope for the best, pucker slightly, and lean in closer. The binoculars whack me on the forehead as she lifts them to her eyes. "Well?" she says, seemingly unaware she just wounded me. "Aren't you going to show me more stuff?"

Thoroughly humiliated, I rub my forehead. *What are you waiting for* clearly didn't mean the same thing to her as it did to me. Did she know I was trying to kiss her? Is that why she moved the binoculars? Should I be humiliated? Before I can apologize, she cries, "Oh, no! Look at that huge cloud!"

I follow her gaze, but the sky — almost totally dark now — looks perfectly clear to me. "What cloud?"

"That long one!" She waves her arm in an arc clear across the sky. "Is it going to mess everything up?" Her eyes search mine in a panic.

I'd laugh, but my mood is kind of low right now. "That's not a cloud. That's the Milky Way. You're looking at the edge of our galaxy."

"Huh?" She bends her neck back and stares. "I'm sure I would have noticed that before."

"You have to be somewhere like this, far away from any city lights. A few hundred years ago everyone on Earth could see it." I swallow my wounded pride and say, "C'mon, we've got to keep moving down the list."

"Uh-huh," Tabitha replies, still staring at the Milky Way. "Whatever you want."

If only that were true.

○

After returning to the scope and finding the last few early-setting objects, we take a break before embarking on the next round. I set up Tabitha's GoTo while she munches on a carrot. I'm holding my red flashlight with my teeth to free up my hands and to give myself an excuse for not talking. I can't believe I thought she wanted me to kiss her. What was I thinking? I'm not the guy girls want to kiss. I'm the guy they want to copy homework off of. My mother once told me I would "come into my own" in college. I hope she's right because it's no fun pining away for someone who would never be interested in you. And right now it would be a whole lot easier if that someone wasn't right next to me in the dark. I stall a little longer by attaching my camera to my scope. Focusing on the North Star, I set the lens to f/8, the ISO to 100, and open the shutter for a long exposure.

The longer we stay here not talking, the more I just want to crawl into a hole. I need a break. I pick out a set of star charts and hand them to Tabitha. "Here's the information you'll need to enter. Just type in the coordinates listed next to each object and your scope will find them."

She looks down at the pages in her hand. "What are you going to be doing?"

I glance around helplessly. "I'm going to see if anyone needs help. I'm the Youth Advisor, after all." She can't argue with that.

She waves the charts in the air. "But then you won't be able to do the Marathon."

I shrug. "It's okay. I'll do it next year." I turn away before she makes me change my mind. I feel slightly guilty. It's not Tabitha's fault that she doesn't feel the same way about me as I feel about her.

She calls after me. "I'll be fine. Don't worry about me!"

I take a deep breath and keep walking. Of course she'll be fine. She's always fine. She knows exactly who she is, what she wants to be, and what she needs to do to get there. I don't know any of those things. All I know is what I don't want to be, and that's not the same thing at all. I see groups of club members huddled behind their scopes, but instead of stopping, I walk right past them. I walk past the break tent, and past the scouts who somehow managed to get pizza delivered in the middle of the desert. I debate going back to get one of my sandwiches, but I don't want to risk a confrontation. When I get away from most of the crowd, I lie down on the hard ground. It's been getting progressively colder since the sun set a few hours ago. I wish I had put my warm clothes on. I stare up at the sky, so familiar to me. Turning to the western horizon, I easily find Venus, the evening star, the brightest in the sky. Tabitha is like Venus. She has this presence that's brighter than everyone else's. Soon Jupiter will rise, surrounded by its moons of ice that could hold the building blocks of life. If Tabitha is Venus, I'm like Europa, a big ball of ice that might have a few surprises inside me if anyone bothered to look. I close my eyes and try to imagine I can feel the turning of the earth beneath me.

"Hey," a voice says softly, kicking my toe. I quickly sit up. It's Tabitha. She's holding the blanket, my sweatshirt, and her sleeping bag.

When I find my voice, I say, "What are you doing here? You can't be away from your post for too long, or else—"

She shrugs. "I thought you might be cold."

"How did you find me?"

She points to the binoculars around her neck, then tosses me my sweatshirt and spreads open the blanket. "Room for one more down there?" Without waiting for a response, she lies down. I lie next to her, barely breathing. Then she puts the sleeping bag over both of us.

"So," she begins. "Tell me a story."

"About what?" I ask, my voice cracking.

"You said you had to learn stories about the stars for your Sky Puppy pin, right?"

For the first time she doesn't laugh when she says *Sky Puppy*. I nod in the dark.

"One of those, then."

I notice she's using her bunched-up sweatshirt as a pillow, so I do the same. "Well, I only remember one of them. It's sort of a poem. A Native American poem." I can't tell if the heat radiating through my body is from the sleeping bag, or from her nearness.

"That's cool," she says. "I like poems."

I take a deep breath. "It's called 'The Song of the Stars.' It talks about these three hunters, and they're the three stars in the handle of the Big Dipper. See it up there?" I point, and a few seconds later she nods. "Okay, so the hunters are the handle, and there's a bear, too. He's the cup thing at the end of the handle. Then the Milky Way is like a road. That's what you need to know beforehand."

She nods again. I take another deep breath and can feel the heat from the side of her body electrifying my own. Staring upward and trying to focus, I recite:

We are the stars which sing.
We sing with our light;
We are the birds of fire,
We fly over the sky.
Our light is a voice;
We make a road for spirits,
For the spirits to pass over.
Among us are three hunters
Who chase a bear;
There never was a time

When they were not hunting.
We look down on the mountains.
This is the Song of the Stars.

She's so quiet for a minute I'm afraid she fell asleep. When I get up the nerve to turn my head toward hers, I can see tears silently flowing down her face. The poem is pretty good, but I doubt it's worthy of tears. She hastily wipes them away.

"Tabitha, what's wrong?"

She doesn't look at me. Finally she says, "Do you know why I want to be an astronaut?"

Surprised at her question, I reply, "Well, I figured it was something to do with wanting to explore outer space, do experiments, see the Space Station."

She shakes her head. "When I was eight, and my parents were fighting all the time, and we were moving again, I saw this picture from one of the space shuttles. It was a picture of Earth, seen from space. Just a blue and white marble, surrounded by blackness. It was that blackness that interested me, that endless nothingness. That's why I was never really interested in learning about the stars. They just interrupted the dark. I thought, if I could get up there, if I could see the Earth like those astronauts did, if I could see it as it really is, then my problems wouldn't matter. I'd get a true perspective of things. I'd be above everything. But I realized something tonight. If we're looking at stars whose light is millions of years old, we're not seeing those stars as they really *are*. We're seeing them as they *were*, millions of years ago."

I nod and clear my throat. "That's true. That's why I love taking pictures of the sky so much. It's like taking a snapshot of the past, and of a past that only exists from our exact vantage point. At any other position in time or space, it would look different. It's like taking pictures of ghosts." I've never said anything like that to anyone before.

"Exactly!" she says, leaning up on her elbow to face me. "So my image of Earth isn't real, either."

"Well, it's still *real*. It's just not the whole picture. Does that matter so much?"

She sighs. "I'm not sure. It just means I'm going to have to look at things differently. Maybe that's not such a bad thing. Why do you want to be an astronaut?"

Well, now or never. "I don't," I say simply.

Her brow wrinkles adorably. "You don't what?"

I meet her gaze. "I don't want to be an astronaut."

Her eyes almost pop out of her head and she sits bolt upright. "Because of what I just said? I don't know what I'm talking about, you can't go by—"

I smile, sitting up, too. "No, not because of what you said. I've actually never wanted to be one. I'd much rather take pictures of outer space with my feet planted firmly on the ground."

She shakes her head in bewilderment and lies back down. "Then why? Why did you work so hard all these years?"

I glance around us, but no one is close enough to hear. I lie back again, too. The darkness is complete now, and without a moon, it will be this way for many more hours. The sky is so crowded with stars that it's dizzying. I know they're not the only thing making me dizzy. Under the sleeping bag Tabitha puts her hand on my arm.

"Peter, tell me why. Why did you say you wanted to be an astronaut?"

She squeezes my arm a little, and I flash back to class the other day when she gripped it so tight. That feels like so long ago now. "I said it because *you* did."

"Huh?"

I can't help but smile at her confusion. "If you had said you wanted to be a chimney sweeper that day in fourth grade, we might be in a competition to see who could sweep the most chimneys right now instead of lying here."

She stares at me like she's never seen me before.

I continue. "Don't get me wrong, I'm really glad you said astronaut. Otherwise, I never would have learned about the stars. Plus, I think the ash in chimneys would be bad for my allergies."

She laughs. "You're crazy."

"Maybe."

Then she leans over and kisses me square on the mouth and stays there. No build-up, no time to obsess over where my lips should go on hers, what I should do with my tongue, if anything. No time even to close my eyes. All I can see is her face, her beautiful hair, and thousands of stars behind her. I kiss her back, and am surprised at how much this tops anything I could have imagined. My fingers instinctively lace with hers and we hold on tight. We stay like this for an hour, not talking, our bodies pressed together in the deep blackness. Her stomach growls and mine growls in return. We both laugh.

"You wouldn't have any more Charleston Chews, would you?"

I shake my head. "But I have peanut butter and fluff sandwiches."

We slowly untangle ourselves and get to our feet. My body misses hers already. As we head back, she says, "It takes a secure man to admit he eats fluff sandwiches."

I take her hand and flick on my red flashlight with the other. "I also still watch cartoons. And not the cool ones on at night. The Saturday morning ones."

"I sleep with seven stuffed animals," she says. "And two dolls."

"You win. You're the dorkiest."

When we reach our scopes, I go check my camera while Tabitha gets the sandwiches. I'd set the exposure for eighty minutes, and it had just ended. Flicking on the screen I call Tabitha over to show her the results. Hundreds of concentric circles made of light.

"Wow, you're really good. How did you do that?" she asks,

looking from the screen to the sky overhead, and back again. "I don't see anything that looks like those streaks of light."

"Those are stars."

She looks closer, puzzled. "How can those streaks be stars? The stars aren't moving like that."

"Ah, but they *are* moving like that. We just don't see it because we're moving, too."

She sighs and steps back. "Just one more way that reality tricks us."

I shake my head. "We'll never have a true picture of reality; it just doesn't exist. But I'm real, and you're real, and those fiery balls of gas up there are real, and right now that's all I need to know. That, and if we hurry, we might be able to catch up to the Marathon. We're two hours behind, but if we work with both scopes we might be able to do it."

She looks at my camera screen again. "*Or*…we can go back where we were and get under the sleeping bag again. You know, to see if we can catch the stars streaking like that."

"Yeah, yeah, let's do that one."

⊙

I awake at five AM to cries of *M30! M30! Hurry!* coming from all directions. Tabitha is just waking up, too. My first thought is to protect her from my morning breath. My second is that I can't believe Tabitha Bell fell asleep in my arms. Her smeared makeup and tousled hair look so sexy I literally can't bear it. If Charles Messier were alive he'd be getting the mother of all thank-you notes from me.

A bullhorn sounds. "C'mon, everyone! You're almost at the finish line! Don't give up now!"

Our eyes meet. She narrows hers. I narrow mine. She grins. I grin back. In unspoken agreement, we throw off the sleeping bag and take off in a run. We may have missed most of the Marathon, but we are NOT ones to miss a challenge. I reach my scope first, and am glad I had the foresight to put the dew cover on before we left. Tabitha grabs for the star charts and frantically presses buttons on her GoTo. I search for Capricornus, and then use the eyepiece to starhop down the chain of stars off to its left. I barely have time to move the scope before the coming dawn obliterates the pattern of stars I just left. I don't think I'm going to make it in time. All over the world people are looking for M30 right now and I'm going to miss it. I risk stealing a glance at Tabitha to see her progress. She feigns a yawn and says, "Will you hurry up, already? Some of us are ready for breakfast." I turn back and peer into my eyepiece again, but I know it's hopeless. My scope just isn't powerful enough to cut through the light.

I hold up my hands in surrender. "Okay, okay, you win. You found it and I didn't."

"Wanna see it?" she asks coyly.

I hurry over and put my eye to the rubber eyepiece. Her scope is so powerful the globular cluster glows, even in the twilight of dawn. I can even make out the colorful double and triple stars that surround the core. "Thank you, it's really beautiful," I say, not caring if that sounds corny. I might have to change my opinion of computerized scopes. And who knows, maybe my mom was wrong. Maybe I won't have to wait till college to come into my own.

A little later the man with the bullhorn comes by with a stack of certificates. "So how'd we do?" he asks, his magic marker at the ready.

"We made it to the finish line," Tabitha proudly announces.

"Wonderful!" the man booms. I shake my head at Tabitha admonishingly.

She reaches out to stop him from handing us a certificate. "But we missed the eighty objects before it."

"Ah," he says, tucking the papers back under his arm. "Well,

I'm sorry it wasn't a more successful night for you. You can always try again tonight if you're not too exhausted."

Tabitha whirls around to face me. "You mean it's not just once a year? I've been crazed all week when I could have done this later on when I was more prepared?"

"There's a block of a few days when there's no moon out that'll work," I admit. "But it wouldn't have bought you much time. Most people chose last night because, well, it was a Saturday night."

"So what do you think?" the man asks. "You up for coming tonight? A bunch of us will be here again."

I look at Tabitha. "What do you think?"

She contemplates for a minute, and then says, "Well, I never did get to see the Ring Nebula...."

I feel a grin spreading across my face. "We'd have to miss school on Monday. We never miss school. But it *is* for a good cause...."

"Definitely an educational pursuit," she adds, slipping her hand in mine. "And this time we'd actually do it though, right?" She blushes and the pink on her cheeks match the approaching sunrise. "I mean, we'd do the *Marathon* this time. And not for our college apps, but just because it's fun?"

I smile. "I knew what you meant. Yes, we'd really do the Marathon this time. Well, except for between midnight and two when no new objects rise or set."

"What would we do during that time?" she asks teasingly.

Instead of answering, I lean in to kiss her. I'm a few inches from her lips when I hear the guy with the certificates clear his throat. I'd totally forgotten he was there!

"So you're in, I take it?" he asks wearily.

I quickly un-pucker and step back. "We're in."

"We're definitely in," Tabitha confirms.

"*Teenagers*," the man mutters. He shakes his head as he walks to the next group.

We turn to each other and laugh.

"What should we do now?" I ask.

Tabitha picks up my star atlas and settles into one of the beach chairs. "*I'm* going to read this cover to cover so by tonight I'll be able to teach *you* something. What are you going to do?"

I sit down across from her. "I'm going to watch you read that cover to cover."

"I don't think that will be a very exciting use of your time."

"Oh, yes, it will," I argue.

"Whatever you want," she says with a shrug, and opens the first page. For the next four hours I watch her face as she teaches herself thousands of years of astronomical history. I watch as the patterns of the stars take up residence inside her head. When she turns the last page, she pushes the book into my hands. "Thank you, Peter," she says so earnestly I want to scoop her up and run around the field with her.

So I do.

In her eighth grade yearbook, **Wendy Mass** was bestowed the dubious honor of Most Likely to Solve Rubik's Cube because she spent so much time fiddling with it instead of paying attention in class. Always fascinated by the night sky, she took Astronomy 101 in college. It was so complicated that she never got higher than 45 out of 100 on any exam. Fortunately, neither did anyone else and the professor graded on a curve. She got an A! She loves writing about astronomy now, and tries to make it so easy to understand that the reader will fall in love with it, too.

Wendy is the author of eight novels for young readers, including *A Mango-Shaped Space* (about a girl with synesthesia), *Jeremy Fink and the Meaning of Life*, *Every Soul a Star*, and *Heaven Looks a Lot Like the Mall*. She lives in northern New Jersey, where she can be found staring up at the sky with her telescope, or down at the ground with her metal detector, hoping to find gold. She can do Rubik's Cube in less than two minutes.

What kind of geek are you?

Gaming Geek
Tabletop, online, or tournament, you keep notches on your bedpost of all your kills.

Music Geek
Band geek, record collector, or rock star, no matter how hard you try, you can't tune in that station from your bedroom.

Science Geek
Chess master, biochemist, computer whiz, or sidewalk astronomer, robots make emotionally unavailable life partners.

Skiffy Geek
Fluent in over six million forms of communication, including Klingon. At this rate, you'll have your own *Battlestar* in no time.

Fantasy Geek
Speaker of Elvish, no matter how you feel, elf ears will never be covered by your insurance provider.

Comic Book Geek
DC, Marvel, or indie, that original piece of artwork is way too valuable to be in your bathroom.

IT'S JUST A JUMP TO THE LEFT
by libba bray

"How did she get ahead of us?" Agnes whispered to Leta.

"I can't believe her. She came earlier than us on purpose," Leta said.

Five people up in the line, Jennifer Pomhultz, in a rabbit-fur jacket and side ponytail, executed a perfect step-ball-change while her older sister and a handful of others applauded.

Leta sneered. "There's the dance move. I knew she'd do it. Like we're supposed to care that she got a callback for Six Flags."

"I don't care. Do you care?" Agnes asked.

"You can't imagine how little I care."

If there was anyone Leta and Agnes hated, it was Jennifer Pomhultz, and for very good reason. For six months, Leta and Agnes had a Friday night routine: At eight o'clock, Leta went to Agnes's house. At nine, they started getting ready—plumping their lips with Bonne Bell Lipsmacker, experimenting with eyeliner, torturing their hair (Leta's was shoulder length, stick-straight, and brown; Agnes's, long and blond and wavy-thick) with curling irons and Aqua Net. By eleven-fifteen, their parents would drop them off at the Cineplex for the midnight showing of *The Rocky Horror Picture Show*, and Leta and Agnes would take their places in the long line that snaked from the box office around the side of the Cineplex and into the back alley. Waiting in line was as much a ritual as the movie itself, and the girls delighted in singing along to "The Time Warp" and comparing props—toast, bags of rice, newspapers—with the other moviegoers. *Rocky Horror* was their church, and they were devout. But Jennifer Pomhultz had only been coming for a few weeks—anyone could see she didn't even know the lyrics to the songs—and already she was acting as if she'd been a Rocky devotee for years. She wore a stupid hairdo and too much blusher and a jacket made from bunnies. Maybe that's what ninth graders did, but Leta and Agnes didn't have to approve.

"Look at her! She's trying to be Magenta. Last week, she was Janet."

"You just don't do that. You don't switch characters," Leta agreed. "God, she is such a fake."

"The fakiest of the fake," Agnes said, and she slipped her arm through Leta's in solidarity.

Leta and Agnes had been best friends since third grade when they'd both been hall monitors and discovered a mutual love of horse models. But now, Leta and Agnes were fourteen and in the second half of eighth grade, and that demanded certain concessions. A deal was made, terms agreed upon and sealed with a vow said over the Ouija board: By summer, they would give up *Teen-Beat* magazine and start reading *Cosmopolitan*, which they had only glimpsed in the drugstore. They would buy at least one pair of cool jeans from the mall. And before the school year was out, Leta and Agnes would each have their first kiss.

Leta hoped hers would be with Tom Van Dyke, who worked behind the concession stand. Tom was a high school junior and beautiful, with shaggy brown hair and heavy-lidded brown eyes, which reminded Leta of Tim Curry, who played Frank-N-Furter. Tom drove a red Camaro and played drums in marching band. Often, when she had been banished to the bench during gym class—Toni Benson deliberately hit her in dodgeball and Coach Perry did nothing about it—Leta consoled herself by imagining she was Tom's girlfriend. In these fantasies, Leta cheered him on during halftime concerts as he marched across the field in measured beats, taking his place as part of a perfect formation—a sunburst, a castle, or the Crocker High School mustang, which was their mascot. Sometimes she closed her eyes and imagined Tom kissing her in the rain over at the Frankenstein Place, and she was as beautiful as Susan Sarandon, who played Janet.

"Is he here? I don't see him," Leta said as she and Agnes pushed past the pimply-faced door guardian who asked for tickets and checked IDs, turning away anyone who wasn't seventeen. Leta and Agnes had been granted a pass from the theater manager who used to go to A.A. meetings with Agnes's mom.

"He's behind the counter, same as always. Get to it," Agnes answered, and Leta felt her heartbeat quicken.

Tom's hair shone in the glow of the popcorn machine. "Can I get you something?" he asked.

"Can I have a Sprite, please?" Leta felt she should say something more, to keep the conversation flowing like she'd read in a *TeenBeat* article, "Snag Your Crush!" "I really want a Coke but I have an ulcer? And my doctor said I can't drink Coke anymore because it gives me a stomachache?"

Tom jiggled the cup under the stream of pale, foaming soda. "Bummer."

"It's the same with popcorn, bad for my ulcer," Leta continued. "I had to have a barium swallow. They call it a 'delicious strawberry milkshake' but it's like drinking strawberry-flavored chalk. I almost barfed it back up."

"Hey, Tom, I can cover for you if you want time with your girlfriend," the other guy at the counter snickered, and Leta's face went lava-red.

"Shut up, Marco. That'll be a dollar twenty-five," Tom said.

365

Quickly, Leta dropped her change on the counter. Agnes pushed her toward Theater 2. "Smooth move, Ex-lax. At this rate, you'll never get kissed. Come on. I don't wanna get stuck in the back with the virgins."

Leta and Agnes settled into their seats, third row center. When the lights dimmed and the familiar red lips and white teeth glowed on the screen, the audience erupted into cheers, and Leta felt that surge of excitement in her belly, the thrill of sitting in the dark with strangers sharing an experience that made them all seem like friends. She and Agnes sang along to every lyric. They threw toast and shouted comebacks. But once Columbia was on-screen, Leta was alert, her feet miming the steps below her seat, her hands making small motions on her lap. Only once did she look away, her eye drawn by a flash of gold on the front row. There sat Jennifer Pomhultz wearing her sister's gold-sequined baton twirler's outfit with fringe at the shoulders. So Jennifer hadn't come as Magenta at all but as Columbia, and Leta felt a surge of panic mixed with hatred as Jennifer also imitated Columbia's moves. Leta elbowed Agnes and pointed.

Agnes's mouth hung open in disbelief. "That bitch!"

Someone on their row—a virgin—made the mistake of starting up the battery-powered carving knife way too early. Its electric growl disturbed the mood, and the audience pounced with a chorus of shushing.

◦

After the movie, Leta and Agnes waited out front for Mr. Tatum to come pick them up. It was brisk in the parking lot—the flatlands of Texas could be surprisingly cold in winter. Leta crossed her arms to stay warm and brooded over Jennifer Pomhultz. "I can't believe her. She can have anyone else, but Columbia's mine."

366

Agnes waved it away. "Don't worry about it. By next week, she'll be Riff Raff."

But Leta did worry. That's why she had an ulcer. Even now, her stomach burned with acid, and she wished she'd brought her Maalox along.

"Hey, aren't you Diana's sister, Agnes?" A guy with dark hair and a Led Zeppelin T-shirt walked up to them, tossing his cigarette in the parking lot on the way. Leta recognized him from her brother's high school yearbook. His name was Roger, and he raced motocross. "I'm Roger. I've seen you around."

"Yeah, I've seen you, too." Agnes said it really cool, but she was smiling in a way Leta had never seen her smile before.

Mr. Tatum was late as usual, and for a half hour they stood around talking and trying to stay warm. Roger made fun of Agnes but it was really a compliment, and when Agnes fake-punched his arm, Leta could see she wasn't insulted at all; she was thrilled. At last, Leta saw Mr. Tatum's old white Buick edging into the lot from College Drive. Mrs. Tatum had taken their new car when she left to "find herself" on an ashram last year, leaving Agnes and her sister Diana in the lurch with a dad who was no more than a shadow in their house.

"Your dad's here," Leta warned, and Agnes moved away from Roger.

"So, you wanna go see a movie tomorrow or something?" Roger asked Agnes.

"Sure. Okay."

Mr. Tatum drove up and honked the horn. He sat in the driver's seat staring straight ahead. Agnes jotted her phone number on the back of an old napkin and offered it to Roger with a smile that gave Leta an uneasy feeling in her stomach, like the climb on a roller coaster when you've glimpsed the first steep drop but there's nothing to do but hold on till the end.

Two weeks later, on a Saturday, Leta spent the night at Agnes's house. Aggie's grandmother had suffered a fall, and her dad was in Kansas arguing with the siblings about what should be done. This left Agnes's older sister, Diana, on duty, but she'd gone off with her friends. In exchange for the girls' silence, she'd promised them one monumental favor, no questions asked, to be collected at a future date.

Leta and Agnes enjoyed having the house to themselves. They pretended they were stewardesses sharing an apartment in New York City, where they entertained rock stars and heads of state. Leta said her name was Astrid Van Der Waal, and she was also a Swedish princess. Agnes called herself Agatha Frank-N-Furter until Leta objected, so she changed it to just Agatha, like Cher, and said she was a spy. When they tired of that game, they cooked Tuna Helper in a small black pan, adding in canned corn because it was a vegetable. They scooped it all up with Doritos and washed it down with lemonade concocted from water and neon-pink powder in a jar. They'd lost count on the spoonfuls and the lemonade was puckery tart. It left a coating on Leta's tongue that made everything taste slightly off.

"You know what you say to corn?" Leta said, giggling.

"No, what?"

"See you later!" Leta laughed so hard some of her Tuna Helper fell out of her mouth. When Agnes didn't laugh, Leta explained, "See you later? Because corn comes out in your poop?"

Agnes rolled her eyes. "You probably shouldn't say that around guys. They'll think you're gross."

Leta felt confused. They always laughed at poop jokes. Always.

"Guess what?" Agnes said. "Roger invited me to a party."

Leta took a bite of Tuna Helper. It still tasted like lemonade powder. "When is it?"

"Friday night." Agnes did not look at Leta when she said this.

"But that's *Rocky Horror* night."

"Yeah, sorry. I'm not gonna be able to go this weekend."

"But we always go to *Rocky Horror* on Fridays. And Jennifer's still dressing as Columbia. I need you as my wingman. You have to come."

Agnes glared. "Oh, Leta, grow up."

They spent the rest of the night not speaking. As she lay in her sleeping bag, her mind going over and over the conversation like a rosary, Leta noticed that Agnes's horse models weren't on her shelves anymore. Instead there was a dried-out rose in a vase and a new poster of some motocross champ she'd never heard of. When Leta's mom came for her on Sunday morning, Leta packed her stuff and ran out to the car without even saying good-bye.

THE SWORD OF DAMOCLES

"Who in here has heard of the band Steely Dan?"

Leta's student teacher, Miss Shelton, looked out hopefully at the class. She had on her flared jeans, feather earrings, and kimono top. Her long blond hair hung down straight as a sheet of ice, and her magnificent boobs were pushed into a canyon of cleavage that had every boy in class sitting at attention.

Tracy Thomas raised her hand. "Will this be on the test, Miss Shelton?"

"No, Tracy," she said with a wink.

Miss Shelton had tried to get everyone to call her Amy on the first day, but their teacher, Mrs. Johnston, had looked up from her Texas history essays wearing an expression like she'd just swallowed an egg. "I think Miss Shelton will be best," she said with a smile. But today, Mrs. Johnston was out doing teacher in-service, and Miss Shelton was holding up an album cover that had a photo of a red-and-white ribbon streaking down the middle, like the remnant of a torn American flag.

"This is *Aja*, the new album from Steely Dan," Miss Shelton said, as if speaking of gods. "I'm going to put this on, and we're going to talk about what you feel when you hear the music."

Miss Shelton dropped the needle on the record, and the record player's ancient speakers crackled and popped. The song sounded slightly Chinese and floaty, and it reminded Leta of when she and her brother Stevie were kids bobbing down the river in giant inner tubes. She closed her eyes and saw Stevie in her mind as he was then, his head lolling back against the black rubber. He was singing some stupid novelty song about not liking spiders and snakes, giving it an exaggerated country twang, making her laugh. Sometimes, if she thought really hard, she could still see Stevie the way he was before the accident. But it never seemed to last long.

Miss Shelton passed between the rows of desks. "What does this music make you feel? Remember, there are no wrong answers. Anyone?"

"Horny," Jack Jessup whispered, and the back of the class erupted in laughter.

"Besides horny," Miss Shelton said, giving him a playful swat.

"It makes me think of flying through clouds." It was Cawley Franklin. He and Leta had drama after school together.

"Good, Cawley! Anyone else?" Miss Shelton stopped at Leta's desk. "Leta, how about you? What does this song make you feel?"

Leta's mind was flooded with images. Roger driving Agnes around the neighborhood on his motorcycle. Stevie propped up on his navy bedspread in his room, watching afternoon TV, babbling words that made no sense, his useless left arm and hand curled against his side like a sea creature forced from its shell. Her dad packing his shoehorn and shaving cream into a small case that fit into a larger suitcase that fit into the trunk of the car that drove him to a job in another state.

"Nothing," Leta said. "Sorry."

Cawley Franklin caught up to Leta in the hall after class. He was tall and rangy, with the hunched, loping walk of someone who hadn't completely moved into every part of his body yet. His long, blond hair hung like two curtains on either side of his freckled face. Cawley had transferred to Crocker Junior High last year, and now he lived with his grandmother out past the mobile home park near the Happy Trails Drive-In where you could watch old horror movies for a buck.

"Whad'ja think of *AAAA-ja*?" he sang, imitating Donald Fagen's nasally tone.

"I don't know. Kind of weird. I like Pink Floyd a lot better. What did you think?"

"Dunno. Mostly I couldn't stop looking at Miss Shelton's boobs."

Leta rolled her eyes. "Nice. You going to the Popcorn tomorrow?"

"Indeed," he said, twirling a fake mustache.

"You're weird," Leta said, but she was laughing.

OVER AT THE FRANKENSTEIN PLACE

After school, Leta let herself into the house. She could hear her mother talking on the phone, so she slipped down the hall to Stevie's room and knocked. He wouldn't answer, she knew that, so she pushed it open. Her brother sat on his bed watching the small black-and-white TV in the corner.

Leta took a spot on the floor beside the bed. She'd learned not to sit too close to Stevie. Sometimes he spazzed out, his arms making uncontrolled movements. Once he'd accidentally smacked Leta in the face, busting her lip. The seizures were the scariest, though. He'd had four since he'd come home from the hospital. Each one seemed to be worse than the last.

"Hey," Leta said. "What's happening on *Lost in Space*? Dr. Smith up to his old tricks?"

Stevie's left hand twitched, and Leta automatically moved back. His hair had grown back straight and brown over the indent in his left temple where the bullet had gone in. On a clear, cold day in October, Stevie and his best friend Miguel had been down at the lake shooting at snapping turtles. They were just packing up to come home when the gun discharged by accident. In an instant, the bullet pierced Stevie's temple and did its damage, taking a detour down into his lung where it lived still, a bud of metal that might bloom at any moment and kill him. Sometimes it felt like that bullet had traveled further, though. Like it had flown right through their family, splitting them into a before-and-after that couldn't be put back together.

The TV hiccupped with static.

"Adjust," Stevie rasped.

Sighing, Leta trudged to the gigantic Magnavox that was so old it still had rabbit ears. She moved the antennae back and forth, stealing glances at the snowy TV, trying to see if the picture had sharpened.

"Better?" Leta asked, her hands still on the antennae. Her brother's hand twitched. "Stevie," Leta said slowly and firmly. "Is the picture better now?" Sometimes she had to repeat things two or three times until Stevie understood them completely, and even then, he might answer with the wrong words, a sentence frustratingly out of order that you had to decipher like a secret code.

Leta gave up. "You need anything else?"

"Yes," Stevie said, shaking his head no. "I'm the robot."

"Great. You're the robot. Just what we need in this family."

"Robots in the house!" Stevie insisted.

Leta's stomach flared with a familiar, burning pain, and she took a deep breath. "Okay, then. Don't watch too much. It's bad for your eyes."

"You adjust, adjust," she heard him say as she walked away.

In the kitchen, Leta's mom was putting the finishing touches on a casserole. It seemed to Leta that her mom had gotten older just since Stevie's accident. Like someone had let a little of the air out of her, and now her features didn't have enough to puff them up anymore.

"I'm putting this in the freezer because it's not for us," her mother announced as if she were answering some urgent question on Leta's part, which she wasn't. "It's for the progressive dinner at church on Friday night."

"I'll call the papers."

Her mother turned, hands on her hips. "Was that necessary?"

Yes, it was, Leta wanted to say. She couldn't say why it felt so very necessary to be angry with her mother all the time, but it did. She would walk into a room where her mother sat reading or grading papers and be consumed with a sudden need to wound that would be followed moments later by a terrible guilt and an equally ferocious longing to be forgiven and comforted.

Leta opened the fridge door and waited for something to announce itself. "Friday night is *Rocky Horror* night. It's your turn to drive."

"Well, I can't take you. Get Agnes's dad to do it. And close the refrigerator door!"

Leta closed it hard and her mother glared. "Mr. Tatum is going to some convention."

"Ask her sister. Ask Diana."

"They're going to camp out for concert tickets."

"Well, that's just too bad," her mother snapped.

"Mo-o-o-om!"

"Cry me a river, young lady. You'll just have to skip it this week."

Leta thought of Jennifer Pomhultz in her sequined baton twirler's outfit dancing her Six Flags routine onstage, silhouetted by the eight-foot-tall reflection of Columbia as Tom Van Dyke stood clapping in the back, a look of love in his eyes.

"This is important to me! Why can't you just understand me for once?"

Her mother slammed a bag of frozen peas onto the counter, turning it over and over to break apart the icy scar tissue connecting them inside. "Oh, yeah? Well, why is it always *my* job to do everything? When did I sign up to be mother of the world? That's what I want to know."

"I didn't ask for a kidney," Leta mumbled, fighting back tears. She reached into the fridge and quickly grabbed a Coke.

"I heard that. And you know you can't have Coke with your ulcer. If you think I'm going to pay for another barium swallow, you've got another think coming, young lady."

Leta slammed the Coke onto the refrigerator's top shelf. Her mother whipped around, pointing the bag of peas at her. It sagged like one of those melting guns in a cartoon. "Break that refrigerator and just see what happens."

Leta rolled her eyes. "I'm not going to break the stupid refrigerator."

"You bet you won't," her mother said. "It's five o'clock. Drink your Maalox."

"Fine!" Leta took the Maalox bottle out of the cabinet above the sink. She swallowed down the white, chalky spoonful of medicine, trying not to gag. Three times a day, she had to drink the stuff, letting it coat her insides with a protective film.

In the back of the house, Stevie was shouting at the TV. Leta's mom flinched. "Go see what he needs, please."

"You do it. He's not my kid," Leta shouted, running for the front yard where she stood panting, trapped on all sides. Next door, their neighbor Mrs. Jaworski clipped at her roses with short, hard snips. Mrs. Jaworski was seventy-five and wore a flowered housedress and frosted orange lipstick outside the lines of her lips like a clown. She hated kids in general, teenagers specifically, and Leta in particular. As Leta tried to sneak back in without being noticed, she was caught by the tinny sound of Mrs. Jaworski's voice. "You kids better stop throwing your Coke cans in my yard, young lady."

"Sorry?" Leta answered.

"You'd better be sorry. I found three of them in my yard just this morning. Look!" With her snippers, she pointed to the grass where three crushed soda cans had been carefully laid out like the dead. She'd actually posed them. It was unreal.

"Those aren't mine," Leta said.

"I'll tell your father!"

"My dad's not here," Leta answered back, but Mrs. Jaworski wasn't listening.

Leta crept around the house to the back bedroom, which had been her father's old study, and let herself in quietly through the window. She never came in here, really, and now, her mom's decoupage supplies took up half of the room. Leta's dad had moved to Hartford, Connecticut, four months ago when his company relocated, but they'd stayed behind because her parents said the housing market was in a slump. "No sense selling until we know for sure whether this job is going to be permanent," her dad had explained as they sat at a table in Luby's Cafeteria in the mall while her mother ignored her beef Stroganoff and kept a hand pressed to her mouth like a dam. When she finally spoke, she only said, "That which doesn't kill us makes us stronger, Leta," but she looked at Leta's dad when she said it, and the next week, he was living in Hartford, and Leta was helping her mom with Stevie.

At first, Leta had really missed her dad. But now sometimes she forgot he existed. When that happened, when she'd remember him as an afterthought while blow-drying her hair or finding a pair of his slippers in the laundry room, she'd be hit by a wave of guilt. She knew she should miss him more, but she didn't, and now that he was gone, she began to realize that he'd never really been around much. Even her fuzziest memories were of her dad hunched over the newspaper at breakfast or sitting in his study at night "crunching numbers." In these grainy memory slide shows, she saw him walking to his car in the mornings, coming home for dinner at night an hour after Leta, Stevie, and her mom had eaten. Later, on his way to the back of the house, he'd appear in her doorway like an apparition.

"How ya doin', kiddo?"

Leta would look up from her magazine. "Good," she'd say.

"Whatcha reading there?"

"*TeenBeat.*"

"I thought you liked those, whatchamacallit, those Nancy Drew books?"

"Yeah. In fourth grade."

"Ah, gotcha. Well, turn on a light. Reading in the dark is bad for your eyes."

And then he'd be gone again and Leta would be left with the impression that they'd never really had a conversation at all.

Back in her room, Leta dropped the needle on the *Rocky Horror* soundtrack. As Tim Curry sang, "Don't Dream It, Be It," Leta powdered her face to a chalky finish and drew wire-thin eyebrows above her own with a Maybelline pencil that used to be her mom's. She sighed as she came to her hair. It was all wrong—lank and brown, not short and punkish-red like Columbia's. On the other side of the wall, Stevie moaned and shouted random words—"Robot! Fire! Adjust! Car!"—while her mother cooed to him, but her voice still sounded angry underneath.

"Shut up, shut up, shut up," Leta murmured to no one. Her mother called for her, and Leta blared the soundtrack, singing ferociously this time, twirling around her room till she felt dizzy and sick and the glittery surface of her ceiling seemed to move like an alien thing waiting to eat her.

TOUCH-A, TOUCH-A, TOUCH ME

The next afternoon, Agnes was waiting for Leta at her locker. They hadn't spoken in a while, and Leta found she was elated to see her friend.

Agnes waved her over. "We need to talk. Can you ditch gym?"

"What if I get in trouble?"

"Go to the nurse. Say you got your period and your mom is coming to pick you up. Then meet me in the girls' bathroom on the first floor. Here, wrap my sweater around your waist like you're covering up a stain on your pants."

It took some doing, but Leta managed to convince the school nurse—who really did not want to know too much information about Leta's periods—to give her a pass. Then Leta met Agnes in the girls' bathroom. Agnes stuck her head under every stall to make sure they were alone.

"What is it?" Leta asked.

"Promise not to tell anybody?"

"Promise."

"Double promise," Agnes insisted.

"Okay, I double promise!"

They sank to the floor with their heads under the sinks.

"I let Roger finger me," Agnes said.

Leta's stomach made a small flip, and her head felt light and dizzy and full of white noise, as if she'd finally taken that first plunge on the roller coaster ride. "You *what*?"

"I let him put his finger in my—"

"I know what fingering is, Aggie. Jesus," Leta interrupted. Her heart beat against her ribs. "Did it hurt?"

"Sort of. You get used to it pretty quick, though, and then it's not so bad."

"Not so bad, or good?"

Leta could practically feel Agnes's shrug. The doors swung open. A small girl came in, glancing nervously from Agnes to Leta and back.

"Go ahead," Agnes growled, and the girl raced into a stall. In a second, they could hear her peeing in fits and starts like she wasn't sure she should be.

Agnes lowered her voice to an excited whisper. "He said

he really, really likes me, that he could maybe fall in love with me."

"Wow," Leta said, matching the urgent quiet of Agnes's tone. "Did y'all do anything else?" She wanted to know. She didn't want to know.

"Not yet," Agnes giggled, and Leta felt the words like two quick gunshots. "We have to get you a boyfriend, Leta."

Leta zipped her hoodie up over her mouth. "I'm working on it," she said, her voice sweatshirt-muffled.

The bathroom rumbled with flushing, and the girl came out of the stall with her head down. She rushed for the bathroom door, not even stopping to wash her hands.

"Gross," Agnes said. "Seventh graders. What can you do?"

WILD AND UNTAMED THING

Wednesday afternoons Leta spent at the Popcorn Players Community Theater — "where the play's the thing!" The theater was housed in the city civic center, a big drum of a building with an indoor walking track around the perimeter on the second floor. When Leta walked in, Cawley was perched on a ladder in the center, attaching papier-mâché flowers with a staple gun.

Seeing her, he bellowed, "Juliet! Forget thy father and refuse thy name!"

"Cawley!" Leta hissed, embarrassed. She dropped her jacket and purse on a folding chair. "What did I miss?"

Cawley hopped off the ladder and squinted up at the civic center's walking track, where two older ladies race-walked in circles, their jewelry glinting under the harsh fluorescent lighting. "Well, those blue-hairs in the matching pink track suits have gone around about fifteen times now. I think they're going for the gold. Oh, hey, look what I found in the props box." He pulled out a gold lamé tuxedo jacket. "I know it's not exact, but I thought you could use it for *Rocky Horror*. I mean, it's sorta close to Columbia's."

Leta slipped it on. The jacket was a man's and too big, but it could work. "This is great. Thanks."

"Sure." Cawley pulled a package of vanilla wafer cookies out of his backpack and offered one to Leta. "So, where's Agnes today?"

"With Roger at some motocross thing." The force of the words sent wet cookie fluff flying from her mouth to her cheek.

"She's into motocross now?"

"No. She's into Roger." Leta thought of Agnes's confession in the girls' bathroom. It made her stomach hurt. "I need some milk."

They took the stairs to the dark cool of the civic center's basement where the wheezing vending machines lived. Leta pushed A7 and a plastic carton of milk ka-thunked its way into the tray below. She gulped it greedily, but her insides still burned.

"I shouldn't tell you this," Leta began. "Agnes let Roger finger her."

Cawley's eyes widened. "Whoa."

Leta buried her face in her hands. "God, I shouldn't have told you that—she'd kill me! Don't say anything! Promise me!"

"I promise. Are they doing it?"

"No! Gah, Cawley. Don't be gross."

"Sorry." Cawley tucked his hair behind his ear. "So…have you ever, you know?"

Leta felt the blush to her toes. She laughed too loud. "No! God, no. I mean, not…I mean, no."

"I wasn't trying to say that you did or anything or, you know, I was just—well, since you said that about Aggie…"

He let the words die and they each took another swig of their drinks. Leta stared hard at the sign on the wall that said MAIN-TENANCE. AUTHORIZED PERSONNEL ONLY.

"What about you?" she heard herself ask. "Have you ever, you know, *done that* with anybody?"

"Huh-uh," Cawley said, and his hair fell forward again, covering his face.

"Actually, I've never been kissed." Leta didn't know why she said it, but she couldn't take it back now.

Cawley let his hand rest on top of hers. "I'd kiss you. If you want."

Leta had imagined this moment. She'd imagined it with Tom. Tom breaking form in marching band to pull her to the field, where he would gaze into her eyes, kissing her passionately while the marching band formed a perfect heart around them. She did not imagine this: strange, quirky Cawley with wafer cookies on his breath offering to kiss her as some sort of charity mission, like he could collect karma points for it to post into some little karma booklet and trade it in for prizes later.

Leta pulled her sweater down over the roll of softness around her middle. "Um, thanks, but…"

The metal stairs clanged with the arrival of the senior-citizen exercisers. Cawley took Leta's hand, leading her quickly into the dark of the rarely used men's restroom down the hall.

"The door has a lock," he said, and she heard it click. It occurred to Leta that she should probably be a little scared, but it didn't seem like this was really happening to her.

"Okay, here goes," Cawley said.

In the dark, Leta sensed Cawley's face homing in on hers from above. He was a good four inches taller than she was, and Leta had to angle her head up and to the side. There was a bit of ticklish fuzz on his upper lip, and his breath was warm and vanilla-cookie sweet. They went in for the kiss at the same time and bumped noses hard.

"Ow!"

"Sorry," Cawley said.

"It's okay." Leta rubbed the sting away.

Cawley touched her arm. "Try again?"

This time, Cawley angled her face slightly sideways, a slight adjustment that avoided another nose collision. His lips mashed against hers. Leta held perfectly still and wondered what she was supposed to do now. Was she supposed to be overcome with passion? Was it supposed to come naturally or did you have to practice? God, she should have tried Frenching her pillow like Agnes told her to, because now, here she was in the community theater men's bathroom trying to kiss a boy and feeling nothing but embarrassed and slightly repulsed. His hand found her waist and she flinched at his touch.

Cawley pulled away. "Sorry. Did I get your boobs?"

"No!" Leta laughed in embarrassment.

" 'Cause I wasn't trying to, I swear."

"No, it's fine if, um...it's okay."

Cawley's mouth pressed against hers again. His hand slipped back to her waist and Leta tried sucking in her stomach but then she didn't have enough air to actually kiss and she had to let it go. His tongue lay on hers like a piece of fish she hadn't decided whether she wanted to eat or eject. Should she do something with it? If so, what? Maybe she should dart it in and out quickly, cobra-style?

Cawley stopped. "Not so wide," he whispered.

"Sorry," Leta said. She'd opened her mouth big like going to the dentist, in order to give his tongue room. Now, she closed it, and it was a little better. They kissed for a few more seconds and Leta broke away. Her face was warm and her upper lip was sweaty; she had the overwhelming desire to escape. "We should probably get back before somebody comes in."

"Okay."

"I'll go first and you can follow. But not too closely, okay? Count to twenty. No, count to fifty. Okay? Fifty?"

"Your wish is my command," Cawley joked.

While Cawley was counting to fifty in the bathroom, Leta

made a beeline for the smoke-filled theater management office to ask if she could stuff envelopes for the upcoming pledge drive instead of painting flats. The manager, Mr. Weingarten, handed her a fat stack, and Leta wedged herself in a far corner between a file cabinet and an enormous fake plant where she couldn't be seen. The kiss was a letdown, not at all like the kisses she saw on TV. She wasn't even sure she wanted to do it again. Leta spent the rest of the hour licking away the memory of it until her tongue was dry as cotton. At five o'clock, she bolted, but Cawley caught up with her at the civic center's front doors.

"Sorry," Leta said, her words rushing out on a weak stream of breath. "Weingarten made me stuff envelopes."

"Drag-a-mundo." Cawley smiled. "Hey, thanks, you know, for earlier."

Leta's face grew hot. "Sure. Well, I gotta go. My mom's waiting."

Cawley leaned in, and Leta practically fell through the doors, running for the safety of her mother's car.

"Hey, see you over at the Frankenstein Place," Cawley called after her.

Leta pretended not to hear.

HOT PATOOTIE—BLESS MY SOUL!

"Did he kiss you? Oh, my god—details!" Agnes squealed into the phone.

Leta pulled the phone cord as far as it would allow onto the back patio, closing the door to a small crack. The concrete was cold under her bare feet. Through the window she could see her mother on the couch reading a biography of one of the presidents, her hair in rollers and her mouth set into a hard line, as if the book were disappointing her somehow but she was determined to read till the end.

"Yes. Sorta. I don't know."

382

"What do you mean you don't know? Did y'all kiss or not?"

"We...did?"

Agnes screeched on the other end so that Leta had to hold the phone away from her ear. "Oh, my god! I can't believe you kissed Creepy Cawley!"

"He is not creepy. He's actually pretty funny. And nice."

"For a weirdo."

"You know what? Forget I said anything. God."

"I'm sorry," Agnes said, but she was still laughing a little, and Leta wasn't sure she really meant it. "So, tell me—was he any good? Oh, my god, did he try to feel you up?"

"No—"

"Did you know he's adopted? Like he thought his grandma was his mom but it turns out his Aunt Susie in Oklahoma is his *real* mom. She gave him up to his grandmother so she could go to college and get on with her life. I guess he found it out last year. He asked his mom—his real mom—if he could come live with her in Oklahoma, and she said no."

"Oh," Leta said. She didn't like that Agnes knew something about Cawley that she didn't.

"Jay McCoy told me they got drunk once in a field and Cawley got quieter and quieter, and then, all of a sudden, he stood up and started screaming at the top of his lungs and hitting at this old oil drum. Remember last year when he broke his hand and he said it was a botched alien probe? Well, that's what really happened."

Leta could see Cawley in her mind then—the uncooperative blond hair, the crooked smile, the gap between his two front teeth, the secondhand-store bowling shirt he wore that said "Eugene" on the pocket. All those things she'd always found comforting about him now seemed turned; he'd gone from dorky-cute to intolerable in one phone call, and she couldn't seem to reverse it.

"Roger and I almost did it today," Agnes said suddenly.

Leta sank to the ground out of sight of the window. "You *what*?"

"I want to do it with him," Agnes said as if she were planning a class trip.

"Are you sure you want to have…" Leta lowered her voice to a whisper. "*Sex* with him?"

"Who are you on the phone with?" Leta's mother appeared on the porch, startling her.

"The Kremlin!" Leta snapped, her heart beating wildly.

"You shouldn't joke about that sort of thing. You never know who's listening in."

"What's your mother's problem now?" Agnes snarled on the other end.

"She thinks the FBI's tapped our phones."

"Sweet Jesus," Agnes whistled.

"Give me the phone." Her mother made a swipe for it, but Leta dodged her. "It's nearly ten o'clock, Leta Jane. Tell Agnes good night."

"I'm not finished."

"It's late!"

"I'm not finished!" Leta held fast to the phone.

"Well, don't stay on too long. It's a school night," her mother said. She padded silently to her room and closed the door with a soft *thwick*. Leta knew she'd won this round, but suddenly, she wished she hadn't. It didn't feel safe; it was like she'd taken her first steps in space only to find that her line wasn't anchored to anything and she was hopelessly adrift.

"I better go," Agnes said. "My dad just got home."

"We have to talk, though," Leta insisted. "Do you wanna go to the mall tomorrow?"

"Can't. I'm going to Roger's."

"Oh," Leta said. "Okay."

"Not for *that*," Agnes scoffed. "I'm sitting in on his band's rehearsal."

"Wow."

"Yeah, I know! Isn't that so cool?"

"Wow," Leta said again.

"Don't let your mother drive you too crazy."

"I won't." When Leta hung up, she realized they'd never finished talking about her sort-of-maybe first kiss, and all her unasked questions settled inside her, heavy as sand.

That night, Leta embraced her pillow, imagining Tom's face in the whiteness above her. "I love you," she said, because you were supposed to say that when you kissed. She pressed her lips to the pillow. Her tongue ventured out, meeting with an unwelcoming, cotton starchiness that robbed her mouth of all moisture.

With a sigh, she flipped the pillow over, wet spot down, and stared at the wall. In the next room, Stevie's TV was on. She could hear the drone of it, all the shows and commercials blurring into one another. Stevie was talking, too, saying words that she knew didn't match — cat when he meant house, football instead of man. She wondered if it made any sense to him and if it mattered that no one else understood. Was it lonely not to be able to communicate with other human beings, or was it a relief to stop trying?

Across the hall, soft, strangled cries came from her mom's bedroom. It reminded Leta of a nature show she'd seen once where a bear cub had caught its foot in a trap. It cried for help, and when none arrived, its cries became a muted yelp it used to comfort itself until sleep came. Leta turned away from the sounds in her mother's room. She pressed herself closer to the wall and let the TV's soft, repetitive noise lull her to sleep as if she were five and her parents were having a dinner party, their muffled voices in the living room a soothing wall of sound that stood between her and the rest of the world.

Leta awoke to the sound of Stevie screaming and her mother shouting. Still dazed, she stumbled into her brother's room. Her mother had him pinned to the bed, but she was no match for him. His arm caught her across the face and she flew back, blood pooling at her lip. Stevie shook for a second and settled.

"It's over," Leta said, but she was trembling.

"I didn't sign up for this." Her mother stifled a sob. She held up a blood-smeared hand. "I need to change him now."

Leta knew this was her cue to leave, so she turned on the little TV again, working the rabbit ears until the image was clear, letting the soft constant sound numb them all into a sleepful waking.

SCIENCE FICTION/DOUBLE FEATURE

On Friday, Leta went to *Rocky Horror* alone. She'd never gone without Agnes, and as she got out of her mother's car wearing more makeup than usual, she felt adrift. Standing in the lobby by herself, she searched for a new tribe of *Rocky* fans to join, but they all seemed complete already. Jennifer had added a red wig to her outfit, and Leta imagined using Riff-Raff's gun to laser it to pieces.

"Leta?"

Leta turned around to see Miss Shelton standing behind her with some of her friends.

"Hi, Miss Shelton."

"Amy, please!" her student teacher laughed. "Hey y'all, this is one of my students, Leta. Are you here for *The Rocky Horror Picture Show*?"

"Yeah, I come every—well, *most* every Friday," Leta said.

Miss Shelton's eyes widened, and Leta enjoyed feeling like she was part of the secret club. "Cool. Are you here by yourself?"

"Yeah," Leta admitted.

"Why don't you come sit with us? We'll save you a seat," Miss Shelton said.

"Okay. Thanks."

"Who is that?" It was Tom. He was talking to her. Tom. Talking. To her.

"She's my teacher, um, a friend," Leta answered.

"Huh," Tom said, watching Miss Shelton head for Theater 2. He turned back to Leta with a smile. "Sprite, right?"

"Yeah." Leta grinned. He knew her drink!

"Maybe later I'll come find you guys. Save me a seat."

"Sure," Leta said, and it was like she'd swallowed the sun.

This was only the second time Miss Shelton and her friends had seen the movie, and Leta enjoyed playing *Rocky Horror* tour guide, showing them when to throw things, prompting them on comebacks. She didn't even care that Jennifer stood up in front of her seat to dance. Miss Shelton laughed at all the right parts and even some that Leta didn't understand. When Leta sang along to "Sweet Transvestite," Miss Shelton high-fived her, and Leta couldn't wait to tell Agnes about it. Maybe Agnes would be jealous of her new friendship with Miss Shelton, who was super pretty and cool and in college.

Toward the end of the movie, during the floor show, Tom slid in next to Leta, taking the empty seat she'd dutifully saved for him with her jacket.

"Are those guys in makeup?" Tom whispered, and Leta felt it deep in her belly.

"Yeah," she whispered back, relishing the nearness of his perfect ear.

"Huh. This is a weird movie, man."

Leta stared at him. "You mean you've never seen it before?"

"Huh-uh. Not my thing."

"Oh, my god, it's like the best movie ever. Nothing's as good as Rocky," Leta said.

"I know one or two things," Tom said and winked. "You want anything from the concession stand?"

Leta shook her head, and Tom reached in front of her to tap Miss Shelton on the arm. "You want anything? Coffee, tea, me?"

Miss Shelton laughed, and a woman with crimped hair and a maid's outfit shushed them. Tom made a face, and even though Leta didn't want the lady to be mad at her, she giggled anyway.

When the movie had ended, and they were huddled in the harsh glare of the theater lobby, Miss Shelton put her arm around Leta. "That beat hell out of Texas history, huh?"

"Yeah," Leta said, but her eyes were on Tom.

"I gotta close down the place," he said. "But, hey, let's do the Time Warp again."

"Sure. Okay." Leta was still grinning. "See you next Friday for sure!"

"Yeah. See you then. You, too," Tom said to Miss Shelton.

◉

At the Popcorn on Wednesday, Cawley and Leta put the finishing touches on the set for *Our Town*. In the week since their kiss, Leta had managed to avoid him — taking a different hallway to classes, carrying all her books so as to skip her locker, ducking into the girls' bathroom when necessary. But now they were at the Popcorn together, and Leta was determined to keep things strictly professional.

"Could you hand me those?" Leta pointed to a wad of tissue-paper flowers the size of a tricycle.

"Jennifer Pomhultz told Scotty West's brother that she's going to dance with the regulars at *Rocky Horror* this weekend," Cawley said, holding the flowers in place.

"So?"

"So? We gotta show up and take her down." We. He was already making them into a couple. "I've got it all figured out. My grandmother can drive me over around nine o'clock, and drop us off at the Pizza Hut. Then we could just walk over to the Cineplex from there later."

"They're pretty strict about IDs," Leta said, letting the staple gun rip.

388

"But they let you in. Just tell 'em I'm your cousin or something. Your kissing cousin," he joked.

Leta's face went hot. It had been a mistake to kiss Cawley. She couldn't be seen with him, not now that she had a shot with Tom. "Actually, I-I may not be able to go this weekend. I think my dad is coming. And, you know, we're doing, like, family stuff."

"Yeah, but the show's not till midnight."

"Sorry."

"But Jennifer Pomhultz is trying to take your spot as Columbia! You have to go!"

"You're not the boss of me, Cawley!"

Leta's finger slipped on the staple gun, nearly catching Cawley's thumb, and Leta thought of the gun going off, the bullet shattering her brother's temple.

"Stupid!" she hissed, and she wasn't sure who or what she meant by it.

○

That night, Leta's dad called. His flat tones echoed over the phone, all the way from Connecticut, which sounded like a state you had to put together yourself from a kit. "Hey, kiddo, how's eighth grade treating you?"

"Okay," Leta said.

"How's Agnes? Is she behaving?"

"I guess. You know Aggie."

Her dad laughed. "Well, Stevie sounds good." There was a pause. "Your mom getting on okay?"

Leta flicked a glance toward her mother, who was stirring anger into the pot of noodles on the stove. "Yeah."

"Good, good. Good."

Leta wanted to ask her dad when he was coming home. She

wanted to know if he missed them, or if they were faint as the ghostly images on a negative. She wanted something she couldn't name and she hoped he'd know what it was.

"Well, take care of yourself, kiddo. Lemme have another crack at your mom, there, okay?"

"Sure." Leta handed off the receiver, ducking under the cord.

Her mother's voice dropped to a wounded whisper. "I just don't think I can do this anymore, Dean, I really don't."

When her mother had gone to sleep, Leta took the picture of Columbia she'd torn from a movie magazine and taped it to her bathroom mirror. From under the sink, she took out a box of red dye, coating her head and setting the egg timer for thirty minutes. Once she'd washed it out, she chopped at her lank strands, going shorter and shorter until her hair was just below her ears. It didn't hang exactly even, but it wasn't too bad. The dye was darker than she'd imagined—a deep auburn. It made her eyes greener and her skin more sallow. But most importantly, it made her seem older. Leta pulled on her winter cap so that her mother wouldn't see the new hair before *Rocky Horror*. After tomorrow, it didn't matter if she was grounded.

In the hushed dark of the kitchen, Leta swilled antacid straight from the bottle, wiping the gluey liquid from her mouth with the back of her hand. She tested the locks and checked the thermostat before opening the door to Stevie's room a crack. He was sleeping. In the corner, the TV was all static, and the screen was as white as the surface of the moon.

SUPERHEROES

For the first time in nearly two months, Agnes and Leta were together on a Friday night, but they wouldn't be together for long.

"You little shits better not get into trouble," Diana said. "If I get grounded because of you, you're both dead."

390

"If I get in trouble, you get in bigger trouble," Agnes said.

"Don't make me kill you," Diana said. She flipped them the bird before driving off.

The girls waited in the parking lot. From here, they could see the cars cruising the strip, making the endless loop from the Pizza Hut at the south end to the Sonic at the north.

Agnes ruffled Leta's short red bob. "Your hair looks amazing."

"Thanks. You look pretty. You've got protection, right?"

Leta and Agnes had seen films in their sex ed class about how easy it was to get pregnant, even if it was your first time. To Leta, watching the films seemed like trying to imagine living in a foreign country.

Agnes unzipped the pocket inside her purse to show Leta the small foil pouch. "All taken care of."

A minute later, Roger rode up on his motorcycle. He nodded to Leta. "Hey."

"Hey," Leta answered. That was usually the extent of their conversations.

Agnes got on the back of the bike and put her arms around his waist. She rested her head against his back. It was funny how some people just seemed to fit.

"Don't let Jennifer Pomhultz take your spot!" Agnes shouted. "And good luck with you-know-who!"

For a few minutes after Agnes left, Leta sat on the car hood, searching for Tom's Camaro.

"Hey, I thought you couldn't make it tonight!" Cawley called, startling her.

"I . . . it was sort of last minute," Leta stammered.

"Cool! We can sit together." Cawley slid in next to her on the car hood and put his arm around her shoulders.

"Um, I'm sort of meeting some friends here."

"Okay, so we can *all* sit together." He nuzzled her neck, and Leta flinched. "What's wrong?"

"I'm just not—people might see us, you know?" Leta said, swallowing hard.

"What, are you embarrassed to be seen with me or something?" Cawley asked.

"I didn't say that!"

"So what is it?" Cawley looked her in the eyes then, and she knew he wouldn't go until she gave him the truth.

"I'm waiting for a guy," Leta said at last.

Cawley shoved his hands in his pockets. "You could've just told me you didn't want me to come."

"I didn't say I didn't want you to come, I just..." She stopped and pressed the backs of her hands to her eyes. She was making a mess of things. Why was it that the one person she wasn't sure about was the only person who was sure about her? "I just wanted to go out with somebody else, okay? I'm allowed to do that, aren't I? I mean, it's still a free country and everything."

"Yeah. Free country." Cawley slid off the car hood and walked away from her, toward College Drive.

"I'll see you at the Popcorn," Leta added. It was a stupid thing to say. In response, Cawley kicked a trash can hard and it spun, nearly toppling over.

"Dammit, Janet," Leta said to no one but the cars.

In the litter-strewn field behind the Cineplex, Leta finally found Tom in a tight huddle of older kids. She approached the pack cautiously, trying not to attract too much attention, waiting for them to notice her. When no one did, she cleared her throat.

Tom's head popped up. He squinted at her.

"It's me, Leta," she said, patting at her new hair.

"Oh. Right. Hey, Lisa," Tom said.

"Leta," she corrected softly.

"Wanna party? Hey, make room for Lisa," Tom instructed and Leta was ushered into the fold. A joint came her way, and she passed it to the pimply ticket-taking guy on her left.

"I can't. I have an ulcer," she offered by way of explanation.

"Don't old men get that?" he asked, taking a hit.

"Some people just produce more stomach acid?" Leta said and immediately wished she hadn't. "Anyway, it's okay. I took my medicine."

"How come you're all dressed up like that?" one of the girls asked.

"For the movie. I'm Columbia."

One of the guys snickered. "You're Columbian? Can we smoke you?"

They all laughed then, and Leta didn't understand why, but she wished Agnes were here and they were sitting in the warm movie theater throwing toast and singing like before.

"Hey, Leta!"

Leta turned to see Miss Shelton wobbling over on platform sandals. Her boobs quivered like unset gelatin. Everyone stared.

"Hi, Miss Shel—Amy."

Miss Shelton gave Leta a little hug, like an older sister, and Leta was overcome by happiness. It would be okay. Everything would be okay. "I didn't know you liked to party."

"There's a lot people don't know about me," Leta said, hoping it made her sound mysterious, a spy working undercover whom everyone took to be a dork but whose hands were actually lethal weapons.

"That was the last joint, but if you want to get high, I've got some primo weed in my car," Tom said.

Miss Shelton grinned. "Let's go."

She hooked her arm through Leta's and they followed Tom through the parking lot, over potholes and broken stubs of concrete barriers meant to keep the cars from banging into one another. Leta stole a glance behind her. A clump of fans stood behind the rope, and Leta had a fleeting wish to be with them.

Tom's car smelled of cigarette smoke and new leather. Leta

climbed behind the seat into the back while Miss Shelton and Tom sat in the front.

"Got this from a friend who was in Mexico," Tom said, licking the rolling paper and forming a tight white missile of weed. Leta's stomach fluttered. She didn't want Tom to think she was uncool, but she didn't want to get high, either.

"Ulcer," she mumbled apologetically, and Tom handed off to Miss Shelton who took a hit and held it for a long time.

"You go to Texas Community?" he asked her.

"Umm," Miss Shelton choked out. "Poly sci."

"Cool."

The joint went back and forth a few times, and Leta's head felt balloon-light from the secondhand smoke.

"Nice car," Miss Shelton said, exhaling smoke.

"Yeah? Thanks." Tom's eyes were glassy; his smile seemed liquid. "You like Ozzy?" He popped *Blizzard of Oz* into the Camaro's stereo. "Crazy Train" filled the car.

"Bose speakers," Tom shouted over the searing guitar licks. "Just put 'em in yesterday."

Leta glanced nervously at the line forming for *Rocky Horror*. It snaked into the parking lot. "We should probably get in line."

"Nah, it's cool. I'll just sneak us in the back way," Tom said, his fingers lost in their air-drumming reverie, his eyes still on Miss Shelton.

Just then, Leta caught sight of Jennifer, who had added a bowler hat to her ensemble. "Are you sure we can get seats? That line looks pretty long and they're letting people in...."

"It's just a stupid movie. You've seen it a million times, haven't you?"

"Yeah, it's just..." Leta stopped. How could she explain that it was more than a movie to her? It was her home — the one consistent thing in her life. It didn't matter how many times she'd seen it, she still got that funny feeling by the end that she'd been somewhere, that she had somewhere to go still.

Miss Shelton sat up and turned around in the front seat. "You know what that movie's about, don't you?"

Leta nodded. "Um, it's about this couple who gets lost and they find this castle inhabited by aliens, and it's a takeoff on all those 1950s horror/sci-fi movies where..."

"Sex," Miss Shelton interrupted. "It's about sex."

"All right!" Tom gave a laugh and a high five to Miss Shelton.

"Come in!" Miss Shelton shouted. It was a line Leta never really got in the movie and she didn't get it now, but it made her uncomfortable. She wanted out of the Camaro. She wanted to be standing in that line ahead of Jennifer Pomhultz, Agnes by her side singing out loud. She wanted to find Cawley wherever he was and say she was sorry.

"I'm just gonna go get in line," Leta said.

"Suit yourself." Tom opened the door, and Leta stumbled into the parking lot. In her fishnets, gold jacket, and new short hair, she felt suddenly exposed, as if people could see all the way through to her soul. Behind her, Tom gunned the Camaro's motor and drove off with Miss Shelton, leaving her alone.

The movie was already starting when Leta sneaked in. She'd missed making a big entrance with her new hair and outfit. The place was packed, and Leta had to take a seat on the far left, stumbling over annoyed people on her way in. For the first time in months, Leta didn't sing along. Instead, she watched the audience illuminated by the bright of the movie screen, their worshipful faces washed in a flickering blue, the light as inconstant as everything else. They sang, laughed, and spat back lines on cue. When the "The Time Warp" began, Leta was too tired to get up. Instead, Jennifer Pomhultz went onstage. The crowd urged her on, and by the end, she owned the part of Columbia. Jennifer took a little bow to wild applause while Leta sat numbly, her hands tucked under her sweaty thighs, feeling the fishnets bite into the skin of her palms.

When Frank-N-Furter sang about going home, a small spot of pain flared behind Leta's ribs. Sitting here with everyone singing the same words, she suddenly felt lost and small, like an alien whose spaceship had crashed on a foreign planet where there were three moons and nothing in the sky looked right to her. The film ground to a halt, freezing on an image of Frank-N-Furter tossing playing cards so that the cards hung in the air. The audience booed and hissed as the lights came up and a manager walked to the front.

"Leta Miller? Is there a Leta Miller here?"

Leta raised her hand shyly.

"You have a phone call. Follow me, please. Sorry, folks. We'll get the show going again in a minute."

Leta's cheeks burned as she moved up the aisles, past the annoyed audience members. Behind her, the lights dimmed and the movie started up sluggishly.

In the manager's office, she took the call. "Hello?"

"Leta?" Her mother's voice sounded small and desperate. "I'm at the hospital. With Stevie."

"Is he okay?"

"I can't leave. I called Mrs. Jaworski. She's coming to pick you up. Wait out front." And she hung up.

Mrs. Jaworski showed up in her Impala, her hair still in rollers, and they drove in silence to the hospital. It had rained, and the asphalt shone under the street lights.

Leta stared out at the road and felt her heart beating faster. Was Stevie dead? She allowed herself to imagine that moment: Her father coming home, neighbors and church members bringing by casseroles, her friends consoling her, Cawley forgiving her. Maybe then her mother could stop feeling so angry and pay attention to Leta again.

Mrs. Jaworski pulled the Impala up to the bright white lights of the hospital's front entrance. She kept the engine running.

"Thanks," Leta said.

Mrs. Jaworski patted her leg, and when Leta looked at her face, she could see that the old woman had taken the time to put on her orange lipstick. It lit up the dark like a flare. "I have a brother, lives in Alaska. A real pain in the ass. Family. They're nothing but trouble."

Leta nodded numbly and went in. On the way to the ICU, Leta caught a glimpse of her face in the mirror by the nurse's station. She didn't recognize anything about herself and it was startling. Quickly, she put her hat on, tucking the ends of her new hairdo underneath, but it didn't help.

Her mother sat in the waiting room on an orange vinyl chair whose stuffing was popping out at the seams. She held fast to a white Styrofoam cup. In the corner above their heads, a TV was on but the sound was off.

Leta slid as quietly as possible into the seat beside her mother. "What happened?"

Her mother's voice was flat. "He had a seizure. I found him on the floor, coughing up blood."

"Is he gonna be okay?"

"It was a bad one. But he's stable now. He's stable."

"So he's gonna be fine," Leta said, and she found that she was relieved after all. "Did you call Daddy?"

Her mother nodded. "He was going to fly home from Hartford, but I told him it was okay. We're okay."

We're not okay, Leta wanted to scream. "You should have let him come."

Her mother waved it away like she did most of what Leta had to say. "He's working on that big account. And besides, the flights are so expensive."

Her dad should be here. More than anything, she wanted him to be here. She wanted them to sit at the kitchen table and admit that everything had changed and none of them could stop change from happening; change was no one's fault. They'd all been so careful, but Leta was tired now and she wanted to come off watch. She removed her cap, and her mother paled.

"Jesus God Almighty, Leta Jane Miller, what did you do to your HAIR?"

Leta put a hand to her newly shorn locks. It felt good against her skin, like freedom. "It's just henna. It's not permanent."

"Nothing ever is." Her mother crushed the flimsy cup and dropped it into the wastepaper basket. "I was going to start my master's degree, but I guess that's gone now. I guess I'm just not supposed to do anything. I should never make plans."

"Stop it," Leta said. "Just... stop."

They sat in the hallway on unforgiving plastic seats under hospital lights that bleached them into gray ghosts of themselves while orderlies moved up and down the hallway, pushing carts stacked with laundered sheets, plastic water pitchers, tissue boxes, cups of ice — small comforts for the sick and weary.

"I'm sorry we're too much for you," Leta said, and she wished it hadn't come out sounding sarcastic, because she meant it sincerely.

"That's a terrible thing to say," her mother answered, but she hesitated, and the pause held the truth. Leta's mother reached over like she was going to hug her. Instead she picked a piece of popcorn off her sweater. "We've just had a scare is all. Everything's okay now."

A doctor called Leta's mother over for a hushed conference by a gurney. Leta stared up at the ceiling until her eyes burned. She blinked fast, but the tears came anyway. It seemed a good time for tears. She cried for the way things had been, the way they would never be again. She cried for Agnes in a backseat with Roger, Agnes who had left Leta alone in a between-world of horse models and *Rocky Horror* and kissing boys in bathrooms. She thought about Jennifer's perfect dance steps, the way she'd let that faker steal the moment from her, and she cried harder. A nurse passing patted her shoulder and then she was gone.

Later, Leta took a cab back to her house while her mother stayed on at the hospital. It was late, around three in the morning, and the street was hushed. A soda can glinted in Mrs. Jaworski's grass. Leta picked it up and tossed it in the big green trash can beside her garage.

"Leta?"

Leta started at the sound of Agnes's voice. She was sitting on the front porch, huddled under Roger's jacket, looking small and frail.

"I was waiting for you. I figured you'd be home about an hour ago."

"I was at the hospital. Stevie had another seizure."

"Oh, my god! Is he okay?"

Leta only shrugged. "For now. I thought you were at Roger's."

"I was. Roger and me, we…you know. We did it," Agnes said, and Leta couldn't be certain if there was pride or sadness in it.

"Oh. Um, congratulations. I mean, was it…are you okay?"

Agnes' bottom lip quivered. She started to cry. "I'm so stupid."

"Aggie. Hey. What happened? Did he do something… weird?"

"No!" Agnes said, laughing through tears. "He was super nice to me. Look, he gave me his motocross ribbon." She opened the jacket so that Leta could see the red ribbon pinned to her shirt.

"Hey, you won first place in the Losing Your Virginity contest," Leta joked. Agnes burst into fresh sobs, and Leta felt a surge of panic. "Sorry. It was just a joke…."

"It's not the stupid joke." Agnes dragged her fingers over her eyes and wiped her nose on her sleeve. "It was fine, I think. It was nice. He told me I was pretty. I just…" She shook her head and took two deep breaths. "I'm different now. I can't go back. You know?"

399

"Yeah. I know."

Agnes's face screwed up into fresh crying. "I started thinking about my mom, how I wished I could tell her about it. That's totally stupid, isn't it?"

"No," Leta said. "Of course not." Her breath came out in a puff of dragon smoke. When Leta and Agnes were kids, they'd put straws to their mouths and blow out, pretending they were smoking like the smiling women they saw in magazines who played tennis or lounged poolside, looking impossibly glamorous. In the yard, the trees stood small and naked. The sky above the houses was dark and unreadable, and Leta shivered in the cold.

"I really do love your hair. It's totally cool."

"Thanks," Leta said. "My mom had a cow."

"Even better," Agnes said with a giggle. She quieted. "If I call Diana to come pick me up now I'll never hear the end of it. Can I stay here?"

"Sure," Leta said.

The house was full of shadows. Leta turned on a lamp that only illuminated the emptiness of the living room. Leta gave Agnes a pair of her pajamas and they pulled the quilt off Leta's bed and spread it over the carpet in her room.

"Oh, Charlie!" Agnes took Leta's Appaloosa from its place on the horse shelf and gave him a kiss. She tucked Roger's jacket under her head and clutched Charlie to her chest. The girls lay together on the floor, shoulders touching, and talked about who was the cutest guy in *TeenBeat*, whether Leta should let her hair grow out or keep it short, if it would be totally *fourth grade* to stage *Rocky Horror* with the Barbies in the morning. As Agnes's words became softer and fewer, fading at last to a light snore, Leta stared at the glittery flecks in the ceiling and imagined they were stars winking out a message only she could understand.

Libba Bray is the author of the *New York Times* bestselling Gemma Doyle Trilogy, which includes the novels *A Great and Terrible Beauty, Rebel Angels*, and *The Sweet Far Thing.* She is also the author of the comedic novel, *Going Bovine*. Besides *Geektastic*, she has contributed stories to *Restless Dead, Up All Night*, and *Vacations from Hell.* Sometimes she tells people she's won the National Book Award, but then M. T. Anderson comes by and asks for his back, 'cause he's grabby like that.

Libba is a longtime geek and is fluent in many geek languages including, but not limited to, theater geek, showtunes geek (yes, they are different), music geek, sci-fi TV geek, bad movies geek, "Rocky Horror" geek, campy geek, Hammer Horror geek, and *Valley of the Dolls* geek, which deserves a category all its own. As a teenager, she saw *The Rocky Horror Picture Show* every weekend for nearly two years. Any photos that surface of her in a gold lamé top, heavy eyeliner, and tap shoes are absolutely fabricated, especially if the subject in question is sporting a mullet.

About the Illustrators

Hope Larson is the author and illustrator of several graphic novels, including *Gray Horses* and *Chiggers*. Her short stories have been featured in the *New York Times* and several anthologies, notably the Flight series and Image Comics' Tori Amos–inspired *Comic Book Tattoo*. Larson has been nominated for awards in the United States, Canada, and Europe, and is the recipient of a 2006 Ignatz Award and a 2007 Eisner Award. She holds a BFA from the School of the Art Institute of Chicago and lives in Asheville, North Carolina, with her husband and four cats. She used up all her geek points when she started drawing comics professionally.

Bryan Lee O'Malley was born in London, Ontario, Canada. In high school he joined choir, chess club, the trivia team, and the computer programming club, got his first job in order to purchase a Sega Genesis, attended LAN parties, played Starcraft from dusk 'til dawn while drinking Coke and eating pizza, tried to get his friends to read comic books that he thought were really cool, and hung out with the theater and band geeks. The head of the arts department still speaks of him fondly. O'Malley went on to become an award-winning cartoonist, with a film, *Scott Pilgrim vs. the World*, in development at Universal. He lives in the United States.